*In this sweeping saga of one of the most s[...] Leavell brings alive the stories of unsung Am[...] ten. I love the interaction of real life and well-drawn fictiona[...]* [...]n *events that really happened.* Gideon's Call *is exactly the kind of historical novel I love.*

DONNA FLETCHER CROW, AUTHOR OF *GLASTONBURY*

*Not only do I find* Gideon's Call *completely engrossing as literature, but it occurs to me Peter Leavell is the kind of history teacher we all wish we'd had in school. He tells the stories as if he lived them himself—and that makes them real and memorable.*

MICHAEL EHRET, EDITOR OF THE *ACFW JOURNAL*

*Concerning a little-known episode in Civil War history, Peter Leavell has written a meticulously researched, heart-tugging tale that is both captivating and inspiring.*

NANCY HERRIMAN, AUTHOR OF *THE IRISH HEALER* AND THE FORTHCOMING *JOSIAH'S TREASURE*

*Peter's ability to embody American history and bring it to sparkling life through these characters is frankly alarming, and his obvious passion for the Civil War period shines in every carefully rendered scene. A remarkable debut.*

MICK SILVA, EDITOR, WWW.YOURWRITERSGROUP.COM

Gideon's Call *boldly throws open the plantation doors to give readers a view of life in the Civil War-torn South. Painted with vibrant characters and historically significant scenery, Peter Leavell's debut novel deftly takes us on a journey to a time and place where boundary lines are becoming blurred over a common goal . . . freedom.*

JENNIFER ERIN VALENT, AUTHOR OF *FIREFLIES IN DECEMBER*, *COTTONWOOD WHISPERS*, AND *CATCHING MOONDROPS*

Gideon's Call *is one of those books that, once it comes along, touches a core and scratches an itch you may not have known you had. Leavell's narrative captures the feelings and emotions that still resonate in the heart of the Civil War South, while shedding new light on one of America's darkest periods. Join young Tad on his journey from slave to freeman to independent thinker. You will laugh and cry, but most of all, you will appreciate* Gideon's Call.

RAY ELLIS, AUTHOR OF THE NATE RICHARDS SERIES

Gideon's Call *explores what is possible when we sacrifice personal desires to address the needs of others. Friendship. Love. Honor. To the final page and beyond, Peter Leavell's fresh portrayal of past bravery renews my faith in humanity and my hope for the future.*

DIANA PRUSIK, AUTHOR OF *DELIVERY*

# Gideon's Call

## PETER LEAVELL

WORTHY
PUBLISHING

Published by Worthy Publishing, a division of Worthy Media, Inc., 134 Franklin Road, Suite 200, Brentwood, Tennessee 37027.

HELPING PEOPLE EXPERIENCE THE HEART OF GOD

eBook available at www.worthypublishing.com

Audio distributed through Oasis Audio; visit www.oasisaudio.com

Library of Congress Control Number: 2012947226

Scripture quotations are from the King James Version. Public domain.

For foreign and subsidiary rights, contact Riggins International Rights Services, Inc.; www.rigginsrights.com

ISBN: 978-1-617951-17-6 (trade paperback)

Cover Design: Christopher Tobias
Cover Images: © VisionsofAmerica/Joe Sohm (plantation);
© Eileen Hart/istockphoto.com (man)
Interior Design and Typesetting: Cindy Kiple

*Printed in the United States of America*
12 13 14 15 16 17 LBM 8 7 6 5 4 3 2 1

*For Laura Towne,*
*founder of the Penn School.*

*And for those who educate the less fortunate*
*at great cost to themselves.*

# Part One

# O N E

*T*ad stared at the ancient plantation house shrouded in live oaks and Spanish moss.

His friend Collin paused beside the porch. "C'mon."

"Ain't going in." Tad's mouth was so dry he could barely speak. "Mammy, she done say hags and witches—"

"That's old slave's talk." Not a trace of fear showed on the boy's white face.

"Wasn't right to steal pie, Collin." The odor of decay mingled with the smell of fresh apple and cinnamon from under the golden crust. "Now we make the devil happy."

"Dr. Jenkins won't miss one little pie." Collin stepped onto the porch. The planks creaked and bowed.

Tad stepped closer. Streaks of sun peeked through leaves, covering the battered porch in speckled light. He looked up at the ceiling and almost wailed. "Look, look, color is black. Ain't no way we survivin'."

"Old slave's talk." Collin took a few steps toward the front door that hung by a single hinge. "You're a darkie, Tad. And you make as much sense as one too."

Tad stared at the peeling black paint, his mouth open wide and fists clenched. Someone had died inside the house before it was abandoned. A place cursed with death, and then forsaken, was dangerous beyond words.

Collin stared at the porch ceiling for a moment and swallowed. He swept aside a strand of hair and reached for the doorknob. The heavy, wide door crashed to the porch and crumbled into a pile of rotten wood splinters. The dust cleared, and he stepped over the mound and disappeared into the dark interior. "We can eat the pie in here." His voice echoed from inside.

Tad whimpered. "Abraham, Moses, deliver we." He clutched his hands together. It wasn't the first time Collin had gotten the two in trouble. But because he was Massah's son, and Tad was a slave, Tad knew he'd be the one blamed. That's how it had been since they were born.

His fingers clasped around the silver cross that hung from a leather strap around his neck. "Lord, protect we." He followed his friend into the dark house.

Inside, through a broken window, a ray of light lit the stairway. The ceiling sagged, as if ready to crash down on them. Wallpaper hung in strips, drooping like willow branches. Tad felt the musty dampness in his nose and choked back a sneeze. "I'm leavin'."

A wave of hunger washed over him, and his mind swirled. He reached for the banister to steady himself. Collin leapt up and slipped an arm around his waist.

"Sit down, here." Collin helped him rest on the bottom step. Tad leaned his head against the wall.

Collin crossed the room and picked up the pie he'd set down, and Tad felt his friend's warm skin as he settled close.

"You look terrible." Collin dipped his fingers into the pie and grabbed a handful of cooked apples. "Eat this, you'll feel better."

Collin dropped the handful into Tad's palm, and Tad felt the warm, moist pie on his fingers.

While Collin found trouble now and again, he always looked after Tad.

Collin grabbed a handful of cooked apples and shoved them

into his mouth. "This pie is delicious." He smiled, a piece of crust stuck to his lip. "Go ahead, Tad. You need it."

His mouth watered at the sweet smell. Tad hesitated. "You hear that?"

Collin lifted his head. "I didn't hear anything."

"Sounded like a whistle."

"Probably just a bird."

"No. A whistle. There." Tad put a clean hand behind his ear. "You hear it that time?"

Collin jumped. The pie dish clattered on the floor. His eyes grew wide.

"Witches, come t'git us." Tad dropped his piece and clasped his head. A strong desire to run came over him. Run and climb a tree.

"Let's get out of here. The back door." Collin darted past the staircase. He froze. His hands lifted slowly into the air.

Tad shrieked. He dashed toward the front door and slammed into a body as solid as a brick wall. Massive arms wrapped around him.

"Lemme go!" He stared up into the man's stern black face.

Laughter filled the decaying house. "Caught you." Another man stepped forward. "Been looking to catch you for quite some time, boy."

The strong arms spun Tad around, and he looked into a shriveled white face as sour as the breath that hissed from the toothless mouth.

"Mistah Spencer, we ain't doin' nothin'." Terror filled Tad as he struggled against the iron grip. Spencer, with his own black slaves, led patrols across the island, reporting any slaves that misbehaved. Usually he took matters into his own hands.

Behind Spencer, Collin wrestled with a member of the patrol. "Let us go!"

Spencer ignored him. Instead the old man stared into Tad's

eyes. "I watch you, boy, running free with Collin like you own this island. You should be in the fields with the other darkies."

Collin's voice was firm. "Not your job to say." He wrenched from his captor's grip and dashed to Tad's side. "My father's slaves are his to control." He stood, hands on hips, his red face glowing in the dark room.

Tad didn't like being called a slave. No one talked about it, but it was true: he did roam the islands with Collin, as if they were brothers.

Spencer wasn't rich—he owned three large slaves, slaves who now hauled Tad, with arms pinned behind him, back to Dr. Jenkins' plantation.

Collin followed, arguing the entire way. "He didn't do anything. Wasn't him."

Spencer seemed in no mood to argue. "Stealing pie's a mighty big offense. You let one slave steal, they all wanna steal. Your daddy's got to teach you better how to handle slaves."

Little attention was paid to the small group that crossed the shaved grass to the side of the big house. Spencer ordered a slave to find Dr. Jenkins.

Soon, Mr. Spencer's assistant led a man in a dark suit from the garden, through groups of wedding guests. He strode forward with all the confidence that came with thousands of acres and hundreds of men and women under his control. He clutched a wineglass in his hand. Tad couldn't breathe.

"What's going on here?" Dr. Jenkins downed the rest of his drink.

"Just a slave from the Frogmore who stole a pie. Your pie." Spencer grabbed Tad and hauled him forward.

Dr. Jenkins' eyes turned to Tad then back to Spencer. "*This* lad? He's a good boy, he wouldn't do such a thing."

"He did, stole a pie. I watched him, followed him, and caught

6

him eating it." Spencer spit.

Dr. Jenkins turned from Spencer, a look of disgust on his face, then leveled his gaze on Collin. "Did Tad steal the pie?"

Tad looked at his friend. Collin took a deep breath. His eyes darted from Dr. Jenkins to Spencer. Between the two men, he looked small, his hands twisting in front of him. He licked his lips and then shrugged.

Tad felt as if a knife pierced his heart. His head drooped.

Spencer's grip tightened. "Slaves got to be punished."

"You don't have to tell me my duty." Dr. Jenkins' voice was sharp. He sighed. "Tad, I expected more of you." He turned to Spencer and spoke softly. "I don't see why this is my responsibility. He's not my slave."

"I'm just letting you know what I'm going to do." Spencer tried to hold back a smile, but Tad could see the corners of his lips turn up.

"Just because you patrol for runaways doesn't give you the right . . . " Dr. Jenkins thought for a moment, then sighed. "Just do it away from here, at the slave quarters."

Tad stared in horror as Spencer's grin stretched across his face. "Right, most understandable." He swept off his wide hat. "You see, it's not that I like this sort of thing, it's just my job."

Dr. Jenkins held up a hand. "Just . . . go."

Tad's arm was nearly wrenched from his shoulder as Spencer's slave dragged him through a small grove of trees, along a well-traveled path to several cabins that lined either side of a small road. Slaves gathered to see the cause of the commotion. This seemed to please Spencer.

"I'll teach you, you little wretch." The old man cried aloud so all could hear. "No more thieving for you."

Tad tried to get his feet under him, but his legs left a trail in the dirt. He tasted salt from the tears that streamed down his face.

They entered a small clearing. In the center, an old oak with long, spindly arms stretched wide, as if reaching to snag them. A thick branch crossed the yard, the bark rubbed off from wear. A rope hung from its middle.

"No!" Tad pulled against Spencer's iron grip. "Please, no."

Spencer grabbed the dreaded rope.

Tad couldn't control his breathing. He scrambled to get away, broke from the old man's grasp, but Spencer's slave grabbed him.

The slave catcher bound Tad's hands until the rope bit into his wrists. He was hoisted up, his arms wrenched high above. His shoulders popped and pain burst from his arms. His feet kicked wildly; his toes stretched to touch the ground.

"Can't whip me," Tad muttered, the tears pouring freely. "Can't whip me. No lash for Tad, no lash. I did wrong? No lash." He had never been whipped before, but had seen it done, had seen the limp bodies fall to the ground afterward, looking like butchered meat.

"Can't whip me!" He screamed and flailed like a fish on a line pulled from the water.

Spencer leaned close. "You fight, boy, the more's gonna hurt." Tad could feel the man's spit with every word.

Tad's arms ached. Sweat dripped into his eyes. Trees and slaves, slave catcher and sky all became a blur. Spencer grunted, and the assistant pulled the dreaded black snake from a cloth bag. Panic surged through his body. He couldn't keep his eyes off the whip, curled, as if ready to strike.

Tad spun in a slow circle and stretched his neck to see Collin.

"He's too small to lash." Collin stepped forward. "Look, he can't touch the ground. His back is stretched too tight, he'll tear in two."

Spencer fingered the long strap, letting the leather slip from his hand. With a flick of his wrist, the whip snapped into empty air. Tad yelped. Several egrets near the marsh squawked and fluttered into the sky.

Spencer chuckled, slowly at first, then a full laugh. "You're getting mighty old, Collin, to be letting your daddy do all the work around your place." He thrust the whip's handle into Collin's hand. "Your turn."

Collin stood frozen.

Spencer snarled. "You want to take his place, boy?"

A small glimmer of hope dawned on Tad.

But with trembling hand, his friend reached for the whip.

"Take it, boy, or I'll tell your daddy you was too weak to whip a Negro."

Collin took the whip. The knife Tad had felt in his heart earlier was nothing compared to this new feeling of betrayal. Years of companionship sifted through his mind, the joy of youth and carefree days all crashing like a wave against rocks.

Collin pulled the whip back, whirled it, then swung forward.

Tad winced, but only a light slap touched his skin.

"Boy, I'm warning you." Spencer's voice was a growl. "You treat this slave like the animal he is, or you take his place."

"Don't." Tad whispered from the side of his mouth toward Collin. "Please no. I ain't done nothin' wrong."

Tad spun, his back to his friend. He could hear Collin's breath come in short gasps.

Dr. Jenkins' slaves were silent. No one moved.

Collin let out an angry growl, the whip snapped, and pain pierced through Tad.

After it was over, Tad hung limp. It seemed as if fire burned his entire body.

Spencer stepped into his blurry view. The old man's grinning mouth spat tobacco. "That'll learn you proper." He paused then reached for Tad's neck. "This is too good for a slave."

He felt the necklace snap from his neck. "No, it's mine!" Life filled Tad's aching limbs and he kicked Spencer in the stomach. His reward was a slap across the face and a bucketful of saltwater against his back.

He let out a bloody scream.

# T W O

$\mathcal{T}$ad couldn't decide what hurt worse: the stripes on his back, or Collin's treachery.

After the lashing, Collin had run. A slave from Jenkins' plantation had helped Tad home. When they made it to the Frogmore, Massah was there. Through the fog in his mind, he saw Massah's stern face. He'd said nothing, just left the kitchen.

Mammy carefully settled next to Tad's bed. "Mankind's the only creature in God's earth that enjoys givin' pain to others." She rubbed a salve on his back, and he groaned. After a moment, the sticky mess worked its magic and the ache softened. "They says you was caught stealin'."

Tad turned his face and looked into her red eyes. "No, Mammy, I didn't take nothin'. And I get a lashin'." He lowered his head facedown on a mattress stuffed with Spanish moss.

Mammy touched a clean cotton bandage to his skin. She took a deep breath. "You're different, child. Whole bunch of Negroes who steals anythin' they find, God knows they's been earnin' it. But you don't touch nothin' that ain't yours, I knows you don't. Lordy me, I done some stealin' in my time." She chuckled to herself. "But not you, boy."

A shadow crossed the plank floor, and Tad carefully lifted his head. He sighed and dropped his head back on the pillow. Just his friend Peg.

"Auntie Mammy, he dyin'?"

"No, he ain't dyin'; he'll be fine." Her voice, deep, seemed to scold Peg. "Now you set right next to him for a bit and sing. I'll make somethin' to eat."

Mammy's large body bumped Peg on the way out the door. Peg stumbled and her hand brushed Tad's shoulder. He clenched his teeth.

"Sorry." She sat next to him. "I know how it feels."

"I know you do."

"Didn't use a stingin' whip on you." Her hand felt cool on his brow. "They used a cuttin' whip." A ray of sun sent a steady stream of orange through the door, lighting dust that sometimes floated up, sometimes down. The light reflected concern off her round face. She sang in a squeaky voice.

*"Wake up, Jacob, day is a breakin', I'm on my way;*
*I want to go to heaven when I die, do love the Lord."*

"You mad, Tad?"

He sniffed. "I s'pose."

"Mistah Spencer, he's an evil man. Of the devil, I think."

"Collin's of the devil." He lifted his head and pain shot through his back, biting stronger than the anger.

"Why Collin?"

"Gave me the lashin'." Tad bit back a sob. "Give it to me hard."

She brushed at a dry tear. "Can't believe he'd do the lash. Not Collin."

Collin. No, *Judas*. That was who he was. *Judas.* "Sing anuddah song, will ya?" He didn't want to talk about his troubles.

He'd always been different from the rest of the slaves, playing with Collin, long hours in the sun. Now he was like the rest of them. And the worst . . . Collin had done it. Tad closed his eyes.

With the windows locked and the door closed, Mammy's kitchen cabin—a separate building from the big house—kept the rest of the Frogmore plantation out while Tad lay on his bed. The afternoon heat turned stuffy, and he drifted asleep. Dreams haunted him; a phantom pain shot through his brain. Sweat trickled from his body. A blaze roared. Flames licked at him, burning his back.

He awoke with a yell. The fires of hell jumped in front of him. With an arm, he wiped his sweaty, blurry eyes until he could see clearly. Across the room the fire burned, split logs adding to the summer heat. He'd been moved from the kitchen to the praise house.

The cabin was filled with slaves. They lined the walls, faces looking toward the rafters, their white eyes reflecting the orange glow. Mammy stood nearby. He glanced at her, and she nodded toward the fire.

Three men, just shadows in front of the blaze, waved their hands and sang a deep, sad song. One came close, his face filled with deep wrinkles like rows in a cornfield. The man lifted his head and the song changed. This time they all sang.

*"Help me bear de cross, for I weep, I weep, I can't hold out; if any mercy, Lord, oh pity me."*

Their teeth flashed, lit by the fire, and they rocked from side to side. Samuel, a big man, driver of the plantation, stepped forward. He motioned to Tad then pointed down, as if he wanted Tad to join him in front of all twenty of the Frogmore's slaves.

The scabbed slashes on Tad's back cracked as he struggled to his feet. With Mammy's help he set his legs under him and took a few careful steps. He stumbled forward until he stood with Samuel.

The song, faster now, rose in pitch. Five young girls circled Tad and danced. They swayed, their eyes closed, rolling their hips as they circled the small space in the middle of the room. A few more girls joined them, and then two men.

Samuel stepped forward. In a deep voice that filled the room he quieted the song. "Our boy here, he done face the mighty lash. He know the pain of death. He know the pain of life. He know we do as Jesus do, and take our lashes. Until Moses lead us from here, O Lord, we take our lashes." He raised his hands and the slaves burst into song, singing the same words over and over, faster each time.

Tad had gone to many a worship *shout* before, but never one in his honor. Never to celebrate a first lashing. It filled him with hope, as if he'd been forsaken by Collin only to be accepted by someone better.

Peg stood in the doorway, a pie in her hands. She weaved back and forth to the chorus, crossed the plank floor, and set the dish down on a small table. "Apple." The corner of her mouth turned up into a wry smile.

Tad clutched his stomach. He couldn't eat.

Voices lifted to the rafters. The dancing shook the floor and the noise flooded his head. He shoved through the dancers, out the door, and into the darkness. The cool night relieved some of the pain in his back. He thought of climbing a tree, but instead ducked into a bush. The branches scratched at his scabs.

He paused a moment and tried to resist the tears. But they came.

The same thoughts kept running through his mind. Was there a time when he'd believed he wasn't a slave? He had been a slave the entire time, was still a slave, would always be a slave. Why did he feel like someone had just died?

The bush rustled. He rubbed away the tears in his eyes. "Who's there?"

"That you, Tad?"

"Leave me alone."

Peg settled next to him and brushed dirt and leaves from her brown dress. She took off her scarf. "You hurtin' inside? Looks like you been cryin'."

"You can't see, it's dark."

"I can hear just fine." She leaned close. "And the moon's shinin' just enough."

Tad looked toward the big house. Two stories high, with a porch along the front, and two chimneys.

He sighed. "What's it like to live in there?"

"Just 'cause I live inside don't mean I got it easy." After a moment, she added, "I guess you never seen inside? You livin' with your mammy in the kitchen."

Tad shrugged. "Many a kitchen burns down. Suppose it's good they don't build it right in the big house."

"Collin never let you see inside?"

Tad crossed his arms and bit his lips. He shook his head then reached for the small cross around his neck. It wasn't there.

"You lost it?"

"Mistah Spencer took it."

She leaned forward. "I see'd him," she whispered fiercely. "I see'd him come by, when Massah come, earlier. He gave a necklace to Miss Mary."

Tad gritted his teeth. "Why'd he do a thing like that?"

"She almost marryin' age, silly." Peg took his hand. "Tad, come back to the *shout*. Mammy and me done up a pie, just for you, and we ain't had a pie in so long. Besides, you'll hurt your mammy's feelins'."

"I ain't goin' back."

"Fine, but I'm eatin' your pie."

"Which room's Miss Mary's?"

"Upstairs, end of the hallway. Why? What you thinkin'?"

"Ain't thinking nothin'; jis' wondered."

He watched her approach the praise house, stop, and turn back to peer into the night. Her shadow stretched from the open door before she disappeared inside.

He'd owned one item in his life, and that was Pappy's necklace. He'd never known Pappy. There was a dream that came sometimes in which he heard his voice. But the necklace reminded him when he was awake that there was one thing Massah couldn't take, and Mr. Spencer and Collin stripped it all away.

Tad turned to study the big house. No lights, no movement. He took a deep breath. He crawled out of the bushes and limped toward the house, through the jasmine, and paused at the back door.

# T H R E E

*T*he moon's silver glow lit the back door. Tad took a step up the single stair and the wood plank groaned. He paused. The sounds of alligators and frogs filled the night. From the praise house came cheers and clapping, then silence.

Massah let them worship as they wanted, late into the darkness, well past when he and his family went to sleep. The distant sounds didn't seem to bother them.

Tad's heart thundered in his chest as he opened the door and slipped inside.

His bare feet touched the cool, polished wood floor, different from the rough planks of the slave cabin. He crept forward and stopped in the shadow of a hutch. The sound of a pendulum clock ticked in the darkness.

He shivered.

By the front entrance, two doors stood open on either side of the hall. The moonlight drifted through a window and onto the stairway.

The stairs creaked as he worked his way up, his throbbing back against the wall.

He reached the top of the staircase and looked down the hallway that stretched the length of the house.

At the end, a door stood open. Tad waited at the top of the

stairs. A drop of sweat trickled down the side of his face and dropped from his chin. He wanted to dash back down the stairs and out into the open where fresh air could touch his aching back, but he stayed.

Another step, then another, toward the dark room. He stopped between bookshelves and waited. Dust from the book covers hovered in the air and tickled his nose.

He stole inside. Two beds, one with wood stands on the four corners, another with an iron headboard, held the forms of Massah's girls. He watched their even breathing. Something moved. He froze. Wide-eyed, he slowly turned his head.

Against the wall hung a looking glass, his dark figure reflected in the room. He held a hand against his heart and let out a long, quiet breath.

A jewelry box rested on a dresser. In the soft light, Tad ran his fingers across the smooth wood. A tug on a knob and the top drawer opened easily. He sifted through several bracelets, a hair comb, two rings, but no necklace. He slid the drawer closed then held his breath again.

Was that the downstairs door?

He looked wildly around the room. Where to hide? He crouched against the wall, beside the bed. The small figure under the covers sighed and turned toward him, the gentle scent of perfumed sheets drifting in his face. She slept, her breath brushing his forehead. He closed his eyes.

The sound of footfalls came from the stairs and a dark figure appeared in the door. Tad made himself smaller.

Peg.

She crossed the room, pulled a blanket from the foot of the bed, and spread it near Tad. Her small form curled a few feet from him, so close her body heat touched his skin. Smoke from the praise house drifted from her clothes.

Peg settled into the blankets. Within minutes her breath evened.

In a way, he felt sorry for her. If Massah's girls needed anything in the night, Peg had to do it, anytime.

She hadn't stirred.

He stood and stepped over her body. He paused at the door to look back.

Peg screamed and scrambled to her feet.

⚞

Tad watched the morning light touch the tops of the trees then set the marsh grass ablaze with gold. He tried to stretch, but his hands were bound behind him. A rope bit at his ankles. His back burned in pain, splayed across a wagon wheel.

Marshes crossed the miles in front of him, from the Frogmore on St. Helena Island to Hunting Island. In between the two islands, Station Creek filled and emptied with the tide, a rush of saltwater driving upstream then draining to let freshwater take over. The vast empty flat was broken by an uninhabited piece of land crowded with trees, rising above the marsh like a single warship on a lonely ocean.

He leaned his head against a spoke. Last night, Massah didn't say a word, just tied him up and left him. How could Peg wake Massah like that? It was her fault he was here, her fault he shivered through the cold night, and her fault he didn't have the necklace. He clenched his bound hands. If only his back would stop burning.

Mammy had wanted to spread mud all over him, but Massah wouldn't allow it, so swarms of mosquitoes bit at his flesh all night. He felt like alligator bait. At least the morning sun warmed his skin.

A shadow blocked the light and a deep voice broke the morning quiet. "Boy, you done wrong." Strong hands gripped the wheel, lifted it from where it leaned against an oak, and set it on the ground. Tad groaned. Samuel, the Frogmore's driver, slipped a knife through the ropes at Tad's feet. "You ain't runnin'." His wide eyes met Tad's. The driver's eyes burned with anger.

The big man scared Tad. "Yes suh."

"You ain't sulkin'." He cut the ropes at Tad's hands. The knife gleamed in the sunlight.

"Yes suh."

He reached down, wrapped huge fingers around Tad's arms, and lifted him to his feet. Tad's raw back tore from the wheel. The scream caught in his throat.

Samuel towered over Tad. The driver wore a dirty vest over a torn linen shirt, and his trousers were a colorful patchwork of fixes. Muscles rippled under the thin cloth. A wide-brimmed hat covered his head.

There was little sympathy on his face. "Follow." Samuel turned and hurried toward the creek. Tad limped after.

Down a narrow path that dropped off the bank and led into the marsh, Tad struggled to keep up. Marsh grass tickled his legs as his feet sank into the mud. Samuel reached down and picked up two buckets. "You know the land we cleared, by Seaside Road?"

He and Collin had watched the oaks fall and bushes burn earlier that summer. Tad nodded.

"Needs mud." Samuel held out the buckets.

"Ain't yet time to mud the fields."

Samuel dropped the buckets and grabbed Tad's shoulders, almost lifting him from the ground. "Don't you talk back, boy. You's in a world of trouble, and the end of your free days has come. Mud the field."

The big man paused, pulled Tad close, and glanced at his back. Samuel let out a stream of air that whistled. He turned without a word and scrambled up the bank.

Tad stared at the buckets. His first chore as a slave. He lifted them.

He didn't care that planters insisted the fields needed fresh mud every year to help the cotton grow. He pictured cold weather biting the islands, when slaves were forced to march through bone-numbing marshes at low tide to drag freezing mire to the fields. He knew at the end of the day that he'd be like the slaves he'd watched mud fields before: he would fall asleep by the fires, too exhausted to eat. Dread filled him.

Ten acres of raw dirt flashed in his mind, ten acres of land that needed mud.

He swallowed his despair.

He grit his teeth, tried to ignore the tiny crablike bugs that scurried about, their single large pincers snapping at him. He neared the water where the mud was deepest. A fish leapt as he dipped one bucket and hauled it up with a loud sucking sound. Water filled the small, rotten smelling hole. He gagged.

Once the second bucket was filled, he tried to lift them both. He paused to catch his breath. A heron glanced his way then ducked its head back underwater.

He hauled the buckets out of the marsh, across the gardens, past yellow cornstalks, and into a pine forest. Clouds blocked the sun, as if a morning storm was coming. He slowed and sniffed the fresh air. The small wood had been a perfect place for Tad and Collin to play, usually armed with sticks—one branch a sword in hand and another holding imaginary reins, fighting like George Washington on horseback.

He continued through the forest. From the side, a figure appeared in the distance. Peg came running, a smile on her face. Tad ignored her.

She called out. "Tad, Tad, wait up."

He kept walking.

She hurried between the large pines, a bucket clutched in her hand. "I come to help."

"Go away." He continued his struggle through the forest.

"Lemme help!" She tugged on his arm.

He dropped the buckets and mud sloshed on his feet. "Go away. I don't want you here." He rubbed his shoulders.

She took a step back, confusion in her eyes. "I'd be a good help."

"No." He sounded like an angry dog, but he couldn't help it. "Your fault I'm here, so leave me be."

Her voice trembled. "I'm sorry, Tad."

She wasn't sorry, not like he wanted her to be. The sun burst from behind a cloud and the light sifted through the trees. He turned and stomped away. "Don't need no help."

"I feel—"

"Shut your fat face."

Peg jerked back as if he'd hit her. A soft cry came from her throat and she bit her thick bottom lip. Her bucket dropped to the forest floor and she rushed away.

Tad watched her disappear. In his mind, he saw Mammy's stern face, and he shivered. What had Peg ever done to hurt him before last night? Usually she tried to take care of him. "Peg!" He started after her and ran for several feet, but a man stepped from behind a tree. Tad's feet skidded to a stop on the dead pine needles. "Massah," he whispered.

Massah shook his finger at Tad's face. He spit as he yelled. "Don't misunderstand me when I say, the lash you received is nothing, do you hear me, nothing compared to what I will give you if you *ever* slow at a chore. If you even look up while you work, I will lash you."

Tad couldn't breathe, Massah's anger washed over him like a hurricane.

"I will sell you so far downriver you will never hear of Mammy again."

Tad brought a hand to his head, a light penetrating behind his eyes. He desperately wanted to find a tree and hide. "You *can't* sell me. Please."

Massah's face turned as red as a crimson rose, his outstretched fingers reaching toward Tad's neck. "Never, ever step foot in my house again. And never, ever look at my daughters. Ever!"

Tad hefted the buckets and held back the tears.

While Tad walked, Massah followed. "No more running when you're angry. No more bunking with Mammy. You stay with Johnny and Bo. And never speak to Collin again."

Tad strode forward. After a few moments of silence, he risked a look back. Massah had walked away, his white cotton shirt flapping in the wind.

Bucket after bucket, bleeding hands, tears, sweat mixed with hatred. What was the song last night at the *shout*? He mumbled the words.

*"Help me bear de cross, for I weep, I weep, I can't hold out; if any mercy, Lord, oh pity me."*

He sang it again, louder. He lifted his voice to heaven, and his heart and lungs beat with the song. The buckets in his hands and the scabs on his back weren't forgotten, but lighter, somehow. He worked and sang until late in the day, when Samuel stopped him. He collapsed in Bo's slave cabin without eating.

※

In the morning, Bo nudged Tad in the ribs. Tad's stiff muscles wouldn't move without loud grunting, the pain nearly over-whelming. He opened his hands, and the dried blood cracked as he spread his fingers.

"Bread there." The old man motioned to the table.

The cabin creaked as he stepped out the front door. The whitewashed planks and wood shingles were better than sleep-ing outdoors as he'd done the night before. Tad ate his bread in the gray morning light.

Tad shivered from the cold marsh water, but hauling buckets

to the empty field warmed him. He had just begun to feel the sun on his back when Samuel stepped from the tabby barn and motioned. "Come, time to pick."

"Pick?"

"You heard me, c'mon."

Other slaves from the Frogmore had gathered in a field near Seaside Road. Men wore wide hats and loose shirts and the women dressed in brown dresses with scarves over their hair, tied under their chin. A few young children ran naked in the lane.

Magnolia trees lined the field, and the scent from their flowers drifted in on the breeze.

Samuel called, and the slaves turned to him. "Warm sun, and the cotton pods bust open. We gotta pick. We all here, so we get started, fast, before rain comes."

One by one they picked up a cloth bag and slung it over their shoulder. Tad lifted one and tried to fit the bag over his head.

"Like this." The driver stepped toward him and with huge hands, adjusted and tightened the strap. "You's small, that's all. Now, you never picked before, so listen here. Fill your bag, then dump it on a sheet I put out for you. Don't get no dirt on the cotton, and take out any bad that don't belong, like leaves." He sighed. "And those hands . . . "

Samuel reached into his own bag, pulled out a strip of cloth, and tore it in two. He wound it around Tad's palms. "Won't do to get blood on the cotton. Now listen here, you're gettin' a lashin' tonight."

"No!" He looked into the big man's eyes.

"Won't be too hurtful, it'll sting some."

"Why I gotta get a lashin'? My back—"

"Never you mind. I don't like lashin' you, don't want to, but I's gots to do it."

What more must he endure? Tad looked away.

Peg watched him, quickly turned away, and disappeared into the field. He started to follow, but stopped. He sighed, his heart heavy. He squinted his eyes from the glare, the cotton a sea of white, and entered the field.

He reached for a cotton puff and almost crushed the soft and sticky ball. Tiny leaves and branches stuck to the fibers. He picked at it for a few moments, then, satisfied it was clean, stuffed the ball into his bag. He pulled another off the plant, his hand barely big enough to surround the cotton. The ball rolled from his fingers and dropped into the dirt.

A quick blow from his lungs and the dust with tiny leftover bits of leaves fell off. He reached for another ball. This time was a little easier.

He glanced at the elderly woman in the row next. With two hands grasping at different plants, she yanked the cotton faster than Mammy shelled corn. Her bag was nearly full. After thirty seconds, she hurried to the start of the row, dumped the bag onto a sheet, then returned.

Someone's deep voice started singing, and others joined.

*"Gospel train's a'comin', I hear it just at hand,*
*"I hear the car wheel rumblin' and rollin' thro' the land.*
*"Get on board, little children, there's room for many more."*

Tad cleared his throat to sing, wiped his brow with his sleeve, and picked cotton.

At the end of the day, Samuel weighed each sheet on a scale in the tabby barn, then lifted it onto a hook with two large hands. Tad's sheet only took one hand to lift. "Yours was lightest, Tad." Samuel, with a soft look in his eye, stood over him. "Got to whip you."

Tad bit his lip and nodded, understanding the warning now, and let Samuel lead him to the front of the big house. He stood miserable and naked while the whip slapped at his back. The fresh scabs ripped open, and he cried, mostly because Massah was watching, not from pain.

Tad let Mammy bandage his back before he ate and stumbled to his cabin and bed. Raindrops pelted the roof as he drifted off to sleep, while Bo and Johnny sat at the table and talked in the dark.

Thunder woke Tad. Bo's snores filled the room. He tried to cover his ears, but a sound caught his attention. Voices from outside.

Tad thought about waking Bo. At least the old man would stop snoring, even if the voices weren't important. He sat up.

The door broke open. Two men rushed into the room. "Nobody move."

Mr. Spencer's ugly face lit up as lightning crossed the sky. "Nobody move," he said again. He and his assistant, both with rifles tucked under their arms and lamps in their hands, flipped over the table. The unlit candle spun across the floor. They checked under beds and poked blankets. Spencer recognized Tad and shoved him against the wall. The two men slammed the door.

Bo helped Tad to his feet, then laughed.

Tad was confused. "What's he doing? Why did he charge in here like that?"

Bo's old bones cracked as he righted the table. Johnny picked up the candle and lit the wick. He set the flickering light on the table and sat on a bench. Bo settled his frame in the chair across from Johnny. Tad crawled into bed.

Bo pointed at the door. "See if it's open."

Tad shook his head. He didn't want anything to do with Spencer.

"C'mon, boy, I bet you can't open it."

Tad crept across the floor, tried the door, but it wouldn't budge. He glanced at Bo.

"Locked, from outside."

Bo's face wrinkled in a look of amusement, his eyes locked on Tad's. "They's lookin' for someone."

A gust of wind shook the cabin. Rain beat against the door. Despite the pain, Tad dove back into bed. Sweat beaded on his forehead. He wanted to get out but couldn't. He was trapped.

Johnny ran his fingers through his hair. "Bad night to run."

Tad shook, and wrapped his arms around his knees. "Somebody run?"

"Somebody run." Bo gave Johnny a knowing look. "Samuel."

"What? Samuel ran?" Tad brushed his nose, curious.

Johnny nodded.

"I did once." Bo looked up to the rafters as if an ancient memory were hidden somewhere near the cabin's apex. "Done got caught. Them dogs are of the devil. Got sold downriver, to here."

"The North ain't no place to run. They send you back, even if you make the North."

"Moses." Bo gave a sure nod. "If Samuel finds Moses, he be home free."

Tad didn't understand what they meant. "Why'd he run? Who's Moses?"

"Why does any slave run?" Bo shrugged. "But he didn't like lashin', for sure."

Tad sniffed. "He lashed me."

"Ain't why he run." Johnny laughed. "'Cause he had to lash you. Nope, we know he was runnin'." He stuck his chest out.

"You *knew*? How? He tell you?"

Bo sighed, stood, and stretched, his eye on his bed. "Don't know much, do ya?"

Johnny glared at Tad. "If you'd worked in fields, 'stead of playin', you'd know."

Tad felt ashamed and angry at the same time, and wanted to shout at Johnny. But he held back. It was true.

Bo settled into his bed. "Lie down, Tad. You was too small to be a good field hand, anyhow. That's right, settle in there. Now tell me, you remember whose voice first sang today?"

"I reckon I don't." Tad thought back. "Samuel?"

"That's right." Bo's few teeth gleamed in the candlelight. "He told us that he's jumpin' on the gospel train and goin' to run. They call it the *Underground Railroad.*"

Of course. Tad thought back to the words. *Gospel train's a'comin', I hear it just at hand.*

Johnny leaned forward, his seat creaking. "And Moses helps slaves, once they find him."

"He does?"

Johnny lowered his voice. "They say he's a spy. Reckon he'll free the lot of us. All we got to do is run."

Tad wanted to run. How beautiful, to run.

# FOUR

$\mathcal{I}$n the morning the door unlocked and opened just as the sun's full light filtered through oak leaves. Massah led Tad, Bo, and Johnny to the meeting tree, an oak whose tall branches filled with moss stood guard in front of the big house where Tad had been lashed the night before. Frogmore's other slaves stood in a half circle around the tree, just far enough away to keep from the dripping leaves.

Massah broke away and spoke to another man, not far off.

Tad approached Mammy, watched her face, and stood next to her when he saw her smile.

Massah scared Tad. He kept tight control over the Frogmore. But the gentleman next to him—his suit gray, pressed, a gold watch chain hanging from his vest—made Tad's knees shake. He glanced at the man's shoes. Not a bit of dust, and two slaves waited nearby with towels on their arms, ready to shine them when he crawled back into his carriage. This man was more important than Dr. Jenkins. This man was Massah Coffin.

Tad imagined what it would be like to be Coffin. He owned the Frogmore and left Collin's father in charge because he spent most of his time in Beaufort, on the mainland. To be Massah Coffin meant to be the most powerful man on the island and surely the richest.

29

Tad watched as Coffin's arm waved and hushed the crowd's murmurs. He moved slowly to remove his tall hat and handed his cane to a slave. "I've come to squelch rumors. Nasty rumors that aren't true. I believe it is important that you know what is happening."

Tad glanced at Mammy, who watched with the same eyes she used when she thought someone was lying.

Coffin continued. "Samuel, your driver, has run because of these rumors, and I fear for his life."

Tad saw Bo and Johnny nod at each other.

"The Yankees are stealing our servants. A war has started, against us, to take you and sell you to Cuba."

Cuba. Tad had heard about how slaves were treated in the sugar fields. It was a slow, painful death between rows of heated sugarcane. No one lived five years picking sugar.

Coffin spread his arms wide. "But you are my family, and I would not have you ignorant. The Yankees steal our property, rape our women, kill those we love."

"Please, Massah Coffin, please save us, save us," someone called.

"Thankfully, one Southern boy can whip ten Yankees." He smiled. Then his face turned grave. "I am concerned that Samuel is dead, or on his way to Cuba. That is why I warn you of the war. But fear not!" He raised a hand. "For the Lord hath given us hope."

He reached into his coat pocket and pulled out a small but thick, black Bible. A ribbon marked the place he opened the book. "Daniel, chapter eleven."

Coffin cleared his throat, set spectacles on his nose, and read. "*And the king of the south shall be strong, and one of his princes; and he shall be strong above him, and have dominion; his dominion shall be a great dominion.*"

He glanced over his spectacles and smiled. "*But out of a*

*branch of her roots*—meaning South Carolina—*shall one stand up in his estate, which shall come with an army, and shall enter into the fortress of the king of the north, and shall deal against them, and shall prevail.*" He closed his Bible. "We shall prevail. But we must pray."

"Oh yes, Massah, we pray, we pray."

"Pray for Master Rhett, Master Fripp, Master Chaplin, Dr. Jenkins, pray for them all as we defend ourselves, and defend you." Coffin returned to his carriage, Massah close behind.

Tad watched the horse. Horses weren't rare on the island, but Tad hadn't seen one so beautiful. He glanced at Mammy, who shook her head. "Lordy me. I hope he ain't right 'bout Samuel."

Tad slipped into the gardens, hurried along a hedge, and hid in a bush not far from the horse. The beast's chestnut flanks reflected the morning sun. With no one looking, he crawled from the thicket and reached forward. The black muzzle twitched as he touched her velvet hair. He closed his eyes and rubbed his cheek against hers. She snorted.

He ran a hand past the carriage's riggings then over the mare's strong back. Bumps in long stripes crisscrossed the rump. He glanced toward the carriage, Massah and Coffin's feet the only part of them he could see.

Tad whispered into the horse's ear. "You and me, horsie, we a lot alike. We both saw the lash."

He could hear the men's conversation. "I've read the papers too." Coffin's voice. "The fleet in New York could attack several places."

"But larger than the Spanish Armada? They can attack anywhere!"

"Perhaps," Coffin said. "But if Manassas is any gauge, ten million men and ships cannot make inroads against us. Your job is to finish this harvest. Quickly now."

Massah's feet shuffled. "They made war on King Cotton. What fools."

Coffin's voice lowered. "All the same, Mr. Rhett has called together the local militia. Chose a new driver to care for the Frogmore and joined them. Nothing to fear. Steady. The Rhett family won't let a fleet enter Port Royal."

# FIVE

*T*ad and Peg jumped off the road as horses ridden by local planters thundered by. The two brushed dust from their clothes and scrambled back to the lane.

Peg sneezed, wiped her nose on her sleeve, and then turned to Tad. "Why there so many riders?"

They'd been told to deliver papers to Dr. Jenkins—papers, Tad guessed, that were an excuse to keep Massah from serving in the local militia. He clutched the wrinkled letter in one hand and wiped sweat and dirt from his face with the other.

"Tad, you still mad at me?" Peg's voice was quiet. Her large eyes searched his.

He shrugged.

"Tad, don't be mad at me. Wasn't in me to give you away like that, and you knowed it. I'm sorry. I'm sorry like the Israelites was sorry for their sins."

Tad's will gave way. It was her brown eyes, the honesty. He was about to speak when something like distant thunder split the sky. "You hear that?"

"Hear what?"

"Sound like . . . cannons?" Tad took a few steps forward.

"How you know what cannons sound like?"

Tad wiped dust from his nose. "There. Cannons. We can see from Dr. Jenkins' place." He ran down the lane.

"A storm, Tad, a storm."

He hurried ahead, on toward Dr. Jenkins' plantation. Was this why so many men on horseback galloped along Seaside Road? Were they getting ready to stop an attack? Ahead, a dozen armed men in a small bunch turned down the plantation lane. Tad ducked into the thicket. Peg crashed into him.

"What they doin'?" She wheezed, trying to catch her breath.

"It's war, Peg."

"Tad." She grabbed his arm. "You goin' to war?"

"Don't know, but I wanna see it."

Cannons again.

"C'mon."

Buggies and carriages lined the road where a wedding had been a week before. Between the plantation buildings and Station Creek, horses reared and whinnied. Women waited on the house's wide front porch, fanning themselves and pointing east. Planters lined the marsh and peered across the wide flat to a rise far away. Some men wore blue uniforms; others looked out of place with fancy suits and tall hats. All had rifles slung over their shoulder.

Tad shielded his eyes from the sun's glare to see smoke drifting over the distant island. The war had washed into Port Royal Sound.

"Peg, take the letter." He handed the envelope to her, then sprinted across the yard and into the forest.

Branches slapped at his skin. He jumped a rotten log, didn't quite clear it, and slammed onto the forest floor. He scampered to his feet and raced ahead, toward the deep rumbling, a constant sound now. Land's End would be the best place to see— from the beach he could view all of Port Royal Sound.

Ships dotted the horizon, their masts thrust into the air. The fleet looked like a forest springing up from the water.

He guessed there were more ships than there were people

on St. Helena Island. They seemed to be waiting . . . waiting for what? Tad glanced down and noticed the tide was out, and his heart skipped a beat. The tide! Any moment the rising water would carry the ships toward the inlet.

Two forts guarded the opening to the sound, one on either side, their guns thrust through holes in palmetto log walls. The battlement on Tad's side of the water, Fort Beauregard, fired hopelessly at the ships that waited offshore. Shells splashed into the rolling waves well short of their target.

Plantation owners had joined Tad at Land's End to watch the battle begin. He was the only slave there, but no one seemed to care. They whispered to each other, pointing to the defenders that lined the beaches, prepared to push the Yankees back to sea.

Ships' bows slowly turned toward them. Sails opened, billowing in the breeze, and paddle ships belched white clouds of steam into the sky.

Smaller ships, gunboats with cannons on their bows, hurried in on the tide. The Yankee flags fluttered like angry whips in the wind. They pressed toward ships with the South Carolina flag—a crescent moon over a palmetto tree—that fought against the tide to meet their attackers. Cannons thundered in the morning breeze, the white smoke appearing in a puff of cotton, then drifting to the north. Behind the Yankee gunboats, steamboats appeared with huge sailing ships close behind, cannons bristling in the morning sun. He saw a rope strung between several ships. The steamers pulled the massive sailing ships! Tad laughed and hoped that someday he would be so clever.

The gunboats pushed the defending ships away, and the steamboats closed in on Fort Beauregard. Fire burst from the defenses, but it seemed as if nothing could hit the ships. The Yankees paddled closer to the fort then veered to the side, pulling the sailing ships with them. Long rows of cannons pointed toward the walls.

The air split with a blast, ripping at his ribs. The ships disappeared in smoke. In less than a second, the fort exploded. Sand and wood soared into the air, and blue smoke choked the inlet. When it lifted, Tad saw Fort Beauregard smoldering in ruins.

With perfect formation, the ships paddled across Port Royal Sound toward Fort Walker on the other side. Again, thunder tore the air, and the fort trembled under the attack. The Yankee guns continued until only one South Carolina cannon fired. The ships turned back to Fort Beauregard and pummeled the broken walls, the two defending cannons falling silent.

The ships attacked Fort Walker, then circled one last time until both forts were crushed. Tidal waves pushed the gunboats up the sound past Tad, pressing the defensive ships upstream. He glanced at the planters around him, their nervous discussions turned to arguments. Some dashed to their carriages and sped away.

The ocean filled with rowboats, packed with blue troops. They drove toward shore. A trickle of sweat dropped into Tad's eye and he brushed it way. His elbow bumped against something soft. Beside him, Peg stared at the ships, her eyes open wide.

He reached for her. "North attacked."

"It's bad." Peg nestled closer. "Men dyin' out there."

He tried to calm the excitement, the thought that planters were falling before the Northern guns, but he couldn't stop his feelings any more than he could stop the tide. He didn't want to. They were new, fresh, and life surged through him. "Yep, men's dyin.'"

The smell of gunpowder finally reached his nose, and he breathed deeply. Peg coughed. "Power o' God." Her voice was shaky. "Almighty power of Elijah, calling fire from heaven."

Tad couldn't take his eyes off the battle. "Wish I was on a ship, setting us free."

"You know they've come to free us?"

"I know if I was on that ship, I would."

He felt her arm wrap around his. "You'd free me?"

Tad looked at her. "You and Mammy, sure, and the rest." Mammy! Someone would have to tell her what happened here. "I gotta go, Peg."

She called his name, but her voice drifted away as his bare feet slapped the dusty Seaside Road.

The forest drowned out the battle noise. The miles melted as he replayed the fight in his mind. What did it mean to have the Yankees attack? Why here? Did this mean he didn't need to mud the fields tomorrow? Never before had Tad seen a man from the North. Did a horn grow from his forehead, like the rumors said?

Mammy would know.

He dodged horses, buggies, militia, and slaves, all running back to their plantations.

The newly mudded field slowed him, but he hurried across, then through the pine forest, past the empty slave quarters to the tabby barn. He rounded the corner, then stopped dead.

At the dock, two boats were filled with supplies. Mammy was there, Bo and Johnny, and most of the other Frogmore slaves. Massah held a pistol.

Tad backed around the corner of the tabby barn and watched.

"Get on board." Massah towered over Bo.

The old slave flinched. "Ain't goin'."

No one moved.

Massah's face turned red and he roared, "Load the boats now, or by God, I will fire." He lifted the pistol.

The distant sounds of cannons drifted from the creek. A few slaves looked up, then climbed aboard. Most didn't budge.

"You'll row this boat to Charleston. All who go will be safe in the Charleston house."

Bo shook his head. "No, Massah. I'm stayin'."

Johnny nodded eagerly. "Needs a crew to farm for you, Massah. I'm stayin'."

Massah turned to Missus, distracted. "Where's Collin?" He turned to Mammy. "Find him." She didn't move.

He shifted the pistol, first at her, then at Johnny, as if confused. "Get on this boat, now." Massah's hand shook.

Johnny glanced at Bo, then stuck out his chest. "Ain't goin'."

"Last warning, get on board."

Johnny shook his head violently.

Massah pulled the trigger. Tad turned away. A splash echoed against the barn. Tad choked on a cry. But he turned back, afraid for Mammy.

Bo and several others scattered, but Massah reached for a second pistol at his belt. Bo ducked and the shot sailed past his head, smacking into the side of the big house.

A handful of slaves boarded the boats as Massah reloaded his pistols.

"Run, Mammy, run," Tad whispered, but she was too large.

He waited, unsure what to do, staring at Johnny's body floating in the marsh. If Massah shot Johnny, then sure as sweet grass Massah would shoot Tad. It didn't matter. He scrambled to his feet and rushed forward.

A hand grabbed his arm. "Tad, stop."

Tad turned, wide-eyed. "Collin, what you doing? They're looking for you."

Collin's face was pale, his eyes darting in panic. His voice was earnest. "I've got to go with Father, but I'm sorry. I should've taken your lashing."

Tad's fist clenched, and with all his might he slugged Collin's shoulder. "You should've."

Collin gave a weak laugh and rubbed his arm. "It's been eating me up inside. I'm sorry, I really am. I wish . . . "

"If there was time, I'd dunk you for sure."

"There isn't enough time." He held out a hand, his face earnest. "Peg told me why you were in the house. Here." A necklace slipped from Collin's outstretched fingers, but he caught it before it fell. "This yours?"

"Pappy's necklace!"

Collin dropped it in Tad's hands.

Massah's voice bellowed. "Collin!" They both turned toward the river.

"I have to go." Collin grabbed his arm. "Tad, listen, I will come back. You're my best friend. When all this is over, I will return."

Tad glanced at the white skin against his black, and nodded, confused. Return to what? Return to be a new massah? He held up the necklace. He was a jumble of emotions, hatred, anger, shock. He opened his hand and stared at the silver cross.

"I'm grateful, Collin." He squeezed his hand. "And you'd best take care."

Massah's voice drifted around the tabby barn. "Collin, we're loading the boats."

They both peered around the corner. Tad gasped.

Massah held a pistol to Mammy's chest. "Get on board."

Tad jumped up, but Collin pulled him back. "Let me go."

Collin raced toward the dock. "Father! Here I am."

Massah glanced up, then looked at Mammy. "Get on board."

She put a hand to her heart and took a step back. "Ain't leavin' my boy, Massah, and that's a fact. Shoot me if you must, but I ain't leavin'."

Massah swore as Collin reached his side. "Get in the boat," he snarled, then leveled his gaze back at Mammy. "You'd sink the boat anyway." He climbed into a vessel and pushed off.

Tad crept from behind the barn and joined Mammy on the banks of the stream. Both stood, watching Massah row away.

Gun smoke still hovered in the calm air. Tad couldn't keep his voice from shaking. "Charleston, Mammy? How they get to Charleston? I saw the water, it's full of Yankee ships."

She glanced down. "There be waterways from here to Charleston, no doubt about that."

Tad took a deep breath. "Mammy, they running, all of 'em. From here to Land's End, there ain't gonna be a massah left on this island."

"Praise be," she said quietly. "Maybe's I's free."

Tad looked again at Johnny, his back just above the murky water. He shuddered. "Better move him before a 'gator gets him."

Tad felt a hand at the back of his neck, saw Mammy's eyes swollen with tears. "Reckon we can let Bo take care of that?"

"I reckon."

# S I X

*T*ad had always wondered why an alligator would snap at birds and take them under. What did the birds ever do to the alligator?

But when the slaves destroyed the island, he understood. Tad felt the sting on his back every day from his lashing, and if he'd been treated that way all his life, he might snap at the massahs too, like an alligator after a duck.

They buried Johnny in the family cemetery, next to the white folk, and they spent the night talking on it, how Massah would be fit for killing them all if he knew his mammy and pappy was buried next to a slave.

Not long after, Tad cornered Mammy near the marsh, where she'd just come from the tabby barn with a basket of potatoes.

"Mammy, when this is all over, will Pappy come back?"

"Lordy me, child, what brings on your nonsense questions? And a time like this too."

"Just wonderin', that's all. I dream of him sometimes. Saw him, Mammy, a big man, me hidin' in the bushes, waitin' for somethin' the other night."

Mammy's eyebrows creased. "Don't be thinkin' on him now, or the Lord will punish you for wastin' time."

"It couldn't be Pappy, could it, Mammy? I mean, in my dream? 'Cause he was so big, and me kinda small."

Mammy shifted the basket to her other arm. "You is tiny for your age."

"But where did Pappy go?"

She waved a hand and started for the kitchen. "Texas, I do believe. Now I's gots cookin' to do. Just 'cause Massah gone doesn't mean we stop eatin'."

Bo wouldn't let anyone in the big house. Tad stood with the other residents of Frogmore and listened to the old driver, standing on the porch over them, speaking like a preacher. "We've got to think this out." Older than Samuel, and smaller, Bo worked smarter, not harder. His accent wasn't local, but from northern regions. "We got to survive, 'cause Massah ain't around no more to care for us. We got a barn full of cotton, and we've got all Massah's animals, and then the food. But we need to think on next year, and the crops we want to grow. I reckon corn instead of cotton.

"Work, and us is eatin'. Don't work, and we gonna be like the Israelites in the wilderness."

But soldiers marched through the Frogmore over the next week and stripped the plantation of furniture. Tad studied the uniforms, stripes on their shoulders, thick blue coats with smart buttons. Their heavy boots tramped through gardens. They slung packs over one shoulder, a rifle over the other. The gun Tad noticed most of all.

The army cleaned out the tabby barn and left no food for the coming winter. When Mammy and Bo complained, all an officer in blue said was, "You touch the cotton, you'll be shot."

A few days later, two men pulled up to the big house in a small carriage. They wore suits with gold chains that dropped from a buttonhole into their vest pocket. Their mustaches were waxed to the sides of their faces. Bo stood on the porch, hoe in hand, to fight them off.

They slugged him. Mr. Lincoln had sent them, they said, from the North. Agents. Cotton agents.

The agents moved into the big house.

That afternoon Tad half-closed his eyes and leaned back against the wall next to his bed. When Massah left, he'd decided to stay with Bo and not return to the kitchen cabin. So Peg had moved in with Mammy.

Bo nursed a bruised head and gently touched his eye.

Peg swung a wet rag in the air to cool it then set the cloth on Bo's swollen face. She touched his white hair. "He a good man," she whispered to Tad. "No reason to hit him, he just defended what he thinks is ours."

"I'd have helped if I'd been there." Tad thought of marching into the house and throwing the two men out.

"Massah was right, the North ain't no better." Peg crossed the room and sat at the edge of Tad's bed.

"We ain't no freer than with Massah." He sat up.

"Reckon we are, some. But the tabby barn's empty. They took the cotton and sold it for Uncle Sam."

Tad glanced at Bo, who mumbled something in his sleep. "They say if we work, they pay."

"You believe that?"

Tad leaned back, slipped his hands behind his head, and stared at the rafters. "No, reckon not."

"What you gonna do?"

He opened his mouth to speak, but when he looked into her eyes, he hesitated. "I think . . . " he finally said, " . . . I think my pappy was a soldier, so I'm gonna be a soldier."

She laughed. "You're too small to be a soldier."

He clenched his teeth. "I wanna be a soldier."

She stood. "You's too small, boy. And what's more, they ain't never gonna let no black boy into the army, no how."

He covered his ears. "Someday I will, and ain't no one gonna say nothin' about it." He would be as big as Pappy. Then he'd show them.

If Bo were a soldier, those men wouldn't have hit him. His uniform would have kept them away. He would be respected, would get everything the Frogmore needed.

They wouldn't be starving.

# SEVEN

*E*dward Pierce slammed the book shut and leapt to his feet. At the edge of the desk waited a copy of the *Boston Morning Journal*, the *Atlantic*, and his favorite, mostly because of the pictures, *Harper's Weekly*. He turned his eyes away, then paced in front of his desk. If his law practice were to enjoy continued success, he needed to bury his nose in books, not public events.

But public events held a certain appeal, and lately the world changed at an alarming rate. A war to abolish slavery endeavored to destroy a country. True, books such as *The Federalist* and *Democracy in America* made sense of some of the last century's debacles, but in the end, Pierce knew that young men who kept up with the latest happenings, coupled with a classical education, held incredible power to mold events. But Pierce wasn't young anymore, in his thirties. And time ticked by without a mind for regrets.

Pierce wandered to the window and brushed his brown hair back. Through the thick pane of glass, he saw travelers with heavy coats and scarves being whipped by the winter wind. Horses blew cloud streams from their iced muzzles. At one corner, a man cried out for volunteers to fight. At another, a man preached repentance.

He turned back to his fire, stirred the coals, and threw in

another log. He snatched the *Atlantic*, opened it, scanned his article, and wished he'd worded his ideas a bit differently. He tossed it aside and grabbed a stack of papers from his desk. There was a law practice that needed his attention.

A knock from the front door pulled him away. Pierce called to his secretary, but received no answer. With a sigh, he hurried down the stairs and flung open the door.

A black man filled the door frame. His head just missed the lintel and his shoulders blocked the cold wind.

Pierce couldn't hold back his surprise. "My good man. Come in out of the cold, quickly now."

The man swept off his tattered hat and brushed a few snow-flakes from ragged clothes. He removed the scrap of cloth he used as a coat. His pants were a calico patchwork of repairs.

Pierce glanced down at his own fine suit. "Let me take your things." He fussed over the coat and hat and set them on the stand by the door. "Can I get you a drink? Maybe something to eat, perhaps?"

The man shook his head. "You Edward Pierce?" His deep voice echoed down the hallway.

"Yes, yes, I am. Come, come sit in the parlor where you can warm yourself."

"Thank you kindly, suh."

Pierce stepped into the parlor and motioned to a seat. He watched the chair's thin legs as the man settled between the arms.

"A drink?" Pierce looked up as he stirred the fire.

"No suh, a drink ain't necessary."

"I'm at a disadvantage, I'm afraid I don't know your name." He took a seat across from the man.

"Name's Samuel. I heard . . . " The man took a deep breath, then continued. "I hear you can help runaways."

Pierce winced. "Who told you that?"

"Down ways. I reckon it's hard to remember, when I've come such a far piece." He rubbed his head and the weight of his latest fortunes seemed to settle on his shoulders. The chair creaked as Samuel slumped in exhaustion.

They sat in silence for a moment. A dull sadness filled Pierce. "There's not much I can do for you. It's illegal to help you, or recently was, before the war. Fugitive Slave Act. We must return all slaves back to their owners. Dreadful law, but a law nonetheless."

Samuel grimaced, nodded, and leaned forward to stand. "I'm sorry to bother you, suh."

Pierce held out a hand. "Wait, just wait a moment." He felt curious. "I may be able to help. But first, where are you from? How far have you traveled? Why did you run?"

Samuel brushed his tired, swollen eyes. "I ran 'cause I needed to run, and that's why any slave would run."

"Of course."

"I reckon I just got tired of beatin' ones that don't need a beatin' and bowin' to Massah's every whim. So I hid in the marshes and swamps. I followed the drinkin' gourd, North Star, and it led me north. But clouds covered it, so I found some soldiers in blue. They took me to their commandin' officer, man named Butler, I think. He wanted work from me, but I'd told him I was goin' north. He give me your name and a map to Boston, so here I am, askin' for help."

"In a moment you and I will find some food."

"Yes, suh. Thank you, suh." Samuel lowered his head. "I reckon I need favors now."

Pierce stood and crossed the room to look out the window. "Butler, General Butler, was my commanding officer. I enlisted for ninety days. Was stationed at Fortress Monroe." He looked at Samuel. "That's how he and I know each other."

The man returned the gaze.

Pierce put himself in the big man's place and recognized a lost and lonely feeling. "The Underground Railroad is almost at an end, my friend." He tapped the man's thick shoulder. "Times are changing."

"Then what's I goin' to do?" Samuel's voice was quiet and sad.

"Not all is lost." Pierce turned and stoked the fire. "I have a friend, Mr. Garrison, who will help you."

"They say you a smart man, Mistah Pierce, that you wrote books."

Pierce looked up from the fire. "I have, yes."

"They say you wrote a book on the Underground Railroad."

Pierce stared at him. "Wrote a book? On the Underground Railroad?" He stretched his arms and readjusted his jacket. "Do you perhaps mean this?" He reached for a bookshelf and pulled a thick leather-bound volume. "In 1857 I completed a treatise on railroad law."

Samuel shrugged.

Pierce patted the freed slave's shoulder. "Steady, you're in sympathetic hands."

Samuel nodded.

"Energy and persistence conquer all things, or so says our famed Benjamin Franklin. So action will be the order of the day. Let's find Mr. Garrison, he will help you."

A knock came from the front door. "It seems we are of some import today." He left the room and opened it to find a young boy, dressed in a thin, brown jacket. "What can I do for you?"

"Telegram for Mr. Pierce."

"Yes, thank you." He took the envelope and handed the boy a halfpenny. "I hope you don't mind," he said when he'd returned to the room, and opened it.

*Edward Pierce, my compliments. If you incline to visit Beaufort in connection with contrabands and cotton, come to Washington at once.*

*Sec. of the Treasury, Salmon P. Chase.*

Pierce stared at the note, read it again, his mind racing. Beaufort. Where had he heard the name? He said the name aloud. "Beaufort?"

Samuel leapt to his feet. "What about it?"

"Where is it?"

"Mistah Pierce, Beaufort was a town off my home island. What happened?"

Pierce stuffed the note in his pocket. "Come, quickly." He smiled at Samuel. "An adventure is set before both of us."

❧

The Underground Railroad, Pierce discovered, had adjusted its philanthropic ideas from whisking runaways out of the country to feeding and clothing them until the Lincoln administration decided what to do with them. Samuel fell into Garrison's care.

Pierce took a train to Washington, hired a cab, and crossed the city straight for Chase's office.

Secretary of the Treasury Chase, modestly dressed in a thick black jacket and ribbon tie, smiled warmly when Pierce shook his hand.

Chase brushed back the two puffs of hair that protruded on either side of his balding head "Good to see you, lad. It's been too long. Your health holding up?"

"It is." Pierce eyed the books that lined the shelves. There weren't many, and the few that Pierce had read spoke mostly of ambition and democracy.

"And your law practice?"

"Successful."

"Of course." Chase settled in the chair. His round stomach barely fit behind the desk. "I'd offer you a seat, but it wouldn't do any good now, would it, knowing your energy?"

"The journey was tedious." Pierce glanced out the window that overlooked the White House, a view thinly veiled by falling flakes. He let his eyes rest on the snow. "Not enough light to read by, bumpy roads. I will take a seat." Pierce sat in the mahogany chair and sighed.

"You've done well since I saw you last." Chase motioned to the *Atlantic*. "Excellent article. Scholarly, but yet understandable to the masses."

"Thank you. You've progressed as well. The Republican Party seems to like you."

Chase's eyes darkened. "I didn't win the presidency." He leaned back and folded his hands over his stomach. "Yes, of course, I lend my talents to them. But the true measure of success is how I can help this country, not the party." He pointed. "You're still a Republican."

"I see change needed," Pierce admitted. "Slavery, mostly, and the Republican Party holds against slavery."

"A blasted abolitionist. One more is all we need. But Lincoln must tread carefully, and he walks a dreadful line. When the Peace Democrats hate you because of the war, and the Republicans regret nominating you for your weak stand on slavery, there are many sleepless nights."

Pierce took a deep breath.

Chase continued. "No one would have guessed the resolve of the rebels. Farmers, all of them. Some are planters with slaves that can grow cotton, others just poor, mindless thugs." He closed his eyes. "Bull Run, awful bloody mess." He paused a moment, as if deep in thought. "But never you mind. That's not why I called you here. I need your help."

Pierce stood and paced by the window. Winter clouds blocked the sun and the late afternoon darkened the office.

Chase motioned. "Light some lamps while you're up." The secretary tossed a box of matches and Pierce caught them.

He struck the match and touched the wicks. The tiny flames lit the room.

"That's better." Chase straightened his jacket. "Now let me see, where was I? Ah, the war, and how you fit in. We know you come from an excellent family. So let's discuss your education."

"Brown University then Harvard Law."

Chase nodded. "And next you worked with the Free Soil Party, then the Republican Party, even before Lincoln joined."

Pierce smiled at the memory. That's where they'd met, through their abolitionist ideals in a political party.

Chase snatched the *Atlantic*. "I wanted to read a line of your article to you."

Pierce groaned.

Chase's eyes scanned the journal. In twenty years, when Pierce approached his midfifties, he hoped to look as rested and healthy as Chase. Handsome, powerful, confident, Chase was a man who quickly decided what he wanted, then how to get it. Pierce knew the secretary was going to use him, but he let Chase have his way. Nothing short of the presidency would please the aging man, and riding the man's ambitions had its advantages.

"How many times have you been elected as a delegate for the Republican conventions?" Chase didn't look up as he turned the page.

"Twice."

"And you've spoken before the Massachusetts legislators so influentially that the law you argued for was enacted, am I right?"

Pierce crossed the room and stood before the desk. "I suppose. Am I to review my entire life? Why did you summon me?"

Chase set down the journal and looked up. "I'd hoped to satisfy some of my curiosity before we came to the point of this meeting. I bring your education and qualifications to the table to ask you this. Why did you sign up to the army when Lincoln called for volunteers? To be a common foot soldier is far below you. A private, when you could have been an officer."

Pierce sat and rubbed his head. How could he explain why he'd enlisted in the first place? To help the black man? To free him? To see what it was like to be a soldier? "I served under General Butler, an experience I couldn't duplicate. And I had no previous military training."

"I understand your experience with Butler, but you didn't know what would happen when you signed up."

Pierce shrugged.

"And you didn't sign for three years. Just ninety days."

Pierce held back a smile. "The tents had veteran snorers, who we wished had stayed home. Must have been a comfort to their wives to be rid of them."

Chase chuckled, then sighed. "You had no idea, though, your role naming them contrabands."

Pierce hadn't traveled this far to be questioned about his actions. But this felt like a job interview. He let Chase continue.

"Slaves pouring over the lines and the South demanding their return. Of course they couldn't go back to the South, they would just help the enemy's war effort. But the legal implications of keeping them? Difficult. Then General Butler's declaration, a decision, brilliant, in my opinion. The slaves are property of the South, not people, not prisoners. If they are property, they must be treated as such, and are thus contraband of war, and the South has no claims. Butler called it common law. Tell me, Mr. Pierce, was that your logic, or his?"

Pierce felt weary. "Does it matter? I was serving my country, which was attacked because she's loyal to human rights."

Chase's voice was accusing. "Butler put you in charge of those contrabands, and you answered an important question for this country—could the Negro be useful to the North? *We* knew he could, and he was. But listen to your logic." He picked up the journal and read. "*The venerable gentleman, who wears gold spectacles and reads a conservative daily, prefers confiscation to emancipation. He is reluctant to have slaves declared freemen, but has no objection to their being declared contrabands.*"

The words sounded good coming from Chase's rich voice. Pierce rubbed his chin. "I suppose I called out some from the North, claiming they wanted the slaves for themselves."

"You're a hero to the abolitionists, no doubt."

"I admit some dissatisfaction toward President Lincoln. Why didn't some formal order come from the top down, instead of precedence coming from the battlefield and working itself upward into policy? Is this to be Lincoln's standard method?"

Pierce clenched a fist and continued. "We can imprison or slaughter a rebel, but we cannot unloose his hold on a person he claims is a slave!"

"I know this is not a virtue you possess, Mr. Pierce, but be patient. Lincoln will come around. He's a Declaration of Independence man, the rights of every man come first, and all are created equal. But the constitution protects slavery, and to change the written law should not be taken lightly."

Chase took a deep breath and settled a moment. "That is why I've called you. We can . . . spur Lincoln into action, if done properly."

Pierce paused and looked up.

"We've taken a portion of South Carolina's Sea Islands, and there is not a white man to be found. Every master has left. Ten thousand slaves were left on their own."

"Ten thousand? Dear God, truly not."

"The military has martial law in the area, but you know how the army is in these matters."

"Woefully underqualified. Ten thousand?"

"We've sent a man by the name of Colonel Reynolds to take

control of the slaves' well-being. He's also in charge of the cotton agents, who are consolidating last year's cotton crop and selling it. I can't tell you how much the Treasury needs the funds."

"Of course."

"Right now, Reynolds is in charge of the military, but no one is in charge of the Negroes." Chase reached into a drawer and pulled out an envelope. "Here are your orders. You are to travel to Port Royal and see if Colonel Reynolds cares for the slaves' well-being."

"I am your eyes and ears?" Pierce asked.

"First you report to me, and then you report to the papers. It's possible you might goad Lincoln into action, but that isn't our main purpose here."

Pierce laughed. "Secretary Chase, you care for the people?" He reached out to take the envelope, his mind already placing assignments for understudies and assistants at his law practice.

"I will send a letter to Colonel Reynolds, so he'll be expecting you. And some advice, Mr. Pierce. I want you to find a way to make those men in golden spectacles care about the slaves. Make them embrace emancipation. We need to find a use for the Negro, or this country will never give its consent to free them."

Pierce said his good-byes. He left the office and near the entrance, retrieved his hat. He paused when he saw her.

The clerk waited to hand over his coat. "Sir, do you need assistance?"

Pierce hesitated. "A moment."

Kate Chase walked through the door, her dark hair tied behind in a loose bun, snowflakes resting on it like tiny diamonds. Her calm, brown eyes looked straight ahead. Generous lips, normally relaxed, were pursed in determination. Her flowing, red dress floated across the floor. Kate glided over the marble. She removed her shawl, shook off the moisture, and looked up.

Her resolute lips turned into a genuine smile. "Edward!"

Pierce took a step toward her. "Kate."

She reached out a hand and he took it, feeling the softness. He stared into her eyes for a moment.

With her other hand, she touched his face. "No beard, I see."

Removing her hand from his face, he glanced at the clerk. "This is Washington." He leaned forward and whispered in her ear. "Rumors here spread like wildfire."

"I don't care."

He snatched his coat from the clerk and led Secretary Chase's daughter through a hallway and toward a private bench under a generous window. Gray light filtered from above, reflecting off marble pillars.

A quick glance told him no one was around. He pulled her close, smelling the cold winter day on her clothes, and felt her lips ignite a fire within that warmed him. They didn't see one another enough to make the kisses old. Each one was fresh and new.

After a moment, he broke the embrace.

She opened her eyes and took a shaky breath. "I was on my way to see Father. You've been to see him?"

"Not for what you think."

She feigned a pout, and then blinked and burst into laughter. "What would you say if I told you I've given up on you?"

He held her hands. "My practice isn't settled enough, Kate. And your father isn't president. He'd never consent to your marrying a man who has no power to get him elected."

She frowned. "I wish you weren't right."

He heard footsteps and scooted down the bench, away from

Kate. The man who passed eyed them but continued until he turned the corner.

Pierce slid closer again and put his arm around her. "Look, my love, I have an opportunity that may change things. The slaves in Port Royal have been freed. I've been asked to see what can be done about it, to find a way to integrate them into society. They're starving and need help."

The grin disappeared, and she looked thoughtful, much like her father would when he considered several sides of an issue. "It sounds like philanthropy to me. You can't assist Father unless you're in Washington. With me."

His joy at seeing her faded. He tried to dispel the uncomfortable feeling, but it was stronger, growing every time she referenced her father's ambitions. "I'll be reporting the information I find in Port Royal to the local newspapers. I'll give your father credit for the good things accomplished there."

The concern written in her eyes eased, and he took her hands again. "I must go, Kate. I have cases to finish before I travel to South Carolina. I'm sorry I didn't warn you I was coming to town, otherwise we could have taken in a play together. I was going to call on you."

She leaned in close, and the scent of a winter day was gone. All that remained was the whiff of rose petals. "You will write me? Every day?"

"Every day."

# EIGHT

*W*aves crashed against the side of the ship as the *Baltic* left New York's harbor. Pierce swallowed the rising bile in his stomach.

Chase's final instructions had come late, and a ship wasn't leaving for South Carolina until the thirteenth of January 1862. There was a war on, after all. The orders sent to him aboard ship, however, were disappointing.

He was to *report* to Colonel Reynolds, and to report was to be subservient. That meant limited access to information. His eyes would be diverted from wicked deeds, and ears deafened from the glorious gossip that told the happenings of Port Royal. A letter, fired off to Chase, asked for clarification. With any luck, Colonel Reynolds didn't have a copy of Pierce's orders.

The *Baltic* steamed out of the harbor and into the open ocean. Dark clouds threatened rain, rolling in over a treacherous sea. The coastline disappeared to the west. A strong wind blew across the ship, and Pierce clasped tight the rail with chilled fingers.

"A goodly sight," came a voice from behind, "when a landlubber takes to the Atlantic and won't go below deck."

A sailor stepped up beside him, hands on hips. The gale ruffled the sailor's coat, and Pierce clutched at his own hat.

"Do us all a favor and join the other passengers."

Pierce was forced to yell over the wind. "I don't care to be in the tight confines of my cabin."

"And so you'd rather reside in this tempest." The sailor trudged by, shaking his head. "A loony one, I must say."

"Winfield Scott's blockade, the Anaconda Plan, to send a snake around the whole of the South, how goes it?" Pierce asked.

The sailor paused. "I'd not be knowing about such things. We're not a warship." He touched the side of his nose. "But I did hear, down at the pub, that we're taking vessels here and there, getting some sailors a small fortune."

"They get to split the plunder?"

"Aye, after the sale of it."

The sailor hurried about his work. Pierce wrapped his rubber cape tight around him as a wave sprayed over the bow.

Pierce wondered why a man would choose sailing as a career.

He wiped seawater from his face. Free markets, of course, the idea that a man could get rich. It was why an American did anything. Self-interest. It was self-interest he hoped the slaves would exhibit. If introduced to wages, they might continue to grow cotton. They would contribute cotton to the mills, while collecting pay, and then become consumers themselves.

A nagging thought troubled him. How could a slave, when freed, create a better life? Without a trade or education, the drain on society created hard feelings between those with wealth and those without it. But when people learned a trade and took wages, they not only produced but consumed, making a perfect cycle. As long as the self-interest of preservation and monetary advancement was the chief concern, society could move forward.

Southerners had lost this idea—at least the rich plantation owners had.

Spray washed over Pierce again. He shook his head in frustration over the troubled seas and his personal troubles. There was a great curtain across the United States, at the northern border of states like Virginia and Missouri, hiding the true picture of slavery. Few in the North had an accurate idea of what the bondage truly entailed. But General Butler, and now Secretary Chase, had given him an opportunity to observe the black man firsthand.

Pierce reviewed the two questions everyone in the North wanted answered. The first, could the Negro benefit society, work, follow social mores, and contribute? Pierce felt there was little to worry about. Fortress Monroe proved they could—he'd put the freedmen to work under General Butler's approval.

But he couldn't begin to answer the second question. Could the Negro stand in a line of soldiers, lift his rifle, look his master in the eye, and fire? If the Negro could fight, the North would welcome him with open arms.

After two days, they approached the South Carolina coast.

Palmettos lined the beaches, blocking Pierce's view of the dense interior. He shifted, uncomfortable, nervous, and anxious.

How did the ocean not overwhelm such flat land? South Carolina stretched on into the horizon. Nothing but the low sandy beaches and impregnable jungle met tides and hurricanes.

They neared land, then sailed for an inlet. Pierce could see the shore clearly. The burned remains of a lighthouse a testament to the war. Ruins where a fort had been, charred wood and broken guns strewn about and forgotten.

The lingering echo of a vast evil filled him, and Pierce tried to catch his breath. Was it his abolitionist upbringing and beliefs reacting to what he knew took place here? He couldn't fight the depression, for here lived slavery.

# NINE

*P*ierce hugged the rail to keep himself from vaulting over the side of the ship, splashing into the ocean, and climbing onto the dock. He held back his excitement and waited until the gangway planks dropped.

He'd always been a target for jests, his energy and impatience—an ally in his mind—seemed to bother others.

He departed like a gentleman but was first to exit the boat onto Hilton Head. He looked frantically about to find someone to guide him to Colonel Reynolds.

He gagged, the stagnant marsh smell overwhelming.

Across the dock, men hauled supplies, boxes, and animals. He brushed past them and through a swarm of soldiers.

A small man across the road motioned to him. "Are you Edward Pierce?"

"I am. And you are?"

The man glanced at the crowds, adjusted his uniform, and stood up straight. "I would like a word with you, if you have a moment."

"I must admit I'm in a hurry."

The man, several inches shorter than Pierce, thrust out a chin covered by a well-trimmed beard. "It is a matter of utmost importance. Mr. Pierce, I am Chief Quartermaster Rufus Saxton. It's vital we speak." His earnest eyes pleaded.

Pierce sighed, trying not to show his irritation. "Quickly." "My carriage is this way."

He followed Saxton across the road to a waiting coach. "You're fortunate." They entered, and Saxton shut the door behind him. "Colonel Reynolds is in Hilton Head today. He normally resides in Beaufort, across the sound."

Pierce sat at the edge of the seat across from Saxton.

The quartermaster leaned out the window and called to the Negro driver to find Colonel Reynolds at Headquarters. As they jostled through the streets, Saxton sat back and smiled. "Mr. Pierce, I must say this is well met. I admire your work, from your career with General Butler. Your articles as a private, quite amusing."

Pierce couldn't keep his leg from bouncing impatiently. "Thank you. An abolitionist, I take it."

"A staunch abolitionist. Free Soil in my younger days, but Republican now, if one can be political and hold a military career."

Pierce couldn't hold back a laugh. "With political appointees for military officers, how can one not?"

"Good point, excellent." Saxton grinned. "I'm not a smart man. Not like yourself. Not clever, no, not very clever, but in the end, I hope to do my part. Do you aggressively seek abolition?"

"My personal desires and my actions sometimes conflict in serving my country," Pierce said.

"Let me be frank, for there is little time. Many in Beaufort, Port Royal, and the islands look to make fortunes on the backs of the Negro. They are men hired from the North." His dark eyes turned to fire. "The Negro is in a position to be exploited by men who would fill their coffers with gold instead of helping those in society who are less fortunate."

"And what is my mission here, do you believe?"

Saxton's eyebrows dropped. "I do hope I haven't overstepped

my boundaries, but your reputation has preceded you as a friend to the Negro."

Pierce watched Saxton collect himself with a deep breath.

"I've read your reports." Saxton leaned forward. "I readily agree with your opinions and suggestions."

"Let's be clear. You believe cotton agents strip the area of its wealth."

Saxton nodded. "Are you here to report them to the government?"

"I have no desire to interrupt the state of things." Pierce smiled inwardly. At least, not yet. "Welfare of both the laborer and the businessman is my desire, and a happy equilibrium is all that Washington hopes for."

The carriage lurched to a stop, and Saxton held out a hand. "We've arrived. Please take great care in your choice of words, for these men wish to dispose of that equilibrium."

Pierce nodded, thanked Saxton, and stepped out of the carriage.

Inside the house, Pierce followed an orderly to the parlor. He waited for several minutes, the only sound a ticking clock.

Pierce studied the Southern décor. Rich blue wallpaper accented thick red drapes. A small couch rested on expensive oriental carpet next to the fireplace, where Colonel Reynolds sat after introducing himself.

"I received word you were coming." Reynolds' smile parted his bearded lips. "I trust your journey was pleasant."

"Winter seas." Pierce resisted the urge to interlace his fingers and fidget with his fingernails, a distracting habit to everyone but himself. "Rough weather, a bit tiresome."

"I expect you'd like a tour of the area immediately. But not before a drink, perhaps?"

"Coffee, if there's some to be found." His bones needed a good warmer, and the ship's coffee tasted more of coal than bean.

Colonel Reynolds whistled, startling Pierce. A black woman appeared, her dress a hodgepodge of patches. Her head bowed slightly forward, she made no eye contact with either of them. Reynolds nodded toward Pierce. "Coffee, for my guest. Brandy, for me."

"Yessuh." She disappeared around the corner.

"I've read reports." Pierce motioned toward his satchel. "General Sherman's satisfied with the cotton procurement, as well as the redistribution of foodstuffs."

"It wasn't easy getting my cotton agents in place, I must admit. In the end, the blackies, or coloreds if you will, caused more problems than they helped."

Pierce stared into the man's dull eyes and tried to mask his sudden irritation. He couldn't afford to have Reynolds angry at him. The government needed a man with Northern sympathies who understood cotton. South Carolina's gins were destroyed, so a man with considerable knowledge of textiles was needed. Colonel Reynolds fit the bill.

"In what ways do freedmen cause problems?"

The woman entered and handed him a warm mug, the smell of coffee filling the room. The drink tasted strong and rich. He sighed as the warmth spread through his body.

Reynolds took his brandy. "I'd like to see the work move faster, but I don't see how, given the manpower we have. These slaves aren't Northern men, they don't know hard labor. This may take longer than I first thought." He settled back in his chair. "I received a letter from Secretary Chase to expect you, but I do not know under what capacity you come."

"To observe, I suppose." Pierce cleared his throat. "So you say the freedmen don't work?"

Reynolds downed his brandy in a single gulp. "Don't, or won't. Not if they can avoid it."

Pierce sipped his hot coffee and set it down. Energy coursed through his body. Would it be rude to leave so soon? He stood. "I must start my explorations. Thank you for the drink."

"One last question." Reynolds formed the words carefully. "Do you come with the ability to make changes?"

So Reynolds knew nothing of why he'd come. This suited Pierce, and he smiled. "An operation this efficient . . . does it need changes?"

Reynolds' frown changed to a satisfied grin. "Efficient, a word I like."

"There's one I enjoy more." Pierce sensed the man's growing loyalties and decided to play on them. "Profitable."

⚬

Pierce found a corral with a handful of lean horses set aside for government officials. He saddled the best of the lot, a decidedly thin and tired animal, and turned the horse's head toward Hilton Head.

All along the lane, Negro families, their faces gaunt, huddled with their meager belongings under makeshift shelters. Men stood in groups, either lazy or with nothing productive to do, and Pierce paused long enough to ask why. They'd been removed from their plantation, one said. Too close to enemy lines.

Pierce visited a nearby plantation, where the cotton agents who'd taken control cordially invited him to dinner. Meals were served by the freedmen, their heads bowed and manners pristine.

The next day, at a second plantation, dust filled the air where the slave cabins surrounded a tall gray barn. He pushed the horse that direction.

Several freedmen stood at the entrance, their conversation heated. He dropped off the side of the horse and patted its neck. Soon, he might have to carry the horse.

Pierce approached the small crowd. "What seems to be the matter?"

"This man was on another plantation when it come time to harvest, didn't do no harvestin', so he don't get none."

Pierce took off his hat and ran fingers through his hair. "Are you the driver?"

"I am."

"Why was he on the other plantation?"

The driver lifted a peck of corn. "I'm sayin' he don't deserve none, runnin' off to visit his wife when it's harvestin' time." An angry frown crossed his pockmarked face.

Pierce turned to the worker. "Is this true?"

"Sick I was, and the wife was nursin' me to health. But I done put the time in, plantin' and hoein' corn."

They looked at Pierce, their eyes wide. He glanced from the driver to the worker. It amused him to suddenly find himself no longer debating a case before Massachusetts' judges and gentleman juries, but to now be the judge, jury, and possibly executioner. When compared to fighting over vast tracts of undeeded property and inheritance in Boston, this dispute seemed trivial.

But justice was justice, no matter how small. He motioned to several freedmen listening nearby. He pointed to the worker. "Was this man sick at harvest?"

"Yes, Massah, he was."

"My name is Mr. Pierce, not Master. He was sick?"

"Yes, Mistah Pierce. I done see it myself."

"And had he planted and hoed, as he said?"

"Yessuh."

Pierce turned to the driver. "I think this man deserves his peck, don't you?"

The driver reluctantly handed the wooden box filled with corn to the worker, who took his prize with a smile, bowing his head. "Thank ya, Massah, thank ya." He hurried away.

Pierce despised the name *Master*, but he let the man go, instead turning to the driver. To his surprise, the black man's face held no malice, no anger. He seemed satisfied with the judgment and lifted a box to hand to the next in line. Perhaps this man could teach something to the Northern lawyers and their clients.

"You're a fine driver," Pierce said, and the man's pockmarked face beamed.

He stayed the night at the plantation. The next morning a boat took him across Port Royal Sound to Port Royal, where he rode several miles along an inlet to Beaufort. He watched for snakes and alligators, something of the local fauna that unnerved him, but saw neither, just white birds with narrow necks hunting in the marsh.

Beaufort, the islands' vacation town, was filled with men in blue uniforms who had settled in the large plantation houses. He spent a few days studying maps and the military position of the islands. Soon, he was ready to look over the islands.

In the next week, wherever Pierce traveled, his reputation preceded him. Freedmen were eager to answer his questions, and they asked him to judge between petty matters that plagued the islands.

He listened to several slaves from the plantation of Dr. Jenkins, a man of apparent respect in the community. A physician and planter, Dr. Jenkins owned a home in Beaufort and one at St. Helenaville, a village on the north end of St. Helena Island. He also worked the plantation Pierce surveyed. It was here, he learned, the Southern militia gathered as the Union troops invaded the islands. Near the marsh, hoofmarks pressed deep in the mud gave testament to the freedmen's stories.

Pierce took notes for his reports.

Plantation hierarchy suited the owners' whims, but in the end he noticed a pattern. Of course, at the top, the planter dictated the tone of discipline, tasks enforced, and particular freedoms allowed the slaves. Next on the list, the driver would carry out the planter's wishes, usually with the threat of the lash. Then Pierce added skilled workers to the hierarchal chart, slaves who knew a trade. Carpenters, ironworkers, cooks, blacksmiths, even specialized field hands were used on self-sustaining farms or hired out to make the master cash, something that seemed in short supply in the South.

There were others to be taken care of at the bottom of the list, such as the elderly, who usually worked with clothes, cooked food, or cared for the young. An elderly male often adopted the role of religious leader—someone to lead the plantation slaves in worship on Saturday night, all night—for Sunday was a day of rest, and work was not to be done, not even worship.

After the plantation owners ran from the invasion, it was the drivers who managed the plantations. If the driver had treated the slaves with kindness, fairness, and wisdom, he usually held sway over the others and could keep the local population under some semblance of control. Other plantations were chaotic, as if the parents of children had gone to Europe and hadn't left enough food to get by.

Some sort of governmental authority was needed to regain control over the region. Colonel Reynolds had done nothing to solve the problem. If anything, he damaged the cause by pillaging the islands and destroying the freedmen's trust, something Pierce understood as primary to educating and transitioning to wage labor.

But the organizational factor chilled him. The total slave count from records in Beaufort and the 1860 census was ten thousand in captured territory, and slaves outside captured territory trickled in every day. The area desperately needed teachers and missionaries before planting season.

The bindings of slavery had left them helpless.

Something needed to be done.

❧

"This is my field." Tad looked down on Peg from his perch atop a rock. "I mudded it, chopped back the bushes, and in a week I'm going to plow and plant. It's mine."

She tugged on her brown jacket. "You can't just claim land. It belonged to Massah."

"He ain't coming back." Tad surveyed the field. Tall pines edged one side, Seaside Road the far end, and brambles bordered another side as well as the length that looped around to meet the pines. He loved the feel of owning the field and the trees that surrounded it. "I know how to make it bigger." He reached into his pocket and pulled out matches.

"Where'd you get those?"

He kept his gaze on her.

She bit her bottom lip. "Cotton agents?"

Tad smiled.

"You stole 'em from the cotton agents?"

"One dropped 'em. It's not stealin' if someone drops 'em and doesn't pick 'em up. Means he doesn't want the matches. Now, all we've got to do is burn a bit away, nice and slow. When it warms this spring, I'll plow it up, and grow you corn. You want pone, don't you?"

"I do . . . but I don't think burnin' is a good idea."

Tad scrambled down from the rock. He sat on the ground because Peg was an inch taller, and sitting was a good way to forget he was small. "Look, even if Massah does come back— and he won't—he'll be happy I made the field bigger. Then I reckon he'll give it to me."

Peg took a moment to answer, and when she did, her voice shook. "Fire's of the devil."

He desperately wanted to make her understand. "Look, I'm hungry. Can see my every rib. I know you're the same. Bo's wasting away. Mammy and the rest, we gotta eat." Tad jumped to his feet. "No more talk. Time to work."

He crossed the field at a run. Peg's footsteps sounded behind him. With no shoes, his feet grew cold in the open field.

"Tad, there's a storm comin'."

"Then we've got to hurry." He dropped to a knee and struck the match against a small rock. The wind instantly blew it out. He glanced at Peg. "You ever do this before?"

She shook her head.

"Me either. But I saw it done." He pulled out another match, scraped it against the rock, and this time held his hand around the flame to protect it from the wind. The fire sputtered, but continued to eat up the matchstick. He watched it, mesmerized, until the flame burned low enough to touch his fingers. He flung it away. The flicker died on the way to the ground.

Thunder rumbled in the distance.

Tad looked up, but his view of the sky was blocked by trees.

He pulled out the last match. "I gotta get this right." He scratched the last one, which sparked and blossomed into a bright blue flame. He carefully lowered it into a patch of brown thicket. The fire jumped from the match to the kindling like a rabbit to its den.

Fueled by the wind and abundant dead growth, flames leapt from bush to bush until a large blaze lit the side of the field. The warmth caressed his skin. He inhaled the aroma of burnt weeds and old leaves.

As the fire grew, so did the heat, forcing him to step back. Clawing at the sky, the flames reached twice as high as his head.

"Get back."

He turned to find Peg standing several feet behind him, flames reflected in her brown eyes.

He swiveled to stare at what was quickly becoming a forest

fire. Heat washed over his body, drying out his eyes and searing his lungs. He blinked and retreated several more steps. He hadn't intended for the fire to grow this large.

Low clouds roiled above them and seemed to reflect the orange flames. He turned to look at Peg. "What do we do now?" He had to yell over the crackling roar.

She looked from him to the fire and back again. "I don't know."

*Run.* The word rang in his head, overwhelming him with the urge to escape the inferno. He brushed past Peg and darted toward a cedar with low branches.

"Tad!" He heard Peg's screaming behind him. "Tad, you can't climb that tree. It'll catch on fire!"

Higher he scrambled, into the upper branches.

"No! Come down. Please."

He could see her reaching for the first limb, her face awash with fear. A gust of wind swirled through the branches, bending the tree. Brilliant embers streaked through the air and scurried past her into the pine forest. Tad ducked as light flashed and thunder cracked, cutting through the howl of the fire.

A red cinder landed on the branch below him. Instantly, flames shot upward. He kicked at them, but they singed his naked feet. He tried to knock loose the burning branch. It cracked in a shower of sparks but remained intact.

Several feet below him, Peg shrieked and slapped at her thick hair. Smoke rose from her head.

He eyed the burning branch. If he kicked it away, Peg would be its target. A burst of guilt filled him. He'd left her to face the fire alone.

He clambered to the next branch and looked up. The top of the tree bowed. If he went any higher, he'd fall to his death. If he stayed, he would burn.

"Good Lord. Help me! Help Peg. I won't ever do wrong again.

I didn't really want to clear that field, was just wanting to burn something. Help us!"

Before he finished praying, he felt the first drops of rain.

In moments, he was soaked through, and the smoldering branches below him sizzled and dripped.

He crawled down to Peg, avoiding the steaming branch, and silently followed her to the ground.

With her hair matted to her face and her bottom lip quivering, she looked awful.

He wrapped his arms around her. "You hurt?"

She clung to him, crying. "Oh Tad, oh Tad." Her heart pounded against his chest as they watched the rain drench and subdue the smoking field around them.

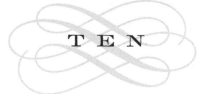

# TEN

*P*ierce returned to Beaufort and encountered Chief Quartermaster Rufus Saxton. They secured lunch together in a small café across from the Verdier House, where Colonel Reynolds had made his headquarters.

He liked Saxton. The small man, earnest in every endeavor, was more relaxed than he'd been in the carriage.

"It is here the North will look for examples." Pierce felt a twinge of nervousness. When he was tired, the sense of responsibility was overwhelming.

Saxton shook his head. "Why do you care for the freedmen? I'm an abolitionist, and I'm sure you are, and with both of us on the cusp of real change for them . . . why do you care?"

Pierce glanced out the window, could almost see his supporter's face; hear his voice; see his light, curling hair; in his fifties. Not Secretary Chase. No, earlier in his life. Senator Sumner. The impact was such that Pierce sent a letter to the senator explaining the righteousness of the cause and to give him strength during a difficult time. To his surprise, Sumner wanted to meet Pierce, and soon the two became close friends, closer than he and Chase. It was through Sumner that Pierce had been introduced to people such as Longfellow, who helped shape his future through philosophy. Sumner thought Pierce far too young to have any political influence. Yet Secretary Chase did not, and in the end, Chase became the door to public work. Still, his love for Sumner was unending.

Pierce turned back to Saxton. "Sumner is my mentor. He taught me—"

Pierce watched Saxton's gaze out the window. The quartermaster stood. "Ah, I see your counterpart has arrived."

Counterpart? A tall, thin man in a tight black suit crossed in front of the window, then opened the café door.

Saxton held out a hand, and the man shook it. "Reverend French, good to see you again. I have someone I'd like you to meet. This is Mr. Pierce, from Boston, on assignment from Secretary Chase."

Pierce tentatively pulled back his chair, rose, and took the man's soft hand.

"This is Reverend French, from New York."

French, in his fifties, tucked his cane under his arm and snatched a chair that rested under a coatrack. He set it at the table. "Are you looking after the freedmen, Mr. Pierce?"

"I hope to."

French accepted a cup of coffee and sat. "I do hope you are enjoying your stay."

"I am. If you don't mind me asking, Reverend French, what is the nature of your visit?"

"Souls, my dear boy, souls. The army does much to free the beautiful black man." French glanced at Saxton. "But does little for their eternal state. They may believe in God, but their fervor must be directed. What is Boston prepared to do in this matter?"

Pierce crossed his arms. Never before had he felt walls built between him and a man so quickly. "I answer to the government. I've been sent to ascertain the conditions of Port Royal in regards to the treatment of freedmen, not garner support."

"New York is prepared to do its part. I've been sent by the American Missionary Agency to prepare the way for more missionaries."

"Missionaries?"

"Why, yes. A small group has already arrived." French looked surprised. "I thought you'd viewed the islands?"

Pierce took a calming breath. He'd not seen missionaries. What was French's game? "I've almost completed my study. I planned to start again this afternoon."

Saxton pulled at his collar and cleared his throat. "It seems the government is not the only agency that cares for the cause."

"That is true." French flashed a wide smile. He tapped his cane on the floor. "What I believe, though, is that the government cares for nothing but profits. It is the souls of a race we must be concerned about."

Pierce gripped the side of his chair. "Their souls, and their physical welfare."

French waved his hand. "The two go hand in hand. But I'm glad to have found a sympathetic ear. Most around Port Royal are less than appreciative of the freedman's plight." French changed the subject. "Abolitionist parents?"

"Of course."

French sniffed. "It is easier for the second generation of abolitionists. More popular to be against slavery than when I was young."

Saxton lowered his voice, so quiet Pierce strained to hear. "Many things go on here." He struggled for words. "General Stevens, one of the generals, decided to gather books found in the vacated houses, to create a library. The soldiers are bored, and some of the drivers can read." Saxton stared out the window toward Reynolds' headquarters. "The colonel took every book. Confiscated them, and shipped them north. They've disappeared."

"Outrageous, completely outrageous," French muttered.

Saxton ran a finger around the edge of the porcelain saucer. "I don't have proof it's Colonel Reynolds, but I've seen furniture shipped north."

French shook his head and turned to Pierce. "This is what happens when the government is involved."

Pierce bit down his anger. "And what would you suggest? Who has the resources to solve this dilemma? Do not be so hasty as to dismiss the government."

French held out his hands, a calm smile on his face. He spoke with passion. "Do not misunderstand me, I agree, the government resources are needed, and we must request their aid—no, in fact, we should demand it, for it was the government who created this difficulty. But I believe you underestimate the sympathy of church laymen." He licked his lips. "Now, you are from Boston, and I, New York. What if we were to garner support for our cause here in Port Royal, and see what funds might come in?"

Pierce scolded himself for letting his emotions get the better of him. "I agree, of course. And I apologize for my tone. Perhaps I'm too passionate about the freedmen."

"Or you care for the government too much. But there is no harm done. Passion in all of us is what is needed."

Pierce stood and paced, disturbing the other occupied table. The waitress stepped in with a questioning look, but he waved her away. He turned to French. "If you rally New York, and I gather Boston's leaders, we can see what support there is in the citizens."

"Good, excellent." French's voice rose, his cheeks flushed.

"I will write a report to Secretary Chase that will probably be published in newspapers. I would like teachers to come, in hopes the freedmen will read."

French sat up and nodded. "With missionaries. To capture their souls."

Saxton snatched his officer's cap from the table and tucked it under his arm. "Imagine the fighting force against the South if we can create regiments of black folk. An unstoppable army with a righteous cause!"

Pierce's breath quickened. "If the Negro can fight, the North's support will be won. I believe it is through the military that the black man can endear his race to the hearts of all Americans."

"Except in the South." French stood, winced, straightened, then shook Pierce's hand. "Do not let me keep you any longer, for you have a report to pen. Write it well, for the world will read it." He gave Pierce a stern look. "And act on your suggestions."

Pierce rested a knee against the flatboat's planks and leaned against a small, wooden barrel. Atop the cask lay a thick stack of papers, to which he added one more finished document. He reached for a satchel and pulled out another blank page, and wrote.

Teachers and missionaries, sponsored from the vaults of private associations, could come to the islands to teach the freedmen. Government wages were sure pay, and in his experience, sure pay led to unknown results. To connect the results to the wages, private funds would ensure the missionaries' fealty to the cause.

His tired horse shuffled restlessly in a holding area behind him, the large surface of the boat unsettling to the beast.

The flatboat slipped next to Dr. Jenkins' plantation, bumped against the dock, and jarred to a halt. Pierce pulled his coat tight to ward off the cold wind and climbed ashore, dragging the horse across the brown gardens and onto the muddy lane. Gray clouds dominated the sky, darkening the day and the mood. Even the horse's head hung inches from the ground.

Several miles down the sodden road Pierce grew tired of

dense trees, cold wind, and light rain. Live oaks reached their long branches along the road, sometimes overhead, and draped Spanish moss like loose sleeves. To the left, an empty field filled with weeds stretched for half a mile. It served as a reminder to hurry. Planting season had almost arrived.

To the right a field slashed through the dense forest, freshly hoed into tiny trenches between wide rows. The light sandy earth, drenched in the winter moisture, looked lush and ready for cottonseeds. The gentle rain slowed and the immense clouds showed signs of weakening. Pierce decided to see who prepared the field.

He didn't have far to look. In an unplowed corner, where a large, burnt portion of the forest stood, a small boy worked with a hoe. The weeds were thick, but his hoe, sharp and agile, cut the soil like a knife through meat.

Pierce dismounted and led the horse along one of the rows until he stood over the youth.

The boy's tattered clothing hung in long shreds and covered wet, shiny skin. His tight, curly hair was littered with field and leaf debris. Pierce couldn't help but notice his skin seemed much lighter than most on the islands.

"Hello, young man. Poor day for hoeing?"

The boy glanced up with small, dark eyes, shrugged, and thrust his hoe deep into the earth.

"My name is Mr. Pierce."

The boy sighed, stood, stretched his back with a groan and leaned on the hoe's handle. "I'm Tad."

# ELEVEN

*W*hat white man ever struck up a casual conversation with a slave? There was always an angle, some task needing done or chore waiting.

But the man standing before him seemed teeming with energy.

Tad liked him. It wasn't the brown eyes that seemed to smile, or the brown hair that puffed out the sides of his tall hat, or even the white skin that reminded Tad of a fresh piece of blank paper that made him feel he could trust Edward Pierce. It was his charm. Bright, energetic, as if his smile alone could stop all the evils of the world.

He watched Pierce glance over the field. "You've done a fine job here. You've had help? Perfect rows, ready for seed."

"Not where your horse just walked."

The man's face turned red as he looked back along a row. "Yes, sorry."

"Easy to fix." The blisters on his hand stung as he picked up his hoe.

"This is a lovely farm. What plantation is this?"

"Frogmore. Bo's our driver." He thrust the hoe into the earth, the rich soil spilling to the side of the mound.

Pierce clicked his tongue. "Frogmore. Frogmore. Where have I heard that name before?" The man sounded like a snake for a moment, making an *sss* sound. "Samuel. That's it. Do you know a Samuel?"

Tad felt as if a runaway horse had hit him. "You know Samuel?" The hoe slipped from his grasp.

"Big man, I came up to his shoulder."

"Samuel! That's him!" Tad jumped up and down. "You see him? He made it North?"

"He came by my office." Pierce smiled. "He's well. Safe in Boston."

"I gotta tell Mammy and Peg." With a single bound, Tad leapt over a row, and then the next, on his way to the kitchen.

He rushed through the slave cabins and past Bo, who was sharpening an ax and hoe on the big stone. Tad didn't slow, but kept running and called back, "Man said he saw Samuel."

He leapt up the steps and burst inside, where Mammy sat with a knife, slicing through a squash.

"Mammy! Mistah Pierce say Samuel is alive and well."

"Lordy, who is this man? Mr. Pierce? How does he know?" She put down the knife.

"Said Samuel came in his office."

She stared straight ahead, biting her lip. A small smile crossed her face. "Better run'n tell Peg. She'll want to know. She's by the birdbath."

Of course—Peg. She'd always seemed close to the big man. He backed out of the kitchen cabin, turned, and ran across the open space toward the tabby barn. After searching down the lane at the birdbath, with no Peg in sight, he wandered back to the cabin.

There was a knock on Mammy's door. Mammy opened it and there was Mr. Pierce. She stepped forward and they spoke for a moment, Mammy wiping her hands on her stained apron. She let the man inside.

Peg would have to wait to hear the news about Samuel. Tad leaned his head against the closed door to listen.

"You cook for the entire plantation?" Pierce asked.

"Lordy me, I cook for most. Some can cook for themselves too. Seems like they do more their own cookin', now Massah's up and run away."

Tad could hear Pierce or Mammy leaning back in the chair, the wood crackling under the weight.

"I met a man near the barn who said Tad was your boy."

"My one and only."

"Seems like a bright lad. Working the field, that's impressive. He's nine?"

"My boy is twelve, Mistah Pierce. He just kinda small is all. And he is mighty smart, if I do say so. Sees things others don't see."

"Is his father here?"

"Lordy, his father ran long ago, when I needed him most. But I reckon he's in Texas somewheres."

Tad sucked in a deep breath. Pappy ran?

"I'm sorry, ma'am, I'm not sure how to address you."

"Everyone just calls me Auntie Mammy. Even those I ain't aunt to."

"Auntie Mammy." It was strange to hear it come from Pierce's voice. "In the North, not many understand the plight of the freed slaves. I've come across many young men, but none working in the fields."

"He wants to own that land. And be a soldier." Her voice caught on the word *soldier*.

Pierce talked slowly. "It's a rare combination in one person. There may be a day when I need someone from these Sea Islands to speak to people in the North. Would you be willing to let your son visit me in Washington—when he's older, of course? To speak to Congress?"

What a beautiful thing, to travel to Washington. He burst through the kitchen door.

"Yes, Mammy, yes!"

She recovered from her surprise and thrust her hands onto her hips. "Ain't no way, and you know it."

Tad looked up at Pierce.

"He would be in capable hands, eat the best food, and sleep in comfortable and safe boardinghouses. I would look after him myself."

Before Tad could say a word, Mammy stepped forward. "That boy is my one and only. He's all I got. And he's special. You see it too, Mistah Pierce, by you just askin' without really knowin' him. But how can I send him away from me?"

Tad felt a small fury well within him. She would win. He'd never seen beyond St. Helena Island, except a few boat trips to Beaufort on the mainland with Massah and Collin. And then, he'd walked the narrow streets in their wake, never looking into the planters' houses, catching glimpses of their riches only from the corners of his eyes.

He looked into Mammy's eyes and expected to see anger, but instead saw sadness. Confusion filled his mind, and he stumbled backward, out the door, shoving Peg, who was nearing the kitchen. The frustration of his life wrenched away his desire to work. He scrambled up a low oak branch, crossed to a cedar tree, and hid in the branches.

Station Creek's muddy water stood stagnant, evidence of the outgoing tide. He watched a heron fly alone over the water, and he wished he could join the bird, across the sky, to lands across the sea.

After a minute, he heard voices drift toward him. Peg's high, fluttery voice rose to his ears. "He goes runnin' when he is mad. Or sad." She paused. "And happy. All of it."

"I see." It was Pierce again.

"Tad's probably up a tree. Auntie Mammy lets him work it out on his own, because he come back when whatever's botherin' him don't bother him no more. She says anybody can see that's the way it should be done. Look in the Bible. When prophets of God run, they worked out troubles with God, then come back. Tad's just doin' the same, so don't be too hard on him."

"I won't."

"Ah, there he is. See him? In the tree."

Tad kept his eyes focused across the miles of marsh.

Peg continued. "He a good climber. A real good climber. And runner too. He done run miles like they was just a few rows of cotton. He's a friend of mine, some think a brother, but we ain't related. And Mistah Pierce?"

"Yes, Peg?"

"Don't bother him just now. He don't make much sense 'til he work it all out."

"Can you give him a message for me then?"

"Oh yes, Mistah Pierce. I'm a good listener. And a good re-memberer. And I can sing."

Tad glanced down to see Pierce looking back at him. Tad turned away.

"Tell him I'll return. With food for everyone. And teachers. All of you will learn to read. Can you be brave until then?"

Peg's laughter floated up to Tad. He couldn't resist peeking at her round face and wide smile. "Why, Mistah Pierce! We brave. Remember, when Yankee soldiers come? It was the massahs who ran, not us."

# TWELVE

*P*ierce took Kate to their favorite restaurant in Washington, and then *The Tempest*. He couldn't concentrate on the Shakespearian play, and he barely noticed Kate's fingers as they brushed against his arm throughout the night.

"You've seemed distant." Kate looked out the carriage window at the dark night and lamplight. When they stopped at his hotel, she turned to him. "Are you all right?"

"I'm sorry. I've just been a little preoccupied."

She gave a sad smile. "I'd hoped to spend more time with you."

Pierce straightened his black jacket. "You've been more than patient with me, Kate. I wish . . . I hope . . . "

"I know that look. I see it on my father's face. Your mind is on business." Her voice was light and soft. "Why don't you see him tonight? He's in his office. Then tomorrow you'll be able to focus on me?"

"You don't mind? But I'd planned on coffee with you in the hotel café."

"I really don't." She looked away. "Just . . . finish with the slaves. Come to Washington. Please, tell my father you're done with them."

"Why? I don't understand."

She turned back. "Because South Carolina is so far away, because you're away from me, because no one in Washington can see what you're doing. There are so many reasons."

He shifted in his seat, trying to hide his agitation. Why couldn't she see the importance of what was happening in South Carolina? But he wouldn't ruin the evening with an argument. "Yes, I'll see what I can do."

❧

"Well done, Edward, well done. Your report was published in almost every periodical." Chase slapped Pierce on the back so hard he needed to grip the chair to keep from falling on the secretary's desk. Chase settled in his seat and sipped his coffee. "Report was too long, though."

Pierce studied the secretary's bright, playful eyes. He couldn't hold back a smile. The man only called him by his first name when Pierce had done something that delighted him. Warmth spread through Pierce. How many times had Chase's displeasure been directed at him? When he was Chase's secretary—too many. Pierce decided to bask in the moment.

"I believe the effect we hoped for has spread through the country." Chase balled a fist and slammed it into his other hand. "Good work. Well done."

Pierce needed to pace, his energy overwhelming. He crossed the room then returned.

"Something on your mind?"

Pierce paused. "What effect had we hoped for, sir?"

"What do you mean?"

"Do you truly believe public opinion will sway the policies of this administration?" Pierce sat down. "I didn't mention the slaves' status in the report, and considered them already set free, but you and I know they are not."

Chase gave Pierce a curious glance. "Tell me, which policy do you speak of?"

Pierce took a deep breath and gathered his thoughts. How could he make Chase understand? "The Negro cannot have contraband status forever. They are not contraband or slave, and refuse to be so. We must know their status, the government's official position, and thus proceed."

"Their status?"

"Whether they are free citizens or slaves. Or something in between."

Chase looked annoyed. "What matters of their status? As long as they are treated well."

The political game. Pierce bit his tongue.

Chase slipped a piece of paper from the stack and reviewed it. "Yes, here we are." The paper, small, with a few words scribbled across the top, was covered with coffee stains. "You can get orders from him."

Pierce leaned over and tried to read through the brown streaks. The seal on the bottom was clear, an eagle with wide wingspan stamped in red wax. "A note, from the president?" He made out the first three letters, *Edw*, near the top.

Chase's stern voice cut through him. "Yes, it is an invitation to speak with President Lincoln. Not for me, but for you. Watch what you say about the status of the slaves."

Pierce could barely think. The president? So his report *did* reach the highest level. There was a chance he could affect policy.

He paused. What about Kate?

"I suggest you not bring up any topic he doesn't," Chase said, turning back to his paperwork. "The president's son is deathly ill, and Lincoln's in no mood to be trifled with."

❧

Rumors on the lawyer wires had it that Lincoln was no average president. He was a man who consolidated support brilliantly, much like a railroad baron gathered wealth. He'd launched a country into war, a war he commanded. Never before had a single man in the Union wielded so much power—not even George Washington.

The capital bristled with excitement. Men in top hats huddled on snowy corners. They joked with one another, their chests bulged from the weights of their wallets, gold watch chains looped low. As Pierce neared his hotel, he wandered close to a group and listened. They spoke of Port Royal and the freedmen, discussed how exactly they could go about industrializing a backward South. Freed slaves, millions of man-hours, were ripe for use. Pierce smiled. *His* was the nation's topic of the day.

Pierce returned to his hotel. He washed, shaved, and donned a fine black suit, including a thick vest and top hat. He stepped from the hotel, waved down a carriage, and told the man to drive to the President's House.

Before they rode away, Chase's secretary, out of breath, arrived with a note.

Pierce scanned the contents and told the driver to proceed. The treasury, Chase said, was nearly bankrupt, and financing a humanitarian expedition to Port Royal must prove to be a moneymaking proposition in the long run. If that weren't pressure enough, public opinion must be swayed to believe the Negro was self-sufficient and a help to the war effort. Another burden to set on the scarred backs of the freedmen.

Pierce almost touched the letter to a match.

Brick and stone buildings lined the way as the carriage jostled along the crowded streets.

He stared at his bouncing knee. All his life, Pierce could never decide if he was rarely nervous or always nervous. It drove his parents to madness. Yet in this moment, he couldn't remember a time when his insides hadn't felt as if a feathery bird fluttered about a breadbasket.

Lincoln's White House wasn't as Pierce had imagined. Instead of long rows of soldiers defending the Union's head man, herds of cattle roamed the neighborhood, burrowing their muzzles through the snow to find sparse morsels of grass. Soldiers camped on the south lawn, their bonfires adding smoke to the winter afternoon sky. The smell of cooking meat drifted on the breeze.

At the door, no one asked for credentials. Instead, the two guards looked into the distance, as if they slept with eyes open.

Inside, he barely glanced at the enormous paintings, enshrined statues, and marbled walls. Pierce followed other men, guessing they wanted the same as he, an audience with the president.

In a small room packed with officers, Pierce gave his name and waited in a corner. He tried not to inhale their odor and instead watched out a window. He listened to the conversation of uniformed majors, colonels, lieutenants, here only to request a promotion or inquire why they were passed over for one.

Did they not realize the importance of Lincoln's time? They were, however, only doing as others had done before, looking for recognition of their status first, military skills second. It was partly why Pierce could not extend his enlistment. The military was not for him.

The door to the president's office opened, and the receptionist, a young man, stepped out, his face white, as if he'd never seen the sun. The receptionist glanced at his paper, and called out, "Edward Pierce."

Pierce crossed the room, avoiding the envious glances of others who'd waited for hours, and with a deep breath, strode through the door.

The office furniture was modest but sparse, less luxurious than the secretary of the treasury's furnishings. Pierce had imagined Lincoln's work area to be as disorganized as the previous room, but the office was tidy. The walls were decorated with maps and sconces. A large clock rested on the mantel. A fire blazed in the fireplace, lighting a picture of Andrew Jackson. A desk and chair sat empty near a long table, filled with maps and papers.

Pierce shivered. Great men had discussed national policy in this room. The thought was intoxicating.

On the floor was a long shadow in the shape of a man. Pierce looked at the room's single window and shielded his eyes from the bright afternoon glare. The shadow took a step away from the shining light.

Tall, very tall. Pierce's forehead barely reached his shoulder. Not as unattractive up close as he'd been told to expect, but homely. Rugged, to be sure, as an Illinois man should be, strong but tired. Careworn.

"Yes, come in." Lincoln's voice was far higher than he remembered in speeches.

The receptionist startled Pierce, whom he'd thought had left the room. "Mr. President, this is Mr. Pierce. You asked to see him? Port Royal?"

With a large, slow hand, Lincoln motioned Pierce toward the table. The receptionist closed the door behind him, and he was alone with the president.

As Pierce settled into the chair, he wondered at the men who rested in this very seat. Generals, presidents, dignitaries. He refocused, and took another deep breath. "Good afternoon, Mr. President."

Lincoln gripped the back of a chair with wrinkled hands. Veins ran through his skin like mounds atop the earth. "Tell me of Port Royal."

"Tremendous victory, sir. The soldiers stormed the beaches and took it easily." The anxiety etched in the president's deep-set eyes seemed to ease. The president surely knew this information, but he seemed to enjoy hearing it. "Casualties negligible, and the land we took will set back the South's war-making capabilities."

"Good news, welcome always." Lincoln's lips turned upward into a sincere smile.

Pierce desperately wanted to stand, as the president did, but stayed in his seat. "Unfortunately, the attack has left nearly ten thousand slaves penniless and uneducated, with no masters to see to their welfare. I believe now is the time to prove our intentions toward the freed slave and to treat them with honesty. Let us send teachers and missionaries."

Lincoln's shoulders slumped and the weary look reappeared. He brought a giant hand to his face and rubbed his swollen eyes. "Tell me, Mr. Pierce, why is this matter up to me? Why must this burden be laid at the feet of the president?" His fingers curled and he clutched his stomach. "Why must I be bothered with such details?"

Pierce didn't have an answer. He proceeded warily. "It may set precedence for reconstruction, after the war is won."

Lincoln didn't seem to hear. "I didn't want to free the Negroes." He turned and looked out the window. "But free them we did. And what next, keep them as underlings? Did we better their condition? Can they become our political and social equals, just by granting freedom? I cannot give them what I do not know how to give." He looked up. Pain filled his eyes. "But tell me, Mr. Pierce, why is everyone itching to get Negroes behind federal lines?"

A thousand answers crossed Pierce's mind, but the single thought that surfaced was the little girl under the cedar where Tad had run. Peg. What had she said? "Mr. President," Pierce said slowly, gathering his words. "The Negroes, sir, are no different from us." Pierce leapt to his feet and stood in front of the president. "Their old masters, when the Union attacked, all ran. But the slaves, who had the most to lose, for they'd been told we were evil barbarians and would send them to Cuba, they were courageous. Mr. President, the Negroes didn't run."

Lincoln thought a moment then quickly turned to his desk, dipped a quill in an ink bottle, and wrote on a piece of paper. He held it out. Pierce reached for it.

"Please give this to Secretary Chase. My compliments, Mr. Pierce. Good day."

In front of the President's House, Pierce opened the note. Had the slaves obtained free status at last? *Mr. Pierce is authorized to use discretion in regard to Port Royal contrabands as may seem judicious.* He glanced up at the president's window, with both awe and disappointment. True, he was to take charge of the freedmen, but they still held contraband status, mere items to be captured in the fortunes of war.

The work ahead loomed before him like a mighty wave. He would gather people and money as quickly as he could and send it to South Carolina. Congressmen first, then public appeal. It wouldn't hurt to wire an old friend in Boston to do what Reverend French did in New York. Reverend Manning was just the abolitionist to gather troops for the cause. Pierce rushed to the telegraph office. There was so much to do.

And worse. He would be going back to South Carolina. How would Kate react? He turned his back on Lincoln's window.

He knew what she was going to say.

# THIRTEEN

*T*ad's resolve wavered.

He crept through the marsh, the ground under him nearly frozen, the cold seeping through his clothes. Ahead, a small campfire burned, and he could see vague forms huddled around the flames. The smell of coffee overpowered the rotten mud smell.

He paused in the thick grass and waited for several minutes. With head down, he crawled toward the marsh. A gray blanket of mist draped over the water, hovering on the shore and dissipating with the sun.

The soldiers behind him stirred. He could just make out the blue uniforms.

He studied the marsh carefully, looking for a way across. Swimming seemed the only option. Across the water, nothing moved. He scanned harder, looking for gray uniforms.

This marsh was the front lines.

"Hey you. Come here."

Behind Tad, a soldier in blue stood, his rifle at the ready.

"Let me see your pass. Don't you know you're heading into Confederate lines?"

Tad turned and dove into the water. Icy barbs shot through his skin, the cold sucking the air from his lungs. He struggled to the surface, gasping for breath. He heard a gunshot, and dove deep.

Popping noises continued overhead. He swam underwater, his lungs burning. Finally, he couldn't hold his breath any longer, and he kicked hard, surfaced, and saw he'd made it to the far bank.

Both sides of the marsh erupted in gunfire. Smoke filled the tight space. Tad frantically searched for a place to hide, but the grass was short on this side. The angry exchange of bullets continued.

None found him or landed nearby. The soldiers fired on each other.

He inched up the bank, the smoke covering him in a shroud. No one would see him now. He scrambled to his feet and rushed into the forest—and freedom.

He didn't see any gray uniforms as he ran. But bullets whistled by, smacking into branches and trees, propelling him faster. The smoke disappeared, and the smell changed from sulfur and coffee to the musty stench of a winter morning. It came from his clothes.

Tad paused to catch his breath and watched the sun rise. Birds chirped overhead, bouncing from tree to tree.

The warmth enveloped his skin like a blanket, and his shivering slowed. He closed his eyes. For the first time in his life he felt truly free. No one was ordering him around, telling him what to do and how to think. He was free to visit Mr. Pierce in Washington.

The distant sound of gunfire slowed, and finally gave way to silence.

Another thought struck him. Wasn't Pappy in Texas? Why not visit him there? Perhaps become a soldier, like him.

He could steal food and shoes along the way. Surely there were plenty of barns between here and there to sleep in.

He plunged on, whistling as he went. Perhaps after making a fortune as a soldier, he would come back and get Mammy, so she wouldn't have to work so hard. And Peg? Well, if she wanted to come, she could.

As he walked through an open field, he burst into song. Such a glorious day, and all his.

"What do we have here?"

His heart jumped, and he twisted toward the voice. Several gray-coated men lay in the thick grass, their rifles pointed directly at him. One man leapt up and grabbed his arms. Tad struggled against the man's grip but couldn't move.

One soldier spat. "Looks like a runaway. Quite a bounty for these."

They tied his hands behind his back and shoved him into the forest he'd just left. They marched under oaks and past the ruins of a mansion. Finally, they arrived in a wide clearing. Dozens of white tents stretched across the grass. Soldiers milled about, some at fires, others sitting near makeshift homes, the smell of food making his stomach growl despite the growing fear.

Someone pushed Tad to the ground, and he fell to his knees.

Others wandered close and encircled him. "Now, how old you reckon he is?"

"Six, seven?"

"No, he's more like nine."

One voice broke above all the others, one Tad thought he recognized. "He ain't young. He's just small."

The man stepped forward and spit on the ground next to Tad. His unshaven stubble, white against thick wrinkles, caught some of the tobacco, and the black dribbled down his chin.

"He's just small." The man towered over him. "Name's Tad."

"Mistah Spencer!" Memories of the whipping coursed through Tad's mind. "No, leave me be!" Tad struggled to his feet, more afraid than he'd ever been before.

The old man leaned close. The smell of whiskey, tobacco, and rotten breath made Tad gag. "You're lucky, boy. I've got my whip with me. And I know where your master is. He'll be pleased to see you again."

"Please, let me go."

Spencer snorted. "You deserve to be a slave, boy. You'll be a slave the rest of your life."

"What did I do to make you mad? Just untie me, and I'll leave you alone."

"Wasn't you, boy." Spencer leaned down and whispered in his ear. "Was your pappy."

❧

Cold wrapped around Tad like the blanket he didn't have. His hands were bound with icy shackles, his back sore from the frozen dirt floor. The smell in the tiny cellar grew worse every day. He competed with spiders and mice for space.

Spencer had taken Tad to Massah's Charleston home in the dead of night. Massah shackled him in the cellar.

Every morning for a week, Massah opened the door and let the bright sunshine in while he walked down the steps with a hunk of bread and a jar of water.

And every day, Tad asked, "Massah, why am I here? Please let me go home."

Every morning, Massah answered the same way. "You're pure evil, Tad. And that evil needs to be washed from you like the tide washes the shores. The longer I leave you here, the more you'll appreciate the warmth of your quarters and the gifts I give you."

Gifts? Did he mean the one set of clothing he received every year?

Left with only his thoughts, he dreamed of his field, the hot summer days when corn, *his* corn, would grow tall and straight as a cattail, and he would pluck every weed, fight off every bug and worm. Like a soldier, he'd defend the field, day and night.

He lifted the chains that chafed his wrists. They were a symbol—not of captivity, but of freedom. Only the shackles held him back. They were the one barrier between him and freedom. Massah *had* to chain him. Massah had no choice. A shot of pride ran through him, filling him with hope and strength.

He made several vows. If he escaped, he would never be a slave again. He would never allow himself to be locked in a tight space. And he would not trust someone who said they were in charge.

The Bible said to be meek, that the weak would inherit the earth. That idea only led to slavery, to the chains that bound him to the cellar. He wondered why Jesus would ever say such a thing.

A spider crawled across his shoulder. He brushed it away, and to keep his mind busy, he sang.

*"I want to climb up Jacob's ladder, Jacob's ladder, O Jacob's ladder. I want to climb up Jacob's ladder. But I can't climb it till I make my peace with the Lord."*

He sang loud and strong until his throat hurt.

He dropped his chin to his chest and was almost asleep when he heard the cellar door creak open. A narrow ray of light sliced through the darkness.

Tad shrank into a corner. Massah never came this time of day.

The voice that drifted down was cautious. "Hello?"

Tad sat up. It wasn't Massah. "Help me. Please, help me."

The door opened wider and sunlight burst into the cellar, blinding Tad. He held a hand over his eyes.

A few steps sounded on the wooden steps. "Who's down there?"

Tad recognized the voice. "Collin, that you?"

"Tad?" It sounded as if Collin crashed down the stairs, but

he still couldn't see him. He felt Collin's warm touch on his cold arm. "How did you get here?"

Tad leaned back, a sense of relief spilling through him. "Thought I'd take a break from fieldwork."

Collin shifted. "Why are you chained?"

"Mistah Spencer caught me, brought me here. You gotta help me."

"How long have you been down here?"

"Long time. A week, maybe."

"Have you eaten?"

"Massah brought me bread, sometimes." Tad shifted the chains on his wrists. "I'm mighty hungry."

Tad's eyes adjusted to the light. Collin fumbled with a knife and then snatched a can from the shelves that had long tempted Tad, but that he could not reach. With the blade, he cut open the top, and the most beautiful smell in the world filled the blackness. Peaches.

Collin thrust the can into his hands. "Here. Careful of the edges. I'll be back."

Tad put the can to his lips and tilted back until a peach pumped against his teeth. He let the fruit slide into his mouth, the sweetness tensing his jaws.

Footsteps sounded on the stairs, then paused.

"I regret . . . " Silence in the darkness lasted for just a moment. "I wish I could go back and take that whipping."

Tad shook his head. "Don't feel bad about it. I'd have probably done the same."

Collin paused, nodded, and finished his journey up the stairs and out the door.

Tad finished the jar in minutes, just before the door opened again.

Collin held a blanket. Tad felt the warmth as he carefully wrapped it around his shaking shoulders.

With a smile, Collin held up a key. "Found it in Father's room. I can let you loose, but I can't get you back to Frogmore."

"I'll find my own way." The thought of crossing another picket line made him shiver more violently, but he'd do it in the middle of the night.

"I wish I could go back with you." Collin held up one of Tad's wrists and thrust the key into the lock. He worked it for a moment. "Do you still have that necklace?"

Tad nodded and pulled it out from under his shirt. He'd been relieved when Spencer hadn't searched him. He'd have taken it for sure.

Collin chuckled. "You remember the time we were swimming in the ocean and you lost it? Then swam to the bottom to get it, almost drown doing it?"

"You saved me."

Collin's face turned serious. "You think we'll ever have good times again?"

"Collin, come back with me. We can have a good time now. I've got a field you and I can work."

The lock slipped, and the chain fell from his wrist.

Collin started on the other arm. "It's not that easy. Father's not going to fight in this war, but I am." He looked into Tad's eyes. "I'm to be a drummer."

"You're only fourteen!"

"I don't want to fight, Tad. But what can I do? My father enlisted me."

"Sing, I suppose."

"That's how I found you. Your singing." Collin paused, the key still in the lock. He looked up. "I can't desert the army. I don't have the nerve. I never had your courage." He gripped the key and opened the lock.

Tad tried to stand, but Collin had to help him.

"I'll get you some food to take with you. Father's not around, and Mother's been ill. Besides, no one else knows you're here, as far as I know. It should be easy to get away."

Tad studied the light blue eyes and sandy-colored hair of his friend, searching for the right words. Then he knew. As if Jesus whispered it into his ear.

Tad grasped Collin's arm in desperation. "Come with me, Collin. Please. Come back to Frogmore. Maybe we could be soldiers together."

"Father's honor. My honor. I'm a . . . I'm a slave as much as you were, I suppose."

"Then promise me you'll come to the Frogmore after the war. Please."

"Made that promise before." Collin lowered his head. "But I make it again. I'll come back. After the war."

# FOURTEEN

$\mathcal{D}$o you remember when we first met?" Kate kept her hands in a woolen muff, her large hat covering most of her face.

"At your father's office? How could I ever forget?"

"Actually, it was here." She nodded toward the city park filled with tents and soldiers. What few trees surrounded the clearing looked dead in the winter snow. "During President Lincoln's speech. He was a senator then. You were so young, so handsome. You were enraptured by his common sense."

"I don't remember meeting you there."

"I was a young girl. Sixteen." She paused and looked at him with her large hazel eyes. Her hair, brilliant blonde and brown, curled around her face. "I think I fell in love with you then. You were so aggressive, so energetic."

He tried to remember, but couldn't.

"I wanted to talk to you, but my stepmother wouldn't let me." Her voice darkened. "I was forced to take matters into my own hands."

Pierce couldn't hold back a smile.

She lowered her face, and he noticed red rush to her cheeks. "I bumped into you."

"Wait . . . that was you? I was speaking with Mr. Sumner."

"Too engrossed to be bothered by a silly, lovesick girl."

99

"I remember now."

She looked up, concern etched on the corners of her eyes. "Edward, I'm afraid the same thing is happening again. I've only bumped you, but you're too engrossed with returning to South Carolina to notice me."

He looked into the winter sky, searching for answers. The slaves needed help, *his* help. No one else cared as much as he, except perhaps Reverend French, but his motives were questionable.

"Look, Kate, this is an amazing opportunity. We're sending missionaries—I mean, New York and Boston are. This is a big step, a real chance to effect change. And I'm in charge of them all. It's an honor."

"You have such a bright future." Kate's words were measured, but her tone was one of growing frustration. "If you go to South Carolina, you'll be lost to history forever. You'll never make a name for yourself."

"Then who will help the slaves?" Pierce couldn't hold back his own rising tone.

"Someone else. Anyone else. I hate this! When will we marry, Edward? I fear that when this cause is over, you'll find another, and another. Will I ever be your cause?"

He reached into his pocket, held out his hand, and revealed a silver brooch decorated with a green stone.

She took a step back.

"Please wait for me," he said. "I know it will be difficult, but it will be worth it."

She hesitated, took the brooch, and then fell into his arms. "Oh, Edward. I'm sorry. Yes, of course I will. Just please don't be gone forever."

The warmth of her lips against his remained long after she'd said good-bye.

❦

On March 2, 1862, Pierce and his handpicked teachers from Boston crowded into a railroad car and took a short trip to New York. At the dock, he pulled his coat collar high around his neck and dashed through the pelting rain. Thick clouds rolled off the harbor. Steamboats blasted their horns, and he covered his ears at the shrill whistle. The harbor smelled of rotten mud, more like the marsh smell of Port Royal and Beaufort instead of the fish smell of Boston. Not even the freezing rain could dispel the odor.

Boston's men were educated at Brown, Harvard, Yale, and other excellent schools. The freed men and women of Port Royal would receive the finest education. In all, combining Boston's men with New York's delegation, there would be just over eighty teachers and missionaries.

Tackle lines crisscrossed the dock, buoys lay scattered about, and warehouse workers jostled them, making it difficult to find their ship. Most of the activity revolved around a steamship, its large paddles locked in place. Across the bow, written in red letters, was the ship's name: *Atlantic*.

A large man in short sleeves barked out orders from a nearby ramp. Rain dripped from his nose onto a packet of papers he checked from time to time as workers loaded boxes of food, clothes, seeds, and other goods. Pierce approached and asked to see the passenger list.

"These lists, are these New York's missionaries?"

"Yes, sir."

Pierce rubbed his forehead as he read. This must be a mistake. "Mr. French," he said under his breath, then looked up to the dockworker. "Do you know where I can find Mr. French?"

"Yes, sir, in the warehouse, over yonder."

Pierce passed a group with umbrellas and petticoats, then burst through the warehouse door. "Reverend French!"

"Ah, Mr. Pierce, glad you've arrived." He stood from inspecting a box of white potatoes. "Are you ready for the journey?"

"What is the meaning of . . . ?" Pierce choked then caught his breath. "What is the meaning of inviting women?"

"What do you mean?"

Pierce couldn't remember when he'd been so angry. He stumbled over the words. "Are not the rigors of South Carolina's weather enough? More demands than simple survival will be required of each person."

French's face turned red and he glanced around. "Come, let's talk in private."

A small crowd gathered, and three women shot him irritated looks. French led him into a small office and shut the door behind them.

"Mr. Pierce, let me understand you better. You mean to free the slaves but exclude women's capable help?"

Pierce paced in front of the office window and rubbed his hands together. He forced his mind to clear. "This is not a game, Reverend French. We go to war, in our own way, against the South. I would no sooner send a woman into battle than I would the dangers that lay before us."

"You would take their monetary gifts and deny their help?"

"We will be mere miles from the front lines. It is best that women garner support at home and send supplies, not make a nuisance of themselves with the enemy so close."

French's voice, soft and even, cut through Pierce. "Elizabeth Stanton, Susan Anthony, have you read their works? New era, my friend. We could no longer hold them back than we can stop the rain."

"I understand that women can be of great use." Pierce was in earnest. He looked up to the rafters. How could he make French understand? "But in this case, they will be a burden.

First a drain on resources and next a moral dilemma for the men." Pierce crossed his arms and leaned against the window.

French pulled a chair from under the table and sat down. He scratched his head, looked thoughtful for a moment, then crossed his legs. "Have you ever considered marriage?"

Pierce spun and stared at him. "A topic that doesn't need to be discussed."

French leaned back. "A man your age should be married. I believe you dislike women. What is it? Is there a woman in your past?"

"Completely irrelevant. And out of line."

The older man smiled, an irritating calm. "Perhaps. Perhaps you're right. But if we are to work together, maybe for several years, I need to know the reasons for your aversion to women. What makes you hate them so?"

Pierce turned to look through the thick glass and into the warehouse.

He didn't hate women. But women like Stanton, Mott, and Anthony left him feeling unsettled. There were rules, some written, some unwritten, in regard to social relations. No, he didn't despise women. He esteemed them . . . as long as they followed the rules. Other men he called friends tried to accomplish great deeds in their careers only to be hampered by a decision of marriage they'd made in their youth. He'd always thought to abstain from this burden. But then there was Kate, a woman whose own ambition might brush up against those rules.

Before Pierce could sort through his thoughts and find the words to speak, the door opened. A thin woman around fifty, her wiry dark hair in a bun, stood in the opening. Thin strands escaped her control and spilled around her face.

French stood. "Hello, darling."

Her wide eyes searched Pierce from head to foot. She turned

to French. "Mansfield, they've loaded our items. I'm going to board. You coming?"

French smiled, and his voice betrayed strained patience. "Let me introduce you to Boston's missionary leader, Edward Pierce. Mr. Pierce, this is my wife, Austa."

Pierce hesitated but took her hand, and instead of the kiss he expected her to demand, she pumped his hand in a firm handshake. "Mrs. French, a pleasure."

She pronounced her words carefully. "Call me Austa, Edward."

Pierce smiled. "I take it you're joining your husband on the expedition?"

"Of course!" She glanced at his left hand. "Are you not married, Edward?"

French stood and took his wife's arm in his. "Mr. Pierce and I were just discussing the matter." He patted her hand. "Perhaps he'll find someone in this latest adventure of ours."

Pierce resisted the urge to strangle French.

The reverend's wife looked into her husband's eyes. "I've had a breakthrough on the article I'm writing."

French flashed a patient smile. "Go ahead, dear."

"You are like Moses." She closed her eyes. "You lead us to the Red Sea. The slaves are the ark of the covenant, and we stand on the bank of the sea which we must cross over upon dry land, so that when the waves crash upon the South, we will be safe and can proclaim victory."

Pierce imagined writing such an article for Chase and held back a laugh.

"Lovely, dear." French kissed her forehead. "Go make your finishing touches and I'll be along to look at it in a moment." She disappeared from the room without a second look at Pierce.

Pierce folded his arms. "Reverend French, I disagree with this decision."

"I believe women are invaluable on this enterprise."

"They are your responsibility, then. They have homes when they get there, correct?"

"They are taken care of, Mr. Pierce. You need not bother about them, since it seems you care little for the weaker gender."

Pierce stormed from the warehouse, found his secretary, Hooper, and checked in the missionaries as they boarded. One young woman approached the ramp.

"Wait." He crossed the short distance to her side. "How old are you?"

She looked up into his face. "Seventeen, sir, almost eighteen."

He ignored her fearful eyes. "You're too young to journey to Port Royal, Miss . . . " He glanced at a paper. "Miss Ellen Winsor. You'll have to return to New York."

Her perfect teeth bit her lower lip.

"Mr. Pierce?" The woman behind Miss Winsor brushed her way forward. Her wrinkled face held a determined look that commanded his attention.

"Yes? What do you want?"

She patted the young girl's shoulder. "I guarantee Miss Nelly will be a great asset on this endeavor. It would be a mistake to set her skills aside."

"And you are?"

"My name is Susan Walker."

Pierce knew of Susan Walker and her radical friends. While their cause was just—women's suffrage—he couldn't abide the way they fought for it by attacking social norms. Emotional outbursts didn't justify their logic. Logic should, in the end, justify itself. "Welcome, Miss Walker. It seems you know Miss . . . Nelly, is it?"

"I know her well, and her services are of upmost import."

"She is too young to join this expedition. It is far too dangerous."

Miss Walker gazed into the dark, gray water beside the dock, then looked up. "Mr. Pierce, I understand you've been sent by Secretary Chase."

"Yes," Pierce said cautiously.

"Secretary Chase sent me also." She took a deep breath. "And Miss Nelly stays."

# FIFTEEN

*A*n early spring squall drove against the bow of the *Atlantic*, and not even Pierce could stay on deck. He milled about the hallways and memorized the list of passengers, trying to put names with faces, alphabetically.

Two men seemed to gravitate to him. The first, Edward Philbrick—a man in his midthirties and an engineer by trade—boasted a broad, thick mustache. His wife and children, who he'd left in Boston, had given their blessing to his endeavor. He'd already donated one thousand dollars to the cause.

The second man was a twenty-two-year-old beardless boy, William Gannett. Fresh from Harvard, he taught school in Massachusetts. His deep brown eyes took in the chaotic scene.

Philbrick looked toward the huddled, seasick travelers. "Good group of missionaries. They appear ready."

Gannett's smooth face broke into a bright smile. "Of course we're ready."

Philbrick brushed his mustache. "I must admit, striking a blow against slavery appeals to every bit of my abolitionist self."

Gannett shifted uncomfortably, but Philbrick continued. "The slaves will look to our examples and follow them. Joy and prosperity for everyone."

Gannett looked up to the older, taller man. "Prosperity for you, you mean."

"If a few men get rich in the process, so be it." He frowned and clenched a fist. "But not at the disadvantage of the slave. Never."

Gannett's soft eyes turned toward Pierce. "What think you? Should charity work allow gains for those involved?"

"You are all well paid."

Philbrick cut in. "I don't want luxury, unless gained through honest means." He raised his hand, as if a preacher, and spoke loud enough for all to hear. "A name, we must have a name for our group."

"A name?" someone asked. Everyone looked in their direction.

"Of course. Sam Adams' Sons of Liberty, or, or Poseidon's Tridents."

Pierce glanced out the window at the stormy ocean and shuffled his feet.

"Or Achilles' Heels," Gannett mumbled.

"A name." Pierce glanced at their eager faces. He hesitated, and after a moment, continued. "The freedmen study the Old Testament, almost to the neglect of the New." Paddle wheels thumped the ocean, the only sound in the room as Pierce continued. "One man took a small band of men and gallantly led Israel from bondage to freedom . . . Gideon. Gideon's Band?"

The name was quickly adopted and Pierce, tired of the crowd, slipped away to the stormy deck. An overhang protected him from the rain, but the large paddle wheel blocked much of his view.

"Gideon's Band?" A soft voice drifted over the pound of the ship. "Very smart."

Gannett leaned against the rail, and Pierce fought a sudden pang of irritation. He looked into the young man's face, and suddenly felt glad for the company.

"I admit, I thought of it before."

"Luck favors the prepared." The cold wind turned Gannett's face red. His wavy dark hair ruffled in the wind. "My thought was Lincoln and his Preaching Men. Or Pierce's Preachers."

Pierce laughed and looked into the waves.

"I'm going to miss Boston, I think," Gannett said. "Is Port Royal similar to home?"

"No," Pierce admitted. "Not similar to Boston."

"I suppose it will take time to understand the aboriginals." He stuffed his hands in his coat pockets. "You've worked with the Negro before, at Fortress Monroe. I suppose you know what you're up against."

"Some," Pierce said.

"I want to do my part, but Father is a pacifist. He'd hoped, once I finished at Harvard's Divinity School, that I would take his place at Arlington Street Church, but I couldn't do that. I can't, with good conscience, sit this war out."

"Joining Gideon's Band was a compromise?"

A tear appeared in Gannett's eye. "No, Mr. Pierce, my father is not an abolitionist. I am here without his approval." Gannett stood in silence then shook himself. "I suppose it's just as well. Twenty-three thousand casualties at Shiloh. Someone named Grant, Union commander, gave the South a real fight." He took a deep breath. "I could have been among the dead."

"You're more use to me alive."

"You'll tell me what I need to do, once we arrive?"

"Oh yes, you will be very useful, Mr. Gannett."

He sighed, a slight smile on his face.

⚬

Gideon's Band lined shoulder to shoulder along the ship's side, eager to catch a glimpse of the South Carolina coastline. Pierce watched in amusement, laughing at the men and women he'd gotten to know over the past three days. One of them pointed to the rounded edge of an island where Northern engineers worked to rebuild the fort. Excited voices rose above the pounding paddle wheels.

"Lovely palm trees." Philbrick stepped alongside Pierce. "Almost reminds me of Egypt, the way the sand runs up into the palms."

Pierce shook his head. "They're not palm trees, they're palmetto trees. Locals don't like it when you call their trees palm."

"You mean the slaves?"

"Freedmen, yes." Pierce rubbed his eyes and studied the land. "You've been to Egypt?"

Philbrick's mustache bristled. "Engineering. Took a trip to study their forms of power."

Gannett joined them, a cup of coffee in hand, steam pouring from the rim. "Mr. Philbrick, you're not discussing Egypt again." He smiled. "I'd hoped for a break."

"Look at that." Philbrick waved a hand toward shore. "Tell me, where are the mighty windmills to capture the breeze? I see none. Where are the factories? Mr. Pierce, have you seen any waterworks in Port Royal harnessing the strength of rivers?"

"No, I don't think so."

Philbrick leaned against the rail. "Been an engineer and architect all my life, traveled to many countries, but I haven't seen a coastline as backward as this."

They were silent for a few moments, then Philbrick coughed and spit into the water. "Tell me, will you? Tell me how Adam and Eve grew their corn? By hand. How did they grind the kernels? By hand. The South harvests the same! They haven't learned a blessed thing since day one."

He continued to rant but Pierce turned away. Such obvious disdain made him uncomfortable. But many felt the same as Philbrick and could not hold their opinions in check.

They entered the channel that led them to Beaufort.

After they finished unloading on the Beaufort's docks, Pierce led them past the row of buildings that followed the length of the dock along Bay Street. Empty cans littered the muddy streets, broken pieces of wood were scattered everywhere, and shattered glass made barefoot excursions dangerous. Pierce looked about in dismay.

Small shops once filled with luxuries for rich planters were now mercantile businesses. Because there were no slaves to make clothes and other goods, textiles were imported. Specialists did metalworking. Barrel makers, blacksmiths, and restaurants enjoyed a hearty business. Laundry shops catering to soldiers filled in the empty spaces.

The group wandered past gawking soldiers who called out insults, on toward the east side of town, where the elite in Southern society had made their city homes. It was here they'd come to play when the fevers passed over the islands, leaving slaves to tend to the cotton. But the owners had run away with the invasion and the houses were now filled with soldiers.

Pierce stopped where the town ended at the edge of a marsh. "This is where the men will stay." He turned to the group. "I will leave the women with Reverend French. Reverend French?"

Susan Walker stepped forward. "I believe he and his wife are still on the ship."

Pierce grimaced. "Well, once I know where you're quartered, I will, one by one, take you to the plantation where you are assigned, to do what you've come to do." He looked at the men's house. Bald cypress and live oaks shielded the two-story home, Tidalholm. Palmettos nestled up against the whitewashed walls.

"Go on in." Pierce pointed across the yard, where weeds dominated. "The door's on the other side." The men eagerly rushed by him, leaping over a pile of broken bottles. In their excitement to see their quarters, they forgot the women.

Pierce watched the men for a moment then turned to Miss Walker.

She leaned against the iron gate. It swung a bit then stuck, and she brought a hand to her head. "Mr. Pierce, would you please guide us back to the dock? I'm growing weary, and with all these roads, cutting this way and that, I'm afraid we might not find our way."

"Certainly." Pierce led the women to Bay Street, pointed behind a row of shops, and said, "There's the dock." He removed his hat. "Ladies." He bowed his head as they walked past. He returned the hat and hurried back to the men.

He stepped into Tidalholm and the men crowded him.

"Marble!" Philbrick could barely hold his excitement. "Egyptian marble."

Another voice came from the hallway. "Columns, beautiful rooms . . . windows . . . beautiful!"

Broken furniture littered the rooms, papers were scattered everywhere, but it was livable. They got to work right away, cleaning out the refuse and washing the floors, wallpaper, and windows.

Pierce went for a walk at sunset. Despite the warm glow, a cool, stiff breeze ruffled the hair that crowded the edges of his hat. He pulled up his collar against the wind, stuffed his hands into his coat pockets, and wandered past enormous houses.

Some houses were framed by iron fences, others by vines and bushes, closing in yards with sparse grass, all with an eye toward privacy. Live oaks stretched branches over the road, hanging Spanish moss in clusters.

He soaked in the beauty of the low country.

Pierce's boot caught on a root, and he stumbled. He shook the sting from his foot, then glanced around to make sure no one saw. A low oak branch as round as his torso stretched over the road. "May need to cut that branch."

"Can't do that."

Pierce jumped and spun around.

A Negro stepped from the bushes and onto the road. He glared up at Pierce, his bent frame as gnarled and old as the oak.

"Why not? It's low, too low, and wagons piled high with goods will have a hard time passing under."

"'Cause I won't let you, that's why." He squinted at Pierce and chewed on toothless gums. "Tree's older'n you can imagine, boy."

Pierce let a long breath slip from his lips. "Just the branch, not the tree."

The old Negro stamped his foot. "Ain't takin' the branch, ain't takin' a twig!" He stepped close to Pierce and pointed to a nearby inlet, off the main waterway. "There's where the pirates holed up and slipped into Beaufort, to do what pirates do. Spend gold. But when they cause troubles, like pirates done sometime, the townfolk would haul pirates and hang 'em, right on this very branch. Ain't nobody takin' down this tree. I'm watchin' to make sure nobody does."

Pierce smiled in amusement.

Ahead, in the bright sunlight that streamed through the leafless trees, marched Susan Walker. Her eyes leveled their direction, and she pressed toward them. Pierce glanced at the old man and patted his dusty shoulder. "You keep watching it, make sure no one touches a leaf." He hurried toward Miss Walker.

Her face was red with deep wrinkles that showed her age. Her dark eyes wouldn't look at Pierce. "Sir, may I have a word?"

"Of course, Miss Walker, I am at your disposal."

"I hesitate to come to you because . . . because of your views about women . . . " Her voice trailed, and she looked away.

"Do not hesitate, Miss Walker. I have my misgivings for your safety, granted, but in the end, our goals are the same. Is there a problem?"

"It's Reverend French. I mean to say . . . There are no quarters for the women."

Pierce turned his full attention to her. "What do you mean?"

"It seems as if Reverend French failed to make accommodations for us."

His body and mind went numb. "I will take care of this matter." He tried to control his voice. "You and the others will have warm beds for the night, I promise, Miss Walker. Where is Reverend French?"

She pointed toward Bay Street, then looked up at Pierce expectantly.

"And the rest of the women?"

"Still on the dock. Mr. Pierce, they're getting cold."

"Go back to them, have them gather their belongings." Pierce reached into his pocket, pulled out a few coins, and handed them to her. "Have some of the freedmen help you take everyone to the Episcopal church. Pay them for the task. I will meet you there."

She clasped the money in her hand. "Thank you, Mr. Pierce." She hurried away.

He glanced at the branch overhead and thought of French. And then immediately dismissed the idea.

❧

Pierce thanked the Reverend Dr. Peck for housing the women at the church, a service—the passionate minister claimed—that would be satisfactory for a week.

It was late when Pierce stormed to Bay Street in search of French. After checking a few hotels, he found a lobby clerk who pointed toward the floor above, and Pierce jumped the steps, two at a time. His boots pounded on the hard floor, doing little to keep his presence from being announced. With a curled fist, he pounded on the white door. Austa cracked the door open. "Mr. Pierce, a pleasure." Her face broke into a genuine smile.

"Is your husband here?" Pierce demanded.

"Yes, yes, of course, let me get him." She turned back and motioned, and French appeared.

His long, thin face looked complacent. "Yes, Mr. Pierce, can I help you?"

"Reverend French, I must speak with you," Pierce said in a fierce whisper.

He nodded, slipped out the door, and closed it carefully behind him. "Mr. Pierce, you look . . . agitated."

"You assured me the women would be taken care of when we arrived. Under your watchful supervision, no arrangements were made for their quarters. Their sustenance, their welfare, none of it has been of any concern to you, has it?"

French waved a hand. "It's of little concern when one has faith, young man."

Pierce grabbed a small table in the hall for support. His whisper rose to a low, angry growl. "It has nothing to do with faith."

"In my line of work, Mr. Pierce, one relies solely on God. He will supply all our needs, as unto the Lord."

"But the women had nowhere to lay their heads for the night. It was I who found shelter for them, in a church. Why were the arrangements not made?"

French's body turned rigid. "Mr. Pierce, your view of the world is misrepresented due to your lack of faith. My faith in the Lord has produced results. Where are the women? Will they rest easily tonight? Yes. You see, there is nothing to worry about, for He gives us all we need. I will pray, Mr. Pierce, that your faith in Him is restored. Now, if you excuse me, I must look after some upcoming details."

Pierce couldn't speak. He fumbled for words. "I do hope you have assignments for them."

French held up a hand. "Worry not."

Pierce watched French disappear into his room.

❦

After a week, Pierce had found the women accommodations similar to the men's in the mansion next door. He'd asked Saxton, chief quartermaster, for permission and explained the emergency, and with typical army speed, or lack of, the requisition was granted.

The day after the women had settled in, Pierce spotted Miss Walker on her side of the bushes and made his way over. He cleared his throat.

"Oh Mr. Pierce, I'd meant to speak with you earlier."

Pierce braced himself for the worst. "I suppose the demands on all of us have been strenuous."

She came close enough that he could make out her face through the brambles. "Chivalry, Mr. Pierce. Does it clean cobwebs from cupboards or dust from corners before women move onto the premises?" She gave a small laugh. "We've had to clean the entire house!"

Her levity relaxed him. He returned the smile.

She took a deep breath. "I'm glad it's warming. I'd hoped the land would be better suited for health than it is, but you warned us, didn't you? We have few creature comforts, cots and moss mattresses, a single wooden chair." She clapped her hands and laughed again. "Potatoes for candlesticks!"

"I have a letter to Jefferson Davis, somewhere hidden amongst my maps and plans of the area, blaming him for our conditions. Perhaps a note from you is in order?"

"Most assuredly. I hope to send him more than that. Once educated, I hope Davis finds the Negro his worst enemy." She looked away. "They are little darlings, are they not?"

"I fear we patronize them." Pierce shuffled his feet. "Have you heard the soldiers speak of Gideon's Band?"

"Who cares if they think us sentimental fools? I do tire of the soldiers making us give signs and countersigns. As if any of us could be mistaken for Southern women."

"Planters slip past our lines and return to steal slaves and property. I suppose it's to keep Southerners from terrorizing the town with fire."

"Mr. Pierce, I was wrong about you. It seems..." She struggled for the right words. "It seems you are a pleasant young man."

"Thank you." Pierce hid his reservations. He wondered if the women would ever help in this endeavor.

Back in his room, Pierce poured over maps and plans he'd gone over with Saxton. The division of the plantations into districts, watched over by a supervisor, would start soon. Pierce would escort each to their assignment.

He'd picked a central plantation on St. Helena Island, The Oaks, to be headquarters. General Stevens, Port Royal's assigned military leader, had already approved his plan. Final approval would come from Chase soon. Boston's men kept checking with him every day as to when they could start. New York's, Pierce noted, seemed content to stay at Tidalholm, where there was little to do.

The next day Pierce received permission to move his headquarters to The Oaks plantation. He tried not to dance for joy in the yard. Gideon's Band was on the move.

# SIXTEEN

*T*ad and Peg stood inside the big house.

"Mr. Pierce is comin', Peg. I know it."

Her face, usually round and lively, was hallow and gaunt. "But I'm so hungry." Her words echoed through the empty room. "Mr. Pierce say he would teach us to read. I just want a bit o' bread."

The cotton agents had left. Furniture, books, bedding, everything was gone. Even the food and cotton in the tabby barn had been hauled away.

"Someone's gotta care, Peg. They ain't gonna let us starve." He took her hand. He just wished he could believe that.

❧

The men of Gideon's Band—the women were to remain with French in Beaufort—loaded boxes of food onto a flat-bottom boat. Barrels of pork, flour, and hardtack were lifted from the dock until the final crate settled on deck.

Pierce received a lovely splinter for his efforts. He sighed and pointed where the tools would fit beside a tall pile of goods. Under a warm spring sun, the party boarded the boat. The planks were pulled in and they shoved off.

A horse and rider thundered along the businesses on Bay

Street, rounded the long rows of buildings, and slid to a stop in front of Pierce. A man in Union blue looked down from the saddle and across the short expanse of water. "Mr. Pierce?"

Pierce held up a hand and the oarsmen paused. "Yes, Sergeant, what can I do for you?"

"I've been instructed by Colonel Reynolds to inform you that The Oaks will be off-limits to you and your band. Find another base for your operations." He struggled to keep the horse still, wrenching the reins.

"As you can see, Sergeant, we're already on our way. Please give Colonel Reynolds my regards, but the arrangements have been approved and the lodging is secured. We must be off." Pierce gave a little bow then turned to the men, motioned with his head to continue. Before they'd entered the middle of the inlet, the rider disappeared down the lane.

The heavily laden boat floated toward Ladies Island then to St. Helena Island, where wagons waited. They emptied the flatboats' cargo onto the back of the carts and, under budding trees, mules pulled them the few miles to The Oaks.

"What do the pineapples mean?" Gannett pointed to the two stone carvings atop the pillars once they arrived.

"Hospitality." Pierce flicked the reins and the wagon rolled past the entry. He hoped it was a sign from God.

A vast lawn of ankle-deep grass spread before them, broken by solitary oaks and cedars. Goats crossed the lane ahead, paused to look at the oncoming wagons, and scurried away. The wagon followed the ruts around thick bushes, past dense foliage, and into a wide-open space. Before them rose a tall, white house resting on stone pillars and basking in the shade of tall pine trees. Thin columns spread across the front, holding up two wide porches. Pierce could almost imagine the masters reclining in ease on such a vast estate while slaves worked their every whim.

Several wagons waited along the front—tired mules fastened to the tongues. Instead of food, the wagons contained furniture. Two men hauled a large mirror across the front and loaded it into the bed between bookcases. They rushed into the house.

Before his wagon could stop, Pierce threw the reins into his passenger's lap and leapt from the buckboard. He sprinted up the steps to the front door.

"Who's in charge here?" His voice echoed into an empty house. Dust covered the wood floor, except where couches, tables, chairs, and rugs once rested. Two men carrying a head-board from a heavy bed appeared at the top of the stairs.

"What goes on here?" Pierce waited at the bottom of the stairs as they slowly made their way down.

The first man's thick neck veins bulged. "Move, mister. This is heavy."

"I'm not moving until I get answers." Pierce glanced at the other man. A drop of sweat trickled into his eye and he grunted.

"Take it up with Colonel Reynolds." The man groaned and backed into Pierce.

"You're cotton agents." Pierce stepped to the side.

"Intelligent." They gave strained laughs as they slipped through the door. "Can't you tell by my accent I'm the master of this plantation?"

Despite no furniture, dishes, nor even a candle, Gideon's Band set up headquarters. Freedmen appeared from their tiny cabins and watched with wary eyes. Pierce sent his secretary, Hooper, to explain why they had moved into the Oaks.

After making their rooms somewhat comfortable with the blankets they'd brought, they rested. The next morning, Pierce took a young supervisor to a nearby location, the Tombee plantation. The house was empty, stripped of useful goods, as were the barns. Cotton agents, the freedmen said.

Pierce left the supervisor with some advice and food, gave a short speech to the freedmen, and returned to The Oaks only to find half the house filled with furniture again. Cotton agents had returned, requisitioned half the house as headquarters for themselves, and settled in. They handed Pierce the appropriate paperwork signed by Reynolds.

There were personalities to deal with as well.

Pierce realized he would have to find the talkative Philbrick and young Gannett a plantation, and quickly—both men were irrepressibly impatient. The two seemed inseparable. Pierce decided to give them an assignment together at Coffin Point, on the other end of St. Helena Island. The wide spread of plantations might satisfy Philbrick's drive to prove wage labor over slavery, and Gannett's desire to teach.

After a week, two wagons, the first driven by Philbrick and Gannett close behind in the second, rolled across Seaside Road. At the small village of St. Helenaville on the northern inlet of St. Helena Sound, they turned toward Coffin Point. Pierce studied a map carefully. They passed a gate and rolled down the shaded lane. The wagon stopped and Pierce looked up.

The plantation's majestic house, owned by Thomas Coffin, towered three stories into the sky. Windows, two to a room, stretched across the front. On the single porch a soldier in blue waited, an old musket in his embrace. "Colonel." He walked slowly toward the man. "Hello."

"Get off this land."

Pierce held up his hands. "I'm unarmed, Colonel . . . "

"Nobles." He lifted the musket, but the hammer caught in his long beard. He wrenched it forward and aimed at Pierce's heart.

"Colonel Nobles, we've been sent on behalf of Secretary of the Treasury Chase to help the freedman."

"You come to steal them. But I say never!"

Freedmen gathered just inside the clearing that surrounded the house, their eyes wide. Pierce counted nearly fifty, the largest plantation yet. No wonder this cotton agent refused to give up his territory. "Gather your belongings and go."

"You've no power here!" Nobles stamped his foot. "Be gone, before I strike you down."

Pierce took a hard tone, speaking so the crowd could hear. "You repress the Negro, selling goods at inflated prices, when they have very little money to begin with. If you pay them, it is nothing compared to the work they do."

"You liar!" Nobles screamed. "You mean to sell them to Cuba!"

A crash came from behind. Pierce turned to see Philbrick scrambling to the back of the wagon. A crate of seeds had fallen in his wake.

The engineer straightened. "You're the liar." Heedless of the musket now pointed his direction, Philbrick opened his arms to the growing crowds. "Listen, good people of Coffin Point, don't let others tell you what must be done. You must decide. We are here to teach you to work hard, but for just and honest pay. I can see by your faces what you desire. Freedom. Follow me, and I can lead you to independence."

An older Negro motioned to the side of the house, and all fifty huddled under a budding magnolia.

"Don't listen to him!" Nobles shrieked.

The spring breeze calmed and a trickle of sweat ran down Pierce's neck. He shivered, the beauty of the freedmen's use of democracy filling him with a fierce love for them. Would Pierce leave if they asked him to?

An argument inside the group ensued, and after frustrated gestures, angry faces, and some tears, they silenced.

Nobles rushed the group, but a large woman shoed him away with a blanket, waving it at him until he disappeared into the house.

Pierce's heart swelled. The freedmen would choose Gideon's Band. They were starving and the wagons were filled with food, but what pleased Pierce, tickled him to his boots, was that they simply chose. They were given the opportunity to create a future for themselves, and they took it.

Philbrick and Gannett stayed.

Philbrick could take care of Nobles. Pierce had a larger war to wage. With Reynolds and his cotton agents.

⊗

After a few weeks, most supervisors were in place, and despite the integrity of Gideon's Band, the freedmen's trust was not easily earned. But gaining the freedmen's confidence remained second on Pierce's list of priorities, for the conflict between missionaries and cotton agents had exploded. As the weather warmed, verbal altercations erupted everywhere. Pierce dashed off a letter to Chase, but knew it would do little good. A meeting with Colonel Reynolds was in order.

The Vedier House in Beaufort was guarded by two soldiers at loose attention. Their bored faces turned to him in recognition.

"Puritan."

He refused to look at the soldier. Instead, he stormed inside.

Reynolds had shaven his beard into a long, wispy goatee. He tugged on it as Pierce burst into his office.

"Mr. Pierce, what a pleasant surprise." His face showed none of the goodwill in his voice. "To what can I afford this minor intrusion?"

"Your cotton agents, sir. There has been some trouble."

Reynolds lifted a hand and carefully brushed the gold bar on his shoulder, taking great care to dust the eagle in its center. "Really, Mr. Pierce? I have heard nothing of the sort. In fact, reports show just the opposite, that it is your small band of do-gooders that are crippling the ability to complete my mission."

Pierce paced in front of Reynolds' table. "I beg to differ. Our efforts have been thwarted at every turn."

123

Reynolds slammed a hand down on a stack of papers and he stood. "And your Gideon's Band seeks control where others already have a firm grasp of the situation." He pointed a finger. "Your men know nothing of planting cotton. They offer little but the goods they bring, making the Negroes lazy and reliant."

"I admit the supervisors know little about growing cotton, but we are learning, and quickly." Pierce shifted a chair across the hard floor, sat, and crossed his legs. His voice was earnest. "There is so much more than growing cotton going on here, don't you see? We are getting to know these people better, finding what they need, what they want. And we are in a position to supply it."

"I disagree." Reynolds folded his arms over his uniform and fingered a button. "I see men from the North come to South Carolina, look at the thousands of man-hours the slaves can provide, then seek to emulate the very system earlier deposed. Look at yourselves. A pathetic lot. There is distrust in the Negro, deep-seated, and not even you can change that."

"You know why we're here. To pay them wages, to contract food, clothing, and other items on a fair system." Pierce stood. "This isn't about any of that for you. It's about power—power to pad an already generous fortune."

Reynolds stared at Pierce, then burst into laughter. "Of course it is! Is that not everyone's desire? Is that not what you desire to plant into the Negro, a love for the finer, better way of life, to obtain riches through labor?"

"It is, but within a fair system. Look at Coffin Point. Colonel Nobles sells cloth at twenty-five cents a yard to the freedmen when it's traded for eight cents back home. They will never fit into our society unless they see some successes through their labors. But you have seen fit not to remove Colonel Nobles."

"There is still much work for him." Reynolds had calmed, settled in his seat, and was resting his hands behind his head. "Either way, philosophies matter little. You've far overstepped your authority, and in so doing, the cause of freedom has been compromised by your ineptitude."

"The system works." Pierce felt calmer, his passion spent.

Reynolds shook his head. "The system has failed." He snatched a newspaper from his desk. "Read this. It's everywhere in the North, how your *supervisors* treat the slaves softly, letting them do as they wish."

Pierce knew what the papers said, knew they questioned the lack of results. But how can a starving man work? Once he gets food and regains his strength, fields full of weeds must be cleared. Then rows needed to be dug and finally planted. Pierce glared at Reynolds. "Not much can be done when they don't have the tools they rely upon."

Reynolds stood again, a smile on his face. He walked to the door, opened it, and took a deep breath. "Perhaps you are right, Mr. Pierce. Perhaps the Negro will be part of this society, will brush shoulders with those who once owned them. But they will not do it with goods belonging to their masters. They must find their own way." He lifted a hand, palm upward, toward the hallway. "Good day, Mr. Pierce. I do hope our next meeting will be more agreeable."

Pierce was tempted to lash out, but he knew he'd been beaten. The only channel left to him was Secretary Chase. Letters would be sent, friends contacted in Washington to put pressure on congressmen, but in the end, cotton agents were there to stay. To a government managing a war, a few pieces of furniture and bales of cotton were trifles.

He left the Vedier House. Beaufort's Bay Street was filled with soldiers shuffling along the dusty thoroughfare. Some stared off in the distance, while others stood in circles, laughing at private jokes. One small black child danced to accordion music and soldiers lined the side of the road to watch and throw coins. The boy bowed, set a hat on his head, and scurried away with his money.

# SEVENTEEN

*T*ad leaned against his shovel.

It was nice to have a shovel. Hoes didn't pick up the dirt. Shovels did.

Pierce had sent the Frogmore new tools. And food. That was just the kind of man Pierce was. And now Tad was putting the shovel to good use.

He stretched his tired arms, grabbed the handle, and thrust the flat end into his pit.

Peg kept talking. "With the birdbath so close, I was sure it was in the last place. Reckon we'll find it, just keep diggin'. Good idea of yours, Tad. But what if somebody thinks we're diggin' a grave?"

Tad wasn't listening. How deep would the treasure be? He glanced at his other holes and wondered if they'd gone far enough. A little deeper perhaps?

He heard his name and looked up. Pierce, dark coat jacket flapping in the breeze, walked around the corner of the big house toward them.

As he approached, Tad watched Peg scramble from her hole and rush to the man's side.

"Do you two remember me? I'm Mr. Pierce."

She looked up. "We ain't diggin' graves, Mistah Pierce. Ain't anyone died. We diggin' for other reasons. I'm thinkin' Tad wouldn't like me tellin', so I ain't gonna tell. No. Ain't goin' to."

Tad wiped the sweat from his brow and crawled from his hole.

Pierce stepped close and glanced down. "Goodness, that's about four feet deep." He looked around, shielding his eyes from the sun. "And there's holes everywhere. Are you digging for gold?"

"Silver." Peg's eyes grew large and she slapped both hands over her mouth. "Sorry, Tad."

Tad waved his hand. "Ain't no harm." He trusted Pierce. "Massahs all over done buried their silver—plates, bowls, cups."

"Forks and knives and such." Peg stepped forward.

"Yep. And we're lookin' for it." Feeling a new surge of energy, Tad jumped back into the hole and thrust the shovel into the dirt.

He heard Pierce chuckle. "Everyone wants to get rich."

"But I want to buy seeds for my field."

"I've got plenty of seed back at The Oaks you can buy. On credit."

Tad paused, saw Peg's face turn up to Pierce with a questioning look. "Credit?"

Pierce leaned down to her level. "After he grows his crops and sells them, he can pay me for the seed."

Tad was glad Peg had asked. He didn't want to look like he didn't know what credit was. "I reckon I'll be buying some corn seed from you then."

"Cotton. All I will sell is cotton."

Tad dropped the shovel and stared at him. "Cain't eat cotton."

Pierce smiled at him. "Oh yes, you can."

Peg laughed. "Aw, Mistah Pierce, you gotta be funnin' with us." She paused. "Is you?"

Pierce leaned down and picked up an extra shovel. "Sell your cotton at the end of the year, and you'll have money for corn plus more besides."

A thrill of excitement filled Tad. "Cotton selling high?"

"Very high. England needs it, the North needs it, and the blockade's keeping Southern cotton from getting out."

Tad had pictured his field filled with tall stalks of corn, ready for him to pluck the green husks. But now, long rows of budding flowers turning to cotton seemed like the best idea he'd ever had. "I'll take cottonseeds."

Pierce laughed. "Good man, Tad. No reason we can't find a bit of capital, though." He hefted the end of the shovel into the soil.

Tad couldn't help but smile.

He turned and, with a heave, dug toward the center of the earth. The warm afternoon sun beat down on them. He looked up, saw Pierce taking off his jacket and rolling up his sleeves.

Tad studied the man as they dug. With every shovelful, Tad admired Pierce a little more. And soon, he felt like he would do anything for him.

"Someday I'm gonna get my name changed." Tad paused and looked at Pierce. "Maybe I'll ask Mammy to change it to Cotton."

Pierce continued digging. "You have to change your name?"

"Everyone does." Peg glanced up out of her hole. "Except for me. I ain't got a mammy to change it for me. I'll be Peg forever. But Tad'll be somethin' else."

Nearly an hour went by when someone's voice drifted, calling for Pierce. Tad looked up, saw a fat man in white shirt, suspenders, and sweat stains under his arms wandering through the yard. He stumbled into a hole and caught himself before falling.

Pierce jumped up and helped the older man. They exchanged words just out of earshot. After a moment, they approached.

"I forgot, I'm here to bring a supervisor to the Frogmore." Pierce pulled on his jacket. "I was having too much fun. Tad, this is Mr. Soule. Mr. Soule, Tad and Peg."

The big man held out a hand. "Nice to meet you, young man. And you, little miss. A pleasure." His voice was rich and deep. A white beard hid his chin and bounced as he spoke. "I was speaking with Mammy a moment ago. Lovely woman."

Tad looked at the man's belly. Him and Mammy were the same size.

"I must be off." Pierce reached out and put a hand on Tad and Peg's shoulder. "I'm leaving you in good hands."

After Pierce left, Tad, Peg, and Soule wandered toward the front of the house, the holes long forgotten. Tad couldn't keep his eyes off the magnificent white beard. The old man reached into his pocket and pulled out a small case. He opened it and singled out a thick cigar. "Don't suppose either of you two smoke."

Tad and Peg shook their heads.

He shrugged, reached into a shirt pocket, and pulled out a match. "Well, you work on that, children. Smoking's a fine habit to start."

They both nodded.

He took a draw on the cigar and blew out a dark, gray stream of smoke. It smelled sweet.

"Beautiful." He pointed toward the marsh.

Tad looked. A large flock of birds crossed the sky, soaring above a dense cluster of green trees.

"I don't know what you two think of slavery, or of what we whites are doing here. But I suspect I do know one thing about us all. No matter what part of the country you live in, or how old you are, there's nothing quite like cooling your heels after hard work."

They gaped as he neared the dock and took off his shoes and socks. He leaned down and paused. "You going to join me?"

Tad glanced at Peg. She bit her lip, then nodded.

A moment later, all three sat in a row on the dock, their feet dangling in the water.

"I suppose our toes will feel nibbles from alligators."

Peg's eyes widened. "Oh no, Mistah Soule. They only come out to eat at night."

Soule's pure white toes appeared atop the murky water. "Ah, that does feel better. Look at all those crab things running on the shore."

"Fiddler crabs." Tad laughed. "They got a big pincer, but they scared of you."

Soule sucked in a deep breath. "So, did either of you find anything in those holes?"

"We wasn't diggin' graves." Peg's high-pitched voice echoed off the water. "Silver. We was lookin' for silver."

Soule puffed on his cigar. "Can't have enough of that."

The dock bounced, and Tad saw Mammy standing in the middle of the platform. "Lordy me. This what you up to all day? While I'm slavin' over a hot oven, you sit here enjoyin' God's creation? Well, time for supper, anyhows. Mr. Soule, we'll be eatin' in the kitchen, you're free to join us."

The old supervisor smiled at Tad then Peg. "Well, children, shall we? We've got a lot to talk about." He pulled his feet out of the water, and Tad did the same.

"Oh." Peg jumped up. "I love to talk. What we talkin' 'bout?"

Soule stood at the end of the dock, feet dripping, cigar in hand. "Mr. Pierce. Tomorrow he's going to Beaufort to pick up the women waiting there. He's going to send them to different plantations. I'd like to know what you think of having a woman as a teacher."

They walked off the dock. Tad turned and saw three sets of wet footprints—Soule's big prints, with his and Peg's on either side.

# EIGHTEEN

*A*h, April in South Carolina, much like summer at home."
Philbrick's grand mustache wiggled as he took a deep breath.

Pierce tugged at the oar. Brackish water swirled in tiny whirlpools
as the boat propelled forward. Freedmen rowed, but Pierce and
Philbrick demanded a turn as they made their way to Beaufort.

The sun shone bright off the water. Both men kept their
heads down to protect their eyes from the glare, depending on
a freedman to steer the boat.

"It is warm." But Pierce didn't mind. Chances were, Boston
was still getting snow.

Philbrick shifted in his seat, handed the oar to a Negro, and
sat on the bench across from Pierce. He pulled a piece of paper
from his pocket and scribbled something at the bottom with a
pencil, mumbling to himself.

"Is all well at Coffin Point?"

He didn't look up, still engrossed in the paper. "As well as can
be expected."

"And Mr. Gannett? Has his youth done him in, or does he
excel?"

"He is doing well. He's teaching at a couple of plantations
and he's also supervising." Philbrick looked up, tucked the
pencil behind his ear, and scowled.

"Is something the matter?"

Philbrick folded the paper and thrust it into his jacket pocket. "I'm traveling to Beaufort to borrow soldiers. I must arrest two men. Wish I didn't have to use soldiers. A police force is what is needed on the island, not a gang of paid mercenaries."

"What happened?"

"The men refused to work cotton."

Pierce opened his collar. The heat and humidity pressed down on them. He yanked on the oar. "Seems common."

"We've designed a scheme where they work four hours of cotton daily. The rest of their time is devoted to their own pleasures. Usually they work personal gardens. But two men decided not to work cotton, pulled a knife on the freedman in charge, and demanded corn from storage. Nothing short of simple robbery. But I laid my hand on the man's shoulder, and he gave up his knife."

"Took nerve."

The engineer let go a long breath. "My plantations worked together to plant a field of sweet potatoes. Nearly seventy Negroes in long rows, singing, their hoes swinging in unison." His gaze turned to the green shore, where trees endured the sun's wrath over the dark water. He turned back to Pierce. "So, what's your business in Beaufort? Who's in charge while you're away?"

"Mr. Hooper, my secretary. He's charmed most of the freedmen's daughters." He pulled on the oar. "Today I'm off to gather the women of Gideon's Band. Reverend French has seen fit not to put them to good use. To any use, actually. In fact, they're just there to take care of him. But Reverend French has his uses. The freedmen are quite religious. Not even New York's finest ministers can trump the Negro's passion and zeal for God. The emotional drive of the freedmen fits with French's style of worship, and Boston's Unitarian leanings bore the locals."

Philbrick wore a look of disdain, as if religion had no place

on the islands. "I'm changing my method of operations, paying each person for individual tasks on the cotton fields. Until
they see wages instead of credit, I doubt they'll work to their
full potential."

"How will you pay them?"

"I have funds. My wife has joined me here, in Beaufort,
which is partially why I visit town so often."

"Personal money? You've already contributed so much."

"Without starting capital, nothing is possible. The rewards in
investments may be considerable, but the risks . . . " Philbrick's
voice drifted. "You know, these rowing songs the freedmen
sing, they're much like the songs sung on the Nile."

Pierce well knew the risks of this enterprise. If the crop didn't
fail, then the price of cotton became a concern, especially in a
wartime market. "Any trouble with the cotton agent?"

"Colonel Nobles?" Philbrick laughed. "He's been a lot of
trouble, a powder-keg temper, but I can handle him."

In the distance, Pierce saw a yellow house topped by a wide
platform, occupied by several Union soldiers. From the height
on the roof, the troops waved flags at the ships steaming up the
tide-filled river, directing them to docks. Other ships waited,
anchored offshore.

Their small rowboat dodged several towering ship bows and
touched the pier. With a wave to Philbrick, he leapt ashore and
rushed to retrieve the mail.

Once he had the envelopes in hand, he glanced through the
correspondence. Nothing from Chase.

He opened a letter from Anna Loring, read the scribbled
handwriting, and shoved the paper into his pocket. It seemed
that Philadelphia had sent their own missionaries, and their
representative, Laura Towne, was of a weaker disposition.
Could he, as leader of Gideon's Band, take care of her? It was
what Pierce had feared: a woman who would die of fever the

moment she arrived, a sickly female who sucked the energy from him and the others of Gideon's Band.

"You look angry." Philbrick came up from behind.

"Another group, from Philadelphia this time. It's seems I'm to take care of—" Pierce glanced at the letter for her name. "Mrs. Towne."

"Ah, Laura Towne." Philbrick's wide smile broadened. "She arrived last week. I met her while visiting Miss Walker." He lifted a finger after a moment. "And it's Miss Towne, not Mrs. Towne. You won't have trouble with her."

"I hope not." Pierce turned to leave. "I must gather Miss Walker and the others, probably Miss Towne also, and take them to The Oaks."

Philbrick touched his arm. "Miss Towne . . . she's quite a woman."

He looked into the engineer's eyes for a moment, irritated. He decided to ignore the comment. "I hope you do well; keep up the good work." He gave a final nod and hurried away.

A young Negro woman opened the door when Pierce arrived at the women's house. "Yessuh?"

"I'm here to see Miss Walker."

"Miss Walker's packin', for the big trip to the islands."

She was shorter than Pierce, and he leveled his gaze down to speak with her. "That's why I'm here, to take her and the others to St. Helena."

"Who's that?" a man's voice called from the parlor. "Is that Mr. Pierce?"

The young girl looked up at him.

"I am."

"It's he, Mistah French."

"Let him in, silly girl, let him in!"

She led Pierce to the parlor, where Reverend French reclined on a couch, the plush red and green fabric slightly giving way to his light frame. A silver tea set sat on a small wheeled table in front of him. "Come, sit down, Mr. Pierce. Maggie, drinks. And quickly, pull a chair for our guest."

Maggie wheeled a parlor chair across from French, and Pierce sat. French ordered water with ice. Maggie listened, her head bowed.

He bit his tongue, holding back the sudden rise in anger. Maggie wasn't a slave. "Nothing for me."

Maggie cleared the tea from the table and hurried away.

"Welcome, Mr. Pierce." French brushed back his black and silver hair. His tone was pleasant. "I haven't seen you for a while, nor heard how your efforts have been. Please, tell me, are the freedmen finding God?"

Pierce, conscious of French's grooming, rubbed his own hair. He couldn't keep the cold drink from his mind. "Ice is hard to find. There won't be much left come June."

Maggie brought in French's drink, and the reverend lifted his glass. "Then we must drink while we may." He sipped the water and sputtered. "Maggie, you know I like my ice in small blocks, not chipped. Please, try again."

She glared at him, then reached a trembling hand for his glass.

Pierce grit his teeth and reached for the drink. "I like chipped ice."

Maggie turned to Pierce, and her eyes softened. She bowed, handed it to him, and rushed away.

Pierce took a cleansing breath. "How are the schools, Reverend French? Have they grown? What is the attendance?" Pierce took a long drink and the water cooled his anger.

French waved a hand. "We measure success not by education, but the Bible's blessed standard, looking toward one's own spiritual nature. We combat sin, with all our strength, which is second only to souls. Those two items must progress with all due speed."

The water turned warm under Pierce's heated grasp. Before he could speak, footsteps sounded down the hall. Relieved, he calmed his racing heart, and waited for Miss Walker.

Instead, a woman his age appeared. She paused at the door, pressed either side of her wide, blue dress to fit within the frame, and slid through the narrow parlor entry. Her dark hair, tied into a bun, exposed a slender face, smooth skin, and pronounced jaw.

Pierce leapt to his feet, nearly spilling the water. "I'm Edward Pierce, I don't believe we've met."

"Laura Towne." She flashed a modest smile and held out a hand.

Pierce took it in a handshake he might have traded with Philbrick. Her delicate fingers suggested a metropolitan lifestyle.

He fumbled for words. "Your name precedes you."

She cringed. "Anna?" Her voice was soft.

"Anna." Pierce nodded. "I know Anna Loring. She's a friend. Perhaps you and I have passed by one another in our travels."

"Perhaps. I've heard something of you too, Mr. Pierce. I've read your reports. I enjoyed them thoroughly." Her dark eyes flashed. "Inspiring. I'm an abolitionist also."

French's voice cut in. "Yes, thank you, most of us here are abolitionists." He sat up. "It seems that Mr. Pierce is here to gather the hens and take them away, including yourself."

"We've been preparing for the journey."

"Excellent. I need to run an errand, and will return." Pierce pushed back his hair. "Miss Towne, you are welcome to join me, if you wish."

She looked up, surprised. "Certainly. Let me get an item or two and I will join you on the porch." Her dress rustled through the door and she disappeared around the corner.

Pierce wished French well. He tried to mean it, but felt relieved to pace the wide porch, watching petals from a magnolia tree drift onto the painted planks.

Miss Towne emerged from the house, closed the front door, and smiled at Pierce. "Nice day for a walk." She wrapped a shawl over her shoulders. "I must say, the only joy I've gotten is walking the streets of Beaufort in hopes that soon I'll be put to good use."

"You'll be on the islands today." Pierce followed her off the porch.

She paused, turned to him, and pointed to the stairs. "Why do they have a set of steps up one side and down the other?"

Pierce looked to the porch. "Men use one side, women the other. Modesty, I suppose."

"Oh my, I'd hate to have someone see my ankles." She grinned.

Pierce smothered a laugh.

Miss Towne folded her hands and rested them on the front of her broad dress. "This isn't at all like Philadelphia. I love that grand house there, and look at that gorgeous iron fence. Oh, and the old, sturdy trees. Lovely. It's something to behold. Have you seen the cemetery at the Episcopal church?"

Pierce nodded.

They walked toward the arsenal where arms were stored, first during the Revolution and next by Southern Rebels. Now, powder, shot, hardtack, and extra rifles lined the halls. "Miss Towne, I haven't received information on the group from Philadelphia. Tell me about yourselves."

"We've commissioned the Port Royal Relief Committee, led by James McKim, and I'm their representative. We have several steel barons and railroad presidents who have donated goods, which I am to distribute."

Pierce led Miss Towne past the Maxey house, where secession was first discussed, and he pointed it out to her.

"We've taken the city where the war started. Beautiful irony."

She paused, looked up, and took a deep breath. "Mr. Pierce, I must say, I have a desire to teach, but I also have an advanced education in medicine. I want to help, but yet do not want to interrupt your system." Her steady eyes studied his.

Pierce hid a smile. "We have very little system here, Miss Towne. There are supervisors who run plantations in a general way, and teachers who have tried to gather children, but freedmen hesitate to trust us. We make little or no progress."

She turned away. He studied her dark hair, dappled by sunlight and shadows streaming through the trees.

Miss Towne could be useful as a doctor, certainly. "You will stay with me and Mr. Hooper, at The Oaks. Along with Miss Walker."

She looked back, hope in her eyes. "To teach?"

"No. As my secretary. And as a doctor. Miss Towne, your efforts will be valuable to me." He saw the disappointment in her eyes. "Do you copy well?"

She pulled her shawl tight around her shoulders. "Did Anna Loring write you, telling you how delicate I am?"

Instead of feeling irritated at her persistence, he admired her strength and determination. "If she mentioned it, it played very little role in my decision." He took a step closer, and while not tall himself, he still stood several inches taller than her. "You seem capable of the task."

"Me, a housekeeper." She mumbled as she walked under a towering magnolia. "My family took care of me, giving me my every whim, and I've grown so weary of it."

They strolled back toward the house in silence, until they came close to the entrance. Towering oaks stood sentinel on either side of the stone gate. She paused and scratched her head. "Didn't you have an errand to run?"

Pierce felt the red rush to his cheeks. "To be honest, I find conversation under Reverend French's supervision somewhat repressive."

"You mean that if we don't discuss lost souls, we're wasting time?"

"Something of the sort."

She sighed. "We have done without many conveniences, but the cause . . . "

"The cause?"

"Slavery!" Her face had turned red. "How could they? Have you seen the little darkies running around? Oh, how the darlings can be loved, and are so capable of love! To beat that from them is . . . is inhuman." A redbird swooped across the road, and her eyes followed it. "Ellen Murray, my closest friend, is coming to help. Once she arrives, I will have all I need, any inconvenience a mere triviality."

Her eyes filled with determination, her jaw set, and she nodded.

# NINETEEN

Enormous white clouds choked the sun from St. Helena Island. Pierce's gaze followed them as they hurried out to sea, leaving the trees bathed in yellow. Wagons rolled under the bright sunshine, the old wood planks creaked at every bump in the road. Every dip and rock jarred the women who sat on the benches lining the wagon beds. Fits of laughter struck them all.

Miss Towne, Pierce noted, was the center of much of the frivolities. Spirits rose as high as the brilliant sky looking over them.

Pierce kept his eyes on the long, straight road that shot through the forest. With a tight hand on the reins, he glanced at the broad fields, some freshly planted, others grown over with weeds and saplings.

At a spacious clearing, a noisy crowd of freedmen spread under a large oak in a wide circle. The women pointed toward the raucous crowd, and Pierce knew he wouldn't be able to get past without them demanding a stop. He glanced at Hooper, and they exchanged knowing looks.

Pierce dropped the reins, set the brake, and climbed from the wagon. He walked toward the gathering.

After speaking with them, he returned to the wagons and

looked into the eager faces of the women. He gripped the wagon's side with both hands. "I pray none of you are in a hurry to unpack at The Oaks. There's about to be a wedding here."

Clapping and laughter filled the air. Pierce and Hooper helped the women down to the soft turf. A half hour later, the bride emerged from a small cabin, a cream dress draped over her black skin. Her bright eyes and brilliant smile flashed as she approached. Her groom stood resplendent in a calico patchwork of pants and shirt. His long, gangly neck stretched to catch a glimpse of his bride.

A freedman religious elder was to perform the ceremony, but when they saw an ordained member of Gideon's Band, they had asked for the wedding. Pierce reached into a bag and pulled out his small black Bible. He opened it, and as he spoke, the couple made longing glances toward each other. He didn't know why he tried, since they weren't listening. All they seemed to notice was when he pronounced them man and wife.

Several cakes were laid on a table, and a broom was set just before it. The newly married couple jumped over the handle, then picked up large slices of the cake. A young man started a song, his voice mellow and smooth, and the freedmen danced.

Pierce rested in the shade of an oak on an old wood bench.

He watched the missionaries stare at the dancers, but the two groups didn't interact. He wished he could find a way to break down the barriers between them.

After several minutes, Miss Towne noticed him, and she made her way close, a piece of cake clutched in her fingers.

She smiled. "The taste is good, I admit. But it's heavy as lead."

He picked up his Bible from the bench beside him and set it on his lap. "I've done several weddings for the freedmen. The cake is always the same."

Miss Towne took a bite and settled on the bench. "I never thought weddings would be part of your duty."

"Neither did I," he said, "until I found so many living in sin together. They called their previous arrangements *marrying in blankets*. But what else could they do? The slaves weren't allowed to marry, yet were forced to propagate."

"Austa French seemed to believe that propagation among slaves led only to mixed heritage children, with the mother a slave but the father the slave's master." She took another bite and watched the dance. "I've seen light-skinned slaves in Philadelphia. And look, there's two with red hair."

"Austa French is writing a book on the treatment of slaves. It should be quite a scandal."

After several seconds, Miss Towne turned to him, caught his gaze. "I would like to ask you a personal question, Mr. Pierce, if you have a moment."

He hesitated, but nodded.

"I admit, I reviewed every person's information on my way here. My committee contacted the AMA and your Education Commission to get the reports, and we patterned our agency after yours, in almost every way. Hierarchal representation, fund-raising, it's all similar . . . even wages. I understand you represent Boston, but you left yourself off the salary report, and this made it difficult to determine an appropriate amount for my own compensation. I learned of Reverend French's pay, of course, but I have no desire to emulate him."

"There's a simple reason. I'm a lawyer by trade, but I answer solely to Secretary of the Treasury Chase, not to mission agencies. Monetary compensation is not my desire."

Miss Towne bit her lip. "But don't you have a family to care for?"

"No, no family. I'm free to join this crusade in Port Royal without attachment. I do have a brother, Henry, but neither of us have much time for correspondence." Pierce hadn't written Kate either. He'd spent most of his time writing Chase in hopes of getting answers to problems. The lack of correspondence bothered him less than it should. Best think on that later.

She shook her head. "I'm amazed at the power given you over the freedmen, but yet you choose not to wield it."

He laughed. He found himself enjoying the conversation. "I beg to differ, I use my power. I just . . . choose my moments."

She frowned. "I've never led people in my life. I think that's why I want to teach."

They were interrupted by Mr. Hooper, who'd leapt onto the back of a wagon. He held up his arms, prepared to make a speech. The freedmen gathered.

Pierce groaned. Mr. Hooper had never made a decent speech.

"Good people, what is expected of you?" Hooper held out his hands, his handsome face lit by the sun. "Faithful work. And in return, what is expected of us? Good care, justice, and to teach all to read. Fair wages will be paid."

Men and women around the wagon whispered; some shook their heads.

Pierce cringed.

Hooper kept talking. "We'll write down the amount of work you do, keep the information, and put the wages on account. If you do your work faithfully, those wages will be given to you, once the cotton is harvested and sold."

One tall freedman took a step forward, his thin shirt rippling across massive muscles. "How we know you pay us? Ain't it right to get wages at the end of the day?" Several called out in agreement, and Hooper looked to Pierce for help.

"Your every need will be supplied."

"But we's starvin', Mistah Pierce; we's hungry, and our babies cry at night for gnawin' at their bellies. Growin' cotton for you means we ain't gettin' no food."

"But that's the best part, my fine fellow," came a voice from behind him. Miss Towne, with a broad smile, stepped up. "A

143

few moments with the cotton, and you can return to your gardens. An hour a day, maybe two, and you will have wages at the end of the year. And your gardens will grow, under your hands, no one telling you what to plant."

Pierce held his breath. How did she know all that was required was a few hours a day? She'd been speaking with Philbrick.

The tall man looked down at Miss Towne, his bald head gleaming in the sun. He held his hat in his hands, looked down at it, and finally nodded. "Small-time cotton?"

She gave a warm smile. "Small-time cotton."

He glanced at Miss Walker, and she nodded. "Small-time cotton."

Young Miss Nelly stepped forward. "Small-time cotton."

No one moved, until the freedman stepped toward the women, talked with them, and after a few moments, laughter burst from the group. The freed slaves began mingling. A young man began to sing a song, and soon the dance continued. The missionaries joined the dance, the barrier between the two races broken.

Miss Towne and the tall man continued to speak. Pierce stepped around the wagon so he could hear. Miss Towne pointed to the wagons, explained the food and clothes she brought, and how they would have to work for them.

"We work." His voice was deep, and he spoke quickly. "We work, we work. But we need the guidance." He gave a bow, looked as if he wanted to say more, but turned and joined the dance.

He stepped next to her and touched her elbow.

She turned.

"Miss Towne. When is Miss Murray coming?"

"Soon, I hope, why?"

Pierce watched the dancing and happy mingling of the two races. "Because we're going to need as many women as will come. And quickly."

# TWENTY

*T*he daily scene remained the same. Pierce loaded wagons with supplies, helped a missionary woman to the seat beside him, and hauled the small train to a plantation. The freedmen took to the female teacher on the spot, and relations between supervisors and locals improved instantly.

Pierce came away with eggs, the freedmen's symbol of friendship.

He'd not eaten an egg since he arrived.

But something else passed between the two groups that pleased Pierce most. Trust.

Pierce sat in his office, tucked away in the back of the house. A single candle flickered light against the pale blue flowers that dotted the wallpaper. Mirrors reflected the warm glow.

Newspapers covered the table, and Pierce wanted to feed his desire for current events. Instead of reading, though, he slumped in his chair.

A knock came at the door.

He sat up and buttoned the top button of his shirt. "Come in."

After some jiggling of the knob, the door opened and Miss Towne stepped into the room with a tray. "Mr. Pierce, I've brought some coffee."

"Take some care. You are quickly becoming invaluable, and only after one week."

She held up a tiny plate. "I also boiled an egg."

She set the items on the table where Pierce sat, and her eyes drifted to his paperwork.

"Working late?" She lifted the teapot and poured the drink. She gave a small laugh. "All I could find was army tins for cups. May I intrude?"

"I would be delighted if you would join me," he said, although he wasn't sure he wanted someone to break into his solitude.

She sat across the table, took a sip of her coffee, and folded her hands on her lap. "Mr. Pierce, I understand the need you have for your candle, that you must work late to accomplish all that has been laid upon you. In fact, I'm amazed at the amount of energy and stamina that you maintain. But you have given me much copy work, and my ration is half a candle a week."

"Oh yes, quite right, Miss Towne." He laughed. "I'm sorry. How shortsighted of me. Look, I can't give out any more candles, but you are welcome to share the light of this room."

"I wouldn't be putting you out?"

"No, definitely not."

She left, and Pierce snatched a Boston newspaper off the top of his stack. He read the first article he came across, and set it down, stunned.

"Mr. Pierce, do you feel ill?" Miss Towne stepped into the room and set ink and quill on the desk.

How much did Miss Towne need to know of his private affairs?

"It's nothing. I once again apologize for my oversight." It was all he could do to stall, to give himself time to think through what he had just learned. "I do hope that you're settling in well?"

"I have fallen behind, I admit." She shuffled papers. "Most

freedmen have never received medical attention, so I am giving them inspections and medicines. They have worms, rotten teeth, and they're starving."

A pain suddenly shot through Pierce's heart, and he clutched his chest.

"Mr. Pierce!" Miss Towne jumped from her seat and came close. "You're most assuredly not feeling well."

The pain had come before—when he'd fought through the stress of working the professor's material—but had disappeared when he established his own law practice. Now the ache assaulted him again. Coffee and a bit of rest usually helped.

She waited by his side until he leaned back. He took a slow breath.

He managed a few words. "Something I ate."

Miss Towne returned to her seat. But worry lines continued to cross her forehead. "Are you criticizing my cooking?" She offered a half smile.

Pierce took a sip of the hot coffee and felt the warmth spread to his heart and lungs. He relaxed. "You've done a fine job here, tending the house, cleaning, even making rations edible. Both you and Susannah have done well."

"Thank you." Even in the soft candlelight, he could see her blush. "Susannah's a wonderful cook, and I know you don't approve, but we pay her some wages."

"Miss Nelly is starting classes for children," he said. "And I was hoping you might help, between your other duties of course."

She gave a small cry of delight, and her eyes watered with joy. "That would be . . . most fine."

Pierce glanced at the newspaper and rubbed his chest. "You've earned it."

She turned to her work and spoke aloud as the quill scribbled against the white paper. "Gideon's Band living at The Oaks;

Mrs. Johnson and sister, Miss Donelson, Miss Susan Walker, Miss Nelly Winsor, Miss Laura Towne." She smiled at her own name. "Mr. Hooper, and Mr. Edward Pierce." She looked up. "Mr. Pierce, are you sure you're feeling well. Why don't you lie down?"

Pierce rubbed his forehead in an attempt to slow the coming of a headache. He decided to divert her attention from what was really wrong. "The Department of the South has changed leaders from General Sherman to General Hunter, and General Hunter is an abolitionist. But Colonel Reynolds still holds his cotton agents over our heads." Pierce clasped his hands together. "I suppose I hoped to personally have more impact."

Her lips betrayed a warm smile. "Mr. Pierce, how you worry so! It's true, parts of it. The freedmen won't plant cotton and want to grow corn. And if they do grow cotton, what are the chances they will see much of their efforts turn to cash? I heard a Negro man this morning walking out of church, shaking his head, saying, *Dey don't preach nuttin' but cotton, cotton.*"

He couldn't help but grin at the way she lowered her voice to sound like a freedman.

Her smile stayed. "But if it weren't for you, Mr. Pierce, there would be no hope. You've assembled a group of missionaries who love the freedmen. Their lives are better because of you."

Her eyes flashed in earnest. In the candlelight her sharp features were pronounced, a large nose compared to Kate's gentler profile. Her hair, with troubled waves and loose ends, couldn't compete with the likes of the most beautiful woman in Washington.

She continued. "I do your paperwork for you, remember? I know the troubles that have been placed upon you. God truly would not burden any of us beyond what we are capable." She picked up the quill and touched her nose with the tip as she thought. "The freedmen aren't as bad off as all that. They don't consume alcohol, despite the soldiers' efforts to give them plenty. I've never heard a curse from their lips." She sat up straight. "We can learn from them. Oh, of course they lie, steal. Anyone would if their survival came to it. But they're dreadfully eager to learn and have more common sense than most people I know."

Pierce rubbed his chin, a small trace of stubble evident at the late hour. "It took a dozen generations to build racial slavery. It will take more than one to tear it down."

"If the Union has no patience, we must."

Pierce's mind returned to the newspaper article. He needed some advice. "You have friends, do you not, Miss Towne?"

She frowned. "I have many friends."

"And in the strictest confidence, do you ever wonder if they only keep you close to use you?"

She looked surprised, set the quill on the bottle of ink, and seemed to give the idea some serious thought.

"Only the best of friends don't use others, I suppose." She leaned back. "Mr. Pierce, usually your energy can power a steam engine. Tonight you seem tired. I'm concerned."

Pierce thought of telling her about the new revelation, that Kate Chase found the attentions of another man, a certain Mr. Sprague. The papers boasted the parties they'd gone to, and their courtship was the talk of the capital.

He thought of the look on her face when they'd said good-bye. Had the romance Pierce thought was serious only been a way to keep his loyalty focused on her father? Pain coursed through his heart as he pictured her beautiful face.

But this was not Miss Towne's problem. "Miss Towne, are you of a denomination that prays to God?"

"Yes, I pray," she said cautiously. "I'm Unitarian."

"As am I. Pray with me, that perhaps a miracle may take place? That this experiment may have a chance to succeed?"

"Of course."

The prayer wasn't answered that week. But the next week, Pierce received a report from the vigorous Philbrick that three thousand acres of cotton had been planted, with plans to seed more. A second note arrived with a summons to Hilton Head.

Pierce took a ferry across the sound. On the docks, thousands of mules waited with strict orders for their care. Mules, along with five thousand in cash to pay freedmen for their work, had arrived from Washington. It wasn't nearly enough, not the tens of thousands of dollars Pierce needed, but a commendable promise.

The word *promise* stuck in his mind.

He had promised Kate he would. He would write to her and return for her.

# TWENTY ONE

*T*ad loved the summer—despite the heat—and this summer, he was happy. Cotton grew in his field. The field he mudded as a slave Soule let him plant as his own. He walked the long rows.

Tad liked Mr. Soule—not as much as he liked Pierce, but Soule was kind, helped Tad with seeds for the field, and made sure he'd gotten new tools.

Bo kept the hoes and shovels sharp and tried to help Tad in the field, but his old back couldn't endure long periods of standing. Instead, he simply told Tad what to do.

"Thin all fields of cotton."

So Tad picked out the weaker plants to give room for the strong ones.

While Tad worked, Bo would tell stories of days when he lived up north, when someone else other than Massah owned him. Back then, he'd only been whipped lightly, since a heavily scarred back meant a slave was the rebelling kind and wouldn't fetch a high price. He was sold to Massah's pappy.

"Now all massahs have rebelled, and Union's not holdin' back on lashin' ol' Massah now. Only with a musket." Bo laughed at his own joke.

As Tad worked, he often invited conversation with Bo. "They was a good thing, the soldiers, you think?"

Bo scratched his head, and a leaf fell from his white hair. "Someday, boy, it'll be a good thing."

Dreams haunted Tad, almost nightly. In them, he wandered as a child through brush, hearing the cries of someone in the darkness. He would reach up to push away the bush, a clearing on the other side, but always awoke before he could see.

Tad learned to enjoy *shouts*. While Sundays were used by the Northern missionaries to teach about hard work, the late-night songs and dance brought him closer to God. He swayed as the words lifted to the rafters and beyond, into the starry sky, where God listened with bent ear.

Mammy's voice lifted above them all, but he joined:

*"Walk in, kind Savior, no man can hinder me!*
*Walk in, sweet Jesus, no man can hinder me!*
*See what wonders Jesus done,*
*Jesus make de dumb to speak.*
*Jesus make de cripple walk.*
*Jesus give de blind his sight.*
*Jesus do most anything!*
*Rise, poor Lazarus, from de tomb.*
*Satan ride an iron-gray horse.*
*King Jesus ride a milk-white horse.*
*No man can hinder me."*

Jesus was with him, he felt it. Tad was free, free to feel Jesus, and free to plant cotton and corn, to build a fortune, free to do what he wanted. What did he want? Money? Tad wasn't sure. But as he wiped his brow in the worship house, he knew what he wanted right then.

Cool air.

He opened the door and slipped outside. He was surprised to find night hadn't fallen yet, the orange sun setting just over the line of trees. The breeze washed up from the marsh, bending the grass then stirring his damp linen shirt. He wandered along the marsh to the other side of the house and saw Peg sitting on a stone bench in Massah's old garden, surrounded by bushes and plots of flowers that no one cared to tend.

Tad sat beside her, the stone still warm from the sun. "Not comin' in?"

She looked up at him then turned away. "Don't feel much like it."

"You feelin' kinda sick?"

"Ain't feelin' too sick, just kinda . . . sad."

"I didn't make you sad, did I?"

"Wasn't you this time." She sniffled and attempted a smile.

"What is it?"

She fiddled with a magnolia flower, white against her brown dress. A petal dropped and Tad picked it up, rubbed it between his fingers, the thick and soft touch soothing.

Peg took a deep breath. "What's you gonna do, Tad? You figurin' to plant corn and cotton and potatoes? All your life?"

"You mean, after I'm a soldier?"

Her thick fingers crushed the magnolia. While her face didn't betray anger, her voice did. "Ain't no month of Sundays you're becomin' a soldier."

He puffed out his chest. "I'm free to decide."

She turned to him and punched him on the arm. "You ain't no freer than you was before Massah, Tad. Ain't no whippin', of course." She took his hand and fingered the rough areas on his palm where the hoe rubbed it. "It's a good thing to be workin' in the fields, but what about up there?" She pointed at his head.

"What are you sayin'?"

"The white peoples, they free, 'cause they know things. Free to come here and teach us. I reckon that's a right nicer than anything anybody done for me. I'm feelin' sad 'cause I don't know things. So . . . I'm goin' to learn. I'm goin' to school tomorrow."

"School? You're goin' to school?" Tad dropped the petal, feeling betrayed. He'd heard Mr. Soule say what goes on inside a room with a teacher. Where they would tell him how to live and what to do. Besides, he didn't need to learn. He knew everything he needed.

"Reckon so. I been thinkin'. Bein' free's about knowin' what you can do." Peg turned away and added in a quiet voice, "I's thinkin' readin's a mighty fine thing to learn."

"I ain't goin' to school." The thought of being trapped in the room scared him.

She looked into his eyes. "Mammy'd be proud of you if you would. Mighty free, to know how to read 'n' write. Even prophets of old know how to read."

"If it's like Sunday school, I reckon I ain't goin'."

"It's just at Oaks."

"Too far." He shook his head.

"Tad, you knows you can run farther'n that. Ain't like you never been there before." She crossed her arms.

"I reckon I don't see a need for goin'." Tad stood.

"I don't care." She looked up at him. "Anyways, it's a dangerous walk, there being gators and snakes, reckon I'll have to call on a real soldier to walk me to school. Someone who ain't so . . . small."

What did she know about real soldiers? "Fine. I'm goin', but just to walk you." He turned and ran away, but heard a quiet giggle from behind.

❦

A small lane led from Seaside Road to Land's End Road, stretching nearly a mile or two north, with Tad's reckoning. Then another half-mile walk under tall pines, flowering magnolias, mighty oaks, and trembling palmettos.

The sun baked the exposed mud, the tide rushing away so

fast that, if Tad stared, he could see it move. But Peg marched ahead, past two pillars topped by carved pineapples, then through a small herd of goats. Tad reached out a hand and pushed on their rough horns. They seemed to enjoy that.

Well-tended fields lay on either side of the road, and Tad sucked in a breath as he studied the perfect rows. The fields made his seem small.

He hurried on, following Peg.

As they approached the house, Tad found out why The Oaks had such perfect fields. They used mules. He crossed the gardens and patted a mule's neck then ran a hand over its back. No ridges. They treated him good. A plow, tied behind the mule, lay tipped on its side.

Hoes had been Massah's favorite—not a plow to be found at the Frogmore.

"You sure like animals." He looked up to see Peg waiting for him.

"They's all God's, He made 'em all." Tad gave a final pat on the mule's rump then pointed toward the big house. "Others goin' in to do school. Reckon I'll head back."

"Tad, walk me to the door."

He rolled his eyes and joined her near the large porch where others waited. Most children were younger than Tad and Peg's thirteen years, the few older ones just there to dodge fieldwork.

"Ah, two more." A young white woman stood near the rail. She crossed the porch, took a few steps down the stairs, and leaned over. Her beautiful face smiled. "My, it's wonderful to see so many children here. My name is Miss Nelly. And what are your names?"

"I'm Peg, this is Tad." She pushed him forward.

"It gives me such a nice feeling to have you come to our school." Tad couldn't keep his eyes off her warm and pleasant face. "Are you ready to come in?"

"I gots work." Tad's mouth was dry. "Can't be stayin'."

"Oh." Miss Nelly's bottom lip shot out in a cross between a pout and a frown. "Of course, we all have things to do. Can't let them wait, can we? How about coming in for a moment, just to see what it's like?" She leaned close, so only he could hear, and gave him a sly smile. "You aren't afraid, are you?"

Tad puffed out his chest. "I ain't."

"Then come in, and see what we do." Her dress swished as she returned to the porch and clapped her hands. "Let's go in, children, and meet our teachers."

Tad couldn't hold back his rising curiosity. His dread gave way to resignation.

The students entered the house and walked across the hardwood, their feet slapping with every step. Tad kept silent as whispers filled the hall. Miss Nelly whistled happily until they reached the back of the house and filed into a crowded dining room.

Rows of benches were filled with children. Tad sat in back. Peg brushed by him and shot to the front, sitting between two eager girls.

A picture of George Washington hung near a window next to a long blackboard. Miss Nelly stood at the board, and scribbled something with a piece of chalk.

"Hello, my name is Miss Nelly."

Tad pulled at his shirt and tried not to notice the stuffy heat, the room crowded and loud. Sweat dripped into his eyes.

Miss Nelly continued. "We will be joined today by two others, Miss Walker and Miss Towne."

She pointed to the two teachers, stationed in the corners of the room. "Now, if you have a question, just raise your hand and wait until I call on you."

A hand rose.

Miss Nelly pointed. "Yes, young woman?"

"You teachin' us to read writin'?"

"That's what we are here for, but to teach you other subjects, like numbers and how to study maps and other things."

Tad sat up when he heard they would study maps.

"I can count to five," one girl said.

"You may be able to," Miss Nelly said in a low voice. "But you don't know how to raise your hand."

Tad dreamed of the ocean, the long cool swims with Collin. Heat washed over him. The crowded room seemed to grow smaller. Flies buzzed in his face and he whisked them away. He glanced at the door behind him. A quick jog to Land's End and a long swim . . . he could do it.

"While Miss Towne hands out *Hillard's Second Primary Reader*, I will write a verse that will help you to read." Miss Nelly continued to write on the board.

Tad's legs bounced so hard the bench shook. Trees needed to be climbed. Rocks on shore wanted to be thrown into the rivers. The field needed a good hoeing. He knew enough to get by, anyway. The tight confines and packed room crowded into his brain. His mind flashed to the cellar he'd been trapped in for a week.

Miss Towne set a small book in front of him. She leaned over. "You are making too much noise with your legs." She smiled, but put a finger to her lips.

Pressure rang in his ears. He tried to hold still. The room grew unearthly quiet as the others opened the books. Tad felt as if the book held a chain, and the heavy metal wrapped around his neck to hold him down. One desperate glance at the board told him everything he wanted to know about school. His breathing grew quick and his eyesight blurred.

"No!" he screamed, then picked up his book and flung it against the wall. He pushed back, leapt to his feet, bumped into Miss Towne, and dashed through the house into the hot sun.

The bright light blinded him and he slammed into someone.

"Tad, are you all right?" The voice of Pierce came from above.

"I'm free!" Tad knocked the hand away and scrambled to his feet. "Ain't no one trappin' me."

"No one's trying to trap you." Pierce held out his hands. "Just calm down. Everything's all right."

A rustle of dresses from behind brought Tad's head around. He stared at Miss Towne, then backed away.

Pierce reached for him. "Tad, no one's going to hurt you, I promise."

Miss Towne looked at Pierce. "It seems we have a runaway."

Tad tried to calm his breathing.

"Miss Towne, have you met Tad?" Pierce asked.

"No, I haven't had the pleasure." Her voice was soft, and she smiled.

"Tad's an incredibly bright boy from the Frogmore, where Mr. Soule is supervisor. They don't have a teacher there yet." Pierce turned slightly and Tad looked up at him. "You came this far to run away?"

Tears flooded Tad's eyes and tickled his cheeks. "I ain't meek! Ain't never been, 'cause if I was, they would whip me. And the meek don't ever inherit nothin' but a beatin'! And that's what you tryin' to get us to be. Meek."

Miss Towne took a step toward Tad and leaned down. "Tad, what do you mean?"

Tad backed away. "Meek is the slaves, and I'm free."

Miss Towne reached out a hand. "Tad, no one said anything about being meek . . . " She turned to Pierce with a sharp look. "Miss Nelly wrote Matthew 5:5 on the chalkboard." Her dark eyes turned back to Tad and widened. "You can read?"

He could be hung for knowing how to read. Now Miss Towne and Mr. Pierce knew.

Terror filled him. "I hate you!"

She looked at him in horror.

Tad turned and ran.

Brush slowed him down. He leapt over the shorter thicket and pushed through branches. Into the forest he stumbled, tears streaming down his face. Why had he told? They tricked him. He would run forever, swim the wide sound, and keep running to Texas. And fight by Pappy's side.

A flash of Mammy's face filled his mind. She would be sad, would tell him he was wrong, they were only trying to help. He felt washed in guilt. He tried to think only of the wrongs the missionaries and cotton agents had done. He kept running, although he was confused, then looked around for a tree to climb.

A cackle came from behind, and without slowing, he turned his head.

He tripped over a stone grave marker. His body flew through the air and landed awkwardly on a left arm that folded in a place that shouldn't bend. His head slammed into a tall stone pillar.

No pain.

Everything went dark.

# T W E N T Y   T W O

$\mathcal{P}$ierce and Miss Towne sat on The Oaks' porch alone, listening to the laughter from inside where the teachers traded stories about the first day of school.

The sun settled and the wind died. Mosquito swarms could be heard buzzing nearby.

Pierce glanced at the porch ceiling. The powder blue color was thought to keep the bugs away—wasps, mosquitoes, and flies.

"It's beautiful here." He hoped she would smile, but her face remained sullen. "Like you said before, the charm of this place comes forth. It appeals after a time."

She nodded and looked away. With thin fingers she gently pressed a braid against the side of her head.

"Tad's a good boy. I'm sorry you had to meet under these circumstances. Peg, the young girl from the Frogmore, explained it to me. He gets these funny emotional journeys, and I suppose they just need to run their course."

Miss Towne tilted her head toward him.

Pierce leaned forward, his elbows on his knees. "Peg says he wants to become a soldier. I fear when faced with battle, he will flee. His answer to every dilemma seems to be running. And that could shatter his spirit. We need to take great care with

Tad. He's intelligent, very quick. I had no idea he could read. Or where he learned his letters."

With a firm grip on the arms of her chair, Miss Towne pulled herself forward. "The way he connected the Beatitudes to his own plight . . . "

"Exactly what I mean. His mind is agile."

Miss Towne fell quiet and fanned herself, the delicate lace edging of the fan waving lightly before her face.

"He didn't mean he hated you. He hates all of us, if he really hates anything. I wonder where he learned to read."

Her eyes held steady to the porch planks.

Pierce decided to change the subject. "General Hunter is drawing up plans to recruit Negro soldiers, so I'll speak to him this week. Thank God Tad is too young. Any word on Miss Murray?"

Miss Towne shut her eyes and shook her head.

Pierce knew how much she missed her best friend. "Miss Towne . . . is there anything I can do?"

She bit her lip, then swallowed.

He reached out a hand to touch her shoulder, wondering if she felt as awkward as he felt clumsy.

Miss Towne sprang to her feet and pointed at a small figure emerging from the forest.

He turned around and saw Peg running toward them. She stumbled, then caught herself. She stopped at the foot of the porch to catch her breath.

Miss Towne hurried to the young girl's side, and Pierce followed. Peg collapsed in Miss Towne's arms.

"Tad . . . didn't come home." She coughed. "Bo, behind me."

Bo hobbled down the lane trying to catch up, his old frame bent and twisted as if in pain.

Pierce ran to him, slipped an arm under his shoulders, and helped him to the porch. Bo collapsed on the steps.

"Mr. Pierce." Miss Towne finished taking Peg's pulse and put a hand to the young girl's forehead. "Peg needs to speak with you."

Pierce dropped to a knee beside her.

"When Tad runs, it's always in sight of the Frogmore." Peg's eyes were bright in the growing darkness. Her voice rose into a frantic pitch. "He's never gone long, maybe an hour, but he ain't returned. I'm afraid alligators done eat him. Or worse, he run off again like he did to Charleston."

Pierce pressed a hand on Miss Towne's back. "Go find Old Robert. Tell him to get the horses ready, and a wagon." Old Robert, The Oaks' driver, knew the island better than anyone.

A few curious missionaries stepped outside and Pierce motioned them close. "We've a missing boy. Help us find him?"

"Of course!" one said.

Soon, Old Robert led two mules pulling a wagon to the front of the mansion. Several freedmen followed.

Pierce gave directions. "One person will drive the wagon down Land's End Road. We'll spread out on each side of the wagon, like a fan."

They nodded, understanding looks on their faces.

Miss Towne helped Peg to her feet, then stepped to the side of the wagon and took the reins from Old Robert. Pierce began to voice his disapproval, but she gave him a stern look in the waning light. "Tad may need a doctor."

He withheld his objections. She motioned to Peg. The young girl crawled up the wheel's spokes and into the wagon next to Old Robert and Bo.

Fifteen men and women, Pierce included, spread out from either side of the road, all within shouting distance. Miss Towne's wagon rolled in the center.

Their voices rang through the evening. The shadows lengthened. Once the darkness spread across the island, Tad would be nearly impossible to find amongst the deep thicket. Pierce felt like cursing.

The group burst into a field of cotton. To his left, the wagon continued ahead while the others pressed through the tall bushes. They pushed into the dense thicket. Low branches tugged at Pierce's legs, he felt his feet tangle in the vines, and he nearly fell. With a deep breath, he paused to listen. The distant sounds of thunder rumbled. A tropical air fell through the woods, the thick canopy locked in the humid air.

A week ago, Old Robert had killed an alligator on The Oaks' lawn, and the memory crossed his mind. While a five-foot alligator wasn't large enough to eat Pierce, Tad might make an excellent snack.

"Tad!" His voice was growing hoarse.

Fifteen minutes later they crossed Wallace Creek, and after half an hour the sun was nearly gone. The voices, earlier loud, were now desperate. Figures on his right and left drifted in and out of the shadows.

Peg's scream cut the night, and Pierce raced toward the sound.

He crossed the road, passed the empty wagon, and ran deeper into the forest.

In the center of a clearing lay a small body.

As he closed in, he made out the figure. Tad. Freedmen from The Oaks surrounded the boy, leaving Miss Towne alone to work over him. Missionaries who'd heard the scream filtered into the clearing.

Pierce raced to Tad's side. The boy's arm was splayed at a terrible angle. Dried blood covered his head. He wasn't moving.

Miss Towne looked up as Pierce approached.

"He's alive," she said quietly. "But we need to get him to the house quickly. Preferably before he regains consciousness."

Pierce and several young men gently slid Tad onto a blanket and prepared to lift the corners.

"Wait." Miss Towne leaned down, gripped Tad's wrist with one hand, and grabbed his broken forearm with the other. She yanked.

Pierce felt his stomach turn as the loud crunch reverberated off the surrounding trees. He glanced up. The curve in Tad's arm remained.

Miss Towne felt the bone again and looked at Pierce. "I need your help. Hold Tad, near his armpit."

Pierce dropped behind Tad and gripped under the boy's shoulder. Tad's head slipped to the side, and a missionary set a blanket under it.

Miss Towne lifted the boy's arm. "I'm glad he's unconscious," she mumbled then turned to Pierce. "Brace yourself."

Pierce held tight.

Miss Towne put her foot next to Pierce's hand and held tight to Tad's arm. She whispered. "One, two, three."

She yanked. Pierce almost lost his hold but managed to hang on to the boy. A loud scrape filled the night, and Miss Towne relaxed. The arm was straight.

"Finished." She nodded. "Let me tie it up."

She grabbed a branch, and with two ribbons from her dress, wrapped the stick directly to his arm.

"He's ready."

Pierce took a corner of the blanket, freedmen gripped the other three, and they carried Tad to the forest road. Bo and Old Robert helped haul the boy up into the back of the wagon.

Pierce snatched the reins as Bo and Old Robert joined Peg and Miss Towne in the back.

"We'll walk," a missionary said, the rest nodding in agreement. The freedmen agreed to go with them.

Pierce pointed to the coming storm, but they waved him on.

He took a calming breath, then started the horses forward.

"Speed, Mr. Pierce." Miss Towne's firm voice came from the back. "Do not bother with smooth. He cannot feel it."

The mules plodded along, despite Pierce's coaxing. The beasts had never run a day in their lives, and weren't about to. Tree frogs croaked wildly as the wagon passed by. He did his best to avoid holes.

With care not to be noticed, Pierce turned every now and again to watch Miss Towne. Wasn't she supposed to be delicate? She'd proved to be just the opposite. In the waning light she looked up and saw his eyes on her. He turned quickly away.

He rolled off the main road, crossed a small bridge that spanned Wallace Creek, and approached The Oaks.

Miss Walker and others waited on the porch, and they hurried to the wagon.

Pierce pointed to the second floor. "My bed."

Four men carried Tad up the porch stairs into the stuffy house, to the second floor, and into Pierce's room. They set him on the mattress.

Peg held Tad's left hand while Miss Towne adjusted his head and limbs under pillows. Miss Walker brushed at the dried blood with a damp rag. Miss Nelly went for water. Everyone else cleared the room except Pierce, who waited by the door jingling coins in his pocket.

Miss Towne, with a candle in hand, opened Tad's eyelids, studied his pupils, and turned to Pierce. "Would you go downstairs and pace? You're making me nervous."

He left the room, but from the hallway he heard her say, "Most men can't handle this." The other women agreed.

Missionaries chatted in the parlor, the only black man in the room Bo. Pierce sat in a corner, waiting for news. A wave of nausea passed over him.

Outside the window, Old Robert was leading freedmen in prayer.

After a moment, Miss Nelly appeared and all turned to her. "He'll be all right." Her pretty young face was blotched with red. She gave a weak smile. "He's unconscious right now, which is good, I think. Miss Towne says he'll have a headache in the morning, and his arm's broken. But he'll live." She brushed back her hair. "Someone should tell his mother."

The room fell completely silent. No one wanted to face Mammy's predictable reaction. She'd not wanted him to go to Washington in case something bad happened. And now, just miles away, Tad had broken his arm and lay unconscious.

Bo struggled to his feet. "I's goin', I's goin'. No need to tell this old man twice, I reckon."

Pierce felt relief, and guilt. But not enough blame to stop Bo. He helped the freed slave to the door. "Thank you."

"Reckon I's too old for this."

"Take a mule."

Bo bowed his head. "Much obliged."

The room cleared as the young women found quiet corners to talk. The freedmen outside wandered back to their homes.

Pierce singled out Hooper, and stood next to him. "I'll be leaving for Hilton Head tomorrow. I'll need you to come with me."

The secretary rubbed his eyes. "I better turn in. It's been an adventurous night."

"Yes, of course. Very good."

He watched Hooper hurry upstairs, passing Miss Nelly on the way. They smiled at one another.

Pierce slipped outside and slumped into a rocker. He caught a whiff of the sweet night air. Wind whipped the trees and lightning flashed across the sky. Huge drops of rain pelted the earth. Swarming insects hovered near the windows where lamplight shone through. He closed his eyes.

The front door opened and quickly closed. He looked up and saw Miss Towne step past him and lean her head against one of the thin white columns. She squeezed the bridge of her nose between her fingers.

"Miss Towne, are you feeling ill?"

She jumped and put a hand on her heart. "Mr. Pierce, you frightened me."

"I'm sorry." He spoke over the falling rain. "I didn't mean to."

"I just . . . I thought I was alone."

Pierce stood. "I will leave you to your thoughts. I apologize."

She held out a hand. "You can stay. Please. The company is most welcome tonight."

He settled into the rocker and leaned back, gently stretching his aching bones. He never thought he'd feel old when he entered his thirties, but age slows for no man.

Miss Towne gripped the pillar for support, as if her own age pressed against her body. "He'll be well. Pained, but well. He awoke, babbled something, then fell asleep."

"I let Bo take a mule to tell Mammy."

There was a moment of silence, broken by a clap of thunder. She tilted her head toward him. "I appreciate you giving me the opportunity to teach today." She paused, fought for control. "Perhaps I'm not meant to be a teacher after all. I should get some rest." She turned quickly to leave.

Pierce reached out and caught her arm.

She looked down at his grip, and then into his eyes, tears streaming down her face. "I must go."

He held her arm, the compassion of a leader for one of his missionaries overwhelming him. Another feeling stumbled forward. One he hadn't felt for a long time.

Her words tumbled out in a sob. "Thank you, Mr. Pierce, but I think I will continue with my medical practice instead."

"Why the change of heart?" He let go of her.

She wiped away a tear. "It seems my skills with children end at medical care."

"Oh Miss Towne, what happened this morning isn't your fault." He waited while she wept against the column, his heart beating in sympathy. He watched the rain pour off the porch roof, and finally spoke. "You know, Tad did the same when I first met him. I wanted to take him to Washington, but when his mother told him no, he ran. Climbed a tree. This isn't your fault, it's mine, for not following him into the woods this morning."

She turned to look into his eyes. "I just wanted to help."

Pierce ran his fingers through his hair then rubbed his chin. Tad's final words as he left, *I hate you*, echoed in his brain. "I wish I had more answers, other than to say that Tad is indeed a special boy. I'm sure he didn't mean what he said."

"It seems I'll have to take your word for it." She turned away.

"He can read, isn't that something?"

"You're right, of course." She nodded, straightened her shoulders, and wiped her cheeks. "It is impressive. I'm very sorry, I must be tired. I will retire now. Perhaps, with the sun, events will brighten." She gave a small bow and he let her go. The door closed quietly behind her.

"Good night," Pierce said to empty air. He wanted to follow, to cheer her, but he stayed.

The next morning, Pierce checked on Tad, who, Miss Nelly sleepily informed him, had drifted from unconsciousness into a deep sleep.

The boy groaned. His dark head rested on a thick white pillow slip. With slow, even rhythms, his thin, naked chest rose and fell. Pierce touched Tad's warm skin, said a prayer, then crept downstairs and stepped into the cool morning.

Hooper had rigged a sulky and stood nearby. "Tad feeling better this morning?" the secretary asked.

"Still asleep. Let's go."

The half-hour ride to the ferry was quiet. Thick drops of water rested on the green shrubs, and mist rose wherever the morning light touched. Through the air the sounds of singing drifted with the dense steam.

Pierce and Hooper passed below the arches of a live oak. They ducked under the Spanish moss that draped over the limbs, then passed a field where freedmen worked the land. Pierce stared through the mist as the hoes swung in unison to the rhythm of the song. He strained to hear over the horse's hooves.

*"Oh Massah, take dat new bran coat*
*And hang it on de wall,*
*Dat darkee take dat same ole coat*
*And wear 'em to de ball.*
*Oh, don't you hear my true love sing?*
*Oh, don't you hear 'em sigh?*
*Away down in Sunbury*
*I'm bound to live and die."*

At Land's End, Pierce and Hooper crossed Port Royal Sound on a ferry, another hour swiftly flowing by. Army headquarters were situated on Hilton Head, away from the islands, at Pierce's request. The freedmen knew the soldiers' swearing and drinking well enough already, and distance between the two seemed a good idea. Port Royal, Beaufort, Ladies Island, St. Helena Island, and others were thus partially isolated from the soldiers' abuses, other than patrols and guard duties. It amazed Pierce that the army listened to his request, and he was determined to ask General Hunter why he'd taken such a favorable action.

A long dock built by the Union army stretched deep into the sound, where a dozen steamers unloaded. Pierce's ferry, dwarfed by the warships, dodged anchored vessels and finally bumped against the pier. Lines were thrown to make fast. He and Hooper jumped to the dock and crossed toward shore.

"Mr. Pierce! Mr. Pierce!"

Pierce glanced about for the owner of the voice, and recognized the man from Philbrick's plantation, Coffin Point. It was the cotton agent who'd given so much trouble, Colonel Nobles. He stood on another pier.

"What is he doing here?" Pierce said to Hooper.

Nobles held up a packet of envelopes. "Mail, Mr. Pierce. I've mail for you." He ran toward them.

"How did he know you'd be here?" Hooper backed away. "I don't trust him."

"Can't afford not to, especially if he has our mail."

Nobles weaved past dockworkers and sailors. He smiled and held out the envelopes. "Mail, Mr. Pierce."

Nobles held the packet with his left hand and Pierce reached for it. The cotton agent's eyes flashed, and his fist swung wide. In a panic, Pierce lifted his arms to protect his face, but the blow smashed his jaw. A dull slap sounded in his head. The envelopes were flung to the side and blows rained down like hail.

Nobles swore. "This is for ruining my business." A fist connected with his temple, and Pierce fell to the dock. The world spun.

Through a long, dark tunnel Pierce heard people running across the dock. Hooper tried to pull Nobles off, but the enraged man connected a boot to Pierce's ribs. Voices filtered through his brain and the pummeling stopped. Someone helped Pierce upright.

"Sir, are you all right?"

Pierce heard Nobles scream, "I hate you, I hate you!" His voice faded into the distance.

Pierce struggled for breath, tried to clear his thoughts, and brushed his jacket. Hooper helped him to his feet, but Pierce's knees buckled and he collapsed.

He could just make out Hooper's face through the thickening fog in his mind. "Just rest, sir," the secretary said. "Everything will be all right, just take a moment." The young man turned his head, and called, "Doctor! We need a doctor!"

# TWENTY THREE

*T*ad's raspy breath rattled Pierce's head. The fog slowly lifted from his muddled brain. He opened his eyes to see Miss Towne staring down at him with an amused look. "Well, Mr. Pierce, it seems as if you've had your little bit of martyrdom."

"Ugh, I feel terrible."

"I don't know why you didn't let the doctors at Hilton Head care for you." She set a wet washcloth on his forehead.

The coolness soothed the burning in his brain. Why did he ask to come back?

"You've received quite a thrashing, you should not have traveled so far for care."

Pierce stumbled over his excuses. "I . . . thought I could keep my meeting with the general. Hooper . . . Hooper wanted to come back anyway, so he brought me."

She laughed then turned when Tad groaned. "He's coming awake again." She stood over the boy. "Tad?"

"I'm sick." He sounded as if his mouth were filled with cotton. "My arm hurts."

"Stay still. You broke your arm."

He groaned again, then licked his lips. "I'm thirsty."

Miss Towne poured a glass of water from a pitcher and let the boy sip. When he finished, he rested his head on the pillow and moaned, not quite asleep.

"That's the third time I've told him he broke his arm." Miss Towne settled next to Pierce's pallet.

Pierce sat up, the floor hard despite the blankets. He reached up and carefully touched his face.

She leaned close and spoke softly. "This morning a rider came in with news. You'll be glad to hear Colonel Nobles has been shipped to the North."

"Now, there *is* good news." He paused and checked his teeth. All firm. "Court marshal?"

"I think not."

Pierce flexed his fingers. They felt fine. "Any letter from Chase?"

"One. It seems Mr. Nobles did, in fact, have your mail."

He touched his temple and groaned in pain.

"It's a lovely yellow color." Her frown was an obvious attempt to keep from smiling.

"What did the letter say?"

She smiled. "Everyone knows what it says. Mr. Hooper opened it. The letter gave you permission to force those who set high prices, such as cotton agents, to pay the freedmen back. It seems that Colonel Nobles understood you were about to bankrupt him."

She glanced at Tad, who'd sat up in bed.

The boy slowly turned his head toward Pierce. "I broke my arm."

"You gave us quite a scare, lad," Pierce said.

Miss Towne reached forward to touch Tad's head, but he brushed her away. "I'm all right."

Tad looked at him with eyelids squinted. "Mr. Pierce, you fell?"

"I was beaten by a cotton agent, but doing well."

"I hope you gave him more than he gave you." Tad looked at him expectantly.

Pierce pushed away the feeling of annoyance. Should he have attempted a blow against Nobles?

"I'm glad you're feeling better, Tad." Miss Towne sat at the end of his bed. "Would you like something to eat? An egg perhaps? Chicken? Corn bread?"

"I reckon chicken and corn bread'll do." He managed a smile.

"How about you?" she asked, turning to Pierce.

"Yes, please, the same."

As she left, Pierce leaned back on his mat and closed his eyes.

"Mr. Pierce?" Tad asked.

Pierce kept his eyes closed. "Yes?"

"You didn't win the fight, did you?"

Pierce sighed. "No, Tad, I didn't."

There was a moment of silence then Tad asked, "Mr. Pierce?"

"Yes, Tad."

"You didn't even give him a knock, did you?"

"No, Tad, not one little jab." What if he had fought back? Would the outcome have been different? He felt a bit ashamed. Either way, it was time to change the subject. "Where did you learn to read?"

Silence filled the room. Tad finally said, "Collin, he taught me on the sly. And Mr. Pierce? You not fighting him, that's good."

Pierce opened his eyes. "Why do you say that?"

"Jesus didn't fight back neither. And He died."

"Imagine what He could have done if He hadn't died."

"Now, Mr. Pierce, I reckon you'd know better'n that. He died for our sins. Good Book says so. He won in the end, I reckon."

Pierce had always been skeptical. Was that good enough to go to heaven? God looked at works, intent, not entirely faith.

Tad wasn't finished. "Jesus, He done set the lot of us free. I know it, and love Him. He died, and came back to life. I believe it, 'cause the Good Book says it." Tad winced in pain and caught his breath.

They were interrupted by heavy footsteps climbing to the second floor and a voice filling the hallway. "Where's my baby? What done happened?" Mammy's huge frame filled the doorway. "Lordy me! There he is, and I reckon I've seen him a bit worse, but you, boy, I can't see if you're feeling bad. So tell me, boy, you feeling well?"

Tad reached his good arm toward her, and she rushed to the bedside and wrapped him in a tight embrace.

The boy's back was exposed. Ragged scars, thick and long, stretched across the boy's back. He studied the light, puffy skin. How could anyone beat a child in such a brutal fashion?

Mammy laid Tad back down and touched his head. "You're cut, boy, and Bo done say you hurt your arm. Broke it? Well, it mends, it mends." A tear trickled down her face. "Don't know how I let you out of my sight. I would've come sooner to see you, child, but Bo didn't want me comin' in darkness. And that mule Mistah Pierce give Bo, he's slow pullin' carts."

"I'm sleepy, Mammy." Tad licked his lips. His eyelids drooped.

"You'd best get your sleep, and when you wake, I take you right home."

He nodded, closed his eyes, and smiled.

"Lordy me, Mistah Pierce, why you lyin' there too?"

"A fight, and I received the worst of it." He rolled to the side, reached for a chair, and attempted to pull himself up. "Ma'am, we are doing all we can to keep Tad quiet, and I must assure you, his recovery will be complete." He leaned against the wall. "There, you see? I've been healed. Looks as if we're in capable hands. But, ma'am, I'd like a word with you, if you could, while Tad sleeps."

"He done bad?" She backed quietly out of the room.

He kept his voice low. "No, no, quite the opposite, in fact." He followed her out the door and reached for the small table in the hallway. The porcelain dishes rattled as he leaned against it for support. "He's quite intelligent."

"I know it."

Miss Towne, down the hallway, stepped close. "Did you know he can read?"

"My baby can read?" Mammy shrieked.

Miss Towne held up a hand. "Please, quiet, I have other patients."

Mammy held a hand to her mouth. She spoke through her fingers. "Lordy, we's in trouble now. Old Massah would have beat him for sure. I'm praying you won't do the same."

"Quite the opposite. He now has every opportunity to learn. The boy is young, he's attractive, intelligent, and he doesn't have a thick accent. Most of you speak Gullah, and little else. He would be a wonderful spokesman, representing your color in Washington."

She leveled a fiery gaze at him. "Mistah Pierce, we gotta fight this again? My boy ain't leaving my side, no, not ever again."

"I'm afraid he must, at least for a short time." Miss Towne straightened her neck, as if trying to implement doctoral wisdom. "He can't be moved. Another blow to the head and he may receive permanent damage. He must remain here for several days."

Pierce saw in Mammy's face the struggle of wills, one for her son's welfare and the other for her own piece of mind. Finally, she gave in. After a few more hours with her son, she impressed her stern warnings about Tad's safety into Miss Towne's capable hands, and left with Bo.

# TWENTY FOUR

*T*he sun streamed from the window, and Tad wiggled his body so he lay in the warm rays. He turned to his side and felt the tingle of cool air on his back. He rolled to the edge as the bed and the blankets slid over the side. He stretched his toes one at a time, and then took a deep breath.

His head spun, and he pressed a hand against the soft quilt to lie down again. But a noise from outside the window caught his attention. He took a step forward, the legs of his linen pants tickling his ankles.

Both legs shook, but he took another step. He grabbed the dresser, glanced in the mirror at a white bandage wrapped around his head and arm in a sling, and limped toward the door.

He staggered down the stairs and through the hall. By the time he reached the open front door, his strength had returned.

Miss Walker greeted him with a smile. "I'm glad you're up!"

He stepped onto the porch. The front yard spread before him.

Instead of the lawns that most plantations boasted, The Oaks now grew potatoes and corn in large plots. Freedmen in tattered clothes milled about with hoes, and a circle of women plucked dead chickens. A soft breeze lifted feathers into a pine forest.

Near the lane a mule bellowed. A freedman wrenched on a rope in an attempt to pull the animal, but the beast struggled, backing away from the man and his cart. With a club, the man swung at the mule's knees and it crashed to the ground. Miss Towne brushed by Tad and ran to the man's side. "Be kind to him!"

The man laughed. He held the mule by the head as it struggled. "Just a dumb animal. Best is to show who's boss man."

"That's a terrible way to treat God's animals."

Tad crossed to Miss Towne's side.

She held up a hand. "Tad. Don't go near."

The mule bellowed and struggled to rise, but the man slammed his fist across its muzzle.

Miss Towne grabbed the man's arm.

The mule dug its hooves into the soft earth and stood. It reared back.

Miss Towne held out a hand toward the beast, but kept her distance. "Easy, boy."

Tad didn't want the mule hurting anyone. But the animal was backing toward the women plucking chickens, and the freedmen seemed unwilling to move.

Tad stepped between the beast and the women.

"Tad, back away," Miss Towne said. "You cannot take another blow to the head."

The mule's eyes flashed, and it reared again. Its front hooves slammed into the dirt, kicking up a cloud of dust.

Tad held out a hand to the animal. "I know. Sometimes we do get our beatings. Like ol' Mr. Pierce, he got his, but he didn't fight back. I think that's the way the good Lord wants us to do sometimes."

Tad took a step closer and looked into the mule's brown eyes. Its lungs heaved and its teeth shone in the morning light.

"I hope you can be a good mule and do what they tell you to do, 'cause we all have to do it. It's being free that gives you the right to do what they tell you. What's your name, boy?"

Tad touched the coarse muzzle, then wrapped an arm around the mule's neck. The mule's ears twitched.

"I'm thinkin' your name is Buster. And you're kinda small, like me." He patted its nose, looked up, and noticed the man was gone.

"Ain't no right to treat animals such." Tad looked at Miss Towne. "They're not slaves."

"It's shameful how cruel some are to beasts." She wiped her sleeve across her forehead and closed her eyes for a moment.

Tad turned back to Buster and scratched the rough fur between the animal's ears. He took a deep breath, knew he needed to say the words to Miss Towne, but they were hard. "I'm sorry, 'bout what I said to you. I don't hate you none."

Miss Towne stepped forward and laid a hand on the mule's back. "I understand, Tad, how difficult this is for you. These changes must be very hard."

Tad stuck out his bare chest. "But I've a field of my own to grow."

"Very good." She pulled a loose strand of hair behind her ear. "That's a very important skill."

"Maybe."

"And you can read, which is even more important."

"I read mostly in the outhouse, Bible hidden in there. Collin gave me one. He taught me to read it. And I didn't even tell Mammy, in case someone found out and I got in trouble. I'm not in trouble?"

"Of course not." Miss Towne stood up straight and stretched her back. "Who is your favorite Bible character?"

"Favorite person in the Bible? Moses."

"He's one of my favorites too, along with Luke."

Tad paused and turned his head to make sure no one was near. "I reckon they say Moses is back." He lowered his voice. "They say he frees slaves, Georgia, North Carolina, other places. Moses come back to free slaves."

"I'm glad Moses gives the slaves hope."

A small group of black women walked to the house to buy clothes. Miss Nelly stepped out to greet them.

Tad watched Miss Towne's gaze turn from the women to him. "I'd like to give you a book or two to read. If you can read the Bible, you know far more than the others. Would you like to read something for me?"

He nodded reluctantly, and Miss Towne rushed inside.

Buster nudged his muzzle against Tad's arm and looked up as if feeling sorry for him.

"It's better, Mr. Buster. Miss Towne, she's done right by me, I reckon."

He pulled the mule's head close, then let him go as Miss Towne stepped off the porch.

"Here." She held the book open to the first page. "Read this."

Tad cleared his throat and read aloud.

She snapped the book closed with a flourish. "You're quite ready to read advanced works. This is George Washington's rules of etiquette."

"I like stories of George Washington."

Miss Towne motioned Tad inside, entered the parlor, settled in a rocker, and opened the book.

She read the first several paragraphs.

He walked in front of her as she read, then to her side, then looked over her shoulder. He wandered around her again, until she put her book down.

"Tad, is there something the matter?"

His head dropped and nodded.

"What is it, dear?"

"Miss Towne, do you not hug me 'cause I'm black?"

She stared at him a moment, her mouth open, then spread her arms. "Come here."

# TWENTY FIVE

*P*ierce trudged across the path toward the main house. His boots felt as if they were filled with rocks. Depression pressed on his mind. Three days after the beating, he still hadn't fully recovered.

Freedmen milled around stacks of clothes and food in the front yard, attended by Miss Walker and Miss Nelly. The freedmen had been paid wages, meager to be sure, but the goods sent from the North weren't expensive. A token price was set on each item to teach the freed slaves to weigh each purchase carefully in hopes they would save for luxury items.

A dog barked, but he ignored it.

He eyed a mule resting in front of the steps leading up to the porch.

Miss Nelly paused her sales and looked at Pierce. "Tad's new friend, Buster."

"He must be feeling better."

"Much." Miss Nelly turned back to her customers.

Pierce patted Buster's muzzle and continued into the house.

The door felt heavier than usual. His mind, normally quick to sort through problems, seemed sluggish, as if wading through the marsh mud. He tried to take a deep breath and pain seared through his heart. He grabbed the door frame.

"Mr. Pierce, are you feeling ill again?" Miss Towne rushed from the parlor to his side. "Tad, why don't you see if Susannah has a chore you can do with one hand." He felt her touch on his elbow. "Come, quickly, to the kitchen, sit down."

She led him down the hall and to the right, past the formal dining room and into a small kitchen where she helped him to a bench.

Miss Towne leaned toward a cluttered counter and pots crashed to the floor.

"I'm sorry, most relaxing sounds, I'm sure."

Pierce rested against a small table. "I'm just tired. In college, these pains in my heart always came when work was the hardest. A doctor believes it may have something to do with my stomach."

Miss Towne nodded. "I'll fix you some tea and buttered bread, and you'll be about your business in no time."

He sighed. "I suppose. Been a long day." The sunlight slanted across the kitchen floor. Three o'clock and he felt as if it were time for bed.

She turned to him, studied his face, then set the kettle over the fire and set a slice of bread on the stove. "Did you see General Hunter today?"

The smell of fresh bread filled the room. His stomach rumbled. Perhaps food was a good idea. "I visited him, yes."

"Good news?"

"I suppose that depends on your point of view."

Miss Towne brushed a strand of hair that crossed her cheek. "I trust he was in good health?"

"Is any general in good health?"

She smiled. "A choice few." She pulled the dark bread off the stove and buttered the slice. Thick, rich grain, unbleached flour, a favorite of the freedmen. As slaves they were forced to eat bleached flour, an item they quickly discarded. She poured hot water in two small cups and whisked the silver tea strainer in both. "Drink this."

"General Hunter has plans for the freedmen's future. As I did when we first started."

She blew at the top of her cup. "Perhaps you are too close to the affair to see the changes. Schools have started, crops planted, it's better than anyone could have hoped."

Pierce let the warm drink fill his empty stomach. "Secretary Chase has recalled all the cotton agents now that their work is complete. The secretary is slow, but at least he listens." Pierce felt guilty for the letter he'd sent the day before, bringing the secretary to task over Colonel Nobles. "He'll leave a single cotton agent to deal with this year's bounty."

"Not Colonel Reynolds, I hope."

Pierce tried to hold back a satisfied smile. "His records show a 10 percent discrepancy compared to the inventory. He has some explaining to do."

"From my perspective, that is excellent news. Is it true that General Hunter intends to create a Negro regiment?"

"I don't know, it could be. He refused to give me a straightforward answer." Pierce took a bite of the bread. "This is delicious, thank you. Though I doubt it's possible to recruit freedmen. The funds must be raised through Secretary of the Treasury Chase, then we need approval from Secretary of War Stanton. If that weren't difficult enough, Stanton and Chase would have to convince a president who's shown nothing to make anyone believe he will allow men of color to carry a rifle."

"Your report did say how important it was to prove that the Negro could fight."

"And it is." Pierce leaned back took a deep breath. He felt the tension release from around his chest. "Times are changing, Miss Towne. Tomorrow General Hunter will declare marshal law. Hilton Head, Port Royal, Georgia, and Florida will be un-

der his direct control. He will declare all slaves under his juris-
diction as free."

"You mean they'll have a status after all?"

"They will, but I must admit misgivings. He's doing this
without approval from Washington. If the freedmen hear of
it, and the status is revoked, how will they ever learn to trust
us? Status *must* come from Washington, not a general on the
field."

Miss Towne stared out the window and they sat in silence.

"There was a man who helped ease my arrival on the islands,
the first I met here, in fact. His name is Rufus Saxton. He was
the chief quartermaster. Small man, military, but abolitionist
to a fault."

"I met him once."

"Chase has decided to restructure the experiment here. He's
given Saxton a promotion to general, a well-deserved advancement, I'm sure." He took a deep breath. "General Hunter is in
overall command of the area, but General Saxton has replaced
me as leader of Gideon's Band. He's now in charge of the freedmen."

Miss Towne's face froze. "That means . . . "

Pierce cleared his throat, the lump rising threatened to bring
tears to his eyes. "Secretary Chase did mention a hope that
General Saxton does as fine a job as I have in organizing this
difficult situation."

"Oh Mr. Pierce, I'm so very sorry." Her calm demeanor
changed, and she slammed her fist on the table. "They can't do
this. The freedmen trust you!"

"Miss Towne, please don't be angry with the administration."

"Why shouldn't I be angry?"

"Many reasons." He felt a wave of sadness wash over him.
He'd only asked Chase about the longevity of his position, but

the secretary had jumped at the chance to replace him—to put the entire operation in military hands. "I'm a lawyer with a law firm and clients. The workload is overwhelming for my seconds. Secretary Chase has given me the option to resign and return to Boston."

There was a long, awkward pause.

"I think I may rest for the evening. Miss Towne . . . " Pierce stood, rubbed his forehead. He took a few steps toward the door then paused. Her Christian name slipped from his lips. "Laura . . . "

The back door burst open. "Mistah Pierce! I'm looking for you." Tom, a young man who worked at The Oaks, stood panting in the doorway. "I come to ask you to marry Miss Moll and me."

"Moll, who works with Susannah?"

"That's the right one, suh," he said. "Marry us, today, if you please, suh."

Pierce felt his energy completely drain away. Before the interruption, he'd wanted to tell Miss Towne that he didn't want to leave.

Miss Towne took Tom's arm. "How old are you, Tom?"

"I'm fifteen, I reckon."

"And how old is Moll?"

"She done turned fifteen too."

"A smart age to marry." Miss Towne led Tom out of the kitchen and into the hall. Pierce could still hear her voice. "We must do this with fashion, Tom. There are many plans to make, dresses to mend, food to prepare. It may take a week!"

"I reckon," came the disappointed answer.

Pierce sighed and slipped upstairs to his room.

# TWENTY SIX

$\mathcal{T}$ad found Buster near the porch steps and leaned against his warm body. Miss Towne and Tom came from the house, her arms waving about as if disconnected from her body, Tom nodding his head. The two wandered to the nearby slave cabins.

The sun was settling in for the night and cool breezes crossed the island. His arm ached, and it seemed as if the cooler weather made it hurt even more. Headaches came and went.

Shouting brought his attention to the road. A long row of blue uniformed soldiers marched toward him. Tad scrambled to his feet and ran down the porch stairs, Buster close behind. The column halted about a quarter mile from the big house and fell out on either side of the road. White tents went up quickly.

Tad couldn't pull his eyes away. He stood beside an oak and watched bonfires flare around the camp. The smell of cooking food drifted on the wind.

Residents from The Oaks stood and observed for a short time then hurried to their cabins. As the sun settled and a bright moon turned the darkness to silver, small groups of soldiers marched into the brush and disappeared.

Pierce flew by Tad without a word. In the moonlight, he looked tired, but he hurried down the road to speak with the soldiers. An officer stepped close to Pierce, and they entered a tent.

"Tad," said a voice from behind. He turned to see Tom walking toward him. "We's got to talk."

"Why?"

"We's all got to know 'bout the soldiers, and you're friends with all the white folk, so come."

Tom led Tad to a small cabin, much like the one he and Bo shared. A small fire burned in the fireplace, flashing light on the newspapers that covered the walls. Three beds lined the edges, where old freed slaves sat. The younger folk, like Lucy, Moll, Tom, and Rina, stood along the walls. Old Robert and Susannah huddled near the fire, their aged faces ghostly in the light.

"Tad, we's questions." Old Robert's voice was somber.

"Why the soldiers here?" Susannah asked.

Tad looked toward the others in the room, maybe twenty in all. They stared at him expectantly. "I reckon I don't know."

"They's here 'cause the old massahs have come back," Old Robert said.

"Maybe." Tad met each person's gaze. "Maybe they've come to get us?"

"The boy don't know." Susannah put a hand on Old Robert's arm. "We's got to pray and sing to the Lord for deliverance."

A knock came from the door, and Old Robert motioned for Tad to open it. Miss Towne's bonnet shone in the moonlight. She swept it from her head.

"Can we come in?" Miss Nelly and Miss Walker waited behind her.

Tad looked back at Old Robert, and he gave a single nod.

Miss Towne stepped up and in the dim light looked from face to face. Her white skin looked ghostly. The other women crowded behind her. "I don't know what's going on," she said in a whisper.

Susannah's face looked old and wise in the firelight. "We's thought the old massahs had come back to take us."

Tad watched Miss Towne give the idea serious thought. "That might explain this activity. Mr. Pierce went to find out, but hasn't returned." She bit her lip. "We're as scared as you are."

No one spoke. The silence ate at Tad, until he had to say something. "Mr. Pierce, he's a good man to be talking for us."

"That's right," Susannah said. "He a good man. He'll do what's right."

Old Robert's voice started low, and the rest joined in song. Sleep came to no one during the night as they waited for the dreaded sound of gunfire. No one left the cabin.

⊗

Morning lit the moss that hung over the slave cabins. Birds jumped from branch to branch, cheering the new day with song. Tad followed Miss Towne and the others from the cabin past the tiny houses toward the big house. They rounded the corner and stopped. Miss Towne gasped. Tad couldn't turn his eyes away.

Blue soldiers marched along the lane by the hundreds. Rifles against shoulders, their backs straight and faces stern, they drilled two by two around cypress and pines. Before an oak, in front of the big house, twelve men stood in a battle line, their rifles held at the ready.

Mr. Pierce argued with an officer. Both looked as if they'd been at it all night.

"He a captain," Tad said to Miss Towne. "You can tell by the two bars."

She stood behind him and put her hands on his shoulders. The others from the cabin joined them.

"Old Robert, look." Miss Towne pointed toward the white tents.

Tad shielded his eyes from the rising sun and gazed toward

the camp. In a ring, made by soldiers with bayonets, several hundred black men huddled in a group, their heads down. No one in the circle spoke.

From the other side of the big house, soldiers marched two dozen black men from The Oaks. They halted near Pierce, and the twelve infantrymen rushed to help contain their bounty.

A voice startled Tad. "You men, there, hurry along." A soldier had come up behind them, the muzzle of his rifle pointed at Tom.

Miss Towne sucked in a deep breath then whispered at Tad. "Mr. Pierce will protect you." She looked up. "All of you."

Tad, Tom, and Old Robert joined the twenty-four others from The Oaks. Tad huddled in the center of the circle, hidden by the height of those he'd grown to know. Women and children stood off to the side, clinging to one another.

The captain called out above the sounds of wails from the women. "Second platoon, some order here. Get the Negroes in a line."

The soldiers fell out, and with bayonet jabs, shuffled the men in a ragged row. Again, Tad found himself in the middle.

The women cried so loud the captain had to yell to be heard.

"I've been ordered—" The captain thrust his thumbs into the black belt around his waist. His saber at his side rattled as he spoke. "I've been ordered to conscript every colored man between the ages of eighteen and forty, to create the First South Carolina Volunteers."

Tad wasn't quite sure what *conscript* meant, but it didn't sound as if volunteer matched it well.

The captain paced before the men. "I'm looking for any who will join without fuss." The man's beard ruffled in the wind and his glossy black boots crushed the cornstalks as he walked. "Now is your opportunity to fight against those who oppressed you. All men of valor, of bravery, who will fight for me, fall out."

Tad, with head high, chest out, eyes straight ahead, stepped forward.

"By God and all that's holy!" screamed the captain. "No one other than a boy—with a broken arm at that?"

The yard fell silent. When Tad spoke, all could hear. "Captain!" He kept his eyes forward. "I am a soldier. I will fight for you against those who oppress us!" He tried to mimic the captain's strange accent. An unfortunate squeak sounded as he formed the *s* sounds.

The captain halted in front of him. "What's your name, son?"

"Tad, sir."

"Tad, I'm Captain Stevens. How old are you, ten?" His breath smelled old.

Tad bristled. "Close on fourteen."

"Tad you listen here. Your bravery won't be forgotten. You stand over with the women, learn your letters, study your numbers. When you've learned to read, join the infantry."

Tad tried to restrain himself. "Captain, I can already—"

"Over there, now!"

Tad knew he shouldn't argue with a captain, but he knew how to read. He'd watched soldiers enough to know he could be a good man in the ranks. Before he could say a word, he felt a hand on his shoulder. It was Pierce. He led Tad to the porch.

"It won't last," Pierce said as they made their way to the stairs. "There's more to this than you know, Tad. These men won't be soldiers."

"But, Mr. Pierce—"

Captain Stevens continued to berate The Oaks Negroes.

On the porch, Pierce whispered, "Tad, some men in Washington are trying to gain support from border states, such as

Maryland, states that could still join the Union. A black regiment won't do much to help the effort. Not right now."

Tad watched Pierce nervously rub his head. "Mr. Pierce, I just want to be a soldier."

"This is not the way to win volunteers. What are we to do, force service?"

The captain blasted the circle of Negro men. "What is owed you? Nothing. And you refuse to help those who freed you?"

The men sagged under his barrage, a look Tad remembered well from Massah's anger.

"Second platoon, form ranks," the captain ordered, and the soldiers hurried to the front. "Prepare to fire!"

The women screamed. One fainted. The children hid behind their mothers.

"I will say this once. You will volunteer, join this army, or my soldiers will fire upon you!" Captain Stevens took a step back as the soldiers lifted their rifles. "Aim."

Pierce jumped off the steps. "You can't do this!"

Captain Stevens pulled a pistol from his holster and pointed it at Pierce's face. "I've been authorized to shoot."

Tad stared, and felt as if he were watching from above, not from the porch.

Pierce didn't move. "This is utter nonsense."

The captain screamed, "I will fire!"

"You will not!" Pierce's face was red.

Miss Towne stepped between the soldiers and the freedmen. She faced the captain, her arms folded across the front of her blue dress. "That is quite enough, young man. You've overstepped your bounds." She thrust her hands on her hips. "You will have to shoot me before you shoot any of these darkies, so you best get it over with."

"You keep me from my duty, madam." A look of uncertainty crossed the captain's face. "Prepare to fire!"

"Yes, yes, you said that already." She rolled her eyes and shook her head. "You fool. Honey and vinegar. Watch."

Tad was shocked with her language.

She turned to Old Robert, who was obviously over the age limit. "I'd like to talk to all of you. Can you help me get them together?"

"Ain't gettin' shot." The old man shook his head.

Miss Towne turned her head and shouted at the captain, "Lower your weapons."

The captain hesitated.

Miss Towne barked out the order. "Lower your weapons!"

The rifle's muzzles lowered without a command from their officer.

"That's better." Miss Towne's voice grew calm and she walked along the line. "Now it seems we must listen to these men, at least for the moment. I know your desire to stay with your crops, but I'm sure you will return soon. Go for a short time, learn what you may, and then come back to us."

Tad thought Miss Towne sounded just like Pierce.

"They roundin' them up to go to Cuba," a woman wailed.

Miss Towne glared at the captain.

"We won't take you to Cuba," he said.

"I can't go," one man said. "I gotta plant cotton."

Tad almost laughed. No one wanted to plant cotton.

Miss Towne held out her hands and spoke quietly. "Your education goes well, you learn quickly. This may be a good opportunity to show General Hunter and the North that you're not only good farmers, but good soldiers." She held out her hands. "Surely you can do that."

The men huddled to talk things over. Miss Towne motioned to the members of Gideon's Band who stood on the porch.

Miss Nelly, her skirts rustling, passed Tad as she hurried to Miss Towne's side. Miss Towne reached for the young woman's arm. "My wallet, quickly."

After several minutes, Old Robert stood by Miss Towne. "They's goin'. I reckon I gotta stay, but I'm takin' care of the women while they gone."

Under guard, the men were forced into single file and marched toward the holding area. Miss Towne stood by the side of the road and handed each man a half brick of tobacco and fifty cents. After the last man passed, she hurried to the keening women who watched their men leave in their field clothes, wide hats atop their heads, and not a good-bye said.

Moll fell to her knees. "My Tom, my Tom, where is my Tom to die?"

Tad didn't see Tom.

Captain Stevens stepped up on the porch where Tad watched with Pierce. The captain lit a cigarette. "Dismal way to run an army. I would resign my commission, if allowed."

"You put such energy in the chore," Mr. Pierce said sullenly.

"I may disagree with the orders, but they are orders none-theless." Captain Stevens turned to Tad. "You, my boy, show promise." He nodded and left.

Tad glared at the captain, then turned to go inside. If he had promise, he would be marching with the other men.

"Tad, wait a moment." Miss Towne left the women and climbed the porch stairs. "I ran out of money, but here is some tobacco. Maybe you could trade it."

"You're mighty kind." Tad took the small brick.

For a moment, he watched the soldiers, his heart aching with regret and longing. He turned away.

⚯

Tad woke up in a sweat. For a moment he struggled to remember where he was, but his aching arm and Pierce's snoring brought him to reality. He'd been dreaming. Again.

The same dream came every night now. He always pushed through thick branches, drawn toward mysterious voices in the dark night. What was happening? Who was talking? It was at that moment he always awoke.

❧

Tad demanded to go home.

Miss Towne sighed and reached into her bag, pulling out a book. "I hoped to get a freedman's opinion on this. A woman named Mrs. Stowe wrote it, and I wondered how true it is. It's very popular in the North."

"Why you wanting to know?"

"In the North, no one knows much about slavery." She shielded her eyes from the afternoon sun, and pulled her bonnet over her head. "No one really understands what it is like to be a slave."

"I want to read a book about animals."

"Please, Tad, this is important to me."

She was in earnest, so he finally agreed. He thumbed through the pages. "Shouldn't take long."

"Thank you, and when you're done, return it, and I'll check on your arm. Please tell Mammy hello for me. Will the walk be too far?"

"Ain't too far." Tad hurried into the forest, anxious to check his field before he saw his mother.

# TWENTY SEVEN

$\mathcal{M}$r. Pierce, may I ask you a question?"

He noticed Miss Towne's sunburned face. They'd returned from speaking with General Hunter, who'd released many of the freedmen—most of them plantation drivers—from military service. They stood on the dock at The Oaks.

"I wish you would." He'd been frustrated by her silence.

"Do you understand my passion for the Negroes?"

"Of course."

"No, I think you do not. This is not Philbrick's passion, or Miss Walker's, not even Mr. Soule's or Mr. Hooper's. What is *my* passion?" Her voice was earnest.

"You want to teach." Her questions bothered him. Why ask about passion? "You want to heal the freedmen."

She huffed and crossed her arms. Her feet shuffled on the planks.

He glanced at the slave cabins and it dawned on him. "You love them, don't you?"

Her face softened. "And what is your passion, Mr. Pierce? Law?"

He swallowed the lump in his throat. Emotions filled him, feelings he didn't understand. She wanted to know why he was leaving. "Miss Towne, your confidence in this matter would be . . . appreciated."

"Have I given you reason to doubt my confidence?"

Memories crossed his mind, the weddings she helped plan for the freedmen, the patients she'd cared for on the porch, the copy work he'd forced on her late into the evening, sometimes just to gain her company. "No, you haven't."

"I've done all you ask of me, and it is of little consequence that I do all gladly, because I love the freedmen. In all of it, I have hidden your secret dispatches, so what is one more?"

"You mean to ask why I leave? Why I don't share your passion?"

She nodded.

"There are several reasons. I will give the least important matter first indulgence. It *is* law, Miss Towne. My Boston practice is failing. I am almost in financial ruin, and if drastic steps aren't taken immediately, I may be finished."

She cocked her ear to the side and nodded as he spoke.

He continued. "Many lawyers have fortunes to fall back upon, investments and the like. I have nothing. My family is not rich, and while I enjoy a lineage of military legacy and political involvement, I have no secret stash, no treasures in waiting. My income is a result of my hands, my minor genius, my energy."

"So the position General Hunter spoke of wouldn't pay enough?"

He cringed. "No, it wouldn't. It's a military position." So Hunter had told Miss Towne about the position under Saxton. He'd hoped she wouldn't find out. "The sound of it, Colonel Pierce. I care for it none at all. I'm here on Secretary Chase's bequest, to create a way to integrate the freedmen into our society. My position leaves me no salaried work and the new employment under General Saxton will not garner enough money. Philanthropy, it seems, pays too little." His energy was gone and depression filled him again.

"Will you take charity? My funds are more than adequate."

A rising love for the woman burst forth. He rubbed his face to keep tears from forming. She cared, believed in him, and he wondered why he felt no one else did. Kate had given up on him long ago. Granted, he hadn't given her much reason to continue their courtship. "Of course I can't take charity. Honor, and the rest. But the offer is appreciated, more than you know."

"Mr. Pierce, please do not be angry, and I know it is none of my business to ask . . . but there is someone for you in Boston? A dowry perhaps?"

He kicked a rock into the water. "I don't know." He bowed his head. "I'm not one to listen to rumor, but . . . well, rumor has it she's found another."

"Who is she?"

"Does it matter?"

Her lip quivered. "No, I suppose it doesn't."

# TWENTY EIGHT

*W*hen Pierce returned to The Oaks two days later, he found Miss Towne sitting in the afternoon sun with her face in her hands. He climbed the porch steps and she looked up, pulled a handkerchief from her sleeve, and wiped her red eyes.

"What's wrong?"

With a sigh, she stood. "Just stories of the freedmen. Loretta's pregnant. She hasn't had a child born alive. All killed by the lashings she took."

Above them, three mockingbirds twittered and flapped about in a cage.

"Where did those come from?"

"Tad." She smiled. "He brought them to me as a thank-you. He took Buster too. I hope you don't mind."

No one was to take a mule from the premises without permission, but Tad was the only person he felt would properly care for the animal. Pierce took a deep breath. "Miss Towne, I apologize for the troubles between us, or if I've caused you dismay, I'm sorry."

"No, do not apologize. I must admit, I am honored you would confide in me your troubles." She paused, then took a step toward the stairs. "I believe a walk might be in order."

"Is company welcome?"

"Of course." She smiled.

They wandered through the slave quarters, the whitewashed cabins with sunken roofs pleading for repair. A large fire pit in the center of the common area burned hot, where an iron pot filled with boiling soup gave a dark, beefy smell.

Moll burst from behind a building. "Mistah Pierce! News, suh, good news. My Tom's come back!"

"Wasn't Tom part of the conscription?"

Breathless, she pointed. Tom walked from behind the cabin, dark skin glistening in the humid air.

"Wasn't caught. They looked for me, but I'm free, and ready to marry Moll." His white teeth gleamed.

Miss Towne's eyes showed shock, but then she turned and looked into his eyes, studying him earnestly as if pleading with him.

Pierce smiled. "You can't wear those clothes to a wedding. Go change, quickly now."

Moll squealed and clasped Miss Towne's hands, then hurried away.

Tom pumped Pierce's hand. "Thank you, suh, kindly much, thank you." He disappeared into a cabin.

Pierce looked down at his own brown pants and tan shirt. "I suppose I should change as well."

Miss Towne gave him a wry smile. "It's customary."

Pierce retired to his room and donned fresh clothes. He saw no action out his window, so he read for an hour, then two. Darkness covered the yard. Pierce paced until a dull glow crossed the gardens. More lights appeared, like stars. He brushed back his hair, glanced in the mirror, and hurried down the stairs, Bible clutched in his hand.

Freedmen stood along the porch like sentinels. They held torches, the flames slapping like blankets in the breeze. Members of Gideon's Band emerged from the candlelight behind him onto the wide porch. Behind Pierce they stood, Miss Walker, Miss Nelly, and Mr. Hooper, dressed in their finest. The groom, in dark pants and work shirt, fidgeted with the rope that held his britches tight. Susannah, Old Robert, Rina, Lucy, and Jane surrounded him, all fellow freedmen.

Then Miss Towne stepped in the doorway. Her evening dress flowed around her. It was the color of purple lilacs, with white lace that touched the nape of her neck. A large jade stone hung from a golden chain about her neck, with a smaller gem below, and a still smaller one below that. Dark braids wrapped around the side of her hair, held tight with gold combs. She stood near the other teachers and dimmed their presence with her radiance.

Pierce's heart beat faster.

Moll marched into the light, her blue shift and brown cap a lively picture. The instant she spotted Tom, she burst into giggles. Tom lifted his chin and stuck out his lower lip as if in defiance to the world.

The bride finished her journey to her groom's side.

Pierce gave her a stern look in hopes to calm her. She gave him a sheepish smile and bowed her head.

It took but a few moments for Pierce to join the young couple in marriage.

The young freedmen kissed then rushed into the darkness. Thirty of their family and friends followed to harass them throughout the night, a long-standing tradition from the days when the church or government didn't formalize the marriages.

The teachers waited on the porch in silence until Pierce turned to them and said, "I thank you for coming on such short notice. It is vital we show the importance of these events."

They nodded their agreement and walked away. Miss Towne stayed.

"Mr. Pierce, do you have a moment for a word?"

"Of course, in fact, I was thinking a late-night walk was in order. We didn't get our earlier stroll."

"The pines, in the dark? I would like that."

Though trees blocked the moon's glow, tiny drops of silver filtered through the needles.

"You did well tonight." Her voice remained pleasant.

"I've had plenty of practice." He stuffed his hands in his pockets. "The consequence of an education in divinity before studying law."

Frogs along the marsh thrummed a deep, melancholy call, so loud the couple had to raise their voices to be heard.

"Mr. Pierce, I must ask you to reconsider your leaving. The sweet darkies, they love you, trust you. They come to you with every little worry, every care, and you put their minds at ease. You are too valuable to leave these islands."

Pierce looked at the treetops. Everyone he'd written to for advice expected him to take the position under Saxton. It was salaried, after all. But lost power could never be regained. As director of Gideon's Band, he answered only to Chase. Under Saxton, the lines of communication would be complicated.

Chase had written to tell of his disappointment that Pierce would be leaving. A small comfort, to be sure. But another question dominated his mind. Did he really want to return to the life in Boston?

And what of Kate? Could he give her up without a fight? With Laura Towne by his side, it was easy to forget about his Washington romance and the pressure of performing to Kate's exacting standards in politics.

He looked at the teacher and physician who walked with him through the pine trees.

She liked him. Perhaps it was his position as leader of the freedmen, or maybe his modest looks and potential future. He knew she admired his ability to organize and administrate. She understood why he'd denied her a teaching position at first, and for that he was grateful. Miss Towne had much to learn when she arrived, but now she seemed ready to take on any challenge.

He looked at her moonlit face. She was lovely. Not beautiful, like Kate. But she had a strange inner beauty, and it surrounded her like a soft blanket weaved by angels.

He shook his head. She made him poetic. And that was the heart of the matter. He liked who he was around her.

"I take by your silence you're giving it reasonable consideration."

He stuttered. "The people are important, all of them—not only the children, but the elderly and the lame, and those in Gideon's Band as well. I've enjoyed my time with you, Miss Towne. But you know the financial impact this is having on my future."

She thrust her hands on her hips. "Do you understand the impact this will have on the freedmen? You demand normalcy for them but refuse to deliver it yourself."

Pierce reeled from her harsh tone. "My future is at stake."

"Your future is with the Negroes! They trust you. They love you . . . We all love you."

"Perhaps I wish not to be tied down," he replied quickly. Too quickly.

"The freed slaves bind you?"

He lifted his arms in frustration. "I mean to anything, to everything."

In the darkness, he could see her smile past the tears. "I begin to understand you better. And I would like you to understand me. I have watched you for several months, seen your intense energy put to good use. You work incessantly, long after others have failed or given up. Every movement you've made has been for good reason. But in this decision, I believe you are wrong."

He looked into her eyes. "There is something inside me that hopes you are right." He tried to hold back his ramblings, but the emotions tumbled out of him. "My time here was short from the very beginning. Secretary Chase never meant me to stay. He has other contacts down here as well, Miss Walker one of them." With a bold gesture, he reached out and touched her hand. "I would stay, if I could."

She took his hand. "When will you tell the freedmen?"

"Sunday. And I'll leave the next week."

"It won't be a popular decision."

Pierce couldn't hold the tears back, and they trickled down his cheek. He turned his face to hide them. "I don't want to leave. And when I face them Sunday . . . oh, how can I?"

She held tight to his hand.

They walked through the plantation, under wide oaks and tall pines, in silence.

❦

Pierce stared at the fresh-cut, bright blue hydrangeas covering the front of the pulpit. Freedmen filled the pews and leaned through the open windows of the brick church to hear Reverend Horton. The heat was insufferable.

Horton called out his name and motioned. "Just a few words, Mr. Pierce."

Pierce stood in front of the podium. He would hide behind nothing as he told them. "I must return North." His mind went blank. The speech he memorized was gone. He took a deep breath and worked to form the words. "I've done my best to protect you." He felt the shudder that ran through the congregation.

"President Lincoln always thought a great deal about you. He was always your friend. Now, you are more than ever in his thoughts. He is going to send you a protector, a more powerful man than I. A general to care for you, a man who has always been your friend. You must love him and obey him."

Pierce shifted his Bible to his left hand and pointed to several in the crowd. "Each and every one of you are my friends." Tears trickled down his cheeks. He saw Miss Towne crying also, a handkerchief clutched to her chest. Most in the congregation had tears in their eyes. "You will always hold a special place in my heart."

Head bowed, Pierce took his seat. Sounds of weeping filled the church. Reverend Horton slowly approached the podium. After a moment, he spoke. "Every person in this room has been affected in some good way by Mr. Pierce. For those who regret his departure, please rise."

Pierce held his head in his hands and refused to turn around. Horton pointed, and after a moment, Pierce looked. Everyone was standing. Some held their arms toward heaven.

"Thank Ye, Lord, thank Ye for Mistah Pierce," one man said.

Old Robert, bent and aged, struggled to the front and held out a hand. He squinted, and his wrinkled face reminded Pierce of a raisin. "Lordy, we thank You fo' being our Massah. And we thank You fo' Mistah Pierce and his goodness to us."

Pierce sat in the pew and cried as hands and prayers were lifted in thankfulness and sorrow. He felt the coarse touch of cloth against his cheek. He looked up. Freedmen brushed by him, and he reached out to grasp their hands. They didn't want to shake, but to touch him affectionately.

He wandered down the center aisle, reaching out to them. They followed him outside. Under the shade of an ancient oak, Pierce stood and said good-bye to eight hundred freedmen, one by one. Finally, after two hours, the last of the freedmen wandered away, and only Miss Towne, wearing a pink and white dress, remained.

"A blind man couldn't reach you." She reached out her arm. "He asked if I might shake your hand for him."

Pierce took her soft hand in his, her touch sending shivers through his spine. Though her small fingers fit perfectly in his, they held the grasp for only a moment before letting it slip away.

⚛

Mr. Hooper took the position under Saxton. It was a relief to Pierce having his chosen man to be selected. Hooper was more than capable.

Pierce wrote notes to several of Gideon's Band, memos of encouragement, thanks, or directions. He ordered twelve muskets for each plantation, since the risk of Southern reprisal was real.

A few coins in Old Robert's capable hands bought Miss Towne a two-wheeled carriage and horse, the same tired gray horse that had hauled him around many months before. "Promise me, Old Robert, Miss Towne won't hear of this until I'm aboard the steamer."

Old Robert nodded and winked.

Tad had a fever, and wasn't able to come to The Oaks to say good-bye. Pierce dashed off a note to the lad, wishing he could see him once more. But with broken heart, he had to tell him he was unable to visit the Frogmore.

As Pierce finished packing his pens and paper in a leather folder, he heard Susannah scream. He scrambled from his chair into the hall. At the front door of the house, Susannah fanned Miss Towne, who lay on the threshold.

Pierce raced to her side. "What has happened?"

"She done faint away," the old Negro woman said, shaking her head.

"Faint? Why?"

"Mr. Pierce, ain't you heard? Miss Murray, she down on the docks, heading right here, right now."

Ellen Murray. Miss Towne's closest friend had finally arrived.

The two met in the parlor, their voices dignified and controlled, as if they were merely acquaintances. Miss Towne had completely recovered from her faint.

Miss Murray's round face couldn't hold back the joy of seeing her friend. Miss Murray looked more the part of a teacher than Miss Towne. It wasn't until they went to Miss Towne's room did Pierce hears squeals of laughter.

That night, his last night, Pierce sat next to a lamp and discussed events with Miss Towne, Miss Murray, and Miss Walker. Miss Towne's eyes greeted his several times, and the looks lingered.

When he left the next morning, Pierce turned to look once more at The Oaks plantation bathed in morning light. Miss Towne stepped to the edge of the porch and lifted a hand. Regret stabbing at his heart, he returned the wave, and turned his horse toward Beaufort to catch a steamer to Boston.

Alone.

# Part 2

# TWENTY-NINE

*I*t sat on the center of the table. A square brown brick, a compact crush of chopped leaves. Tad couldn't keep his eyes off it. He circled the crude table then sat back on his bed.

Reading *Uncle Tom's Cabin* again would be a good distraction. The characters—Henry, Eva, and the rest—kept his mind busy. He'd struggled to avoid crying the first time he finished the book—when Uncle Tom died. But he died free, which was some small comfort.

His eyes drifted back to the table. Slaves probably grew the plants.

Mammy had seen his prize. "No boy o' mine's chawin' 'baccy," she'd said, but didn't take it from him. The soldiers spit out large chunks of the stuff after the flavor'd gone. And Mammy didn't want Tad doing anything the soldiers did.

So it sat.

Tad thought of smoking a fat cigar, pretending he was a train, like the railroad that divided Beaufort in half. But Massah smoked his tobacco as a cigar, and he refused to be like Massah.

Peg saw the brick on the table when she checked on his broken arm, and her eyes grew large. She put her hands on her hips and shook her finger at him. "It'll make the devil come if you smoke it. The smoke falls to the earth and Satan takes your soul." She turned and ran out the door.

Tad flopped onto his moss-filled mattress. When he became a soldier, he'd chew tobacco like the other soldiers, slowly, showing all that he knew what he was doing. Trouble was, chewing took practice.

He slipped from his bed and rounded the table again. A bit had fallen off the edge, where the brick had been broken in two. He reached out, grabbed a small piece, and shoved the bit into his cheek.

He'd tasted better weeds. He gripped the edge of the table and forced the gritty plant around his mouth. The tobacco turned slimy. After gagging, he rushed outside, parked himself under the pump, primed it, and let the water rush off his tongue. The flavor wouldn't go away.

"Boy, you finding trouble again?" Tad looked up to see Bo watching him.

"The trouble's with the nasty taste of 'baccy." Tad stood and wiped his mouth with a sleeve. "You hoeing corn?"

Bo dropped the hoe from off his shoulder. "Me and the others is done." He leaned on the handle. "Mammy's gonna whip you, boy."

"Ain't gonna be no worse than tasting 'baccy."

"Where you git it? You lookin' to be rid of it?"

Tad stood and scratched his head. "Miss Towne gave it to me when I volunteered for the army. Reckon I could part with it if the price was a good one."

"I could find you a dozen ears of corn."

"If I had a mind to, I could find 'em myself."

"Reckon you could. I'd ask you to teach me to read and I git you somethin' big, but Mistah Soule, he gonna teach me hisself." Bo scuffed his big toe across the dirt. "How 'bout a chicken?"

"Two chickens, and one's to be the rooster Mr. Henry."

"Why Mistah Henry?"

"He hates Buster to no end, chasing him around the plantation."

"Two chickens it is. My lands, Tad, you ain't little no more. The summer's been mighty kind to you. Tall, and a mind for bartering."

"Then we shake on it?"

"Shake on it?"

Tad shrugged. "I saw Mistah Pierce do it, to make a deal."

Tad enjoyed plucking Mr. Henry.

"Mammy, why I gotta have a new name?" Tad took a long drink of water from a tin cup and set it on the kitchen table. "Massah ain't here to make it so." He picked up the hemp bag he'd borrowed and slid the two plucked chickens inside.

Mammy looked up from making her sweet-grass basket. "It's the way it's done, child. Lordy me, you ain't no Tad no more either. You's grown up now, gettin' bigger."

"I like my name, Mammy."

"Let me think on it awhile."

Tad was so worried that as he stepped out of the kitchen he almost plowed into Peg. "Sorry, Peg." He smiled at her. "Can you help me with something?"

She crossed her arms and shook her head. "Ain't doin' nothin' with you again, ever."

He took a step back. "Why? What'd I do?"

"If it weren't for me talkin' you into school, you wouldn't have gotten a broke arm. And 'member, it was me who got you in bad with Massah. I'm just trouble for you." Head down, she drew a circle in the dirt with her naked toe.

"That ain't nothing but gibberish, and you know it." A rogue

213

mosquito landed on Tad's arm. He swatted it. "Now, I've got to have you carry a pot since my arm is broke. And I'm needing some matches. You got matches?"

"I got matches. Mammy give them to me to light the fires in the big house for Mr. Soule." Her gaze wandered to the bag. "Tad, what you carryin' in there?"

"Two dead chickens." Tad pointed to a nearby iron pot, and Peg hefted it against her side. He led her toward the road, whistling.

"Why you got dead chickens?"

"You've got to come see." He started whistling again.

They walked down the road, sometimes in the shade of oaks, at other times in the brilliant sun.

Tad paused his whistling to listen to Peg's voice. The high, squeaky, mouse-like noise was gone, and she drifted into a more mature, velvety sound. "You're taller'n me now, Tad. You been growin' pretty fast. Not enough to be a soldier yet, but reckon soon enough, for sure. I'm not wantin' you to be. Although God do work in funny ways. Like old Betsy, she old but done have a baby, and by the time the baby is old enough to be a soldier, she be dead and gone. Babies are the finest in the earth, ain't they?"

Tad had stopped listening after "you been growin' pretty fast." Why was everyone so surprised he was taller?

Near Land's End, Tad slowed. "Suppertime, 'bouts?"

"I reckon." Peg glanced at the sun.

"Good thing the wind's blowing."

Ahead in a flat clearing, two rows of white tents stretched nearly a quarter of a mile along the road. Rifles rested in clusters, their bayonets locked together at the top, the butts resting on the ground in the shape of a cone. Soldiers in blue milled about, some setting pots of water over campfires, others hitting a ball with a stick.

"Hurry, upwind."

"This is mighty heavy, Tad."

"We're almost there." He ducked into the forest, just out of sight from the camp. "Here."

Peg dropped the pot and rubbed her arms. "That was a long walk." She looked at the piles of cans and trash. "These men is dirty."

"Now we need some firewood." He gathered branches with his good arm and snapped them into smaller bits. Peg held a lit match under the brambles, and after a few moments, flames sprang from the kindling.

Tad opened his bag and pulled out a bladder filled with water. He poured it into the pot.

"Can you put the chickens in?"

Peg nodded, picked up the two chickens, and plopped them into the water. They settled to the bottom.

"I got some spices from the kitchen." He sprinkled atop the water the chopped leaves. "Rosemary."

"Tad, a picnic, with you!" Peg grinned.

"Ain't for us." He stirred the spice into the water.

"Ain't?"

"Smell that?" He waved a hand over the steam. "Before long, the smell will hit the soldiers, and they'll pay to eat the chickens."

Peg bit her lip. "But they got food."

"Have you seen it? More like a tummy ache, for sure."

The water boiled and the scent lifted onto the wind. The longer the food cooked, the stronger the smell, and the more Tad's mouth watered. "Maybe we should eat one of the ch—"

The brush rustled and they both turned.

A soldier called out. "Smell's coming from this direction."

"Over there!" Another soldier burst through the bushes. "Why, it's just a couple of children."

There was a rush to Tad and Peg's fire, and suddenly a dozen troopers surrounded them.

"That's chicken," a soldier said. His narrow face and short hair gave him the appearance of a fish. "Boiling chicken." He licked his thin lips. "Smells better than hardtack dipped in coffee."

"I'm just cooking it for me and my friend." Tad hunched over the pot, protecting it from their view.

The fish soldier glanced at his friends, then reached into his pocket. "Here, I've got a shiny coin, no wait, here's two, one for you and one for your friend."

"They twenty-dollar coins?"

The soldier snickered. "No, boy, they're pennies. Twenty dollars, that's almost two month's pay."

"Don't you got food? This is me and Peg's chickens."

"There's more than one chicken?"

"Two." Peg held up her fingers.

The soldier squatted down to their level and leaned his elbows on his knees. "Well, let me explain about army food. It's horrible. And what's worse, it rarely comes warm. And what you've got there is warm food. Good food."

Tad slowly stirred the water in the pot. "Hard to find chickens, almost have to pay more'n a couple bricks of 'baccy."

The fish soldier brushed his nose. "Soldiering's mighty hard. Sometimes it takes a bit more food to keep us going. What would you take for the chickens?"

"A rifle."

The soldiers laughed.

"This boy would live just fine in New York," the spokesman said. "No, can't trade a rifle. How about a cartridge box? You can hold six ears of corn in it."

Tad weighed the offer. "And four cents."

The fish-faced soldier called for a few Indian heads.

"For a drumstick, I'll give you two," one soldier said.

The soldiers grabbed sticks and speared the chickens. They lifted the food from the pot.

Tad shoved the cartridge box in his bag, pocketed two pennies, and when they were well on their way home, gave the other two to Peg.

She held them up to the sun. "Money makes the pot lighter."

Tad had hoped his plan would work, and now he found himself the proud owner of a prized piece of soldiery. Everyone knew the army had the best supplies.

Peg kept playing with her pennies. "Ain't never had no money."

"There will be more." Tad whistled a happy tune.

Peg interrupted his song. "Tad, what you doin' with your money?"

"I'll find a way to trade for more, to trade back to the soldiers, and keep trading better'n better."

"I mean, what then? You gonna buy a fine horse? Or a nice suit? Oh, or maybe travel? See things there is to see?"

Tad waved his arm. "All of it. Any of it! I'm wanting to do what the whim takes me to do. Can't do that without proper tools, and the ways I learned it, that's cash, or a means to sell for cash." He scratched his head. "Cash. A right good name. When Mammy gives me my new name, it'll be Cash."

Peg was quiet for a moment. "Tad, you ever think on startin' a family? Maybe settlin' down to grow some young'ns?"

Tad eyed her. "Maybe I thought of it, maybe not. Doesn't mean nothing 'til I can trade up to some money. With freedom, we can do whatever we want, long as we got money. And if I ain't soldiering yet, we can be finding cash."

Peg's eyes flashed, and she smiled. Under her breath, she whispered, "We."

⊗

Trading, trading, and more trading. With Mammy. With Bo. With others on the Frogmore. He returned to the soldiers' camp with corn bread, heading straight to the fish-faced soldier. The soldiers put orders in for more corn bread. Lots of it.

"Mr. Soule, I need corn."

The supervisor took a strong puff on his cigar. Tad imagined devils swirling around his head. "Food's hard to come by, Tad. We'll have just enough to get by before the harvest is in." He dropped his cigar in the dirt and leaned against a large red-stained wheel.

"But I can pay, Mr. Soule. I've got to buy two dollars' worth."

The supervisor straightened his vest over his wide paunch and considered Tad. "I'd wonder where you got the two dollars, if I hadn't gotten to know you so well over these past few months. Come on, follow me."

He pulled a long, thick iron key from his vest and walked toward the tabby barn. "We'll measure out some corn for you. I'd hoped to sell the lot I have now, and pay wages with it until the cotton's been harvested. But selling some to you won't do harm. Your buying and selling is wonderful, if you ask me."

Soule swung open the door and Tad walked in first.

After the summer heat outside, the cool air in the tabby barn felt refreshing. Tad's eyes adjusted to the dark, and he dodged poles that stretched to the roof. There were no bins, no stalls, just a large, open room used to store food. A single window let in the sun at the far end. The light fell on a pile of fresh corn, the husks still wrapped around each ear.

In the center of the room hung a weigh scale, suspended from the ceiling by chains. The older man made his way past the scale to the corn. "When I was near your age, corn cost twenty-five cents a bushel. In Beaufort it's selling for a dollar seventy-five." He reached down and picked up an ear and the pile tumbled toward Tad's feet.

"Two bushels for two dollars?" Tad asked, full of hope.

Soule reached into his vest pocket and pulled out a cigar, bit off one end, then struck a match. The light flashed and burned bright as he puffed. He flicked away the match. After filling his lungs with smoke, he blew out a long stream. "Bushel and a half."

"Two bushels to me, and money and corn bread to you? Corn bread from Mammy?"

The supervisor removed the cigar from his mouth. He wiggled the gray strands of hair that stuck out from his nose. He coughed, shook his nose hairs again, and finally nodded. "You drive a bargain as good as any trader. Measure out your two bushels, then set what's yours in the opposite corner. You can store your goods there."

"Thank you, Mr. Soule." Tad felt grown up, warmed to the trading life.

Soule had turned to leave but paused. He looked at Tad with a grin. "We'll make a white boy of you yet."

Tad watched him leave. The thought never occurred to him. Make him a white boy? A white boy like Collin? He shivered. Was there something wrong with the way he was?

He would be better than any white boy, white soldier, white teacher. He would use the Northern invaders, their way of trade, their methods and manners. *They're my slaves. They just didn't know it.* He smiled.

He carefully measured the first bushel, weighed it at seventy pounds, and with the muscles he'd gained in the fields, lifted the entire bag with one arm to his section of the tabby barn. Another seventy meant a total of one hundred and forty pounds of corn, a tidy pile in its own right.

Tad took a bucket of corn to the kitchen to shell. Grasping the ear with his sore arm, he stripped the brown husk with his good hand. He turned the cob with his other hand. Bright yellow kernels fell into a wooden bucket, dropping like rain.

He hummed to keep himself company, then burst into song.

*"Fire, my Savior fire,*
*Satan's camp a fire.*
*Fire, believer, fire,*
*Satan's camp a fire."*

The kitchen door opened. "Lordy me, what's with all this singin' and corn, Tad?"

"Mammy, I done bought corn from Mistah Soule, and I'm gonna cook up some of the best corn bread for the soldiers."

She put a hand to her chest. "You's wantin' to cook?" Her eyes rolled toward heaven. "Lordy, do tell me what has become of my Tad; he done disappeared. I suppose you'll be wantin' my help?"

"I can pay, soon as I get paid."

"Ah, I see, on account, like all them supervisors. I suppose." She snatched an ear, and in five seconds shelled it. "Reckon my boy might as well be my massah. You come by this corn honest?"

"'Course, Mammy." He told her of the latest trade, and the pile of husks grew as the bucket filled with corn. "Am I like a white boy? I mean, I got lighter skin and all. Why's that? And I don't think like some others on the island. I like trading. Why, Mammy, why?"

She sighed. "I can't tell if you're growin' up or if the supervisors done give you all these questions." She shelled two ears, her hands flying over the husks. "You got a mind of your own, boy. One with a head for learnin' like yours'll fit in wherever or whatever you do."

"Didn't make Massah none too happy."

"Bless you, child, there was many a better massah, for sure, and many a far worse."

Corn silk tickled Tad's nose. He brushed it away. "Did Massah sell Pappy?"

Silence hung in the room. Mammy leaned her elbows on her knees, her hands frozen over the bucket, a half-shelled corncob in her hands.

Tad pressed on. "Why am I so light-colored, Mammy? Why am I lighter than you? Was Pappy light-skinned?"

She wiped away a tear. Tad touched her hand. "Your pappy done run, just when I was needing him." She sniffed. "And he was as black as night. Now, I don't wanna talk anymore on the subject. We've got more shelling, then we gots to crush all these kernels. Lordy, where my boy get all these questions?"

The next morning, Tad and Peg walked away from the soldiers' camp with a musket, five dollars, and several rounds of shot and powder.

He and Peg wandered by the Tombee plantation. There, Tad struck another deal for food.

Excited, he raced to the Frogmore, borrowed a wagon, hitched Buster, and returned to the supervisor at Tombee. Tad traded the musket and ammunition for goods. Watermelons and corn, nearly twenty dollars' worth, were loaded on the wagon.

"No harm in this," the Tombee supervisor said. "Best to keep weapons out of the freedmen's hands, and Mr. Pierce's request for guns was never approved. We need the extra protection."

Tad unloaded the food in the tabby barn and split a sweet watermelon with Peg. They basked in the hot, sultry day. The marsh winds cooled them under the oak's shade.

Soule stepped off the porch of the big house and walked slowly over. "Fine work, Tad. I just looked in the barn. You've done well for yourself."

"That's right." Tad wiped juice from the side of his mouth. "Peg helped too."

Her eyes flashed a smile as she spit out a seed.

Soule leaned back and stuck a thumb through his suspenders. Sweat stains on his white shirt stretched in wide, round circles under his arms and down his chest. "I have a favor to ask, which may be an opportunity for you. Mr. Philbrick, the supervisor at Coffin Point, sent several plantations a note asking for food. He's short victuals, and willing to pay. Would you sell him your food? Today?"

Supervisors asking him for favors. This was fine, mighty fine. "I'll go now."

Peg sighed but agreed to join him.

Fifteen miles lay between the Land's End and Coffin Point. Frogmore was in the center. They had gone to Land's End earlier to sell the corn bread, one end of the island. Coffin Point rested on the other.

They discussed school as they walked, Buster pulling the cart behind. Both agreed school was something to take up, and quickly. Tomorrow, if possible. White man's world must be learned. Tad regretted running away, and he admitted it to Peg.

She pointed her nose into the air. "You've got to listen to me more. I knew you'd like it."

Coffin Point bordered St. Helena Sound. The thick marsh odor turned to a delicious ocean smell as they passed the front gate. A canopy of oaks and moss sheltered them from the sun as they walked the lane to the front of the house.

They stopped to stare at the sound. Water stretched north for miles until it crashed against the shore of Edisto Island. Beyond Edisto, the Confederates held Charleston.

Tad and Peg climbed the steps to the porch. The front door was open, catching the cool breezes crossing the water.

A woman stepped aside and smiled at them. "Hello, children. I'm Miss Ware. It's a little late for school today."

She reminded Tad of Miss Towne. "No, Miss Ware, I've come to see . . . " He struggled to remember the name. "Mr. Brick."

"Mr. Philbrick?" She laughed. "Now, why would you like to see him?"

Tad did his best to imitate the Northern accent. "Tell him— tell him I have a business deal for him."

The missionary smothered a smile. "Yes, sir. I will tell him immediately." She spun on her heel and disappeared into the house.

Tad and Peg turned to watch children play along the water's edge.

"Peg, that look fun to you?"

"I reckon it does."

"Me too."

Heavy footsteps pounded across the porch and stopped behind them. They turned to see a tall white man with a fine, handsome mustache. He was a bit intimidating.

His eyes twinkled. "To what do I owe the honor of this visit?"

"My name is Tad, and this is Peg." He pointed toward her.

"Tad, eh? I heard Mr. Pierce speak of you."

"I have food I'm willing to trade." Tad motioned to the side of the porch. They wound around several chairs and a table. At the rail, they leaned over to see Buster and the wagonload of food.

Philbrick sucked in a deep breath. "That's a lot of food."

"I can sell part of it, if you like."

"No, no, I need it, I just didn't expect . . . " He looked down at Tad.

"I'm looking to sell," Tad said after a moment of silence.

"Is this food from your plantation?"

"No, it's mine, I traded for it."

Philbrick glanced back at the wagon and nodded slowly. "I don't have that much cash on me today, Tad. But perhaps, if you're willing to trade, we might have a deal."

"What have you got?"

Philbrick led them across the yard to the barn, where he

swung open the double doors. Inside, tall stacks of cotton bales rose to the rafters. "I can trade one of these for your wagon of food."

Tad groaned. His field was filled with budding cotton. "Got anything else?"

"No, I don't. But this cotton may go for twenty-five cents a pound, depending on who you sell it to."

Tad's interest renewed. "Reckon they're three hundred pounds!"

"That's right."

Tad walked into the barn. He felt along a seam in the bag that enclosed the cotton. "That's near seventy-five dollars, for only one bale."

Philbrick grunted. "You're pretty quick with math."

Tad turned and stuck out his chest. "And I can read." He took a step toward Philbrick. "I won't be taking charity. Half a bag is more than the food's worth."

"It's not charity." Philbrick sat on a bale that protruded from the mountain of cotton. "It's simple. Supply and demand. I've made it no secret I need food. Desperately. No one wants to trade with me, and the food you brought could last us a week. I've got hungry people, and when they're hungry, they can't work."

He continued. "When the masters left, they couldn't take their cotton with them. The cotton agents sold all the bales, but not here, not at Coffin Point. We kicked the agent out before he could sell it. But we've eaten all the food. So we're cotton rich and food poor. That makes the price of my cotton go down, and food prices go up."

Tad absorbed Mr. Philbrick's logic. "And after I trade, I hope the price of cotton will go up."

"Exactly, yes. That's right."

Tad sniffed. "I still see some charity."

"Some. I admit. But remember, when you find more food, who will you sell it to?"

"You, of course." Tad smiled as understanding dawned on him.

They shook hands and went to unload the food.

Tad had burning questions, so he started with an easy one. "Mr. Philbrick, we ain't . . . I mean, we aren't poor, do you think? Compared to where Mr. Pierce lives."

He whistled. "That's a profound question, Tad. To the North, you're wretchedly poor. But you seem happy, your entire race, and in my eyes it makes you rich. You've places to sleep, family, friends, and some food. You don't seem to want much more."

"Then why do *I* want more?"

He stopped to consider. "I don't know. Some of you take to the Northern way of life quickly, as if you've always known how it works. A little training, Tad, and you could be quite successful."

Hadn't that been what Mr. Pierce's last note had said to him?

*Find something to trade, Tad, and take it to the soldiers. If you can trade up, you will acquire wealth, then leverage to find financial success. Do well, and perhaps, someday, when we can, we will see each other again under better circumstances.*

# THIRTY

$\mathcal{T}$he thermometer in the summer of 1862 hovered near ninety-five degrees. As October came, the temperature plummeted to the fifties.

When Tad wasn't hoeing weeds or picking cotton, he continued to trade. He gave Peg cash for melons from her garden and traded them to nearby plantations for corn. He piled up the corn in the tabby barn, and after accumulating a hill of husks, hauled wagonloads to Coffin Point to trade for another bale of cotton.

Was money freedom? Tad decided it was, or at least it gave him some freedoms others didn't have. When he walked along the cabins waving money to entice others to help pick his cotton, eager friends joined him in the field.

Before long, Tad owned several bales of cotton.

Cool weather swept across the island. Tad's muscles were tested by hauling marsh mud, bucket after bucket, to cover his field. His healed arms bulged.

Swinging ax and driving shovel, he expanded the wide swath of land waiting for more cottonseeds. His chest thickened.

In the evenings, after eating dinner with Peg, Bo, Mammy, Soule, and a few of the others, he used a dim candle to illuminate the pages in the books Miss Towne loaned him. Though he attended school with some regularity, the field often needed his attention and kept him away. He learned more from the books, anyway.

Freedmen moved onto the island. Soule sat on the big house's front porch, and Tad asked where they came from.

"Edisto Island." The supervisor pulled the cigar from his mouth. He leaned back in the rocker. "General Hunter sent the soldiers protecting the island to Washington, so no one was guarding the people. That's why they moved the freedmen here."

"Reckon that's why they took Buster?" Tad asked. "The soldiers need him to help the new folks?"

"Probably." The supervisor looked at him with a sad smile.

Later that day, Tad sat and leaned his back against a tree within sight of Mammy's kitchen. He took a bite of thick bread and let the gritty taste calm the raging hunger. He was surprised when, instead of Peg or Mammy, a black man stepped around the corner. He opened the kitchen door and went in. His white shirt and loosely tied silk bow tie made Tad wish he could dress in something other than the rags he wore. And why not? After the sale of the cotton back to Mr. Philbrick, he was rich.

Five minutes later, the door opened and the man left the tiny cabin. He paused and looked around.

The man's gaze rested on Tad and he passed the slave quarters toward him. "Are you Tad?" His voice was as silky as his shirt.

"I am, yes, sir."

"Do you have time for a story?"

"A story? Maybe."

The man hunched down beside him, ducking his head into the cedar's shade. "My name's Robert Smalls."

"You talk pretty, Mr. Smalls."

"Thank you, Tad. I've worked hard to do so. You're not too bad yourself. I'm from around here, or was. I freed myself."

Mr. Smalls sat on a tree root that thrust from the ground. He lowered his voice. "I was the pilot aboard a ship called the *Planter.*"

Tad leaned forward.

"We hauled supplies for President Davis—ammunition, bandages, artillery, food. We were right off the coast, in the harbor at Charleston. My family was also aboard, along with other slaves. Not a white man on deck. The captain trusted me. Let me ask you. What would you do?"

"I'd take to the sea."

He folded his hands and nodded. "It was easy as anything to fire up the boilers and push out into the harbor, leave Charleston behind. A fort waited for us at the entrance, but I knew the code, and blasted the whistle at the right times. We steamed past the forts out into the open ocean, under the morning sun." Smalls laughed. "It was even easier after that. All we had to do was find a blockade ship and surrender the *Planter*. For that, I was called a hero."

Tad sat up straight.

"I still sail the *Planter.*" He leaned back and reached his arm over his head, relaxing. "But for the Union, of course. Have you thought of what you could do for the Union?"

A thrill shot up Tad's spine. "Be a soldier!"

"To be a soldier," Smalls said slowly, "is to be a part of the greatest profession. But that has been denied us by a world that doesn't understand we're given rights by the Constitution, the same as white folks. It's simple, Tad. We've got to convince them we can be soldiers and merchants." He looked into the distance. "And sailors."

"I traded as a merchant, like Mr. Pierce told me to."

Smalls nodded and smiled. "And that is commendable. Almost brilliant, and that's part of why I'm here." He glanced at the surrounding trees and lowered his voice. "General Hunter and General Saxton have failed."

Tad looked up, confused. "They're doing a fine job."

"Oh yes, they are doing well, don't get me wrong. But they have failed, nonetheless. Remember the conscription a while back? The First South Carolina Volunteers has been disbanded. While there are a few hundred soldiers that still drill, they're not paid."

"I don't mind not getting paid."

"Yes, Tad, that's also why I'm here—your enthusiasm. General Saxton has impressed General Hunter to make another attempt at a regiment, this time appealing to the government in Washington. A delegation, made up of Reverend French and myself, are going. We'd like you to come with us."

"I'm not going to be a soldier?" Tad's heart sank.

Smalls shrugged. "Each man serves his country as best he can."

Tad stood and kicked a rock. "I'd like to go, but Mammy won't let me. Mr. Pierce tried once before."

"I spoke with her." Smalls stood, straightened his fine linen shirt, and smiled with a broad, white-toothed grin. "I already have her permission."

When the soldiers came for Tad, Miss Towne was with them. She spoke with Mammy in the kitchen. "General Hunter asked me to review the troops with him. I'll make sure Tad gets on the correct steamer with Mr. Smalls."

Mammy smiled when she heard Mr. Smalls' name.

Eight soldiers stood in formation in the slave quarters while Tad said good-bye to his tearful friends and family.

"You's a special boy." Mammy pressed his head to her ample chest. "Someday the world's got to know how special you are. Lord knows I can't keep you locked on this plantation forever. You got to be free. You just come back to me, you hear?"

"Yes, Mammy." Now that the time came, he didn't want to go. He took a few calming breaths.

Bo slapped his back, and Soule shook his hand. "We're proud of you."

He felt a hand slip into his, the calloused skin sending tingles through his body. Peg leaned against him, kissed his cheek, and ran.

He touched where her soft lips had brushed against his cheek and stared after her.

"Lordy me, the child is growin' up." Tears brimmed in Mammy's eyes. "She's goin' to miss you, boy, more'n you'd guess."

Tad fingered his necklace, then slipped the leather strap over his head. "Tell Peg I'm coming back to get it." He handed Mammy the tiny cross.

He settled in the small carriage with Miss Towne. Next to her were more books for his trip to Washington, and he tucked them into his knapsack.

He enjoyed the hour he spent crossing the island, but he'd never ridden with such a terrible driver. The wheels rolled this way and that while she chatted.

Tad settled into the soft red seat and listened.

"If Reverend French is able to create support for a Negro regiment, then I will think better of him. At least I hope there will be a reprieve from his arguments over sacraments."

"Sacraments?"

"He wants only Baptists to partake of communion, no freedmen outside of the African Baptist. I'm Unitarian, so I'm excluded."

"You mean juice and cracker?"

Miss Towne smiled. "Yes, juice and cracker."

A branch slapped at the roof, and Tad ducked. "Massah let us take juice and cracker, but they asked us first if Jesus came to deliver us from our wrongdoings."

Miss Towne cocked her head to the side. "I think if we are good men and women, there will be nothing to worry about."

"If that was how God worked, wouldn't He let us know when we'd done enough to go to heaven?"

Miss Towne frowned, but nodded.

He reached up to touch his necklace, remembered it was with Peg, and closed his eyes. She was there, in the darkness of his mind, smiling at him, wishing him well on his journey to Washington.

# THIRTY ONE

*T*ad's head ached. Washington's lack of grand houses, fresh gardens, and open spaces crowded in on him. Once Reverend French and Mr. Smalls' carriage pushed through the capital's earthworks and cannons, they entered the overcrowded center of town.

The brick and stone buildings, connected by dirty snow and piles of cans and broken carts, reminded him of Charleston. The roads were narrow passages filled with busy people. The smell of horse manure filled the air.

At home, whitewashed slave cabins were tucked under the umbrella of oaks. He missed the cart paths that passed under tunnels of leafy green. Tad wished he were preparing his field under South Carolina's bright sun.

Smalls and Tad spoke of home, but little else. Reverend French watched out the window of their cab, and after a lull in the conversation, leveled a warning look at Tad. "Remember to keep silent. You're to be seen. Not heard."

Tad held back a reply. French had hardly spoken to him at all, and if he did, it was usually a command.

Politicians and businessmen met them on street corners and in parlors. Robert Smalls took the brunt of Northern curiosity, since he was a war hero, and told any who would listen of how the slaves in Port Royal were learning to be an important part of the free society.

Eyes turned to Tad, but no one spoke to him. While he ate strange food and listened to boring speeches, each night showed him something new. Generals with elegant uniforms, buildings that towered into the sky, or women wearing colorful dresses filled his mind.

"We haven't done any real work yet," Smalls warned.

Tad looked up to the hero. Was any of this work? None of it made blisters.

After several days of watching Reverend French and Smalls meet people, and nights sleeping in a hotel, they met with Secretary of the Treasury Salmon Chase.

"General Saxton has done an excellent job." Secretary Chase sat behind a desk. He twiddled his thumbs as he thought. After a moment, he continued. "And I like General Hunter. He's doing a fine job, despite taking matters into his own hands by creating a regiment. I'm most satisfied he's allowed Tad to come. I know of you, Reverend French, but you, Mr. Smalls, I'd like to hear your story in your own words."

Fifteen minutes later, as Smalls finished the story of the Planter, the room fell silent. Secretary Chase leaned forward. "Most excellent. Fine work. I see a future in politics for you. You would be an excellent voice for the freedmen."

"Thank you, sir." Smalls bowed his head.

Tad gulped down the lump in his throat, glanced at Reverend French, and decided his need to speak was too important to hold back. "Secretary Chase?"

French slowly shook his head.

The secretary leaned forward, his hands folded together. "Yes, Tad?"

"How do you know me?"

"Why, that's simple. Edward Pierce spoke highly of you."

"Mistah Pierce, he done talked with you?" Tad forgot to speak like a Northern man.

"Mr. Pierce and I are close friends." He frowned. "Or used to be. He's in Boston now, with his law practice. I've told him how disappointed I am with his leaving you."

As they stepped out of Secretary Chase's office, French leaned down. "You have done well up to this point." Tad could feel the older man's musty breath on his cheeks. "But you should not have spoken. Keep quiet. We go now to the War Department, where Secretary Stanton holds all our hopes to create this regiment. One word from him, and all can be gained or lost."

Tad folded his hands together and bowed his head. What did he do wrong?

Secretary Stanton sat behind a desk much like Secretary Chase's. The two offices were similar; both had books, both were well lit. Secretary Stanton's beard split into two long gray and yellow streaks that fell in front of his chest. Tiny spectacles rested on his prominent nose. While Secretary Chase's eyes had held mischief, Secretary Stanton's were soft and kind. Tad listened to his voice, deep but sharp, quick, and clear. His questions were direct.

"Are the freedmen willing to drill, or are they lawless?"

French sat straight. "Freedmen drill with perfect obedience, respecting authority and understanding the need for regular discipline."

"Will the black regiments take casualties?"

Smalls gripped the arms of his chair. "He has, and he will."

"The North may not be ready for a black man to take up arms. Do the freedmen understand that?"

Smalls shifted. "No."

"Can we comfortably entrust a black man with noncommissioned officer status?"

"I am a noncommissioned officer." Smalls' face was solemn. "Have I disappointed?"

"We want men of initiative. Tad, will you fight?"

Tad, lost in the questions, jumped. "Will I fight?"

Stanton held out an open hand as if inviting him to speak.

"Yes, sir. I will fight."

Stanton smiled, and said slowly, "Does the idea of fighting your former masters upset you?"

Tad tried not to swing his feet. Excitement filled him. He said the first thing that popped into his mind, from the days he and Collin played in the pine forest together. "George Washington got to fight for his freedom. Didn't he fight against his former masters?"

Stanton's belly bounced with laughter. "Good point, I must say. I suppose if we don't let you fight, we're no better than Southern plantation owners. How do you feel about the Northern influence on your islands?"

"There is good people and bad people. Mostly good."

"Yes, of course. I see. There are bad and good in any race, in any regional division." Stanton pulled paper from a drawer in his desk then dipped a quill into an inkwell. The only sound for nearly a minute was the scratching of his pen.

Tad leaned forward and spoke in a quiet voice. "Sir, I hear you can make things happen, important things. If you say it, it's done."

Stanton looked up, over the top rim of his glasses. "Judicially, yes."

"Can you sign me into being a soldier?"

Stanton considered it a moment. "I will leave that up to General Hunter." He wrote a few more words and he paused again. "You're not the first, you know, to have a commissioned black regiment. I've authorized Massachusetts to train Negro soldiers. They're forming next year."

Stanton handed the document to French, and outside the office, he read it aloud. Tad watched their reactions. The words on the paper made French happy and Smalls grave. It allowed General Hunter, financed through the government, to begin his regiment, officially the First South Carolina Volunteers. The freedmen of Port Royal were going to war.

❧

Abolitionists from Washington threw a party at a mansion that overlooked a narrow river. Tad and his friends were guests of honor.

Two tall, white, thick columns framed the door. As they entered, men and women surrounded French and Smalls.

Tad wandered across the stone floor, under a sparkling chandelier, and settled next to a small tree that grew from a pot. He thought of slipping out the front door, ripping off his fine jacket purchased for the party, and running into the cold night.

He watched Smalls stand on the first step of the staircase that stretched up the center of the room. A crowd gathered to listen to his stories. French joined the war hero, held out his arms, and started a speech.

Tad sighed.

After several minutes, French just warming up, a tall woman slid through the crowd, as if she were a swan on water. Tad couldn't take his eyes off her. Her plain brown dress paled next to the lively blues, purples, and reds worn by the other women. Her black skin and dark eyes stood apart from the white faces. She stood a head taller than most men.

She stopped in front of him, ignoring the ongoing speech. Her long arm reached out and rested her fingers against a statue close to Tad. "Lonely here?" Her voice was deep and somber.

"I is." She scared him, her appearance and forward manners.

"Gullah." She looked at him, an amused look on her face. "Low country?"

"I is."

"I haven't met many from South Carolina." She flashed a wide grin then turned serious. "Was a slave in New York." She looked back to the crowd and sighed. "We's lost in wave of noble sentiment and good intention, ain't we." Her hand slipped from the statue and hovered in front of Tad. "I'm Sojourner Truth."

"Tad." Someone understood his talk, so far from home. He shook her hand.

"Well, Tad, follow Jesus, and all troubles will fly away."

"That's what the Good Book says."

"Well, you just listen to what your mammy and pappy says, you should be fine. We'll be free, one time or another, if it ain't in life, it'll be in death. And the good Lord knows, oh, He knows how we ache. I work with all of them, in the fields, and then run away from the massahs. Like the men. And ain't I a woman?"

Tad wished Peg could meet Sojourner Truth. He was about to ask her what slavery was like in New York when French's voice paused.

Tad noticed people in the room had turned toward him.

He backed into the potted plant. His heart raced.

No one spoke until a man asked, "What was it like, slavery?"

Another man stepped forward. "Why should we let the Negro fight?"

Questions came at him from all sides, and quickly.

"You were a slave?"

"Can you read?"

He nodded.

"Do you like President Lincoln?"

"Can you kill a man?"

"How did they treat you, as a slave?"

The last question rang like a bell through the large room. Tad turned to Sojourner Truth and realized it was she who had asked the question. She repeated it. "How did the masters treat you, Tad?"

Tad's breathing came in short gasps. He wanted to run, but the way was blocked by a mass of suits. Too many people. They stared at him, as if he were a strange brand of cotton the massahs had just produced. He shrank away.

Sojourner Truth stood erect, gave him a little nod, and said in a quiet voice, "I'm a woman, Tad; I can't show them."

Tad realized then what she wanted. If the Negro were to be free, to create sympathy in the North, they would need to know, not through books or rumors, but through their own eyes. He lowered his head.

His fingers trembled as he slid off his jacket and dropped it on the marble floor. He tugged the bow tie from around his neck. Then he pulled on the collar. The first button of his shirt easily came undone, but he couldn't get the second one.

He looked up. No one moved. The silent onlookers tensed.

With a sigh, he unhooked the next button, and the next, until a good deal of chest was revealed.

Tad turned and dropped his shirt to the polished floor.

"Dear God, no!" several cried. Men and women whispered to one another.

Cool air brushed against Tad's naked back. He hung his head in shame.

How could they know how deep the thick scars really were?

Sojourner Truth bent to his side, picked up his shirt, and helped him put it on. "That will do," she said so only he could hear. "Jesus was striped, and so were you. You have a piece of the good Lord with you."

Tad nodded.

She buttoned his shirt and wiped away a tear with a handkerchief. A man with a waxed mustache stepped forward. "Tad, let me shake your hand. You're a hero, boy."

Tad numbly took his hand, and the man pumped it.

Another came forward and offered his hand. "Good lad."

They formed a silent line, and each whispered words of consolation in his ear. "I'm so sorry," a woman said before she rushed away.

Some put money into his jacket pocket. Others simply cried. After the last person walked by, their shock turned to debate on how to free the rest of the slaves.

Tad handed Sojourner Truth the money. "Take this. Maybe more can be freed."

She squeezed his shoulder. "Boy, you may have just done more to change the minds of these rich'ns than anybody else. Jesus bless you. All because you done what's needed to be done."

Smalls gave a speech, thrilling the crowd with his tale of escape, and then the party ended.

Reverend French approached Tad, his tie loosened. "I saw you were given money. Good, now your travel expenses are paid."

"I gave the money away."

"You what?"

Smalls approached. "President Lincoln has paid for our travel. Leave the boy alone."

French paled. "Of course, yes, I wasn't thinking." He took a deep breath and stared at Tad. "We must meet with Lincoln tomorrow, but you are not to come."

Smalls frowned.

French continued. "Lincoln recently lost his son. Tad may bring back painful memories."

Tad didn't understand. "You mean his boy was black like me?"

Smalls burst into laughter, but French shook his head and hurried from the building.

"Mr. Smalls, if I have a day to myself, can I have a request of what to do with it?"

"Of course, what would you like?"

# THIRTY TWO

*T*ad could barely wait for his train ride to Boston to end. Steam billowed from the engine as he leapt from the train car, not touching the steps. Dressed in his fancy suit, he weaved past tall men in uniforms, and women in wide, swishing dresses. A kind gentleman at the ticket office helped him with directions.

Boston streets, many paved in cobblestone, were squeezed in between three- and four-story buildings, some even taller. Not many people of his skin color wandered the city.

Spying his destination, Tad stepped off the sidewalk, passed two parked carriages, and crossed the street to a three-story building. Four steps led to the front door. He knocked softly.

No one answered. He knocked again. Still, no one. Fighting nerves, he reached for the handle and carefully pushed the door open. The hinges creaked. When the door swung wide enough, he thrust his head inside. A young man sat at a desk at the end of the hallway, working intently with a book and pencil. He glanced up, spotted Tad, and grinned. "Why, hello there. Come in. Can I help you? Did you knock?"

Tad crept inside and closed the door behind him. He nodded. "I knocked." He took off his tall hat and held it in his hands.

"Sometimes I don't hear very well. What is your name?"

Tad shifted his weight from one foot to the other. "I'm here to see someone."

From the second story, boots pounded, as if a soldier marched across a hardwood floor.

A man started down from the top of the stairs. "Mr. Donning, please . . . " The man looked at Tad and froze. The papers in his hands slipped from his fingers and floated over the banister onto Mr. Donning's head.

"Mr. Pierce!"

"Tad." Pierce choked, his voice a whisper. Tears welled in his eyes. "Tad!"

Pierce bounded down the stairs.

Tad rushed across the room to throw himself into Pierce's waiting arms.

"How I missed you, Tad!"

"I had to see you, Mr. Pierce. I just had to."

Pierce stepped back, rubbed his eyes, then tousled Tad's thick hair. "I'm so glad you did."

Pierce hadn't changed at all. Tad thought he might be shorter, but he still had brown hair and long, thick burns across his cheeks. "I came to ask you when you were coming back."

"Tad, let me introduce my secretary, Mr. Donning. Mr. Donning, this is—"

"Tad." Mr. Donning held out a hand and winked. "I've heard all about you." He crossed his arms. "And about Miss Towne."

"We miss you, Mr. Pierce. When you coming back?"

He frowned. "I can't, Tad. Too many court cases coming up. How long are you in town? Can you stay for a few days? You'll stay with me, of course."

"I have to leave tonight."

Pierce's excitement noticeably dimmed. "Well, suppose we get something to eat, and I must introduce you to someone. My, have you grown. Look at you in a suit. And your speech could pass as an educated young man. You've changed."

They took a carriage to a small café near the outskirts of

town, where Pierce asked questions, barely pausing for breath. He asked after Miss Towne's health. "I received a letter from her. She wants to start a school in the Old Brick Church, call it the Penn School. I hope you will attend."

Tad finished the last bite of fish. "I already know the things they teach. She lends me books." He set down his fork and settled back in his chair. "Mr. Pierce, Secretary Chase said you were a friend of his, but not much anymore. Why is that?"

A sad smile flickered on his face. "His daughter . . . she and I . . . it's difficult to explain. She and I used to be close friends, but she's found another. I just needed a little time by myself, without her father's influence. Soon, we'll be the best of friends again."

The look on Pierce's face told Tad there was more, but he decided to drop it.

After dinner, Pierce drove him deep into the countryside, where he watched rolling hills rising into the sky like islands. A large bank of clouds threatened rain.

They turned off the main road onto a small lane that bordered a long fence, stopping at a low, two-story house. Tad couldn't remember ever seeing such a large home fronted with such a tiny porch.

Inside, Pierce introduced two men. The first, Robert Gould Shaw, gave Tad a quick glance then returned to his drink and journal. "He's probably my best friend in the world," Pierce said.

The second man was thin but filled with nearly as much energy as Pierce. Mr. Garrison slapped Tad on the back and welcomed him. "I may have someone here you'd like to meet." The bald man winked at Pierce.

Tad sat on a couch while Garrison left the room for a moment. Suddenly Samuel's huge form filled the small parlor.

When he saw Tad, the big man leapt into the air and clapped his hands. "That you, Tad?"

Tad jumped to his feet and rushed to Samuel, but tripped on the center rug.

With massive arms, the driver lifted him and set him carefully on his feet.

"You ran." Tad could barely keep from yelling. "And you're free!"

"I'm free, thank the Lord, I'm free." The big man savored the words, as if speaking them to God. "And what's more, Captain Shaw's going to be leading a regiment. I'm one of the first to sign up."

Tad glanced at Shaw. "Where's his uniform?"

Pierce sighed and motioned they go to another room. When they arrived in the dining room, Pierce kept his voice quiet. "He's a captain—will be promoted to major, maybe colonel. They're to go to Readville to drill, but he's not sure he will take the regiment. I've pressed that he does, as does his father and mother. And what his mother says, he'll do."

Shaw seemed too small to be in charge of anything. General Hunter, back at Hilton Head, wasn't a large man, but looked the part of a soldier, and Shaw did not.

Tad left Samuel and went to stand at the captain's side. "Sir." At Tad's voice, the captain looked up. "I'd like to join the regiment."

Shaw set down his journal and studied Tad. "Where are you from?"

Tad stood at attention. "South Carolina, sir."

"If the regiment ever fights in South Carolina, you can fight with us." His eyes shone in amusement, his voice soft and mellow.

It was the closest anyone had come to promising he could soldier. "Then I'll pray, sir, that you fight in South Carolina."

Shaw clasped Tad's shoulder. "But don't get your hopes up. We're ordered to go to Florida."

After hours of news, telling of Bo's leadership and the field that Samuel made Tad mud so long ago, it was a bitter farewell. The big man assured Tad better times were coming.

Tad boarded the train to return to Washington. He promised to write Pierce.

He joined Reverend French and Mr. Smalls on a steamer to Hilton Head, where they would report the good news to General Hunter. Black regiments would rise to drill, march, and learn to battle. But would anyone let them fight? Would Tad get his chance?

⚜

With General Saxton in charge of the freedmen, Tad enjoyed settling into a routine. The rules for 1863 were in place. But one more surprise came as the new year dawned. Thousands of freedmen were ferried to Smith's Plantation at Port Royal—Tad and Peg among them—for a grand party to welcome 1863.

Certain the party was a trap, Bo refused to go. "All of us in one place, and they send us all to Cuba. I know it."

Mammy stayed behind too, but most of Frogmore's residents loaded onto the boats.

Tad felt every bit of his fourteenth year, the strength and power that came with manhood. He sat in the boat, with Peg by his side, enthused for what lay ahead.

At Port Royal, two long rows of black soldiers stood at attention, rifles held against the right shoulder and pointed to the sky. The white cloth of the tents behind them stood in stark contrast to the blue uniform jackets and reddish-orange pantaloons.

The women, in dresses and wearing white kerchiefs in their hair, huddled in a circle chattering like sparrows. Their clothes used to be brown, before the soldiers came, but now were a patchwork of blues, greens, reds, and yellow. The children, fresh-faced and clean when they left the island, dashed through mud, trees, and grass, only to receive reprimands from their mothers. Men stood with their backs to the children, hands in suspenders or pockets, and discussed the new year and corn. The wind brought sounds of groaning trees.

Teachers and supervisors waited by tables covered with food. "Would you like something to drink?" a teacher asked them.

Tad studied the molasses-water mixture and decided they'd put in far too much water. He shook his head.

Peg picked up a mug.

"I'm going to get a closer look at that." Tad walked toward the artillery, Peg close behind.

He approached slowly, his heart beating to the rhythm of soldiers marching by. With a cautious reach, he touched the smooth spoke, the unmoving wheel almost as tall as he stood. His hand slid to the barrel. Despite the sun's warming rays, the iron was glossy cold. A chill ran up his spine.

"A ten-pound Parrott." Tad turned to see a white officer stepping close and smiling. "I've seen cannons as big as three hundred pounders."

Tad recalled the train ride from Washington, the defenses surrounding the capital. Fixed guns, some almost the size of the train car, lined Washington's border. "I saw them too."

Tad continued his walk. Nearby, a tent flap lay open. He ducked inside.

"You supposed to do that?" Peg called from the other side of the cloth.

Four green bedrolls lay in a pile near the back of the tent. A writing desk guarded the front door. "This is . . . wonderful."

Peg joined him. "Ugh." She brushed her nose. "It smells in here." She sneezed.

Tad shivered, not from cold, but at the majesty of it all. "Up by dawn for a march, a hot meal, a battle, then home by dark with stories."

A bell rang. Tad and Peg dashed into the sunlight. In the distance, crowds gathered around a tall stage, Miss Towne stood near the podium. Her face beamed at the small children around her. Miss Murray helped keep them quiet.

Philbrick took the stage, and Tad felt good to know the supervisor as a business partner, not as someone who ruled over him. The man brushed his mustache and crossed the platform. He promptly spoke on cotton and work. Someone else took the stage and read a poem. Songs drifted from the children, and the air filled with clapping and praises.

A hush fell over the crowd. Tad strained to see. An old man with a cane hobbled onto the stage, his back bent and face racked with pain. He knew the crippled man by sight. Everyone knew him. Dr. Brisbane limped past the flags and generals, the supervisors and teachers, and stopped at the podium.

No one moved. The only sound was flags snapping in the wind.

Before the North invaded the islands, before the war, Dr. Brisbane had freed his slaves. No master wanted his slaves to think they would be freed—hope made for bad control. But word passed quickly across the islands, out of earshot of the masters, and Dr. Brisbane became a hero.

Tad noticed Brisbane wasn't drunk. This was a bit of a surprise, since rumors claimed he loved the bottle. Instead, tears poured down his face. He held a piece of paper in his shaking hands. "President Lincoln penned a letter to you, and to the other slaves, a few months back." He adjusted his spectacles. "I'd like to read it to you."

*"That on the first day of January, in the year of our Lord one thousand eight hundred and sixty-three, all persons held as slaves within any State or designated part of a State, the people whereof shall then be in rebellion against the United States, shall be then,*

*thenceforward, and forever free; and the Executive Government of the United States, including the military and naval authority thereof, will recognize and maintain the freedom of such persons, and will do no act or acts to repress such persons, or any of them, in any efforts they may make for their actual freedom."*

"Tad." Peg nudged his arm. "Does that mean what I think it does?" She gripped him in a tight embrace, and he held her, both speechless.

Finally, Tad managed, "It does. Peg, we're free."

Thousands of freedmen cried silently, until one voice lifted into the wind.

*"My country, 'tis of thee,*
*Sweet land of liberty."*

Several other voices joined.

Like the nearby Broad River, they were all swept away. Mr. Pierce's face came to mind, the bitter fight to find a status for freedmen, and Tad wanted to rush to him, to tell him how much this meant. The air in his lungs felt of precious substance, no longer of the bitter leather that slashed his back, but of colors, of dreams, of gold and silver, of precious life and death.

A colonel was announced as the leader of the First South Carolina Volunteers, Colonel Higginson. He said, "You can sing the song 'My Country' for it truly is your country now."

The regimental flag was introduced, and Tad and Peg danced in circles with the freedmen. Salted pork was served, and it tasted wonderful.

On the boat ride home, Tad held Peg's hand.

# THIRTY THREE

$S$pring of 1863 brought rain to South Carolina's low country. But the forty degrees and wet weather wasn't enough to keep Tad from his fieldwork.

His diet of potatoes, corn, tomatoes, fish, and turtle soup gave him the energy he needed to work long hours outdoors and at night to continue the study of Miss Towne's books by candlelight.

He felt stronger and smarter.

When the time was right, Bo encouraged everyone at the Frogmore to plant the corn and cotton fields in a single day, so that they could return to their personal gardens all the sooner.

Tad worked the cornfield, along with everyone from the Frogmore. Plows, pulled by mules, churned the rich, moist soil. Tad's mule tired, and Soule volunteered to change it out for him. But the new mule smelled food nearby, and burst across the field. Soule's arm, wrapped in the lead rope, snapped like a branch.

Tad helped Soule into a wagon and drove him to The Oaks, where Miss Towne tended the suffering supervisor.

He patted Soule on the back. "I know how it feels."

Tad followed Miss Towne to school that morning. After Pierce had left, she'd set up the Penn School in the Old Brick Church, a short distance from The Oaks. Tad felt she did a good job as leader of the school.

He returned a book titled *Uncle Robin in His Cabin in Virginia and Tom Without One in Boston*. It was the South's response to *Uncle Tom's Cabin*. Tad explained the differences to Miss Towne. It was there she pressed Tad to speak of slavery.

"Wasn't much to tell." Tad looked out the window at a group of children surrounding a teacher. They seemed to be having fun. The temptation to run tugged at him.

"I would like to know more about you, Tad. Do you remember in *Gulliver's Travels* how the main character learned about the world of the Yahoos? I would like to do the same with you."

Tad shrugged his shoulders. After the lesson, rather than wait for Peg, he returned to Frogmore alone.

He ventured into the big empty house and found Soule's old desk. Soule would not be coming back. General Saxton thought the Frogmore had outgrown a supervisor under Bo's aged guidance, so he'd told Tad to warn the others that Soule was to be put in charge of the supervisors on the entire island, stationed at The Oaks. Tad could use the supplies he'd left behind.

He closed his eyes and thought back to the dangerous game he and Collin played, writing each other notes and hiding them. If caught, both could have received severe punishment, probably worse than a lashing.

But it had taught Tad to write.

He reached for a water-stained piece of paper in a drawer. He took a frayed quill, darkened on one end, and scratched the paper with it. The ink was thick and gooey.

They all wanted to know about slavery—Pierce, Soule, Gannett, Miss Towne, everyone except Philbrick, who seemed more interested in the ability to make money, which suited Tad. But they had kept at him, would not stop asking. A letter seemed the only way to tell what happened, how he'd gone from being a happy child to a lashed slave in a single afternoon.

His mind drifted to Collin, to the days so long ago, before

Mr. Spencer stripped away innocence. Tad dipped the quill in ink and touched the paper. *My friend was Collin.* He sighed. *He liked pie, too much.* The lashes, the salty brine thrown on his back, the mistake of entering Massah's house. Tad shivered. The terrible, terrible mistake.

He thought of Johnny, his lifeless body floating in the marsh.

The dream washed over Tad. He was a child again. He peered from behind the bushes once more, felt the sweat, the heat of the dark night, the fear. He heard the gunshot.

He reached out to push away the last cover of bush, to look into a small clearing. A big man, bigger than Samuel, stood alone, legs spread apart. Though he was but a shadow, Tad could see the big man's hands, the shape of a smoking pistol clutched in his fingers. A crumpled form lay below him. The man turned the gun toward him.

Something touched his shoulder. Tad flew backward, knocking his chair to the ground. He scooted into the corner and huddled there, shivering.

Peg knelt before him. "I'm sorry, Tad."

A cry escaped his lips. Tears ran down his cheeks.

"You're shaking," she whispered softly and touched his hand. "What's wrong? Somebody hurt you?"

He struggled to catch his breath, but he couldn't control the sobs. Or ease the ghastly picture from his mind.

Peg slipped an arm around him and pulled his head onto her shoulder. She ran her fingers through his hair, and he cried. He didn't know why, probably because Johnny was dead. Maybe because he sensed the man in his dream—the man standing over the body—was his father. He felt as though a rock, laden with sadness, had hit him and filled his chest. The fear of the dream remained as vivid awake as asleep.

He sensed her lips brush his forehead. She kissed his eye. Without thinking, he placed his lips against her soft cheek and kissed her. She lifted her chin. He looked deep into her eyes and found peace, a strong and gentle calm. He leaned forward and pulled her close. Their lips met. After a moment, they held each other. The house creaked in the gentle winds.

The next morning, Tad rushed to school. He hadn't told Mammy or Bo about the kiss, wasn't sure about it himself, and he didn't want to talk about it with Peg. So he left early, clutching the story he'd finished late last night.

A path led through the forest in a straight line from the Penn School to the nearby marsh. Miss Towne read Tad's story as he walked by her side. Without looking, she nimbly stepped over rocks, around mushrooms, through rotten leaves, and past sprouting saplings. She didn't pause until she finished.

They stood by the dock that stretched into the murky water.

"This is amazing, Tad. Is all this true? No, I didn't mean that. Of course it's true." She hugged him, then backed away, shaking her head. "It's just . . . horrible. I'm sorry."

Tad shrugged and looked away, feeling shy.

"Those in the North have to know."

Tad studied the trees lining the marsh, a thick, impenetrable wall of budding green that bent over the smooth water. "No, I reckon they don't."

"Tad, this is important." She held the paper up, clasped tightly in her hand. "The people *need* to know."

"I wrote it for you. Why can't we let slavery go to the ocean and drown?"

"Because there are no diaries, no words from the Negroes, nothing to tell what it was like. Your plight isn't over. Not many are convinced the Negro should be free. More proof is needed. This may help more people sympathize with you against the slaveholders."

The Emancipation Proclamation should have taken care of

the matter, but now Congress took on the problem of how to implement it, to find out exactly what *free* meant to a slave.

He sighed. "Do what you want with the story."

⚌

Good moods were rare at Port Royal, but Tad wore one like new shoes. Peg, who walked to school by his side, reflected his playful humor. Once Tad learned she wouldn't mention the kiss, he was once again comfortable in her company.

Tad couldn't decide which cheered him the most—Peg, freedom, his field planted with cotton, or the money in his pocket. Philbrick had encouraged him to deposit his money in a bank. Miss Towne was going to Beaufort soon and agreed to create an account for him. It was safer there than in a kitchen.

Shadows stretched from oaks and crossed the road. Birds and rabbits scurried ahead of their footsteps. Peg's voice carried through the sleeping, leafless forest. He could see her breath in the cool air.

> *"Weep no more, Marta,*
> *Weep no more, Mary,*
> *Jesus rise from de dead,*
> *Happy morning.*
> *Glorious morning!"*

She smiled, and Tad's heart fluttered. Peg had changed as spring warmed to liven the islands. Her face had always been childish and round, but now was long, thin, and womanly. Her girlish figure had disappeared last summer, and her clothes now covered a body that stirred new desires in Tad. The voice that cracked had deepened and mellowed. Frogmore residents wanted her to sing the words while they hummed at *shouts*.

In the distance, children walked to school, coming together

with calls and laughter. At the edge of a clearing, a small knot of soldiers watched them pass by.

Tad glanced at Peg. He wanted to take another route, so the soldiers wouldn't see them, but what would Peg think if he avoided them?

The men's blue uniforms stood in sharp contrast to the brown forest. Most soldiers on the island knew Tad, understood his fervent desire to join their ranks, so they left him alone when looking for volunteers. But as the two approached, Tad's hands shook. These men were of the 100th New York.

And they had spotted Peg.

"Hey, darling," one called. Several whistled. "You're too beautiful to be black."

"Just keep walking," Tad mumbled.

The men kept up the taunts. "That boy with you will die digging ditches, and someone else'll keep you warm, sweets."

Tad slowed. His muscles twitched.

"Leave it," Peg whispered.

They continued past.

"Salute me."

Tad kept walking.

A hand grasped his shoulder and turned him. Tad couldn't duck under the backhand across his face. He fell backward.

"Salute," the soldier demanded.

"Leave him alone!" Peg leapt forward, but the soldier grasped the back of her hair and tugged. She screamed.

The soldier's other hand lifted to strike Peg. Tad jumped up and clasped the man's arm in a tight grip, his dark fingers wrapping around the white wrist. The soldier, with Peg in one hand, struggled to pull his arm away, but Tad held it tight like the handle of a hoe.

He flung the soldier's arm back. Peg wriggled loose and ran past Tad, away from the soldiers. Tad turned to run, but the soldier stuck out a foot and he crashed into the dirt. "Where you going, sunshine? We've got to sort this out."

The others circled, closing Tad's escape. He slowly rose to his feet, his muscles pulsing, and he faced his foe.

The soldier stood, his arms wide. Tad studied the man, four inches taller than he was, and thicker. But his own muscles bulged, eager to test themselves against an enemy.

"Careful, Butch," one called. "He's stronger than he looks."

The soldier took three confident steps forward, his head held high. He tossed the rifle to a friend, who caught it by the barrel, and charged. Tad tensed to meet the blow and felt as if a horse had plunged into his chest. Both stayed on their feet, Tad's toes digging into the dirt.

He didn't know the rules to this combat. Tad grabbed the soldier's wrists again and pinned his arms to his side, but the soldier twisted away and slapped Tad in the face. The sting cracked his cheek, waking him to the danger.

He saw hatred filling the man's eyes. He blocked a punch then delivered one into the soldier's belly. Just as quickly he pulled his fist back and launched for the man's white face. He felt his knuckles crush under the blow. The soldier fell against a comrade.

A boot smashed into Tad's back, and he fell to the ground.

The fighting soldier was on Tad in a second. He pummeled Tad's face until numb. A final, heavy fist jarred against his skull, and the world spun. He gasped for breath, his stomach rebelled, he vomited, and finally the world went black.

Peg's scream reverberated through his brain.

❧

Miss Towne laid a wet washcloth on Tad's forehead. Her voice echoed in his head. "Thank God Old Robert heard Peg's scream. Who knows what those insidious troublemakers would have done to you."

Peg rubbed his hand and bent over him, sobbing. "I tried to keep them from taking your money, Tad, I did, but they run off. I's sorry, Tad, I's so sorry."

He blinked until moisture returned to his dry eyes.

A pallet had been laid for him inside an empty classroom in the Brick Church.

He focused on her blurry face. "Peg, you hurt?"

She shook her head and rocked, looking away from Tad. Miss Towne put a hand on her shoulder.

Tad stared at the ceiling and swallowed the frustration. He'd followed the rules, learned the ways of capitalism, the methods of great entrepreneurs, put them to the test, and succeeded. But now, all of it, gone.

He'd done it once; he figured he could do it again. Money was easy to make. He'd just learned the hard way it was also easy to lose.

He reached a swollen hand to stroke Peg's back. She stiffened at his touch. "Peg, nothing to be ashamed of. You did right by me."

She turned to him. "You worked hard for the money, and it's all lost."

Tad shrugged. "I still have you."

Tears swelled in her eyes and her lips trembled.

Miss Towne's cool hands touched his forehead. "We should let him rest, Peg, before you help him home."

Suddenly, both Peg and Miss Towne gasped. Tad blinked and sat up. In the doorway, in all his blessed glory, stood Mr. Pierce.

"There's been troubles on the islands," Pierce said, hands on his hips. "I've come to remedy them." He reached a hand to Miss Towne, who held out her own, and to Peg, who rushed to his side. "Of all things, Secretary Chase has made me a cotton agent."

# THIRTY FOUR

*P*ierce left Tad outside under a tree to recover, while Peg continued classes for the day. The children were called inside from their break to resume their education.

Pierce listened to Miss Towne's lesson.

Halfway through the session, her voice turned monotone, her energy waned, and the children fidgeted. She competed for her students' attention with nearby classes reciting and singing, their voices blending inside the church's brick walls with a mix of confusion.

Miss Murray, on the other hand, held the students' attention with an active voice, flailing arms, and happy cheers as the students answered correctly. The day's subject, shapes, was made exciting for the children.

Miss Towne let him review the correspondence of her little Penn School, and he realized her talents were in administration. While her classes meant so much to her, she was most skilled in garnering funds and gaining publicity for the plight of the freedmen.

He walked through the school in the Brick Church and watched the youthful faces showing an eagerness for education.

There were problems. The children were highly intelligent, something the South didn't want the North to know. He learned of a prank played—according to Miss Norwood—a cat let loose in the schoolhouse.

Miss Towne embraced the childish act. "Who taught them to be children?" she'd asked at the teachers' meeting during the noon meal. "Not I. Not their masters, definitely. Let them be children, for God's sake. Let them act, play, behave as if they attended a school in the North. For I will not lash them. Will you?"

Pierce thought her approach more than adequate. Lively children—not cowering slaves—filled the islands.

A black teacher from Philadelphia, Charlotte Forten, had joined the school, the first black teacher to join the group in Port Royal. She was bright, energetic, gracious, and attractive. She fit in well with the other teachers, and the students loved her. Her popularity with the supervisors was more than even the pretty Miss Nelly enjoyed.

The sun touched the tops of the trees as the school day ended, and Pierce suggested he and Miss Towne walk Tad back to the Frogmore. Through the thick, spring foliage, they walked several paces behind Tad and Peg.

He'd been looking forward to a few moments alone with her since he'd left South Carolina.

Miss Towne pulled her shawl tight around her shoulders. "I'm worried. Tad has suffered two major blows to the head, and a third may cause serious damage. There's no medical proof, but in my experience, three turns to the brain . . . " She shook her head.

Pierce studied the two children walking ahead. "So his hopes to be a soldier will never be realized?"

"His hopes may be closer than you think. I've spoken with General Hunter, and it seems Tad has helped the United States' cause enough to warrant favors. And he's created a minor stir with a story he wrote for the newspaper. He has a following."

"Don't tell him."

She laughed, and they walked in silence.

Among the tall cedars and wide oaks, within the smell of marshes and sight of freshly planted fields, Pierce felt renewed energy.

"Why did you come back, Mr. Pierce? What of your financial condition?"

"I'm being paid. And I'll admit, I missed the teachers and supervisors." He'd relied on her confidence in the past, and he'd do so again. "This may sound strange, but Secretary Chase has given me a secret project. I'm here to pave a way for the Negroes to vote."

She looked at him curiously, as if he was going to answer with more, but Pierce kept quiet.

Finally, she broke the silence. "There's no way to allow women this right as well?"

He shook his head. "And I regret that."

Tad tried to run ahead as they approached Frogmore, but he slowed to a walk when they approached Station Creek, holding his head. Pierce watched in concern.

The evening sun's orange rays touched the murky water, the moss hanging over the marsh lit like torches awaiting the coming darkness. The wind calmed and the shadows stretched across the lawn. Clouds of mosquitoes hovered near their heads, and Pierce slapped his neck. Miss Towne rubbed her ears. The two young freedmen didn't seem bothered by the insects.

Tad and Peg walked onto Frogmore's dock, and Pierce paused by a tree, out of earshot of the two youth.

"This land becomes such a part of you. Even the marsh smell loses its bitterness."

"The sweet-grass baskets are beautiful." Miss Towne leaned against the cedar and looked out over the miles of water and islands. "I could sell them in Philadelphia and make a fortune."

Pierce rested against the same tree and gazed on her profile. He was tempted to think of Kate, but standing next to Miss Towne, the pain of losing her seemed to dull. "The people are so forgiving, so thoughtful. I couldn't stay away, not with the experiment still in question."

Miss Towne turned away. "Look at Tad. You wouldn't guess he'd been completely ruined today."

Tad and Peg dared each other to hold their feet in the cold water. The young man's eyes were swollen and his lip cracked, but he smiled at his companion.

"I'll do my best to find his money, but it's probably already spent."

She rested her head against the trunk. "It's the Negro who has taught *us* to be honorable."

"Of the two questions, the second has still not been answered. The freedmen can learn, there's no doubt. You've done more than anyone to prove they can. And they will not be a drain on society. But there is no conclusive proof the Negro will fight." Pierce lowered his voice. "All that remains in the first line of questioning is what will become of the land."

"What do you mean?"

He turned to her. "This war cannot last forever. To whom does the land belong when the masters return?"

"I suppose all would be lost if the land is not provided to the freedmen."

Miss Towne looked back to the lush marshes and Pierce followed her gaze. A fish jumped nearby, a log floated in the grass. No, not a log, an alligator. It slipped below the surface in a swirl of water.

She looked at him. "I fear for them. I fear they will be subject to their old masters' whims again."

"To reintroduce the masters would destroy any hope of a smooth transition into our civilization."

They stood in silence for a moment, until Miss Towne sighed. "Well, things have changed since your last visit. Miss Walker went home sick. General Saxton married Miss Thompson, and Miss Nelly is engaged."

"Miss Nelly Windsor, the girl I demanded stay home because of her age?"

"The same. To a new supervisor." Miss Towne shuffled her feet. "I suppose we'd better head back, it's getting dark."

Pierce noticed she wrung her hands. He smiled. "Miss Towne?"

She hesitated then nodded. "You're a hero, Mr. Pierce. You created this. With your reports, your energy, you created this system, to help introduce the freedmen into society. And they learn, oh, how they learn. And it's working, *working*."

In the distance, Peg threw a rock and nearly fell in the water. Tad caught her just in time.

Miss Towne continued. "There are problems, though. Those from New York—we call them French's set—are paid as other supervisors and teachers, from their administration. They have *all* come to preach, none to teach. They make money, fifty, eighty dollars a month, live in government housing, take military rations, then ask their congregations or plantations for one thousand a year." Her voice sounded small. "It's gouge, gouge these people."

He wanted to take her hands, but held back. Instead, he leaned closer. "Your school, *your* work, is important. Of all those who came to help the freedman, you embody the perfect balance of charity, compassion, and education."

"I want a school." She held her hands against her heart. "A real school. With a bell. Oh, a beautiful bell, to toll in the morning, to tell the children it's time for classes. And when they're older, when they have children of their own and hear the bell, they will remember what it was like to be a child."

"You intend to stay?"

"My intention is to remain—for the rest of my days."

~≋~

Hilton Head's beach stretched along the crashing waves until it reached the stormy gray clouds gathering to the south. Another bank of clouds, less threatening, blocked the morning sun's glow. Pierce, walking alone, dodged a tidal pool and watched a crab scurry from the calm water toward the retreating tide. Could a lesson be learned there? Running from a safe pool to a maelstrom, knowing its chances were better in the churning waves than in calmer waters, where it could be attacked by a raccoon or bird—a good illustration for a speech or an article.

Sand dunes rose gently from the seaside, giving life to wispy strands of grass that rustled in the wind. Beyond the dunes, palmettoes lined the shore, hiding the dense interior.

Between two trees a man appeared.

"Mr. Gannett!" Pierce cried over the wind. "My, how good it is to see you. I trust you are well." He slapped the young man on the back.

"Good to see you too, sir." A look of obvious pleasure crossed Gannett's face. "How is Mr. Hooper? I haven't seen him for a while."

"My old secretary? As crafty with the ladies as ever."

"He always was." Gannett brushed his thickening goatee.

Pierce studied the man. Smooth skin around his eyes that once boasted of youth had been replaced by careworn wrinkles. A small streak of gray touched the side of his dark brown hair.

"Have you enjoyed your service as supervisor?"

"Always to the point, aren't you?" Gannett gave a wry smile. "Perhaps, if you have time . . . a word?"

"I am at your disposal, you know that."

Both men stared into the ocean. A boat rode the waves, its occupants looking for fish underneath the rolling surface. Pierce thought they might as well search for gold in California.

Gannett stuffed his hands deep into his pockets. "I received a letter from a friend in Boston. He believes I've given up my missionary status and become a cotton planter. I've lost my passion for souls, he said. I've compromised my sacred promise to God and given my soul to the demon economy." His eyebrows narrowed.

Pierce understood the young man's concerns and wanted to tell him to find his own way, to not rely on acquaintances for advice. Why did God grant friends, when already the world was filled with enemies? "Perhaps he's uninformed as to our situation here?"

"I write him often."

Pierce paced along the stiff sand. "And you fear Mr. Philbrick's influence has taken hold in you?"

"I admit it freely."

"Understandable, I agree." Pierce paused, then smiled. "Remember, Mr. Philbrick's only goal was to show that wage labor was economically sound."

"By instituting Egypt's industrial plans in the American South." Gannett laughed. He reached down and picked up a perfect shell, held it up in the sunlight, and blew away the sand that clung to the rich blue casing. "Is money our objective here?"

"It is for Mr. Philbrick."

The young man smirked and handed the shell to Pierce. "I think Mr. Philbrick would sell this if he could."

Pierce dropped it in his pocket. "But that's not your purpose."

Gannett lifted his arms in frustration. "What is my purpose?"

"You understand the bigger picture, that what we do here

will be studied, replicated, perfected, and implemented time and time again. If we fail here, if we cannot make these plantations work, then all is lost. If abandoned, the Negro must find his own way without the tools we give our own children and the South will inflict its anger upon the entire race, blaming them for its misery." Pierce looked into Gannett's eyes. "But some, like yourself, understand all this, see the truth as clearly as the day dawns. It is your efforts, Mr. Gannett, which gives the freedmen tools to enjoy their liberty."

# THIRTY FIVE

*T*ad awoke in the middle of the night, scratched his bare chest, and rolled over. Had someone called his name? He let go a deep breath and settled his head into his pillow.

He drifted near sleep. After a moment, he shot up out of bed. Someone did call his name. The voice was strange, harsh, old, a fierce whisper.

His heart beat wildly. His senses sharpened.

A glance at Bo's dark form told him the old man was asleep. A snore reassured him.

Tad pushed away his blanket and stood, a chill running along his back. Cold planks under his toes made him plunge his feet into shoes. He wrapped a jacket around his shoulders and opened the door.

In the moonlit night, Tad could make out a crippled figure shuffling across the yard.

"Tad." The voice was muffled by a hood.

He hesitated, afraid. But a witch would find him wherever he slept or ran. Best to face the hag here and now. "Here," he whispered, and stepped toward the creature.

The witch spun as quickly as a fox and flew toward him, faster than he thought possible. He stepped back.

"You Tad?"

"I reckon."

The creature sighed. "Thought you'd be taller."

In the darkness, Tad could barely make out her face, and guessed the black woman was just older than Mammy. Her thick, wide lips seemed turned into a permanent frown.

"Who are you?"

She snorted and ignored his question. "Can't all be as tall as we like, I suppose."

"I'm growing," Tad said in a loud, defensive voice, straightening his back.

"You be quiet, boy. I ain't going to have anyone but you knowing I'm here."

He lowered his voice. "But who are you?"

Her eyes appraised his figure. "Here." She lifted a hand. "Yours."

Tad reached out, but paused. Should he trust her? If he didn't, a curse might be cast on him or the ones he loved. He opened his hand.

He felt paper, wide strips, a thick stack.

"Be more careful." She disappeared into the shadows.

He held the bundle close to his face. It was cash.

"Wait!" Tad called. "Who are you?" He followed her, his foot catching on a bucket. He slammed onto the cold ground and scrambled to his feet.

She reappeared in the shadows. "Be careful. Take great pains to be alert. Someone loves you. And the journey you have ahead—danger lies in your path."

Her voice sounded like a witch. She made as much sense as one. Tad brushed dirt from his face. "How did you get this money? Is it my cash that was stolen? What's your name?"

She laughed, a delightful sound, more human than evil. She swept back her hood, revealing thick curly hair. "Good ears take the place of prophecy, boy." She sighed, and a look of sadness crossed her face. "I've heard your name at army headquarters. You're to be called up, and soon. As for the money . . . I persuaded the soldier to give it back. I do good, for all sorts of people. You're just one stop on a long list tonight. But my name—some call me Moses."

Tad choked. Moses. The spy who rescued slaves. A *woman*?

She slipped into the shadows, but he heard her offer one last bit of advice. "Soldiering, bad business. Take care, take great care. For she loves you."

The bushes rattled. After a moment, the sounds of several others who had waited with her filled the night. They drifted into the darkness and were gone.

❧

Tad stood at attention. The sun blazed overhead and the brisk wind threatened to knock him sideways, but he took great pains to show the weather didn't affect him. Ahead, a major spoke to several new recruits, their line straight though their clothes were tattered. Tad tried to listen but was too excited.

He was in the army.

He was a soldier. It was beautiful to be a soldier.

The recruits were dismissed, and as Tad turned to follow the other men, an officer stopped him. "I'm Major Trowbridge, Private. You've been assigned to me. Come this way."

"Yes, sir." Tad saluted and followed the man toward a long row of canvas tents. His stomach churned, his gut aching with nerves. He wanted to do everything right.

"Welcome to the First South Carolina." Trowbridge's broad mustache and wavy brown hair gave Tad the impression the major was more mane than man, but his manner was mild and friendly. "Tad, you've been assigned to me as a special case. A major's staff must be officers, normally, but you will find many exceptions in these strange times, and you are one of them."

They stopped in front of a tent, and the major flung back the flap. "I would like you to be my runner because . . . Well, simply put, my previous runner has run away. I trust that won't be a problem here?"

"The enemy won't see my back, sir." Tad put as much energy into his voice as he could.

"Yes, yes, initiative on the battlefield and all that, very good. Please, step into my tent." Trowbridge sat behind a small field table, the chair such a small, thin piece of furniture Tad thought it would break.

He stood in front of Trowbridge at attention.

The major pulled out a piece of paper and glanced up. "At ease, Private."

Tad took a deep breath but didn't move.

"Thank you. Now, the Second South Carolina Volunteers is being assembled at Beaufort and will return there after a maneuver. We are to act as a retreat point at the docks. Colonel Montgomery is acting commander of the Second." He leaned back at his desk. "Private, I do hope you stay longer than my last runner. You know General Hunter by sight? Colonel Higginson?"

Tad opened his mouth to answer, but the major held up a hand.

"Now, please repeat the part where I spoke about the Second South Carolina."

Tad fumbled to find the words. "That we are to assemble in Beaufort, to act as a retreat point for Colonel Montgomery's troops, and you hope I stay longer than the last runner—"

"Thank you, that's quite enough." Trowbridge laughed. "The memory of freedmen is impressive. I guess since you weren't allowed to read and write, you had little choice."

"I can read, sir."

"Excellent, you've finished your primer?"

"No," Tad admitted. "I read Peg's primer, but not mine."

"And I suppose you can run?"

"Yes, sir, and climb trees."

"I cannot afford to give you a horse." The major shook his head, his voice dull with regret. He leaned forward in his chair. "So you will use your feet." He wrote something on the paper and handed it to Tad. "Go to the requisition office and pick up your equipment. Normal gear, uniform, rifle, boots. You'll be paid eight dollars a month. You'll bunk with the other runners in the tent next to mine."

One half hour later, Tad glanced at his image in a hazy mirror that hung near the door. The small boy he remembered was gone. Instead, a young man five-foot-seven, weighing under two-and-a-half bushels of corn, stood in a blue jacket, short, shaved hair under a tilted cap. His narrow face with its tight jaw and sharp eyes was every bit a soldier's. He cradled the rifle in his arm.

The rifle's cool metal barrel and course wood stock felt better than anything he'd touched before. Now he was any man's equal. If Mr. Spencer or Massah found him, a lash in their hands, Tad would be the master. He nestled the butt against his shoulder, cheek against the chamber, eye sighting down the barrel.

He could barely hold back his eagerness for the first assignment.

Tad marched back to headquarters. Both flaps to Major Trowbridge's tent were open. Nearby, the major's staff huddled, speaking in hushed tones. Most were black, except for one white officer. Tad approached, and they noticed him. One whistled.

"Mighty fine uniform there, boy."

"I'm Tad."

"Well, you certainly is. What's a young child doing in this fine Lincoln army, anyways?"

"He ain't good for nothing other than catching a bullet. Well, I ain't the one telling his mammy when he do."

The white captain pulled Tad's sleeve and led him away from the others. "Don't listen to them. You've been called to the tent.

Go in and make yourself known with a salute. Here," he said, taking Tad's rifle and ammunition. "You won't be needing this. No sense getting anyone killed who doesn't deserve it. There'll be time to train later. Go, go on in."

Tad wanted to protest, but the captain gave him a hard shove in the back. The men in the tent jumped as Tad crashed against Major Trowbridge's desk. Laughter erupted outside.

The major helped Tad to his feet. "A little prank on the newcomer never hurts." He smiled and glanced anxiously at the two men in the back of the tent.

Tad stood at attention. "Orders, sir?"

Trowbridge nodded at Tad with a fatherly smile, as if approving his discipline. Tad's heart swelled.

"At ease, Private."

Tad let out a breath.

"Let me introduce you to my superior, Colonel Higginson."

Tad saluted. Colonel Higginson removed his hat and brushed back his wavy, light-brown hair. His beard was shaved, and Tad memorized his handsome face for future reference. The colonel returned the salute.

"Colonel Higginson commands the First South Carolina." Major Trowbridge pulled a chair and sat behind his desk. He indicated the other man. "This is Colonel Montgomery, commander of the Second South Carolina."

Tad saluted, but Colonel Montgomery ignored him and glared at the major. "Another darkie? Can we trust a volunteer boy?" His wild, black and gray windswept hair and terrifying eyes gave Tad the impression of an insane man. Tad's salute remained frozen at his brow.

Trowbridge stepped away from his desk to put a hand on Tad's shoulder. "We've been watching this boy's education at Laura Towne's Penn School. He's intelligent and trustworthy to a fault. I'll vouch for him myself."

Montgomery looked as if he wanted to argue, but he snapped his mouth shut.

Trowbridge glared at his superior then turned to Tad. "Don't mind him. Colonel Montgomery isn't used to troops of color. He's from Kansas. Fought through Bleeding Kansas, where guerilla warfare was the perfect tactic. A style we need in the Carolinas."

Higginson cleared his throat, stood, and approached a map on the desk. "Mission plans, gentlemen. The Combahee River's been scouted by Moses as a vital link to resources and slaves."

Tad couldn't hold back a smile. To be included in battle plans, after a day in the infantry—he had only dreamed.

Higginson continued. "The South Carolina First is battle tested, so General Hunter believes the Second, with training finished, is ready for the field."

Trowbridge turned to Colonel Montgomery. "We'll march to Beaufort to be your line of retreat in a few days."

Montgomery slapped his gloves against his thigh. "My troops are ready."

Trowbridge's forehead wrinkled, as if in thought. Finally, Tad's commanding officer turned to him. "Tad, please find General Hunter. Give him our compliments, tell him Colonel Montgomery is ready to depart at his command."

Montgomery jumped to his feet. "I've got runners. I'll use mine."

Trowbridge seemed to expect this and had a ready answer. "Surely you wouldn't begrudge a fellow officer training his runners. Yours have much to do to prepare for this attack. Go ahead, Tad. Go tell General Hunter."

Before Montgomery could say a word, Tad saluted and bolted from the tent. Never mind he had no clue where the general was. It wouldn't matter. He would ask. The clerk would know.

His first mission. The joy burst in him like an explosion. He whistled, then sang.

*"My Lord, my Lord, what shall I do?*
*And a heaven bell a-ring and praise God.*
*What shall I do for a hiding place?*
*I run to the sea, but the sea run dry.*
*I run to the gate, but the gate shut fast.*
*No hiding place for sinner there."*

For the next several days, drills dominated Tad's life. When they weren't marching, he stayed near Major Trowbridge's tent.

The bottoms of Tad's feet were calloused from running across St. Helena Island without shoes. But the top of his toes blistered where they touched the end of his boot. He tried to ignore the pain.

Grumbling filled the ranks. Soldiers complained about missing the upcoming fight, until an angry Higginson blew assembly at the flagpole. Tad stood at attention with the other men while the colonel railed against them.

"It was the Second's turn to fight. You've captured Jacksonville and held it for two weeks, fought for salt mines, swept away the enemy like leaves. We had to give the Second a chance. Now, in case they're followed back to Beaufort, we're to go meet them."

Sergeants screamed the men into order, four men across, and they marched north. Tad kept close to Trowbridge, the commander riding a horse.

With knees high, head erect, eyes focused, Tad marched with the others and felt the power of the men around him.

Thunder rumbled the earth. Dark clouds swirled and danced above, holding rain. Lightning tore the sky.

Rain slashed across the land. Mud filled the road, saturating his boots. Water poured off the brim of his cap. Five miles later he saw houses amongst oak trees, where the five hundred soldiers turned onto Bay Street in Beaufort.

Rain pelted their skin while they waited along the dock for the Second's return. No one spoke. A few shivered.

The murky water at the foot of the dock lifted with the tide. The rain cleared, and the clouds pushed out past the thick trees and toward the ocean.

Down the inlet, a ship steamed with the swelling water. Higginson called the sergeants to ready arms. Calls went up and down the lines.

Were Confederate ships following the steamer? Would Secesh troops pour over the marsh and attack Beaufort? Tad tried to control his breathing and not look too eager.

Miss Towne brushed by him, medical bag clutched under her arm. She didn't recognize him in the new uniform. How could she? Mammy and Peg couldn't spot him in a crowd of soldiers. He looked too different.

More teachers and supervisors hurried by, preparing to help the freed slaves and wounded soldiers.

The ship neared, lowered the gangplanks, and a whistle shrilled across the inlet. Pigs, goats, chickens, and other livestock burst from the steamer and flooded the dock. On their heels, freed slaves scampered after their prizes, filling the pier with confusion. Miss Towne scurried to help those who might need medical attention, then paused as soldiers set stretchers onto the dock. Tad strained to see, but there was no need to look. The stretchers were empty.

The Second marched from the ship in good order, to the sound of cheers from Tad and the First. Caps tossed in celebration were blown away from the water by a brisk breeze.

Through the cheering crowds, Tad could see Colonel Montgomery. Beside the tall man with untamed hair walked a small black woman. She didn't smile. Instead, she looked over the soldiers and slaves with concern.

*Moses.*

# THIRTY SIX

*P*ierce learned Tad had a day off to see his mother and friends. The boy had contacted Mammy, who sent a message with Peg to Pierce's temporary home at Hilton Head, and the arrangements were made. A celebratory picnic was in order.

Four freedmen rowed Pierce to the Frogmore, where the party waited for him. On shore, Mr. Philbrick, Mr. Gannett, Mr. Soule, Miss Murray, Miss Towne, and her brother, Will Towne, stood in a circle. Mammy and Peg stood just outside the small group, large baskets by their side.

The boat bumped against the dock. Pierce felt his coattails flap behind him as he lightly leapt to shore. The small group opened to reveal a handsome young man resplendent in uniform. Pierce barely recognized Tad. He was nearly as tall as any of the men in the party. He filled with pride at the sight of his young protégé.

Peg glanced at Tad with her large, brown eyes then quickly turned away. Pierce saw sadness in them and wondered why— Tad looked so handsome. But he dismissed the thought when Miss Towne's smile caught his attention.

With the sounds of cheers and laughter in the air, the boat was pushed from the shore. The bow plowed through the motionless water, heavy under the new load. As they passed through narrow channels of marsh grass, egrets and cranes flew into the air. High above, a hawk whirled in the clear sky, basking in the warm spring sun. On the boat, pink parasols popped open to block the rays.

Pierce held tight to the rudder. The four oarsmen hummed a tune to pace their rowing.

Pierce suddenly felt irritated with Miss Towne for reasons he could not explain. Her tight bun, thin lips, shrewd eyes, and light manner bothered him to distraction. She enjoyed the men's attention too much.

"Mr. Pierce? Are you awake?" Peg stretched her neck to peer over Soule's shoulder at him.

"Yes. Sorry. Was thinking. You were saying?"

"You know who Moses is?"

Pierce saw Tad's shoulder touch Peg's. The touch seemed to satiate the girl for the moment, even lifting her spirit.

He turned the rudder so they curved out from the narrow Station Creek into Port Royal Sound. "She's Moses. That's all."

"You know everyone that comes to these islands." Miss Towne's voice was light and playful. "Who is she, Mr. Pierce?"

He glared at her. "You should know. She's from Philadelphia." His tone shocked the passengers, surprising even himself.

Her eyebrow lifted, and her fingers touched her heart.

There was a moment of silence, and Philbrick cleared his throat. "A military secret, no doubt, and to give away her true identity might harm the ones she loves."

Pierce waved a hand. "Harriet Tubman. She helped slaves run, Underground Railroad and all that."

"Samuel ran," Tad said. "But he did it all on his own."

"Not everyone is so fortunate." He felt as if he were a dead weight, dragging the party down.

Philbrick brushed his mustache. "Always comfortable to know someone looks out for your best interest, though."

"Don't ask Mr. Pierce about caring for best interests." Everyone turned to Miss Towne. Her hands were folded in her lap. "He wouldn't think a woman capable of such a thing."

Miss Murray covered her mouth. Gannett choked back a laugh.

Pierce felt the stab. He'd changed since he first met her. But the comment irritated him more than he already felt.

The talk turned to war, the honor of death with heavy rifle fire, the glory of capturing a tiny bit of ground at the cost of thousands of lives. Pierce's stomach turned. Mammy gasped, and Peg's eyes were large and full of fear.

"Used to play with Collin here," Tad said, changing the subject as they pushed out of the sound and onto the ocean. "On the beaches."

Hunting Island had been preserved by the South as something of a game reserve. No one lived on the island, so animals roamed freely, deer especially. Hunters enjoyed killing the wild game.

Tad told a story of the blockade, of a Union ship catching a small Secesh vessel, but Pierce's mind drifted. Miss Towne was as agitated with him as he with her, but if he couldn't understand his own feelings, how could he hers?

The boat's bow slid up the beach's packed sand, and everyone but the four rowers splashed onto the island. Tad and Peg wandered down the water's edge, while the members of Gideon's Band disappeared into the forest. Mammy and the freedmen rowers laid blankets on the shore and set out the picnic.

A regretful thought passed through Pierce's mind. The scene must have been familiar to Negroes—the slaves setting up a picnic, the masters running about enjoying themselves.

He wandered the beach alone to sort through the emotions. The answer settled on the edge of his brain, but he refused to acknowledge the idea. He watched a bird flap far over the ocean. The wings stopped beating, and it plummeted toward the water and disappeared into the waves.

Pierce thought it died.

In a moment, the bird surfaced and took to the air, the tail of a fish hanging from its mouth.

It was just the omen he needed to take his own dive. He turned, looked back at the small party, where Laura Towne helped set up the picnic. Her smile touched the sunlight. She looked at him. Emotions flooded him.

Waves pounded the shore in rhythm, two small crashes and a large thunder, over and over again. He walked back to the blankets and waited until everyone returned but Tad and Peg. Pierce sat with the others and laughed at stories told of the freedmen's children in school. Tad and Peg's tiny figures grew larger on the shore as they approached. Pierce eyed the young couple.

Tad led Peg into the nearby forest, still visible through the trees. The two stopped, facing each other, and Pierce couldn't hold back his smile as Tad dropped to a knee.

Miss Murray set down a drumstick and looked up. "Mr. Pierce, what are you looking at?"

Pierce nodded toward Tad. They all looked.

The boy soldier grasped her hand. A gust swirled her dress and flapped the fabric around her legs. Tad's hat flew off, but he didn't flinch. He kept his eyes on hers. Peg pulled her hand away. She took a step back and Tad swung his arms wide, a questioning gesture. Peg shook her head, stepped back further, then turned and ran along the dunes toward the small group.

Tad ran away from them. Pierce jumped up and sprinted after him. He flung his coat on the sand as he passed a weeping Peg.

After a few minutes of searching the dense forest off the beach, he found Tad lodged in a tree—an odd sight, a soldier dangling from a branch. "Come down, Tad. Tell me what happened."

"I saw soldiers on the island. I'll go home with 'em."

Pierce reached a hand up. "This is no way for a fighting man to behave, come down."

"She don't want me."

Pierce continued to try talking Tad down, but the lad wouldn't come. After a moment, he gave up, dusted off his jacket, and returned to the small group where Miss Murray consoled a crying Peg.

"She turned him down," Philbrick said in a quiet voice, when Pierce asked.

Tension hung in the air. Pierce, saturated with frustration, mumbled something about a walk and scurried into the forest with little dignity. Palmettos brushed by wind reflected the sun, casting shadows on the sandy soil. Ahead, a stump of a lighthouse stood as if a haunt for children. Support houses lay in ruins, their black carcasses strewn like dead dragons around the lighthouse. He paused in their midst.

"Mr. Pierce?"

He turned and saw Miss Towne approach.

She took a tentative step forward.

He sighed.

"Mr. Pierce, I wanted to apologize for my earlier comments. They were foolish, and I don't know why I said them. We're friends, and I would like to remain so."

He took a deep breath and faced her. "Why did she refuse him? What wrong did he do to deserve her wrath?"

"Love is too strong to be wasted, Mr. Pierce, on the foibles of war."

"I don't understand."

"I don't pretend to understand her reasoning either, but she will not marry Tad before he goes to war."

Pierce looked back to shore. "I must tell her that he won't fight. I've ordered it."

"You've ordered it? Come now, do you truly believe Tad can stay out of a fight? He'll fight, whether you wish it or not. And in the end, Peg believes he will die. Widowhood is difficult to live with. Oh, and remember your concerns of Tad running in battle? A live coward as a husband would torture them both. Either way, she bears the evils of this."

Pierce felt lost and desperate. This schoolteacher had crashed into his life at the best and worst times. His heart ached, for Kate, for Laura, for Tad and Peg. He had to be open with her before his heart burst. "And you, Miss Towne. If you were asked something difficult by a man, would you consider his words or give an answer as quickly as Peg did?"

Her cheeks turned red and her eyes grew large. "I . . . " She stumbled over her words. After a deep breath, she cocked her head to the side. "I believe I am older, more responsible about my emotions, and willing to focus on doing the right thing over . . . over my desires."

He stepped in close, hesitant. "Would you consider leaving this—leaving Penn School, the freed slaves—to come to Boston?"

Her mouth opened.

"Please." Pierce held up a hand. "Just . . . I don't know. I'm sorry, I shouldn't have asked." Guilt flooded him, along with other, impossible-to-define emotions. Had he just proposed?

She reached out and took his hand. "Edward. I think you know how I feel about you. It's difficult for me to hide my emotions. But I told you I would stay here forever and help these children. Are you asking me to leave them?"

Was that her answer, then? "No, you're right, I couldn't ask that."

She held a up hand to her mouth, tears forming, and turned away. Stunned, he watched her run to shore.

❧

The one man who could cheer Pierce stepped onto the Port Royal dock and met him in a restaurant near the customs house. They entered the brick building, the tables filled with fat men, their drinks, and their laughter.

Robert Gould Shaw had been promoted to colonel and given command of the Fifty-fourth Massachusetts, black volunteers. He seemed the obvious choice, from Massachusetts and friends with the Pierce family and other influential members of the government. Shaw also boasted a strong lineage.

"Edward, it does me well to see you in such fine health." Shaw settled in his chair across from Pierce.

Despite his troubled heart, it warmed him to see his friend. "The evils of war haven't done you harm."

Shaw's laughter was like golden bells. His face was childlike, with intelligent but sad eyes, which invoked sympathy. Despite his features, he seemed to command respect from both white and black troops.

"My men are coming ashore now." His face beamed. "Pleasant day for regimental maneuvering."

Pierce looked out the thick-paned glass, where the Broad River mingled with Port Royal Sound. He didn't care for this open area, preferring the closed islands filled with oaks, pines, and cedars. "Are your men ready to fight?"

"More than ready. Drilled marksmen to a man, better troops than we had at Antietam."

"I believe that."

Shaw shook his head, his eyes soft and sad. "They won't let us fight, Edward. For all the bluster, for all the glory and honor, the drills and suffering, we're to dig graves."

Pierce accepted the drink from the waiter and ran his fingers along the wet glass. "Why did they choose you, Rob? Out of the hundreds of colonels, why you?"

Shaw downed his scotch in a single smooth motion, something Pierce knew his friend wasn't able to do before military service. "God knows. Turned it down, you know, but Father and Governor Andrew pleaded, and then Mother . . . " He sighed. "You know Mother."

Pierce knew Shaw's mother well, and he understood the love for his mother that drove his desires. "You'll fight. You'll have to." Pierce sipped his drink. "I've found the blacks feared the whites when slaves. The black soldiers, rifles in hand, trembled, until they saw the fear in their former masters' eyes. It drove them forward. I don't think any government could hold them back from a fight now."

"You've a point there." He blew a long breath so that his small mustache stuck out. "In all honesty, Edward, I'd rather be with my old unit, fighting this war with my friends. Don't get me wrong. I'm more abolitionist than Unitarian, but what can one man do against so many troubles?"

Pierce kept quiet.

"No matter, I'm excited to see what you've done here. Schools, churches." Shaw laughed. "Some say you freed the Negro. That you wrote the Emancipation Proclamation."

"Freed him? No. No, I didn't do that. He freed himself. Here anyway." Pierce studied his glass. "He could have run with his masters when we invaded, but he didn't. He stayed. I'm merely giving him the tools to enjoy his freedom. He can take the skills we teach or not. Choice, I think, is the true freedom here."

After a moment of silence, Shaw's face saddened. "I'm sorry to hear about you and Kate."

Pierce absently tapped the glass with his fingernail. "Is she happy, Rob? Does she love him?"

"Do you need to ask?"

"No, I suppose not. I've some difficulty with women lately,"

Pierce said. "Perhaps it was right to be more attentive of the freedmen and law than the fairer sex. But look at you, you're married. I'm sorry I couldn't attend the ceremony."

"It was nothing. Almost regret the decision. At least this war keeps me busy. Mother didn't seem to approve of me marrying."

A Negro soldier burst through the door. Pierce had to look twice to recognize Tad. The boy marched to the table and stood at attention. He saluted. "Colonel Shaw, a pleasure to see you, sir. I've word from Colonel Montgomery. You are to move out immediately for Simon's Island."

Shaw glanced at Pierce. "I'm glad my troops haven't completely disembarked." He turned to Tad, a questioning look on his face. "You're a runner for Colonel Montgomery? Aren't you the boy I met in Boston?"

"Yes, sir. A runner."

Pierce held up a hand. "Tad volunteered and has done enough to warrant a staff position." Pierce turned to Tad. "But I thought you were a runner for Major Trowbridge of the First. Why are you here for Colonel Montgomery's Second?"

Tad glanced nervously at Shaw. "Permission to speak freely, sir."

Shaw covered the rank insignia on one of his shoulders. "You're among friends. Go ahead."

"Mr. Pierce, I'm sorry, but Colonel Montgomery is a demon from hell spawned only by Satan himself."

Shaw sputtered, then coughed violently. "They learn to speak freely here."

Pierce pulled his chair forward. "Tad, that's strong language, even for you."

"Sir, he requested me to be part of his staff, I reckon, to make a fool of me. Hasn't done it yet. But I'm to bring Colonel Shaw south, where he intends to show how much better the Second is than any regiment from Boston."

Shaw sat up straight in his seat. "That's an opinion."

Pierce shot his friend a serious look. "You'd better take it under consideration. Montgomery's an ill-favored enemy."

After a moment of silence, Shaw spoke. "Private, wait outside, I'll be along in a moment. And I'll see if you can be transferred to my regiment later."

Tad stared for a moment, openmouthed, then saluted, turned, and marched outside.

"Action, my dear Edward, seems the order of the day." Shaw grinned.

*P*roper channels."

Tad tried to hide his disappointment.

Colonel Shaw's look was sympathetic. "You'll be on my staff, but we must follow decorum."

Tad saluted and marched down the grassy slope of Pike's Bluff, Georgia. He dreaded every step closer to the Second South Carolina, and almost ran north to find Mammy. But the thought of facing Peg sent a musket ball through his heart.

Colonel Montgomery stared at Tad when he reported Colonel Shaw's arrival. Tad tried to look into the crazed eyes, but found he couldn't, instead focusing on the gold buttons running up and down the man's uniform.

Montgomery exploded into action. Two boats fired up their boilers while soldiers lined the docks. After they loaded, the vessels pushed out to sea and steamed along the flat coastline. Gulls hovered above. Soon, the bow turned toward the lurking forests where long docks stretched into the water. Tad's boat shuddered to a halt.

On shore, the Fifty-fourth Massachusetts set up white canvas tents under the warm sun. Montgomery spotted Shaw, cupped his hands around his bearded mouth, and called out, "Can you be ready for an expedition?"

Shaw's small figure straightened and he yelled back. "Half hour."

Black smoke poured from an empty steamer, the thick cloud rolling like a storm toward the shore. A gunboat pulled up alongside. The ships paddled toward the dock, where eager Massachusetts soldiers clambered on board. Soon, three ships and a gunboat churned the muddy spring water moving inland. The Second boasted four hundred forty-two men and a spattering of artillery, while the men from Boston numbered nearly seven hundred.

Montgomery and Shaw met on Tad's steamer and traded information. The two men couldn't have been more different. Montgomery's haughty look and energetic passion dwarfed the quiet Shaw. But as the two men talked, Tad noticed strength deep inside the smaller Massachusetts man not apparent at first glance. Montgomery tried to bully Shaw, but the commander would have none of it. He would not put his men under Montgomery's command.

Tad stopped. He shaded his eyes and looked again. Samuel, the Frogmore's giant driver, on another steamer with the Boston soldiers. Tad waved, but the former boss didn't recognize him.

The sun settled into dusk, and Tad rested on the deck next to several soldiers who snored.

He closed his eyes and dreamed of battle, the soldier next to him wounded, the rifle falling into Tad's empty hands. The dying man would whisper, "Kill 'em for me, son." In righteous anger, while lightning streaked the sky, Tad would let loose a roar and unleash his mighty wrath. He would create gaping holes in the enemy line and return to St. Helena Island a hero.

The boat lurched, then ground to a halt. A flow of foul words escaped Colonel Montgomery's lips. Tad lifted his head and in the dying light saw the tide out. He slumped back and glanced at the colonel. There must be no tides in Kansas.

Hours later, he half-woke to the sound of the paddle wheels churning, but drifted to sleep again in the rich darkness. There were no dreams, no sounds but the gentle rhythms of the ship. He fell into a deep sleep.

An explosion jarred him awake. His eyes flew open.

Montgomery stood over him, looking past the bow.

"Fire two!"

Another blast rattled Tad's teeth. Confused, he curled into a ball and covered his ears with both hands. Montgomery's thick boot struck his side. "Get up, you good for nothing."

Tad scrambled to his feet and peered over the side, rubbing his eyes.

He gasped. Thick smoke poured from a house, a trail of black in the morning sky. If it were not for the pines and well-groomed gardens, he would have believed it was home. Two holes knocked into the whitewashed sides showed fire inside. The front door burst open, and a young black woman with two dark children stumbled out the front door. Gray smoke drifted off their forms, as if they were on fire, until the soft wind blew the haze from their bodies. They clutched the porch rail, coughing.

"Fire!" The ship reeled back with the gun's recoil, and the porch exploded. Sharp wood splinters flew through the air and showered the woman and children. The smoke cleared, and the ships continued upriver. Tad strained to see the woman, who struggled against the debris that covered her legs. The two children didn't move.

Tad stared at the burning house in horror. Was this war?

Montgomery's laugh bounced off the deck.

The sun brightened and the spring day turned hot and sultry. Tad lowered his cap and settled against the rail to watch the forested countryside pass by. Breaks in the woods were filled with houses, barns, and fields. Guns roared, demolishing the

plantations, leaving behind smoke, death, and ruin. They continued inland, undeterred.

Ahead, past a wide marsh, the river curled around a small
town. Colonel Montgomery called out orders to prepare for
attack. Another man's voice carried across the water to relay
orders to Shaw's men.

Three troopships separated and paddled toward the village,
while the gunboat protected the flanks. Tad rubbed his sweaty
palms against his uniform and stayed close to Montgomery,
ready to relay any orders. They approached shore. A plank
from each ship dropped and ropes were thrown and secured.
But the soldiers waited on board.

Montgomery watched, waiting for movement. Houses lined
the shore, but appeared empty. Streets were bare. No dogs
barked, no horses whinnied. A bird chirped angrily from an
oak tree.

"Across!" Montgomery called. Swarms of soldiers in orange
pants scrambled ashore. They formed a battle line along the
street, bayonets gleaming in the sun. Shining faces were stern
and hard. Tad crossed with the colonel and stood behind the
line, waiting with the others for the Rebel army.

Shaw's men, in blue coats and pants, formed on the right.
Their eyes were wide, looking this way and that for an enemy
that didn't appear. Montgomery motioned at Shaw to move
forward.

Soldiers' boots thundered through lonely dirt streets, wagon
tracks the only evidence of evacuation. Blank windows stared
down from above. Ahead, on the outskirts of town, vacant hills
looked down on them. Tad wondered why the enemy didn't
roll cannons on top of the hill and pound them from above.

A scream echoed through the tight buildings. Ahead, soldiers surrounded two women, their slaves pushing against the
small knot of soldiers.

"Halt!" Montgomery called. He approached the women and swept off his hat with a bow. His voice was soft and gentle. "Good ladies, I'm afraid we are here to capture your town."

The women studied the colonel's untamed hair, but his manners seemed to command the first impression. "Please, don't hurt us."

"I can only guarantee your safety if you leave, now."

"If we do, please don't touch our homes."

Montgomery held his hat close to his heart. "Dear women, if you would tell me which homes are yours, perhaps I can prevent any problems that might arise."

The women pointed at two houses near the edge of town, along the waterfront. They hurried away, slaves in tow.

Montgomery called his officers together. "Quickly now. Take furniture, silver, and porcelain, anything of value. Load it onto the ships." He turned to Shaw. "Have your men wait on the edge of town with their eyes on those hills. Their army may be waiting beyond."

"Shall I not push over them, to be sure?"

Montgomery's eyes were wild with sudden fury. "Are my orders too difficult a task?"

"No, sir." Colonel Shaw saluted, spun, and ordered his army forward.

The Second dispersed in squads, broke through locked doors, and shattered windows. Soldiers with loads of goods on their shoulders crossed back and forth over the roads to the ships.

Evening settled over the land as the houses, gutted of riches, were bathed in purple and orange. Tad watched with sullen curiosity, wandering with his commander through the settlement.

Montgomery seemed finally to notice him. "Message for Shaw. Burn the town."

Tad stared at the man.

"You heard me, go tell him."

"But . . . why?"

Tad reeled from the backhand. Montgomery prepared to deliver another blow, but Tad hauled himself up and backed away.

"Burn the town. Right, sir." Tad dashed between two buildings on his way to the outskirts of town. City houses turned to country homes, with fences holding large gardens. There were no livestock.

Tad found Shaw pacing along a road bordered by thick trees. "Orders, sir."

"Yes?" Shaw drew close, then glanced at his second in command. "Perhaps we are to give chase to the Rebels?"

Tad couldn't meet his eyes. Instead, he looked at the road. "Sir, Colonel Montgomery requests you burn the town."

Shaw stripped off his white riding gloves and hurled them to the ground. "I will not follow such a dishonorable command."

"Sir, those were his orders."

Shaw pointed a finger at Tad's face. "You tell Montgomery I will not burn a town we've captured without a fight. You tell him it's unethical, immoral, and against the rules of war. Honor-bound gentlemen scoff at such ideas. I cannot, and will not, follow such an order." He snatched the reins of his horse from an aid. He leapt onto its back and wrenched its head to the side. "You tell him all of it."

Tad ran into town then slowed, in no hurry to tell Colonel Montgomery there was mutiny in the ranks. He wandered through the houses, the setting sun casting orange rays across his path. After a few moments, shadows covered the lanes. Long before he felt ready, Tad faced his commander and repeated the colonel's words.

"He what?"

"He refused, sir." Tad took a deep breath. "It is an order he cannot—"

Shaw's voice interrupted from behind. "I cannot have my men use wanton destruction to gain their freedom. This is war, Colonel Montgomery, and the enemy's army must be defeated, not the citizens." His horse's muzzle touched Tad's shoulder.

Tad took a step backward toward Shaw, relieved the brunt of Montgomery's anger would not fall on him.

Montgomery's eyes bore into the smaller man, but his voice remained calm and quiet. "I understand your delicate manners may be offended by the cruel injustices of war, Shaw, but the Southerners must be made to feel this war. If they cannot grow food, they cannot feed their troops, and we will save soldiers for the next fight." He waved a hand. "All must be swept away by the hand of God, like the Jews of old."

Colonel Shaw laughed, a lighthearted sound that, to Tad, was misplaced. "And you deem yourself the vengeful hand of God?"

"I do, and I am. This town will burn."

Shaw gritted his teeth. "I refuse responsibility of this."

Montgomery pulled on his horse's reins. "So be it. On my shoulders then."

In moments, angry flames licked the heavens. Dark clouds of smoke blocked the dim stars. Roofs collapsed in a shower of sparks. Burning embers cast an eerie light on the sweaty black faces of the troops. Tad couldn't tell if the glow was sweat or tears.

Fresh fires spread to the outskirts of town, where Montgomery rode like a conquering general, waving his sword at untouched houses. The light of destruction that flashed in his eyes grew with the inferno. He looked like Satan come up from the depths.

Two houses by the river remained untouched. "Burn them!" Montgomery shouted above the roar of flames.

Tad stepped forward and yelled. "They belong to the women. You told them you wouldn't touch their homes."

Montgomery stared at him for a moment, then grabbed a torch from the hands of a nearby soldier. He spurred his horse toward the houses and paused near Shaw. Tad could just hear him over the crashing around him.

"We are outlaws, Shaw, commanding black troops. If we're caught, the South will hang us without trial." He flung the torch, and a window shattered. Fire shot up the curtains and engulfed the room. "As outlaws, we're not bound by the rules of war."

The flames pushed the soldiers to the river. They boarded the ships to escape the heat. From the deck of Tad's ship, Montgomery stared into what remained of the blazing town, mumbling. "I am God's emissary, using fire, a righteous cleanser of sins, to purge evil from this land."

Tad imagined he could see demons laughing in the dark corners of the fire. Anguished ghosts swirled around the once-stately plantation houses, screaming in terror as generations of memories crumbled to ash.

Tad closed his eyes and covered his ears.

The ships steamed downriver, but the tide quit a mile from the burning town. All eyes turned to watch the glowing sky. As the light dimmed, the soldiers settled on the deck, quietly eating salted pork.

Tad felt a blanket of gloom settle over all of them. He looked up at the stars, which peered back at him, angry and bright, as if the tiny white lights knew what work had been done.

# THIRTY EIGHT

*I*n April, Tad was transferred to Shaw's Fifty-fourth Massachusetts, where Samuel waited for him with open arms. Camp
was moved to St. Helena Island, and Tad was able to visit the
Frogmore to check on his field, which Bo tended with care. He
tried to talk with Peg, but she turned away without a word. He
took his broken heart back to camp.

The soldiers marched and trained, cleared out rattlesnake
dens and slept with mosquitoes. Tad welcomed the warmth,
the rich spring and bountiful summer. He longed for Peg but
enjoyed the late evenings sharing stories and songs while food
cooked over campfires. He was able to share corn bread from
Mammy's kitchen, which made him popular.

On a sunny afternoon, Pierce and Shaw met in the commander's tent and Tad listened outside. They spoke of the Fifty-
fourth. After arming the freedmen and defeating the South,
would the Negroes turn against the North?

Tad smiled and wandered to find Samuel.

"They fear us." Samuel lifted a box of ammunition and set it
into a cart. "Look what they got me doing. I'm toting a pile of
goods from one side of camp to the other, for no reason, 'cept
to keep my mind off fighting. With a rifle, what can't we do? We
could even take Washington."

Samuel was right. With rifle in hand, Tad felt he could take any heights no matter the defenses.

Shaw left the drills to Major Hallowell while he slipped away on a June morning. He wasn't seen for several days. In late June, Tad found out why.

Major Hallowell asked him to deliver a message to the colonel, who could be found at the Penn School. "Quickly now. This is important. Take a horse."

The horse galloped seven miles down Land's End Road and thundered into the familiar Penn School clearing. He spotted Shaw on a bench with the black schoolteacher, Miss Forten.

The colonel jumped to his feet.

"A message, sir." Tad scanned the groups of students in hopes to glimpse Peg. She wasn't there.

Shaw cleared his throat. Tad looked at the colonel's outstretched hand and reached into his satchel. He pulled out the major's note and handed it to him.

Shaw read the paper quickly then turned to Miss Forten. "I must go." Regret saturated his voice. He took her hand and kissed it. "I will see you soon." With grace, he mounted his horse, removed his hat, and gave a nod to the teacher before spurring his horse toward camp.

Tad couldn't keep pace.

Samuel met him at the horse corral. Tad dismounted, straightened his uniform, grabbed a brush, and wiped sweat from the horse's flanks.

"Is it true? Is we going to Charleston? Is we to fight?" Samuel asked.

"I don't know." Tad stroked the soft horsehair until it gave off a brilliant shine in the late sun.

Samuel gripped his hat. "We's gonna fight. After all this training and marching, they finally gonna let us fight."

Tad felt uneasy when Colonel Shaw called assembly and

stood before the long lines of blue, Major Hallowell at his side. "Charleston will be captured." Cheers followed. "The way must be cleared, and we've been called to do it. Not by shovel or ax, but by bayonet."

Tad glanced at Samuel, who was standing next to him. His stoic and serene face showed only one emotion. A single tear trickled down his cheek. "They's givin' us the chance to prove it all. We won't let our kin down, will we?"

Despite his long desire to be a soldier, Tad suddenly wasn't sure.

※

The transport ships pitched in the stormy weather and rain fell uselessly into the gray ocean. Rolling dark clouds blocked the soldiers' vision. A thin, pale line was the only evidence of shore.

Droplets fell from Shaw's cap. "Europe was like this—rainy, dismal." Tad's eyes met his, and the colonel held the gaze. "All the education I've gained, all the languages I speak, and here I am, leading seven hundred men into battle." He looked away. "This is honorable."

Honor, courage, bravery. Tad's heart fluttered with a mixture of anticipation and fear.

"All this experiment is good for," Shaw called over the wind and rain, so that the entire transport could hear, "is to show you've returned to African savagery."

He'd caught everyone's attention.

A smile crossed his face. "Or so the papers say. They think that once you're removed from military discipline, you'll kill innocents." He laughed and lowered his voice. "Not these soldiers. Never have I met such an educated class. Such honor-bound men."

Covered with oiled rain gear, soldiers huddled on deck smoking, talking, or singing. Some sulked in the driving rain. In the sky, a clear patch made its way across the ocean, caught up with them, and gave way for a ray of sun to shimmer against the cresting waves. The bright light shone off their wet slickers.

"Captain Appleton," a soldier called. "It true they taking our guns and giving us pikes to fight?"

"Of course it isn't true."

All eyes turned to the white man with a thick goatee and military perfect posture. He muttered a few words Tad overheard. "As if anyone would take a rifle from the likes of these men." The captain raised his voice. "If they took our guns away, I'd fight still. You're better soldiers than most, and to prove it, I'd charge a bulwark with pickaxes."

The soldiers cheered but Shaw didn't join them. He clenched his jaw tight and with bright eyes scanned the distant shore.

Tad shivered. Somewhere in the thick trees waited the enemy, crouching in the shadows. He suddenly wanted to run.

The boats drove toward one of the many islands, and the Fifty-fourth rushed across an empty shore. Men were sent as pickets, to give warning if the enemy advanced on the shore, in a wide semicircle. Tents were thrown up in the center. Colonel Shaw called the men together and described a victory the Army of the Potomac claimed in the North, at a small town named Gettysburg.

Spirits rose.

Tad took messages to pickets, and found the front lines tense but eager, a distinct difference from the lazy Union men around Port Royal. The distant sounds of cannons brought his attention from the picket line, and he looked toward the unseen Charleston. His breath quickened. The men around him shifted from foot to foot and glanced at one another.

A voice came from behind. "Attack on Fort Wagner."

Tad turned.

Shaw stood with hands on his hips, one side of his lip turned up in a half smile. "I wouldn't worry if I were you. There will be plenty of fight left in them when it's our turn to attack Charleston."

The sounds of war sent a thrill through Tad, and his heartbeat thrummed in his chest. This was a fight against his old massahs, who hated him.

As Tad and his commander walked back to camp, the young soldier let his mind wander. Tad felt he'd given Massah plenty of reasons to hate him. Not only had he been discovered in Massah's daughter's bedroom, he'd been friends with Collin, something Massah surely was pressured by other planters to end.

But Tad had changed. He'd been educated by the finest teachers in America. He saw clearly the victories to be had in freedom, the peace in worshiping as he decided, and the thrill of capital markets. All despite his black skin.

It was no wonder the South hated them so much now. Freed slaves were equals with white men and women.

Another thought struck him. Was Collin among the enemy?

In camp, the colonel paced. Tad stood by, waiting for orders. He sensed something was coming.

"Tad." Shaw punched his fist into his hand. "Call Captain Appleton."

Before Tad could react, the captain, who was within earshot, leapt to his feet and saluted. "Sir."

"Captain, take as many men as you deem comfortable and reinforce the pickets."

Appleton saluted again and rushed away to bark orders. The soldiers jumped to their feet, snatched their new Enfield rifles from the stacks, and slipped into the forest.

Tad was about to ask if he could follow, but Shaw quieted him with a wave. "Do you feel it?"

A bead of sweat trickled down Tad's face.

Thunder erupted nearby. Colonel Shaw slapped his knee. "That's it." He turned to Major Hallowell, who waited nearby. "Let's meet them in battle." Both men shared a grim, knowing look before the major called for assembly.

The rest of the Fifty-fourth clambered for their rifles.

Shaw wrung his hands. "I wish we had the First and Second South Carolina. We could use the reinforcements."

Tad's mind drifted to the regiments at Port Royal, the only full-strength regiments protecting the islands.

"Tad." Shaw's voice was sharp. "Move forward. Find Captain Appleton. Tell him we're coming in full strength, in a line to reinforce his position. We'll be strong on the flanks. Tell him to hold the center."

Tad turned to run but paused. Sounds of battle emanated from the dense forest, punctuated with screams of anger, fear, and hatred. He glanced at the colonel, who was giving orders to other runners, coordinating the nearby white companies.

Prayers. "Lordy." He clenched his teeth, but nothing more came. He dashed into the forest.

Leaves slapped his face, branches clung to his buttons, but he pushed through, closer to the sounds of gunfire. His breaths came in short gasps. Sweat trickled down his hot cheeks. Every leaf seemed sharpened by his alert attention, every movement caught his gaze. The pungent smell of gunpowder touched his nostrils, and he sneezed. All thoughts of honor were left on the beach.

He paused, hearing a buzz overhead. A loud smack and a tree shook. Bullets. Stinging death swarmed around him like bees flushed from a hive. He pictured his father fighting against overwhelming odds, standing victorious against conquered enemies, and pushed forward.

Smoke drifted ahead as blue uniforms came into view. Captain Appleton raced along the line calling out to his men. They kept up a steady fire, rifles pointed out then pulled back to re-load. A high-pitched scream sounded across the entire line, a yell from the Rebels.

Tad competed with the ongoing battle for the captain's at-tention, but finally was able to report. "They should be up any time," Tad said as he finished Shaw's message.

"Tell Colonel Shaw we're holding off a thousand Rebs." Cap-tain Appleton tried to catch his breath. He wiped his wet face with a sleeve. "It's no good if they attack again."

Tad happily fell back away from the battle line. His hands still shook when he reached Shaw's advancing line. He sprinted for the commander.

"A thousand, says Captain Appleton." Tad gave a quick sa-lute. "He cannot hold another attack."

"Double time." Shaw pointed his sword forward, and his men pressed past Tad in a pounding of boots. He followed be-hind the human shields in guilty relief.

Another of Shaw's staff appeared with a message. "The flanks are under heavy attack, but they hold."

"Excellent." Shaw nodded quickly. "The Tenth Connecticut is on our right flank."

They approached the flailing line just as the next attack started. Gray uniformed soldiers halted and fired into the Fifty-fourth's strengthening ranks. A man dropped in front of Tad, though no wound apparent. Another man fell in a shower of red, his head opening like a melon. Tad gripped his stomach and lost the hardtack he'd eaten earlier. His bladder emptied. Breathing heavily, he hurried to Shaw, who stood in the melee screaming orders.

Tad peered at the enemy. A long row of gray pressed toward them. A small man with a straw hat jumped a log, ahead of the others in the line, and with bayonet pointed, charged Shaw's line. His shoulder reared back and his rifle fell, but he pressed on without a weapon, until another bullet found him and he crashed to the ground. Another enemy soldier close by hurled forward and fell face-first.

Tad took a few quick breaths. He turned to look at a fellow messenger but a bullet slammed into the white officer. The man crumpled into a bloody heap.

It was too much. Tad turned to run and crashed into Samuel.

"You's gots to stay, boy, even if that means dying." The big man towered over him. "You understand it?"

Tad wanted to cry, but he fought the tears and nodded. Samuel squeezed Tad's shoulder before returning to the line. The massive driver lifted his rifle, and with a shout, fired.

The din of war covered the sounds of Tad's whimper. As the battle droned on around him, the stings of death dulled.

Soldiers along the line lifted their rifles and fired into an enemy that refused to retreat. Men fell to the earth, some screaming in pain, others never to rise again.

The roar of battle suddenly dimmed, and the attack stopped. A dreadful calm washed over the battlefield, where the dying cried out and a handful managed to crawl back to their lines. A cheer of victory rose from the Fifty-fourth.

"Officers, on me!" Shaw yelled, and they gathered in a circle behind the row of soldiers. "How did we fare?" His voice was high and confident.

"A position of strength." Major Hallowell took a drink from his canteen. His hands shook. "Casualties minimum, spirits high. We held them, sir."

"We've plugged the holes with reserves." Captain Appleton opened the chamber of his pistol and flipped cartridges in with a thumb. "But we held them. We can hold again."

"The first engagement." Major Hallowell dropped his canteen and pumped a fist in the air. "The men held, sir."

"Yes, yes, the men held. You had doubts?"

"No, sir!"

"Then prepare for another attack."

A white captain burst from the bushes and ran along the line toward the officers. Shaw pointed. "He's from the Tenth Connecticut, close in on our right."

The captain shook his head, and with a salute, gave his report. "We're in full retreat. We are to be overrun."

"Overrun?" Shaw swept off his cap. "We've heard very little action from our flank."

The Tenth Connecticut officer's head drooped, and he stammered. "The colonel is certain the Rebs are amassing in his front and are preparing to overrun the position."

"You haven't been attacked yet?" Colonel Shaw's eyes widened. "The action is to *our* front. We can't hold them off without strength on our flanks." He studied the empty forest in front of the Fifty-fourth. "They'll return, there's no doubt." He grumbled to himself for half a minute. Finally, he shrugged. "We'll fight a delaying action, wait on the beach, and hope they don't storm through our defenses. Hold your fire when our backs appear."

The man from the Tenth Connecticut nodded and disappeared into the forest.

A surge of anger swept through Tad. If *he* hadn't run, why was the entire Tenth running? Tad looked up to Shaw.

The colonel took a deep breath and turned to his officers. "One hundred paces to the rear. Re-form there. We shall see the resolve of these Confederates. Now, quickly."

They fell back in good order, across a shallow depression filled with water. Tad thought the command a good idea. The mud would slow the next attack.

Tad saw Samuel, and he nodded.

Wails filled the air, and the Fifty-fourth turned just in time to face the enemy.

Bullets shrieked over Tad's head and he ducked.

"Fire!"

The line erupted in smoke. The gray advance disappeared in a hail of bullets. Over the bodies rushed a second wave. "Reload! Fire at will."

A spattering of shots tugged at the enemy, but on they came. A tall man jerked back, a slug careening off his face in a shower of flesh. His rifle spun through the air and skidded at Tad's feet.

Through the smoke of the battlefield, Tad saw his dark hand reach for the gun. The hot barrel burned his skin, but he felt it as if through a dream. The scuffed stock fit snug against his shoulder. The hammer was pulled back. His finger hovered over the trigger.

He pulled. The rifle jumped in his hands. It was impossible to tell, in the mass of men who charged, if he hit his target, but a man fell from the enemy line.

He turned to Shaw, who glanced down at him. "Keep up the fire."

Tad snatched the belt from the dead man and slung it over his own shoulder. While the regular soldiers fired three rounds a minute, Tad loaded and shot a single round. He'd fired three shots when Colonel Shaw ordered them to fall back.

Dust, sweat, and blood caked their mouths and uniforms as they backed away. Rebels closed in and a clash of steel filled the air. The sound of gunfire slackened as the entire line met the attack with fixed bayonets. He could hear Samuel's roar above the noise and turned to see his friend's massive muscles ripple under his uniform as he clubbed heads with his rifle. White teeth gleamed, his red eyes settled on another victim. Samuel lunged, drove his bayonet into the man's belly, and lifted him screaming into the air.

Tad slashed with the bayonet, catching a man in the chest. He pushed, feeling the blade go deep. It slid so easily. He wanted more.

Next to Tad, Shaw drew his sword. A Rebel came at the colonel from the side, and Tad thrust his bayonet. The tip caught the man in the hip, and he stumbled. Colonel Shaw slashed the sharpened edge against the enemy's neck.

Slowly they backed away, foot by foot, giving ground to the enemy.

The beach erupted in front of them. Sand spewed into the sky. The earth opened up around Tad, preparing to swallow the entire army. A tree shattered, and splinters ripped through the forest like shrapnel. Tad's ears rang with the noise.

"Those cannons are ours." Major Hallowell lifted his rifle over his head.

"Full retreat, to the shore!" Colonel Shaw waved his sword to the south.

His troops streamed out of the forest toward the waiting Tenth Connecticut. Offshore, gunboats supported their retreat with cannons.

Tad stood behind friendly lines and watched the earth rupture in the forest, consuming the Rebels.

Tad paused, tried to feel some remorse for what he did. His mind pressed in on him. His father, no doubt, wouldn't think on it. Mammy and Peg would tell him to run.

Mr. Pierce and Miss Towne would press him to fight. Mr. Philbrick would find a way to make money by pulling the trigger.

But what about him? Strip away the opinions, the conjectures, and at its core, he found pain. He'd been whipped, beaten, humiliated. But those weren't the reasons he meant to fight.

These men would enslave again, if not stopped. Jesus asked to turn the other cheek so the enemy might smite it. But He also ended the reign of Satan's tyranny.

※

The Tenth Connecticut officers readily admitted the black Fifty-fourth Massachusetts troops were heroes of the day. Generals came ashore, along with reporters, and took note of all that had happened. The Fifty-fourth had proven they could fight alongside the white regiments and scrap better than most. The public confidence added swagger to the steps of the Fifty-fourth soldiers.

The fight wasn't over. A few hours later, they were on the march again. Billowing dark clouds rolled up from the south, then unleashed their fury to compete with the man-made war. Torrents of rain washed away blood and dirt but soaked the men. Tad shivered, his boots filled with water.

They reached the end of James Island and crossed slick, narrow planks that engineers had strung across the alligator-filled marshes. Tad slipped and tumbled into the murky water, but strong arms reached down to pull him out. One soldier clapped him on the back. "Can't let our best fighter drown."

He wasn't the only one to fall into the marsh. Several times the line halted while a victim was pulled from the filthy muck. Hour after hour they marched, across another island, then another impromptu bridge. Under the dark sky, lightning lit their way.

As the morning grew light, they paraded on. When the sun touched the top of the sky, they waited on a beach, baking under the hot furnace. They tried to sleep, but just as the temperature dropped to comfortable levels, transport ships appeared. Before they could eat, they boarded. Another storm rocked the boats so violently Tad was glad his stomach was empty.

They unloaded, marched across another island, where more transports waited. Finally, after a long night, they arrived on Morris Island, a thin strip of land that touched the ocean.

In the distance, Charleston burned. Two forts could be seen in the shadow of fires. Cannons belched death toward the earthworks, and smoke rolled into the night sky. Tired, Tad looked up into Shaw's calm face. "Where are we going?"

"The fort in the bay is Fort Sumter, where this war started." The colonel looked down at him and grinned, but it was a sad and forlorn look, despite the smile. "But we're headed to Fort Wagner. That's where the defenses are on the island."

Shaw mounted his horse. "Stay with the men, Tad. I'll ride ahead for orders." The colonel paused, reached down, and set a hand on Tad's shoulder. "You're a fine soldier."

Tad swelled with pride. He watched his commander ride across the beach.

He heard two voices behind him, and turned to listen.

"He knows." Captain Appleton brushed his thick goatee.

"Look at his eyes, how they dart back and forth. And he's been depressed lately." Major Hallowell pulled on a dirty white glove and clenched his fingers. "Explains the friendship with Miss Forten. He told me the other day, 'I trust God will give me strength to do my duty.'"

Captain Appleton gave a decisive nod. "He knows."

"What?" Tad asked. "What does he know?"

Distant flames reflected in Major Hallowell's eyes. He walked over and put a hand on Tad's arm. "Colonel Shaw knows he's going to die."

# THIRTY NINE

*T*ad dreamed of death. Not the recent battle on James Island, but Johnny. Did Johnny know he was going to die? What was his final thought? Did he regret his final action?

Then he was back behind the same bush he'd seen in his dreams one hundred times before. It was an easy thing now to push the bush to the side and view the large man with a knife gleaming in the moonlight. The man looked at him, and they stood for several moments, staring at one another. Hadn't the man held a gun before?

*Run*, the man said. *Run*. Tad told himself to stay, that after the recent battles, he'd seen worse. But he couldn't stop his legs from carrying him through the dark trees. Such short strides. He looked down, his body so tiny. Of course he would flee. He'd do anything Pappy told him to do.

He woke in a fevered sweat. His knapsack lay by his side, and he dug around inside. He pulled out his canteen and took a long drink, then wiped moisture from his lips and looked across the sand. Samuel watched him, leaning against a palmetto in the shade, hiding from the burning sun.

"You sick?"

"Dreams, I reckon." Tad slid the canteen into the pack. "Johnny, mostly. Keep seeing Massah point that gun at him on the dock, the day we were freed."

"No more are gonna die like Johnny. This war ain't about fighting to keep a country together. It about freein' slaves." Samuel swept off his cap and rubbed his head. "That's what's keeping the Union apart anyhow, is us slaves. Once the war's over, the killing stops."

Tad shrugged and hoped Samuel was right. He rested his head against a tree and stared into the dense forest. "You knew Pappy, didn't you? From the old days?"

"Some, I suppose."

"You reckon he's a soldier right now?" Tad shielded his eyes against the merciless afternoon sun.

Samuel looked past Tad toward the sea. "He was a fightin' kind of man, so I suppose he found a way to do some killing."

"Mammy says he ran away to Texas. You think so too?"

Samuel shrugged. "Maybe he did, maybe he didn't."

"But why did he run? Was it so bad, me being his boy and all?"

Samuel's red eyes, tired from the recent fights and marches, opened wide. "It was 'cause he loved you he ran."

Tad sat up. "But why? What happened to make him run?"

"Ain't got time for stories so long." He shook his head and closed his eyes. "Ain't got time. Besides, Mammy wouldn't have it."

"Is it because you're scared of Mammy? Or because my pappy was Massah?"

Samuel let loose a low whistle. "I'm scared of Mammy, that's for sure. Ain't anyone in their right mind wouldn't be scared of Mammy. But Massah wasn't your pappy, not in a year of Sundays. No, your pappy really did run."

"But why?"

Samuel sighed and motioned Tad close, who crawled across the sand to get to the driver's side. "I'll tell you, 'cause, as Mammy would say, Lord knows what may happen in comin' events. It would please me greatly if you wouldn't let on that it was me who told you."

"'Course not."

"Your pappy ran because he had to. Nothing else for it. A man came to sign a bill of sale for you, you being all but three years from Mammy's belly. Said he was selling you upriver, to Virginia or the likes, to make you a breeding Negro. And Mammy had but a few hours to say good-bye because he'd come to take you away."

He was silent for a moment, and Tad watched the Northern warships off the coast pass on the rolling waves, refitted at Beaufort several hours to the south. They returned to pound Charleston and its forts.

Samuel started again. "Your pappy found out about it, and slipped into the woods. He waited in the bushes 'til the buying man appeared on the road. And your pappy killed him."

Tad wrapped his arms tight around his knees.

"Mammy was in a fretful state, 'cause you'd run off that night, but after a bit, you appeared, and Pappy was close behind, though he didn't stay long. He had to run, wasn't nothing else he could've done. But she done something that made his killing the man worse'n anything that could've happened."

"What'd she do?"

Samuel shook his head. "Ain't telling. That's for her to say."

"You going to make me ask her?"

Samuel nodded and took a bite of salted pork.

Tad dug the toe of his boot into the sand and knew by Samuel's tight jaw he wouldn't tell.

The big man swallowed the rations, took a drink from his canteen, and leaned back against the trunk. "Tad, I've got something to tell you, case I don't come back to Frogmore."

"You're coming back."

He shrugged as if he hadn't heard him. "I got relations on Frogmore."

It took a moment for Tad to realize what Samuel meant. He cocked his head. "Who is it?"

"My wife lived on Tombee, but Massah Chaplin ran out of money. Sold me and our little one to Massah Coffin, and Massah Coffin sent us to Frogmore. I heard my missus died, of heartache I reckon."

Realization dawned on Tad like a fresh new day. "Why'd you run away from Frogmore? Why did you leave your relation?"

Samuel's face contorted as he struggled to master his feelings. "I didn't want Peg knowing 'bout her mammy, beings she looked at your mammy as hers. But if I got sold downriver, I reckon it would tear the heart out of her if she knew I was her pappy. You know it would. And she'd die like my woman did."

"So you ran 'cause she had Mammy?"

He clasped his fingers around his rifle and used it as a crutch to stand, took a few steps toward the ocean, then paused and turned back. "'Cause she had you to marry someday."

Pain shot through Tad's heart, and he closed his eyes. Samuel's dreams were ruined, because Peg had given him a choice, marriage or the infantry. He'd chosen the army. At night, alone in his bedroll, he regretted his decision. And now, on the eve of another great battle, he wondered if he could face the bullets again.

When he opened his eyes, Samuel was gone, but he saw a lone figure on shore watching the ships batter Fort Wagner. His hair streamed to the side in the brisk wind. His gloved hands were clasped behind his back, the toes of his boots covered by the incoming tide. The man turned.

Colonel Shaw! Tad scrambled to his feet to take his place beside his commander.

He stopped just beyond the water's reach. Though Shaw's focus was on the battle, his face was so solemn Tad didn't speak.

Soon, officers joined Tad, waiting in silence while their commanding officer looked out to sea. After several minutes, he turned and studied the small group. His eyes were brown and calm. "Prepare your men. I know they are hungry and tired, but we lead the charge. Today, we go to prove the Fifty-fourth."

As the officers turned to give orders to their men, Shaw motioned to Tad. "I'll return in an hour, after I have dinner with General Strong. Be sure to eat plenty of food while I'm gone. You may do an uncommon amount of running, and you will need your strength." Tad felt the pressure of the commander's hand on his shoulder.

Shaw returned just as the troops assembled, and began to march north, over sandy beaches and wet marshes. Tad thrust out his chest as they passed long rows of cheering, white soldiers. He recognized the fish-faced soldier, the one he'd sold the corn bread to.

The soldier cupped his hand around his lips and called out, "Make a door for us! We'll be right behind."

Tad waved at the man.

Shaw continued up ahead, leading the regiment on horseback, and Tad ran to catch him. The column halted, and the colonel saluted General Strong then leaned down to shake their commander's hand before the charge.

Shaw drew his sword, looked back, and swung the blade over his head. He pointed. "Two rows, along here."

After a quick shuffle, the men were ordered to lie down in the sand to rest, but Tad couldn't relax. Instead, he looked over the long expanse of beach leading to Fort Wagner and trembled. Soon, they would be running the length of that field, bullets screaming past. And it was the enemy this time that had cannons.

The men behind him talked quietly. Those who could write traded letters with each other. Some joked to relieve the pressures of pre-battle calm, to push away the tension.

Shaw veered his horse past Tad, toward the crowd of on-lookers who waited eagerly for the coming charge. Tad crawled onto his feet and followed his commander. Pierce stepped forward from out of the throng.

Pierce's dark brown hair waved in the breeze around the edges of his hat. His pale, white face reminded Tad of snow. Tad wanted to rush to the man and embrace him. What was he doing here?

"Colonel Shaw!" Pierce's weary voice cracked. "An honorable day. Thank you again for dinner with General Strong and yourself."

"A valiant charge ahead of us." Tad noticed Shaw's lack of enthusiasm. The commander reached into his uniform pocket and leaned down. "Edward, a packet, for my father, in the event of my death."

Pierce studied the colonel's face for a moment. "I will hold it for your return."

They clasped arms. Shaw looked as if he wanted to say something. Instead, he turned quickly and joined his men.

Pierce, his face serious, motioned to Tad. "A word."

Tad glanced over his shoulder at Colonel Shaw, who again stared out to sea, then off toward Fort Wagner. The sounds of cannons continued to fill the air as the ships pounded the works.

"You've done a fine service for this army." Pierce set a hand on Tad's shoulder. "It's time to let others stand for their country. Come, step out of ranks."

"Colonel Shaw needs me."

"Tad, you're technically not in the army. You're on loan to commanders. You don't have to make this charge. Come, stand with me."

Tad looked down at his uniform, confused. "You mean I'm not a soldier?"

Pierce set his hands on his hips. "Of course you're a soldier. You've proved it. But let's not take this too far."

"Can't let down friends." Tad was upset now. "And I've been drawing pay as a private."

Pierce's head jerked up. "Drawing pay? It doesn't matter. Come, Tad, come away from this fight."

"Mr. Pierce, set down your hat and come with us. Fight for freedom."

Pierce drew back. "What?"

"You didn't feel the lash, Mr. Pierce. You didn't suffer in the fields, didn't pick cotton till your hands bleed. Hauling mud till fingers bleed. Taking hate from massahs and returning in kind. I'm done with it, Mr. Pierce. I die today, or the slaves will all be free. If you aren't going to come, then make sure the papers know what we're doing here."

Tad spun as he would when marching in line and returned to Colonel Shaw. The colonel sent his horse to the rear of the column, then lit a cigar. Tad heard the men around him laugh at a joke. Shaw took a deep puff on the tobacco.

White men with tiny spectacles, tall hats, and black suits stood before the regiment and made dreadful speeches lost in the wind. The wait was torture. Sunshine beat down on them, but the breeze off the ocean cooled his dark skin.

Finally, the Fifty-fourth was commanded to stand. Orders flew by quickly. Check arms, load rifles. Straighten the line. Fix bayonet, twist and snap the long, sharp metal. Load cartridge box as ammunition passed around. Hats on tight.

A spiritual, low and soft, thrummed through the ranks.

*"Gospel train's a'comin', I hear it just at hand,*
*I hear the car wheel rumblin' and rollin' thro' the land.*
*Get on board, little children, there's room for many more."*

Tad tried to fasten the top button of his uniform but couldn't slip it through the hole. Colonel Shaw's shaking hands worked the brass button for him. He nodded at a job well done and grasped Tad's shoulder. Tad saw fear in his commander's eyes.

The ship's cannons silenced.

Hundreds of yards away Fort Wagner rose from the sand, its empty walls stretched across the narrow island. Tad hoped the entrenchment was abandoned.

He took his place behind Shaw. They stood in front of the six hundred freed slaves, eager to move. Tad wished they had been reinforced after losing one hundred men to illness and battle, but it was too late now. The colonel called for the advance, and Tad swelled with pride as the regiment stepped forward as one. He glanced back, nodded a final farewell to Samuel, and pressed ahead. Over sandy dunes they marched, past tall grass and through tide pools. Long rows of men on either side surged ahead, their determined black faces set against the enemy.

Tad saw the smoke before the sound touched his ears. A single cannon shot from the fort billowed white clouds. The ball whistled overhead and exploded, showering bits of metal over the men. Rebels stepped onto the walls, making their presence known. They lifted their rifles toward Tad and the others.

The fort erupted in smoke. Hot fragments of killing metal flew through the air around him. Red explosions, yellow fire, and gray fog clouded their sight. Tad marched forward, keeping an eye on his commander.

Colonel Shaw turned and screamed. "Double time!"

Death struck the lines like a sickle through grain, men at their peak of physical prowess swept away in a single blow. Tad felt no fear, only a distant awareness he was no longer in control of his movement, as if he watched the long lines pressing forward from above the ranks.

A cannonball exploded in front of him, sucking the air from

his lungs. Instinctively, he covered his ears and discovered his head was sticky. He looked at his hand. Red.

A bullet tugged at his uniform, but he pressed on. Another cannonball burst nearby, then three in quick succession.

The force flattened him to the ground.

# FORTY

$\mathscr{P}$ierce stared at the hanging chandeliers and tried to drown out the screams and groans around him.

Each cry of pain was a stab in his heart.

The Episcopal church, in the center of Beaufort, had once been a bastion of religious control for the noble gentry of the South's elite. Sermons against Northern oppression fell not only on the ears of the slaves' oppressors but on the slaves who attended to their masters' every whim, even in the Sunday service. What had once been the center to justify the enslavement of a race now housed wounded and dying Negroes.

He kept his hands in his pocket as he descended the stairs. Elegant wood banisters that led down from the balcony were splashed in blood. Long pews that stretched across the sanctuary now acted as hospital beds for the injured men.

Pierce couldn't stomach the rotten air. He stepped outside.

Under giant, sweeping oaks, graves dotted the yard, protected by a thick, stone wall. Tall headstones had been pulled from the ground and set across shorter gravestones to make operating tables. Four white soldiers held down a Negro man as another sawed through his leg. They tossed the appendage onto a bloody pile of black limbs.

Pierce turned away and walked back inside to return to Tad's pew. Private Gates, a white soldier with a codfish face who rarely left Tad's side, looked up from where he knelt on the floor.

"How is he?" The bandages that wrapped around the boy's head were soaked in fresh blood.

"Same." Gates' face was etched with concern. "He will ask what happened, and I'll tell him, but he never opens his eyes. Asks again a few hours later, like I never told him. Slurs all his words."

"I've called for more doctors from the islands. They should be here soon."

He touched Tad's smooth cheek, then turned toward a commotion from the back of the sanctuary. A woman stood at the church door.

She scanned the room, her eyes dark, her lips taut. The severe bun on the back of her head controlled her hair, but exposed the emotions that played across her face, feelings that seemed to vacillate between anger and concern. She looked directly at Pierce and hurried over.

"Miss Towne, thank you for coming."

She ignored him and settled onto the pew, her dress flowing over the edge. She brushed Tad's forehead with her fingers then unrolled the bandages and glanced at the wounds. The dirty linen dropped to the floor. With her thumb, she gently opened Tad's eyelids, one at a time. "Has he awakened yet?"

Gates looked at her. "Sometimes he stirs. But I don't think it's really waking up. His eyes don't open."

She laid a hand on Tad's bare chest, her fingers trembling. She waited a moment, took a breath, and looked up at Pierce, tears in her eyes. "He's had too many concussions in his young life. He needs a bed, but we shouldn't move him. We must find pillows, blankets."

She stood.

Pierce stepped close but had no words. He wanted to tell

her why he'd allowed Tad to march to war, why she should understand the need for a man to prove himself. He wanted to
explain his own shortcomings, in hopes she would talk to him
again, just a word of approval.

He didn't want to love her.

She straightened and looked him in the eye. "Peg came. To
see him."

Pierce hesitated. "Do you think that wise? Is she angry with
him?"

Miss Towne looked away. "She isn't angry. Some things tran-
scend simple emotions."

Pierce sighed. Perhaps she was here because Tad would
never be a soldier again and she could take him home. "They're
not children."

He shifted uncomfortably as she stared at him. After a moment, he looked away.

She spun on her heels and left the church, her dress swishing behind her. Soon, two shadows stood in the church entry.
Miss Towne's modest silhouette, though beautiful, was paled
by the gorgeous young woman at her side. Pierce hadn't seen
Peg since the day she refused Tad.

Tall and slender, her most noticeable features were her large,
brown eyes that caught the attention of every conscious man
in the room. Soldiers and medics parted, opening a pathway
to Tad's side.

Miss Towne walked straight toward Pierce. Peg followed,
oblivious to the calm that settled in the room. He watched the
girl's eyes. They remained locked on Tad's pew.

She paused to look down on the injured boy, taking in the
gash on the side of his head that oozed blood.

Her face remained stoic.

Peg lowered herself slowly to a knee, by his side, and closed
her eyes. After a whispered prayer, she touched his shoulder.

"What'd they do to you, Tad? What'd they do?" A single tear trickled down her cheek.

Tad's lids fluttered at the sound of her voice and he opened one eye. He squinted at her. "Peg?" The word was barely audible.

"It's me, Tad, flesh and bone. Right here, with you. We'll be making you all better now."

He managed to open both eyes, and a faint smile crossed his cracked lips.

"That's the first time he lifted his flaps." Gates laughed and slapped Pierce on the back.

Tad tried to speak, but his voice rasped and faltered.

Pierce held out a canteen. Peg took it and carefully lifted Tad's head. She set the canteen against his mouth. He drank with passion, water spilling down his cheeks, then tried to sit up. She pushed him back down. "Stay calm."

He glanced at those hovering above him. "What happened?" His words sounded as if his mouth were full of mush.

Private Gates glanced at Miss Towne, who nodded.

"Well." Gates licked his lips. "I didn't see it 'til you come back from the front lines, but we pieced it together from talking to the men, Mr. Pierce and me. I watched you march, and the Rebs in the fort firing into your lines. Slowed the march quite a bit, and the way we hear it, before entering the fort, Colonel Shaw sent you back to get reinforcements. That's when I saw you again, stumbling over a hill. Bleeding." He pointed to Tad's head.

Tad reached up, but Peg held his hand.

Gates pinched his nose. "You was stumbling, almost like you was drunk. You fell into General Strong's arms, and you asked for the reinforcements. But he'd been gravely wounded, and deferred to his officers. They said no reinforcements." Gates laughed, coughed. "You yelled at them, told them they was a pack of no good . . . well, Tad, you swore at them."

Tad pushed himself up, then collapsed. He closed his eyes. "Colonel Shaw—" He managed to open one lid. "The men . . . Samuel?"

Gates bowed his head.

Pierce glanced at Miss Towne, who clutched her hands against her heart.

Gates cleared his throat. "We don't know where Colonel Shaw is. He hasn't returned, perhaps he's a prisoner."

Pierce spoke. "Samuel the same."

Tad grasped Peg's arm so tight she bit her lip. Tears welled in his eyes. "I'm so sorry, I'm so sorry." He repeated it over and over, until Miss Towne mixed a powder in his canteen. He drank it and fell asleep.

Peg laid her head on his chest and wept.

Miss Towne stood, pulled back an errant strand of hair stuck against her cheek, and folded her arms. "Others need me." She hurried away, calling, "He'll live," over her shoulder.

Pierce later found her dressing the wounds of an amputee. The red bandage wrapped around the stub of his leg smelled like rotten fish. He touched her shoulder. "I'm sorry."

She didn't look up, but continued to work on the sweating, groaning man. "For what?"

He swallowed his pride. "For making Tad and Peg's argument ours."

She glanced up, eyed him for a moment, then nodded. "You're forgiven." She blew at the wisp of hair that tickled her face. "Do you really mean to ask me to leave these people, Edward?"

Pierce watched her heft the man's partial leg. She wrapped bandages slowly around the bloody red and black wound. "It would be selfish of me, I know," he said after a moment. "But I've never met anyone like you. It's hard to imagine Boston without you."

She looked into his eyes. "And no man has ever given me

reason to change the course of my life like you. But you will not stay here, and I will not go to Boston."

He was about to respond when a voice drifted across the graveyard.

"Your future is secured. There is good in it." Reverend French looked like Moses in his long, flowing robes. Sunlight glistened off his stern face. Wounded men turned their ears to listen. "You have sacrificed yourselves. There lies the future, as Christ has sacrificed His body for all of us." He waved his arms. "Our Almighty God has given me a vision in the night. He has chosen His side, and it is ours."

Pierce glanced at Miss Towne. Their eyes lingered.

French continued, his face turned upward. "We thank Thee, Lord. We thank Thee for the faithful who have returned. Open Your arms to take in those whom You are about to receive."

His words echoed.

Pierce cringed. He looked at the mangled bodies clinging to life. God's arms would need to be open wide.

⊗

Colonel Shaw was dead. Samuel too. Private Gates—now Sergeant Gates—left, and Pierce, along with Peg, watched over Tad. The boy's recovery was painfully slow.

Pierce wrote Shaw's parents. *Your son gave himself for a country, but has now laid down his life for a race.* Shaw's love for the black man was miniscule compared to his parents' abolitionist views. There would be solace for them in their son's death, he was certain. Shaw's parents immediately sent money to build a church in honor of their son. It was to be located in Darien, the city Colonel Montgomery burned to the ground. The city would be rebuilt.

Pierce felt numb.

Shaw would be remembered. Every newspaper reported

his death and shrines were already in the works. He would be known as the man who died for his men, died to prove the black man worthy to fight. And Shaw hadn't even wanted the position as regiment commander.

Shaw's horse was given to a grieving Miss Forten, at the colonel's final request. It was difficult to say who mourned more, the widow Annie or the newfound friend.

The decision from the generals to replace Shaw shocked Pierce. Of all the men who represented the worst in character toward the Negro, Tad's nemesis, the destroyer of Darien, Colonel Montgomery, would be the Fifty-fourth Massachusetts' commander.

At least the war effort was strengthening for the North. A victory at Gettysburg in the east and another at Vicksburg in the west pushed the South back.

What provided the most satisfaction for him was that the freedman had finally received recognition. While they had failed to take Fort Wagner, the black man proved he could fight. Black regiments immediately formed in almost every Northern state, ranks filled by contraband men who had been slaves in the South.

The experiment was complete. The freedmen proved themselves capable of civilized actions through the uncivilized venue of war. They paid with their blood.

Pierce readied for one last battle. All had been proven on the freedmen's part, from the ability to fight to self-reliance. But one final task remained. Government wavered on land ownership. The ground on which the Negro grew his crops could be swept out from under him at any time—just when trust was at its strongest.

# FORTY ONE

*T*ad closed his eyes and listened to Peg's voice fill the church. The haunting melody echoed from the high ceiling and fell like a gentle, cleansing rain on the suffering soldiers.

*"Brother Robert, light the lamp, and lamp light the road,*
*And I wish I been there for to yedde Jordon roll.*
*O the city light the lamp, the white man he will sold,*
*And I wish I been there for to yedde Jordon roll.*
*O the white marble stone, and the white marble stone.*
*And I wish I been there for to yedde Jordon roll."*

When Tad opened his eyes, he saw Captain Appleton sitting at the end of the pew, smiling. "Yedde?" His words were almost muffled in his thick goatee. "What's Yedde?"

"Hear." Tad struggled to sit up. The ringing in his ears returned. He closed his eyes and leaned against the pew back as the world spun. Peg's voice calmed the roar in his head. "She wishes she was there to hear Jordon roll."

Appleton nodded and put a hand on Tad's shoulder. "You don't look so good. Maybe you should lie back down."

Pierce appeared behind the captain, and the three men watched in silence as Peg calmly walked through the church. "She's like an angel," Appleton whispered. "The way she touches the men's hands, they seem to take strength from her."

"Captain, should you be with your unit?"

"I'm here with a request from the men." Appleton looked at Pierce. "Colonel Montgomery has seen fit to deny all passes for leave. Tad's to be moved to Hilton Head."

Tad felt Pierce's tight grip on his shoulder as the man spoke. "Tad's in no condition to return to duty."

Appleton kept his voice at a whisper, and Tad had to strain to hear. "He's not returning to duty. I'm here to give him a discharge from the infantry. You've done your part in this war."

Tad stared at the church's altar. The past few days had been difficult, almost more than he could handle. Colonel Shaw was dead. Samuel was dead. Appleton had told him both men were buried in a common grave with dozens of other black soldiers.

He closed his eyes. He hadn't told Peg about Samuel's secrets. Words seemed to escape them when they were together. And he couldn't make the words sound right, slurring them horribly. He was satisfied just to be close to her.

He felt a sense of guilt, leaving the infantry, not because he would miss doing his part, but because the thought of entering battle again horrified him. He'd forgotten the reasons he foolishly leapt into the fight, the risks he'd taken. A life with Peg and the field waited for the two of them. A few feet of soil to sustain them and the family they'd someday have was all he wanted.

Pierce snorted.

Tad looked up at him.

His friend and mentor clamped his teeth together and a dark look crossed his face. "Colonel Shaw, against my knowledge, officially signed you into the Fifty-fourth. You'll be getting a pension. Mammy's never going to speak to me again."

Tad rubbed his head. "She'll be glad I'm alive and out of

the infantry." He tried to make his words clear, but his tongue wouldn't work right. He closed his eyes again. "I've got land and the freedom to use it." He settled into sleep and muttered one last sentence. "What more is there to be done?"

# FORTY TWO

*N*o one knew why General Saxton had called the freedmen together at the Brick Church. Until the reason was known, they would treat it as a party.

Pierce saw Tad and Peg under the low branch of a tree, their heads together, talking quietly. Tad's healing was slow, too slow. It had been two months, and while Pierce knew head injuries took time, Tad hadn't been able to tend his fields. Instead, he hired Frogmore residents to work for him. His speech had cleared only a little. But Tad was still able to laugh, something he did more of lately. A few from Gideon's Band joined the two. The mood in their circle seemed lighthearted.

Pierce glanced at Miss Towne. She didn't look well. Miss Murray had come down with the summer fever, and her illness had lasted well into fall. Miss Towne had canceled a holiday visit to her family so she could care for her friend.

She leaned against an oak tree, alone.

He watched Mr. Phillips, a supervisor from a distant plantation, approach her. Pierce couldn't hear, but his words seemed to drive her against the tree trunk. He rushed through the crowd to stand by her side, hearing some of the conversation.

"The Penn School is no longer important for the freedmen," Phillips said. "It is a church first, community center second. There is no room for a school here."

Miss Towne straightened. "Nonsense, Mr. Phillips. There are dozens of churches on these islands. You must put those to better use. We're here to educate these people. And you have no authority." Her voice was soft. She'd lost the fire that once defined her. Her eyes were puffy and dark.

"The church is about to move into private hands. I'm just the messenger."

Colonel Higginson, commander of the First South Carolina, joined them. "Miss Towne, are you feeling well?"

Her eyes pleaded with the colonel. "Please, the school . . . "

Phillips turned to Higginson. "I was informing Miss Towne that the church is built to worship God. The Penn School is closing."

General Saxton shouldered into the group. "Lovely party." He winked at Miss Towne. "Nice weather. Are we ready for the announcement?"

She stared at him, clearly confused.

"In a moment." Phillips drew himself to full height but still couldn't match the three taller men, even Saxton's short build. "I will explain this one last time. Miss Towne must close her school."

Saxton rubbed his bald head. "Now, don't tell jokes on such a fine day. You know her school is the most successful of the island, of any south of the Mason-Dixon."

"There are other places for children to learn."

Saxton puffed out his chest. "I won't allow anything to happen to the school."

Colonel Higginson smiled. "I could send troops."

Pierce added, "Secretary Chase could discuss the matter with President Lincoln."

Mr. Phillips licked his lips. "It will be out of your hands." They watched him hurry away.

Miss Towne smiled feebly. "Thank you, gentlemen."

325

Saxton turned to Pierce, a look of concern in his eyes. "If this idea takes hold—"

Higginson shook his head. "It won't. I won't let it."

Pierce touched his ear. "Keep your ears to the gossip." He noticed a tax commissioner walk toward French and whisper in the reverend's ear. Pierce shifted uncomfortably. Something felt wrong.

Reverend French stepped onto the stage with arms raised. The multitude quieted. The freedmen loved a performance, and French, if not always helpful, could always draw a crowd. Faces looked upward.

The reverend bowed his head. "Lord, You have blessed us. We thank You, Almighty, for Thy generous gifts. You have delivered us a Moses, and Moses has delivered us into the Promised Land."

Pierce looked up. What did that mean?

French waved a hand over the crowd like a benevolent father. "I have spoken with President Lincoln, who welcomed me with open arms and asked about his children in South Carolina. He loves you, he wants you to be happy, and he wants you to be able to take care of yourselves. We know you must have land and that the land you plant is not yours. But we have prepared a way."

The crowd murmured, and French opened a hand toward Saxton. "Let the good general explain it to you."

Saxton strolled onto the stage. He stuffed one hand in his pocket and motioned with the other as he spoke. "All the land is going up for sale. But you have a chance to preempt other buyers. You can buy the land you want, any land, and it will be yours."

Pierce took a step forward. How could this be? He'd been told sixty thousand acres of charitable land were for sale. The three tax commissioners, positions created to squeeze every penny from the land, would surely not agree with Saxton. But yet, there one of them stood, smiling.

Saxton pointed to a structure at the back of the crowd. "Behind you is a cabin. It would only take two or three days to build, and will cost you twenty-five dollars." He stuffed both hands in his pockets. "There will be more details soon, so find the land you want and prepare to buy it."

Pierce paced. This was a mistake. The paperwork filed by the tax commissioners did not allow for preemptions by the freedmen. Chase would have contacted him if Lincoln had signed into law a land option for the freed slaves. Without the president's signature, nothing was guaranteed.

He walked to the side of the stage where French stood and grabbed the reverend's arm.

"See here," French muttered.

"What is all this?" He kept his voice low while Saxton spoke.

"Ah, my friend." A look of recognition crossed French's face. "You see, all will be right in the end. They've worked the land for centuries, and now it's to be theirs."

Pierce studied French's eyes for clues. "I agree. They do deserve the land. But is there legality in this? Will the preemptions hold up in court against other claims?"

"We have found a way." French smiled, his voice confident. "The tax commissioners, especially the one here today, Abram Smith, have been given the right to reward acres of land for good behavior. You cannot deny, Mr. Pierce, that a freedman who earns enough wages to purchase land is exhibiting good behavior. I have met with Secretary Chase on the matter, and he agrees."

Pierce looked up at him, shocked. "He agrees? So every person who earns money can buy land?"

French shrugged. "The *Free South* newspaper in Beaufort is advertising today. Isn't it splendid?"

Pierce imagined standing before a judge, trying to convince him the preemptions were legal because freedmen behaved.

❦

Winter dawned and 1864 arrived with all the bravado it could muster. All freedmen could talk about was the day they could buy land before the general auction in February. But no letter came from Chase in affirmation, despite repeated requests for clarification on Pierce's part. Freedmen hoarded cash, preparing to purchase forty, eighty, even hundreds of acres.

Abram Smith, the tax commissioner upon whose support the preemptions depended, spent most of his time with the bottle. He was drunk daily by ten in the morning, and helped none at all. Brisbane, the head of the tax commission in the islands, was so confident the preemptions would not be allowed, he decided to purchase Port Royal. All of it. Pierce didn't like where the sale was heading.

The freedmen's preemptions were the only way former slaves would ever own a scrap of land, because they had little or no cash. Or they could buy land from men like Philbrick, on credit. If Philbrick would sell.

Pierce kept sending letter after letter to Washington with no reply.

He watched Tad prepare for the land purchase.

One day near Christmas, the boy seemed no longer slow of wit. Tad worked to gather support, funds, and publicity to buy not only the Frogmore, but neighboring plantations. The land would then be parceled out amongst the freedmen according to needs and investment, all under Tad's capable control.

In early February, at the Brick Church, Pierce watched Tad and hundreds of others file for the land. The money was taken and signatures given, land plots set aside, and papers filed away for the official sale.

On February 14, Pierce paced in front of the Rhett mansion in Beaufort. Wooden crates lined the interior halls, the wide porch, and down the stairs. Each crate held preemptions filed by freedmen, with money packed away in envelopes.

A man at the nearby Beaufort dock sprinted across Bay Street and into the house. After a few moments, Brisbane, the head tax commissioner, appeared at the door. He stepped off the porch and walked directly to him. "A word, sir?"

Pierce nodded.

"You're a reasonable man, and a lawyer." Brisbane, much older than Pierce, still contained the energy so needed by government men. "The war is almost over, Mr. Pierce. Southern men will return to this land, land they hold deeds to. These preemptions," he said, waving a hand over the wooden crates, "these documents will never stand in a court of law. I know you understand that. I cannot allow these preemptions."

Pierce struggled for words. "They must hold. They must." But in his heart, he knew it could never be. *Mansfield French!* How could he have done this to the freedmen? Would they ever trust the government again? "The freedmen, what will become of them?"

Brisbane's eyes showed sympathy. "If the government does not act, and soon, the Southern man will return and hire freedmen to work the land. I'm afraid slavery, in one sense of the word, will still exist."

There was a moment of silence before Brisbane explained further. "We just received word from Secretary Chase to ignore the preemptions. We reviewed several filings. Mr. Pierce, supervisors, teachers, preachers—they filed for the land, in quantities that equaled the freedmen. I can't say for sure, but perhaps that played a part in Secretary Chase's decision."

∞

The next day, Pierce watched Tad try to gather the funds from the preemptions held in the crates. But he was a step behind the government, too late to beat the official land sales. The money remained in the envelopes. Frogmore didn't sell, since it was a part of original charitable lands—it continued to be government owned. But Northerners purchased thousands of acres around Port Royal.

Mr. Phillips was successful in blocking Miss Towne's Penn School. Pierce learned he was part of a group that wanted religion and education to have no part with each other, to keep the teaching of Jesus sacred from the general public. No longer able to teach at the church, Miss Towne and Miss Murray packed their things to move to a village at the north of the island, St. Helenaville.

As the women said good-bye to the other members of the old Gideon's Band, Pierce sat on the porch at The Oaks, rocking and reflecting on what they'd learned. The experiment was coming to an end. Many of the supervisors were heading home.

A horse carrying a fine gentleman appeared. Pierce recognized Gannett, who removed his tall hat as he dismounted and greeted Pierce with a warm embrace. "I've come to see Miss Towne. Is she in?"

"Of course, let me call her." He turned his head toward the open door and called her name.

Miss Towne stepped onto the porch, and Pierce started to walk away.

Gannett cleared his throat. "Please stay, Mr. Pierce. I have always valued your advice."

Pierce gazed on Gannett's earnest face, the young man's red cheeks glowing in the winter sun.

"I must tell you of my private concerns, and what I wish to do about them." Gannett shuffled his hat from one hand to the next. "Mr. Philbrick has endowed me with a percentage of the profits from last year's harvest. After paying the freedmen, and all expenses have cleared . . . Well, soldiers make thirteen dollars a month, and we make a great sum of fifty, Mr. Pierce." His eyes flashed in earnest. "I made seven thousand dollars."

Miss Towne gasped.

"It's a sum I cannot have. It feels ill gotten, and I believe the amount can be put to better use than in my hands. Miss Towne, the Penn School. Is it to remain open?"

She shot Pierce a quick glance, then said with care, "I hadn't told anyone this, but Philadelphia's mission agency is building a school directly across the road from the Brick Church for our use. It is fabricated in Philadelphia. But it will arrive any time."

Gannett leaned against the porch rail and crossed his arms. He smiled. "I *am* pleased. My desire is to establish a trust to pay teachers long after we leave. No matter what issues arise, we can still educate the young."

She took his hands. "Oh, Mr. Gannett. That is such welcome news." Energy returned to her voice. She smiled at Pierce. "The Penn School lives. For me, this is a happy day."

# FORTY THREE

*S*ecretary of War Stanton arrived just before 1865. With tight spectacles, a round waist, and a long beard, he drifted from island to island like a king or benevolent overseer. As his straw-colored hair fluttered in the sea breeze, hopeful black faces surrounded him, pleading for help. The residents of the islands demanded land.

If Stanton was king, Pierce was jester. He followed in the great man's wake. Stanton's direct questions and decisions reflected why Lincoln maintained confidence in the man, and Pierce wanted to be near the power. He missed Boston and Washington, where decisions made by men fed on beef and coffee controlled the lives of the freedmen. Freedmen and the rest of America. But the powerful man was here, living, even for a short time, in the midst of the problem. Pierce felt a fierce love for the president and those who advised him.

At Port Royal, inside a brick building, Pierce pressed his ear against a door. Twenty freedmen, including a subdued Tad, sat around a table. They came from all skills—wood, metal, farming, sailing, and carpentry. Each represented some facet of economic strength. These men would press the case of the freedmen, passing information to Lincoln in hopes he could help others become viable citizens in the Union.

Pierce held his breath.

"I don't understand." Stanton's voice was deep, but muffled behind the door. "You want separate schools and different places of worship?"

"Yessuh," one man said. "We's all alike in this. See, we reckon they come back, the old massahs, and when they do, they's gonna be the teachers. I reckon if they don't teach us, then we don't learn no more 'bout slavery. And if slavery ain't gonna be taught no more, then everybody forgets the whole thing, and we live in peace."

Pierce jumped away from the door as it opened, and all twenty men filed out. At the end of the line came Stanton. "Ah, Mr. Pierce. Glad you were here." He thrust his hands into his vest pocket. "I'm going home. I've learned all I need to. Implement Sherman's field order fifteen."

"Sir, I'm embarrassed to admit, I'm not sure what Sherman's order is."

"Land for all." He pulled out a handkerchief and wiped his nose. "Forty acres and a mule. Lincoln will sign it into law immediately. All freedmen will have land."

# FORTY FOUR

*H*onest Abe pulled the plow through the rich soil. Abe was honest, Tad could tell, because of the wide, dark eyes. So he'd named the mule Honest Abe, and did his best not to love the beast too much.

The mule pulled an honest row too. It was strange to plow a field instead of hoe a row, but Tad was open to new methods. The plow worked best for corn. But for the cotton field, he would dig the rows with tools to make the ridges deeper.

One change he rejected was fertilizer, a chemical mix he didn't trust that was sprinkled on the field to add nutrients. Marsh mud was free, so he hauled buckets before plowing.

The sun beat down, and while not hot, warmed his skin. He took off his hat and wiped his brow. Abe's flank, bright with sweat, went untouched by the whip, and Tad let the mule rest often. He patted Abe's snout, then brushed the dirt from his fingers.

Spring had come late, so Tad had been slow getting into the fields to plant. But winter had been busy. He and several others helped Miss Towne put up her new school. Sections of walls had come prebuilt. Strong hands were needed to erect the partitions. With enough classrooms for the teachers—and room to expand—Miss Towne eagerly went to work. She would keep the same name, the Penn School. Her bell, donated from Philadelphia, tolled every school morning, and the children walked from miles away.

Tad decided college wasn't for him, despite pressure from teachers. At least not until he married Peg. They waited on Pierce to marry them, but he was busy helping others get their forty acres, so they would wait, impatiently.

Honest Abe nuzzled his shoulder, and Tad wrapped his arm around the beast's neck.

He heard screams just before Peg burst from the pine forest. Without thinking, he started running across the rows, his bare feet kicking up dirt around him.

"You hear? You hear?" Peg grabbed the sleeves of his shirt. "You hear it, Tad?"

"What, Peg? What? Tell me!"

She wrapped her arms around his waist and swung in a circle. "You hear it? We're free!"

"Yes, Peg, I know."

"No, but General Lee surrendered!"

"General Lee . . . done what?"

"He surrendered. The war's over, and we're free for sure this time."

Tad gripped her tight, kissed her, then spun her in the air. "War's over, and we're free." He pulled her against his chest. "Let's marry, in a few days. We'll have a cake. Mammy can make it. Everyone will be there. Let's marry."

"What about Mr. Pierce?"

"He can come if he wants, but if he don't marry us, then someone else will. Mr. Soule, maybe."

She giggled, took his hands, and spun with Tad in a circle.

❧

"Lordy me. All these vittles and all these happenin's, ain't had time to talk to my Tad."

335

"Sorry, Mammy, with planting and all, I haven't had time to sit with you." Tad ground his teeth into the hardtack left by soldiers. All the food on the Frogmore was held in Mammy's capable hands, ready and kept warm. The beautiful spring day came prepared for a wedding. So Tad ate army rations.

He took a drink to wash down the biscuit. "Mammy, I'm getting married today. You think it's time I know about Pappy?"

But even on his wedding day, she labored over the flaming stove without telling him. She produced the finest chickens, the softest corn bread, the largest, fluffiest cakes.

"I been thinkin' on your new name."

Tad's heart sank.

"I been thinkin' on all the changes come to these islands, and bless me if they haven't come 'cause of Mistah Pierce and all his missionaries. If it weren't for them, I reckon, we wouldn't be capable of learnin'. Them teachers were a help. For my son, most of all."

Tad waited without a word.

Mammy took a deep breath. "Your new name will be Gideon. You ain't a little Tad no more, boy. You earned a Christian name, for sures. So on your wedding day, I'm callin' you Gideon."

Tad stepped out of the kitchen and paused, turning back, looking through the open door at Mammy. Gideon. He had feared this moment—the very idea of a new name. But . . . Gideon. He liked it.

He knew from this day forward anyone he met for the first time would know him as Gideon. But to others, like Peg, he'd always be Tad.

The big house was headquarters for the wedding. Peg was ushered into a room along with Miss Towne, Miss Murray, and Miss Ware to get dressed. Tad and Pierce donned black suits in a different room. Tad had borrowed his, as had his groomsman Bo. Another groomsman, Philbrick, wore his own suit. Private

Gates, the fish-faced soldier, would be the last groomsman, and he wore his uniform. Gannett was pleased when Peg asked him to give her away.

The door opened and General Saxton quietly stepped in. Tad took a few steps toward him, but stopped when he noticed tears on the older man's face. Tad thought he was happy to see him, but another look told Tad different.

Pierce set down his jacket. "General, what is it?"

"President Lincoln has been shot." Saxton's voice cracked. "He's dead."

Everyone in the room fell silent. After a moment, Philbrick stammered. "Dear God, what is to become of our country?"

No one spoke. Each person was lost in thought, trying to imagine life without the man they all felt was their friend.

Tad had never met President Lincoln, but he loved him. He'd brought them freedom. He was their father, and their father had died. Tad looked at the men, saw their tears, and couldn't hold back his own. Without the man who emancipated them, life for the freedmen could turn upside down again.

"Such sad tidings before a wedding." Pierce cleared his throat. "Tad, how can we go on with such sorrow?"

Tad bowed his head and closed his eyes. He searched his heart, imagining what tomorrow would be like with or without Peg as his wife. "Mr. Pierce," he said slowly. "I was born in sorrow and have lived my life in sorrow. Death will be in sorrow. If I must, I will marry in sorrow."

Pierce clasped Tad's shoulder, then nodded at General Saxton. "Tell the women. Let them know about Lincoln. And tell them the wedding proceeds." He smiled at Tad.

An hour later, Tad stood next to Peg on the porch. Her cream dress shimmered in the sun. She'd tied her hair back with ribbons, giving Tad an enticing view of her slender neck. He knew she had mixed feelings of joy and sadness, but her eyes shone like stars.

Pierce married them in a Baptist ceremony. Tad knew it must be difficult for him to preach as a Baptist instead of a Unitarian, but he did, without flinching. Peg repeated the words of the wife, then Tad said the words of the husband.

After Pierce pronounced them man and wife, he shook Tad's hand, then Tad kissed Peg. He held his wife close, keenly aware of her firm, strong body. The bridesmaids and groomsmen all wanted kisses as well, and got them. Then the crowd that had gathered below the porch wanted to greet the new couple. Mammy set down a broom, and Tad and Peg grasped hands and leapt over the wood handle before descending the stairs.

Beside the tabby barn, tables were spread with white tablecloths, all covered with food. Everyone feasted until late in the evening, when Mammy announced Tad's new name.

Tad was about to take Peg to her new cabin, when someone mentioned Lincoln's death. A dark mood settled over the group. Several supervisors decided the time was right to tell General Saxton they were leaving their positions, retiring home to the North. Tad and Peg huddled against the gray wall holding hands, as Gideon's Band came to an end.

Tad nudged Peg and motioned to the cabin he'd had built for her.

"This isn't about everybody leaving," she whispered. "They're just sad about the president dying." She shook her head, stood up, and raised a hand to heaven. The discussion stopped. They watched as the bride glided across the grass to the middle of the crowd. She opened her mouth and sang.

*"Brother Moses gone to the promise land,*
*Hallelu, Hallelujah.*
*Brother Moses gone to the promise land,*
*Hallelu, Hallelujah."*

Tad stood and joined her with his feeble voice. Miss Towne sang along, and soon everyone joined in.

They sang late into the night.

⠶

True to their word, the last of the missionaries had left. Tad was used to farewells, but sadness filled him as he told Mr. Gannett good-bye.

"You're such an honest person." Tad held the man's grip in his own. "Too bad you want to become a minister."

Later in the week, Peg rested on her back and looked at the ceiling while she sang softly. Tad lay beside her and stared at her profile. Her silhouette—reflected against the single lamp—was too beautiful for words, so he just watched her sing.

Her song ended, and she laid a hand against his bare chest. "I'm proud of you."

He sighed, wrapped the ribbon from the front of her nightgown around his finger. "Don't feel special."

"To be invited as a delegate to the Republican convention, that's something."

"I suppose. Mr. Pierce probably had something to do with it."

She pushed against his chest. "You earned it."

"I don't like everybody leaving."

"Feels like we got the islands back."

He bit his lip. "Things are different now."

She sat up, pushed a pillow against the wall, and leaned back. "You're afraid of the old masters?"

He reached up and rubbed the silver cross at her neck, then lay back and pulled her close so her head rested on his shoulder. "Isn't the same, now that we know what's past the marshes."

"We take life as it comes."

He brushed her cheek. "I have held a secret too long from you." He pulled away from her and sat up.

"You've always been full of secrets."

"This is different, Peg." He hesitated but decided just to say it. "Samuel was your pappy."

She stared at him.

"And my pappy killed a man, and then run."

She leaned back and stared again at the ceiling. "Always said you was a good boy." She pulled on his arm until he lay next to her. "It isn't anything, Tad. Mammy told me, some time ago. Back when Samuel run." She kissed him. "As for your pappy, always knew there was a mean streak in your family, but never knew why. Didn't come from Mammy."

"You saying I'm mean?"

She gave a mischievous smile. "You not marrying me long ago, that was mean."

"You ain't mad then?"

She sighed. "Been mad for a long time, Mr. Husband. But I save it for those in deserving."

The door rattled with a loud knock.

They clambered from the bed.

"Tad . . . Gideon. You in there?" It was a woman's voice.

He glanced at Peg, then threw on a shirt. He cracked open the door and peered before flinging it open. "Miss Towne."

In the darkness, he could just make out her red face. Her chest heaved as she struggled to catch her breath. "Tad, I need you."

Peg touched Tad's shoulder and slipped next to him. "Why?"

Miss Towne gave Peg a half smile. "I need Tad for an important mission. We're off to see the president."

# FORTY FIVE

*M*iss Towne briefed Tad on the mission while Miss Hancock, another teacher who would join them, listened.

New York, Boston, Philadelphia, and several smaller missionary societies had banded together to create a government-sanctioned Freedman's Bureau. The organization pushed a piece of legislation through Congress, the Freedman's Bureau Act, to confirm the freedman would truly get Sherman's forty acres and a mule.

President Lincoln had sanctioned the Act, but his support died with him. The executive branch now thought it pointless. The freedmen were about to lose their land—this time irreparably.

Pierce had left the islands immediately to fight the injustice. So overwhelming was the new cause, he had no time to return.

Andrew Johnson, once vice president to Lincoln, sat behind a desk as Miss Towne and Miss Hancock took seats across from him. Tad stood between the two women.

President Johnson's face was locked in a permanent scowl. His bowl-cut hair drooped over his ears, and his long nose and sullen frown so intimidated Tad, he forgot why they came.

Miss Towne did not.

He watched the woman who had taught him how to think

341

on his own use her gift of persuasion against a man who made a life of bargaining and compromise.

"We're here to discuss land given to the freedmen, Mr. President, land set aside in an order from General Sherman, one that is rumored you may take away from these repressed people."

He looked down at several documents, picked up a pen, scratched for a moment, then looked at her. "I have spoken with General Sherman on this matter. He had no intention to maintain Field Order Fifteen permanently, only to settle the Negroes for a short time."

Miss Towne's voice returned in earnest. "And we're here to tell you of their plight."

"Yes, yes, but it's votes we must count, and they have none." He leaned back in his chair. "I know of Edward Pierce's mission to add black votes. He failed. And I know of you, Laura. I've read your letters in the paper. Your work is good. Gideon, I've read of you. You have nothing to worry about. The Sea Islands are quite safe, locked away in charitable lands or purchased during the tax buyouts. We must honor those. They will hold in the courts. But Southern gentlemen will return to their farms, and they must be given every opportunity to pay the taxes owed from previous years. To divide the land and give it to freedmen will keep them from doing just that."

Miss Towne clenched her hands together. "What is to happen to the freedmen?"

"I suspect they will find work." Johnson leaned back in his chair and folded his arm. "Just like the rest of the country. They are no different from anyone else."

Miss Towne's face turned bright red. Tad sensed the anger in her, and knew the president was making a mistake. Her fingers closed into a fist. "Tell me what other race has been subjected to slavery. They ask so little—only a small plot of land and the opportunity for education. It was a government sanction that allowed their subjugation. It is your job to reverse it." She put a hand on Tad's arm. "Gideon has brought a letter to read, written by freedmen."

Tad's hand shook as he reached into his vest pocket. He unfolded the letter before him. He closed his eyes, wet his lips, and took a deep breath.

"Mr. President Johnson. How can it be expected of any man to work for those he has beaten on the battlefield? Is it not just to be the opposite, that they are to be subject to us? How can we ask them for comforts, food, and wood? We have made offers to buy the land from the former owners as they return, but they refused, even at one hundred dollars an acre. We have no confidence in our late owners. Sincerely, freedmen of South Carolina." Tad pushed the letter forward.

Miss Towne smiled. "We speak not for Port Royal's freedmen, but for Sherman's Negroes. This office used to care for the less fortunate, especially those troubled through no fault of their own. Will you not extend the same feelings?"

President Johnson closed his eyes, then slowly stood. He walked to the door, opened it, and turned to Miss Towne. "I am not my predecessor."

§

Tad led Miss Towne through Boston's busy streets to Mr. Pierce's law practice, not for himself, but for her.

As they approached the business front, he could see her hands shaking.

Pierce opened the door before they knocked. His dark hair, which had grown long in Port Royal, was trimmed again, and he had abandoned his attempt at a wispy goatee. "Come, come in. My, it *is* good to see you again." Pierce led them through the hall, past a silent, subdued man at the secretary's desk, and upstairs to the private office. He motioned to two chairs and sat across from them, behind a desk.

Tad stared at the walls. Dusty books, wide and heavy, filled the bookshelves. "You read all this?"

"In the past." Pierce smiled. "But now I mostly read these." He motioned to a stack of periodicals at the end of his desk. "Can I offer you a drink?" Tad and Miss Towne shook their heads. He sighed. "I take it teaching goes well, Laura?"

"The Penn School is—"

A knock at his office door stopped her.

"Yes?" Pierce looked agitated at the interruption.

The door opened, and the secretary's head appeared. "Sir, your eleven o'clock appointment is here."

"Tell them to wait, or come back. I have more important matters."

The door closed. Pierce turned to Miss Towne and leaned forward. "The Penn School?"

She folded her hands on her lap. "The Penn School is changing, and I believe for the better."

"What changes?"

"We teach basic academics, but also trades—woodworking, blacksmithing, sewing, weaving—by any teacher who understands a craft."

Pierce's fingers tapped a pile of papers as he contemplated his words. Finally, with a quick glance at Tad, then back to her, he spoke quietly. "Your school is the only lasting structure in Port Royal. Did we fail?"

Tad spoke. "I don't think you've failed."

Miss Towne cleared her throat. "We've helped some. Who can weigh the impact of a single school?"

"I wanted to show the North how to educate the slaves, to

prove blacks are equal to any race." Pierce lowered his face into his hands. "The experiment was to be repeated across the South."

"We showed them." Miss Towne reached across the desk and took his hand. "But they choose not to see, to understand. They know of Negro potential, as does the president, but nothing will come of it."

"I will fight." Tad slapped the desk. Clearly, schools were the answer, where freed slaves could learn a trade. A thought struck him. "If President Johnson won't help, we must find someone who will, and make him president." He pointed at Pierce. "If we were allowed to vote, then we could make you president."

Miss Towne leaned forward. "Women must vote, also. Why, Edward, you've turned red."

"I am giving up my political career. I have thrown my lot in with the freedmen, and my voice has lost timbre. No one in Washington wants me. Chase is a justice in the Supreme Court, so he can no longer help me." He stood, walked around the desk, and sat on the corner. "It looks as if we come to the end of the endeavor. Tad, you will be asked to speak in front of Boston's finest. Time and again. Miss Towne, I'm sure you will come visit your biggest supporters here in Boston."

"If I must." She smiled.

He took her hand. "Dear friend. I look forward to it."

She turned to leave, but Tad saw he still held her hand tight.

"May I ask, Laura?" His eyes studied her face, which seemed to have turned to porcelain. "One last time?"

"Oh, my dear Edward. You may ask." She gave a sad smile. "But the answer will be the same."

As they left, Miss Towne put an arm around Tad, and gripped him tight, all the way to the train.

# FORTY SIX

*P*eg closed her book. "You know, I'm proud you're in charge of the Frogmore."

Tad looked across the table at the reclining form in bed. "Miss Towne bought the Frogmore, but I doubt she could farm."

"She chose you."

At first Tad hadn't been happy with Miss Towne and Miss Murray buying the Frogmore plantation. He wanted to own it someday. He believed, since the government had set aside land for charitable purposes, that he would be considered as a buyer. But it was deemed that Northern Supervisors could buy charitable lands and the two teachers were allowed to complete the sale as a special circumstance. While a former master would never sell it to Tad, Miss Towne might. And with old masters returning in droves, no one knew what was going to happen. At least the Frogmore was in safe hands. He was willing to wait.

"I'm going to bed, Tad. I can't keep my eyes open."

"Are you sure you don't mind, if it's a boy, we call him Edward?"

"As long as if it's a girl, we name her Laura."

Tad nodded. "I want to finish this chapter. Then I'll join you." He turned the page and tilted the book so the lamp cast its light on the yellow page. Lately, he'd been reading Miss Murray's nov-

els about the American West, where Indians slaughtered helpless settlers, and heroes fought back to protect the innocent.

He finished the chapter, grit his teeth, and forced the book
closed, but found his finger still stuck at the start of the next
chapter. One or two more lines couldn't hurt. As Peg slept in the
bed nearby, he sat at the table in his cotton nightshirt, reading.

After a tale about a harrowing escape, the book settled into a
story of romance. With a clear conscience of putting the good
parts off until tomorrow, knowing he'd have to wade through
the slow bits, he closed the book and blew out the lamp. Moonlight streamed through the open window, lighting the soft bed
and Peg's warm body. He settled in against her.

He drowsed, and dreams began drifting like sea breeze
through his mind. He was a little boy again, in the forest, the
owl above calling out warnings. But his dream suddenly froze
as a different sound filled the night. Tad opened his eyes. Someone had screamed.

Without waking Peg, he slipped on his pants, pulled a shirt
over his head, and stepped outside. He heard it again.

Stars reigned in the heavens, dimmed only by the bright
moon's silver light. Leaves shimmered in the gentle breeze, the
branches etched in white. The cemetery gravestones stood in
somber vigil, glowing gray. He skirted the iron fence and crept
deeper into the forest where the screams grew clear.

A surreal feeling settled over him. It was as if he were in his
dream, replaying it exactly. A touch to his face proved he was
awake. The brush tickled his neck as he pushed through the
thicket. A strong smell of jasmine touched his nose.

He passed a magnolia tree, the white flowers setting the tree
ablaze with stars. Then, voices, one deep voice and a second he
thought he could recognize from another nightmare.

It was Mr. Spencer's voice. The man who had forced Collin
to whip him.

Thick bushes blocked his view of the clearing, the same bushes in his dream. He reached up with trembling hands and parted them.

A big man, larger than Samuel had been, towered over the skeleton form of Spencer. The older man on the ground tried to crawl away, but the large black man kicked mercilessly into Spencer's stomach.

"You was going to kill the boy. I knowed it."

"I wasn't, I promise." Spencer gasped for breath.

"You ain't going nowhere near 'im. I's gonna kill you first." Another kick to Spencer's middle.

"That was just talk," Spencer gasped.

"Talk that'll get you killed."

"Just rumors. I wasn't going anywhere near the boy."

Tad stepped into the clearing, tall and straight. "Stop this."

Both men turned sharply. The big man pulled a pistol and leveled it at Tad. "Who's you?"

"Pappy." Tad heard his own voice, deep and angry. "It's me."

The gun lowered. "Tad? Ain't true, is it? That you, boy? All growed up, tall as me?"

"Killing Mr. Spencer isn't right." Tad took a step forward. "No matter his crimes. There are other ways this can be fixed."

"That's right, that's right." Spencer licked his lips. "Other ways. I wasn't gonna kill nobody."

Pappy turned to Spencer. "You always was evil, that's why I done killed you's brother, and why I'll kill you too."

Tad jerked in surprise. "Pappy, you killed Mr. Spencer's brother, right here in this clearing." He took another step forward. "I was there. I . . . I remember it."

"And I'm telling you the same as I told you then. Run, boy. You run."

Panic filled his mind, like it had before. His leg muscles tightened. He wanted to run with every fiber of his being. But he kept his head high, and he shook a finger at his father. "Ain't running."

"Run, boy, run."

Pappy pointed the pistol at Spencer's heart.

Tad ran, not back to the Frogmore, but at Pappy.

The pistol jumped, and smoke billowed from the short barrel. The retort echoed in the night. Spencer rolled backward and didn't move.

Tad skidded to a stop. "You didn't have to do that, Pappy!"

Pappy's teeth shone in the moonlight. "Been wanting it since I leaved here."

Tad was barely able to speak. "I thought you were a soldier. But you're nothing but a murderer."

"I is a soldier." He stood up straight and faced Tad.

Tad hadn't noticed it before in the darkness, but his father wore a uniform. A gray jacket fitting snugly against the broad shoulders.

"I fought for Texas."

"You fought for the South!"

"Didn't matter who I fought for. I was free."

"But if you'd help them win the war, we'd still live in slavery."

"Not me," Pappy said.

Tad stared at him, his mind reeling. "I'm getting the law."

His father shook his head. "No, you won't. We'll bury him, real quick, and be done with it. Ain't nobody gonna miss him. Then you and me is gonna go West, fight Injuns. Two soldiers."

Tad choked. "Pappy, I'm not going. I fought, in the Union army, for my freedom. You fought 'cause you liked killing."

"Nothing wrong with that. C'mon, the shot'll attract attention. Better head off to the West. That's one o' the reasons I'm here. To come get you now you's free." He looked down at the body. "Heard someone down in Beaufort say Spencer had eyes fixing to kill you. He can't hurt you no more."

"Pappy, I'm getting the law." Tad summoned his courage and walked to Spencer and rolled him over. He lifted the lifeless form.

"Won't be around when they come looking for me."

Tad marched straight toward the big house.

"Tad! Tad, you come back here!"

Several people who'd heard the shot met him and escorted him back. He dropped the body on the porch. With a candle in one hand, Miss Towne pulled a mirror from her bag and held it over Mr. Spencer's mouth. The looking glass didn't fog. Someone volunteered to alert the soldiers and sped away.

Tad looked across the lawn toward the kitchen cabin where Mammy stood with a lamp, Peg by her side. He leapt off the porch steps and raced toward Mammy. He stopped in front of her. "It was Pappy." His voice was a raspy whisper. "He's a bad man."

He reached out to Peg's neck and held the silver cross in his palm for a moment. She didn't move, her chin held high. With a quick snap, he yanked the necklace off. Using all his strength, he hurled the chain into the marsh. It disappeared with a soft splash.

He stood before Mammy. "Samuel said there was more. Tell me, Mammy. Tell me now." He ignored the fear in her eyes. Peg gasped, and Miss Towne held a hand to her mouth.

Mammy nodded and walked to the kitchen with the lamp held in front of her. They followed.

The small group crowded inside, the only light the lamp she set on the table. Using her foot, she pressed against a floorboard near her bed. One end of the floor lifted. With a groan, she settled onto one knee and reached down to pull out a box. Tad helped her to her feet and she set the box on the table, then opened the lid.

Inside was a cluster of loose gold pieces, papers, and trinkets.

She shuffled through them until she reached the bottom and pulled out a wrinkled document. Her eyes glazed for a moment before handing it to Tad. She pulled a chair over and settled in it, her head buried in her hands.

Tad held the paper against the lamp. He could just make out the faint ink. It was a bill of sale. The item sold, on the line, read *Tad*. The date sent a shiver down his spine. January 12, 1854. "Mammy, what is this?"

"I baked cakes and pies, and sold 'em to other plantations, saved money. Lordy, what a day that was when Massah said you was to be sold. I heard it first from a house slave, and Massah admitted it, said if I could come up with more money than the trader, you could be freed."

Staring at her, he whispered. "You had the money."

"But Pappy said I didn't know what I was talking 'bout, could never buy you freedom, so he went to kill the man that was buying you."

"Mr. Spencer's brother." Peg reached over and grabbed Tad's hand. "Mr. Spencer hated me. Reckon I see why now."

"I didn't tell you 'cause a free slave on plantations . . . " Mammy looked up in tears. "It don't happen to be a good thing, unless you go North."

"So I was free? I was whipped, had to work the fields, had to be a slave, but I was free? And Massah knew it?"

An unfamiliar voice at the door shook them all. "Your master was a fool."

Tad looked up.

"Your master is dead. He died in Charleston."

Tad could barely utter the word. "Collin."

"We took our oaths, to honor the peace and promise we would never rise up against the Union again. Easiest oath I ever took."

Tad looked Collin over. "You look like you've been through

a hurricane." Collin's sandy hair had streaks of white running through it.

"Truth be told, I don't know what to do. I promised I'd be back, Tad. I promised that, but now I see that it might not be good to be back. Things are different here. But I won't live with my mother and sisters, and they won't have me."

Tad smiled. "Very different." He looked at those in the room. "I think there might be room for you here, in a cabin." He glanced at Miss Towne, and she nodded.

Collin's shoulders drooped and he took a deep breath. "I heard old Spencer was coming to get you, Tad. He was in the tavern, drunk. I followed him but then lost him on the island. That was, 'til I saw him lying on the porch."

"Pappy must have heard the same thing. Spencer's dead."

Collin's youth returned for a moment, and he smirked. "You mean he wasn't just napping?" He fell silent.

No one moved.

Finally, Collin said, "I fought for the South."

"I fought for the North."

"I killed for the South."

"I killed for the North."

They stared at each other for a moment, until Tad crossed the room, and they embraced.

# ACKNOWLEDGMENTS

$\mathcal{T}$he sun-scorched lawn of the Penn Center played host to a small family. The father trudged across from the Old Brick Church to Laura Towne's tombstone—mother and two children following close behind. Shoulders slumped, all seemed to wilt in the temperature. June in South Carolina's low country can be brutal to those not used to the heat and humidity.

They walked from building to building, wandered to the nearby marsh, and then stood under ancient oaks. After several hours, they stumbled into the main museum, beet red.

The family doing the research was mine. We were hot, exhausted, and inspired. As we entered the museum, we were greeted by smiles and bottles of water. After several hours of bombarding the staff with questions, we were hooked. We'd fallen in love with the Penn Center and the Gullah culture.

Without the Penn Center and their help, this novel would not have been possible.

Behind any historical novel is massive research. Thanks to my wife, Tonya, who not only walked beside me but actually enjoyed herself. Thanks to my children, Jost and Kade Lauree, whose bright smiles and thought-provoking questions opened doors that I never could. And thanks to my parents, Monte and Jeneen, who, when driving around the country, satiated my history habit by taking me to museums and battlefields.

Thanks to Boise State professors Dr. Lisa Brady, who sparked my love of Edward Pierce and Laura Towne, and Dr. David

Walker, who taught me the finer points of war. Both of these professors touched history in a way that came alive for me.

Two editors did the grunt work on the novel, turning my fevered thoughts into coherent language. The first, Becky Lyles, was utterly indispensible. Sending a manuscript to the publisher without her looking at it is like going into battle without ammunition: you're there, but nothing's going to happen. The second is Steve Parolini, whose wisdom and humor kept the process entertaining and educational.

Thanks also to the crew at Worthy Publishing. Especially Jeana Ledbetter, who had to deal with the inpatient questions of a first-time novelist. With a few well-chosen words, she put me completely at ease. Kris Bearss, thank you for your editorial expertise. Morgan Canclini, thanks for being so chipper.

Jeane Wynn, marketing guru for Wynn-Wynn Media, helped spread the story of Edward Pierce, Laura Towne, and Tad. Thank you.

This book would have been impossible without Jerry B. Jenkins and the Christian Writers Guild. The contest and the team made it all happen. You guys rock.

Thanks also to the fellow finalists in Operation First Novelist: Clarice G. James, Jim Hamlett, Kimberley Graham, and Terrie Todd. They helped on a couple scenes and inspired me to be my best.

And finally, thanks to those who are invisible to me. Don't stay hidden forever.

# AFTERWORD

**David Hunter**—General Hunter, after overall command of Port Royal, took charge of the investigation involving the assassination of President Lincoln. He retired from the military a Brevet Major General and died in 1886.

**James Montgomery**—Colonel Montgomery, a villain in the eyes of many, especially Colonel Shaw, resigned his commission in 1864 and returned to Kansas, where he entered the state militia. He died on his farm in 1871.

**Thomas Higginson**—Colonel Higginson, commander of the First South Carolina Volunteers, handed control of the First to Major Trowbridge.

He was a man of many talents. A graduate of Harvard, Colonel Higginson's résumé also included minister, writer, reformer, even poet. Writing to Northern papers, he kept the Union abreast as to the successes of the black regiment. After the war, he turned his efforts to women's rights, and was also an advocate for homeopathy after taking powders from Laura Towne that positively impacted his health. He died at the age of eighty-seven in 1911.

**Edward Hooper**—Captain Hooper proved efficient under General Saxton, after taking the position made for Edward

Pierce, learning financial responsibility. He accepted a post at Harvard as a treasurer. He died in 1901 with pneumonia, although a fall from the second story of his residence probably contributed.

**Edward Philbrick**—An engineer, and a successful one, Mr. Philbrick spent the rest of his life working with sewer designs, making progress toward our modern toilets. He traveled extensively throughout the world and died without having children to carry on his name.

**William Channing Gannett**—The young man to enter the Port Royal Experiment left as a man of reform, eager for change. He became a Unitarian minister, writing hymns and preaching equality, not solely between people of different skin color but between the sexes as well. He married in 1887 and had two children. He died in 1923.

**Rufus Saxton**—Saxton first served as quartermaster for the Union army, and after commanding a battle at Harper's Ferry, took over Edward Pierce's position in charge of the freedmen. After the war he took a post at the Freedmen's Bureau, where he continued to fight for freedmen's rights to the land. Andrew Johnson removed him from the duty. Brigadier General Saxton died in 1908. For the battle at Harper's Ferry, Rufus Saxton was awarded the Congressional Medal of Honor, only one of three given to generals during the Civil War. He is one of three men noted in Laura Towne's diary whom she admired greatly.

**Reverend Mansfield French**—Reverend French attempted to run for public office in South Carolina after the war, but failed, after which he returned north. Reverend French, or Chaplain French, as many knew him, died in 1876 in New York.

**Kate Chase**—Her marriage to William Sprague in 1863 was the social event of the year. Even President Lincoln took time to join the reception. The U.S. Marine Band played a march written just for Kate.

Sprague's unwise investments led him to find help in the bottle, and he became an alcoholic. He accused Kate of affairs, and after four children, they divorced. She returned to help her father's career, and after he died, and her son committed suicide, she lived alone. She died a pauper in 1899. She was, according to the Enquirer, as close to being the Queen of America as anyone ever could. She was buried near her father.

**Edward Lillie Pierce**—The Port Royal Experiment changed Pierce. His energies, once used to help the national government, turned to helping his city government. He married Elizabeth H. Kingsbury, and they had six children. She died in 1880. After donating a library at St. Helena Island to Laura Towne and her Penn School, he married an Englishwoman, his second wife, who gave birth twice. He enjoyed trips to Europe, reading, and taking important positions in Milton, Massachusetts, such as supervisor of the local library.

While he made many speeches and continued to write, he was best known as a close friend to the influential men and women of the day.

Pierce has been forgotten by history for several reasons. First, he didn't press his notoriety to propel him into the more visible positions in government. He chose useful jobs, such as defending the freedmen, and later, the Chinese. Second, he vocally decried the popular Andrew Johnson, President Lincoln's successor. Until the last several decades, Johnson was a popular president, exacting revenge on the South for the war. Pierce's views were not widespread. Finally, the biography of Charles

Sumner, to which Pierce devoted his efforts, is secondary in importance to the more popular characters of the Civil War.

In modern media, he is portrayed incorrectly, usually as a correspondent to Northern newspapers. Instead, philanthropy was his passion.

Edward Pierce died in 1897 while visiting Paris, from all accounts a happy man with the well-deserved love of his children and respect from a healing nation.

**Laura Matilda Towne**—Miss Towne spent more time finding excuses during summer breaks to stay in South Carolina than visiting her family in Philadelphia. Her administration skills kept the Penn School running year after year, despite the North's lagging support. Private funds from such people as Edward Pierce and Lucretia Mott kept the school from closing. The men and women of the island were family to her, and she loved them as her own, taking in children and feeding the poor. She continued in this work until her death in 1901. Hundreds of men and women who loved her sang while surrounding the wagon that carried her body.

Laura Towne's friend, Ellen Murray, died in 1908. Both are buried side by side next to the Brick Church.

Will Towne, her brother, stayed for years, contributing his skills. He remodeled the Frogmore's main plantation house.

Today, the Penn School is the Penn Center. It still teaches, in a variety of ways, about culture, human rights, and other vital information about the islands of the low country.

Laura Towne's bell still resides inside the museum.

**Tad, Peg, Collin, Mammy, Samuel, Bo, Private Gates**—All are fictional characters, but entirely feasible case studies. There are examples in Laura Towne's diary and Pierce's work that describe the former masters' atrocities and kindness, exceptional and dull children, mother and child relations loving or brutal, and soldierly interactions with the freedmen, both good and bad.

**Frogmore**—The Frogmore plantation complex is nestled against Station Creek, a working haven to all that is South Carolina. The Frogmore is privately owned, as it was by Miss Towne and Miss Murray. Over the course of their lives, they made improvements on the land and house—improvements that still stand today.

**Peter Leavell** graduated from Boise State with a degree in history in 2007. He is the winner of the 2012 Christian Writer's Guild's "Best First Novel." He and his family live in Boise, Idaho.


*For pictures and more information*
*about the Port Royal experiment, visit*
*www.peterleavell.com*

WORTHY
PUBLISHING

## IF YOU LIKED THIS BOOK . . .

- Tell your friends by going to: www.gideonscall.net and clicking "LIKE"

- Head over to Peter's Facebook page at facebook.com/ PeterLeavell, click "LIKE" and post a comment regarding what you enjoyed about the book

- Tweet "I recommend reading #Gideon'sCall by @PeterLeavell @WorthyPub"

- Hashtag: #Gideon'sCall

- Subscribe to our newsletter by going to www.worthy publishing.com

**WORTHY PUBLISHING
FACEBOOK PAGE**

**WORTHY PUBLISHING
WEBSITE**